D0486257

THE HARDY BOYS®

COLLECTOR'S EDITION

The Hardy Boys Mystery Stories

Available from ALADDIN Paperbacks

THE **HARDY BOYS**®

COLLECTOR'S EDITION

The Caribbean Cruise Caper
Daredevils
Skin & Bones

FRANKLIN W. DIXON

Aladdin Paperbacks
New York London Toronto Sydney Singapore

If you purchased this book without a cover, you should be aware that
this book is stolen property. It was reported as "unsold and destroyed"
to the publisher, and neither the author nor the
publisher has received any payment for this "stripped book."

This book is a work of fiction. Any references to historical events,
real people, or real locales are used fictitiously. Other names, characters,
places, and incidents are the product of the author's imagination,
and any resemblance to actual events or locales or persons, living or dead,
is entirely coincidental.

First Aladdin Paperbacks edition October 2002

The Hardy Boys® Mystery Stories #154: The Caribbean Cruise Caper copyright © 1999
by Simon & Schuster, Inc.
The Hardy Boys® Mystery Stories #159: Daredevils copyright © 2000
by Simon & Schuster, Inc.
The Hardy Boys® Mystery Stories #164: Skin & Bones copyright © 2000
by Simon & Schuster, Inc.
These titles were previously published individually by Minstrel Books.

ALADDIN PAPERBACKS
An imprint of Simon & Schuster
Children's Publishing Division
1230 Avenue of the Americas
New York, NY 10020

All rights reserved, including the right of
reproduction in whole or in part in any form.

The text of this book was set in New Caledonia.

Printed in the United States of America
16 18 20 19 17 15

THE HARDY BOYS MYSTERY STORIES is a trademark of Simon & Schuster, Inc.

THE HARDY BOYS and colophon are registered trademarks
of Simon & Schuster, Inc.

Library of Congress Control Number 2002105258

ISBN 0-689-85620-2

1109 OFF

THE HARDY BOYS®

COLLECTOR'S EDITION

THE CARIBBEAN
CRUISE CAPER

Contents

1 Flight to the Islands

Eighteen-year-old Frank Hardy slowly turned his head to the left, then to the right. He shrugged his shoulders forward and back, then winced. The flight south from New York to the Caribbean had left him with a major crick in his neck. Airline seats were not very friendly to six-footers like him and his younger brother, Joe.

Joe, seventeen, scanned the crowd of eager vacationers in the San Juan, Puerto Rico, airport. He brushed his blond hair back from his forehead. "Can you spot David anywhere?" he asked.

Frank shook his head. A little jab of pain at the base of the skull made him wish he hadn't.

"Nope," he replied. "Don't worry, though. He'll turn up. He didn't bring us all this way just to strand us."

1

David Wildman, their host, was a playwright. His suspense thriller, *Stairway to Oblivion*, had been an off-Broadway hit. He was now running *Teenway* magazine's teen-detective contest. The five teenage finalists were to spend a week on a luxurious yacht in the Caribbean. There they would compete in solving a series of staged mysteries. The grand prize was a college scholarship.

David had asked Frank and Joe to come along as expert consultants. He knew about their skill and growing fame as detectives from a fellow playwright they had helped.

"This won't be nearly as exciting as tackling real crimes," he had explained apologetically. "These are more like complicated puzzles. But your presence, your experience, will be enormously helpful. You'll love the yacht, the *Colombe d'Or*, and the islands are beautiful this time of year."

The Hardys had agreed. Now here they were in Puerto Rico, and the *Colombe d'Or* was waiting for them and the other passengers a few islands away.

Frank glanced at his watch, then studied the Arrivals column on the overhead TV monitor. "David and the others should be here by now," he remarked. "The flight from Miami landed a few minutes ago."

"Joe, Frank," someone called. "Over here!"

Frank looked around. David was easy to pick out from the crowd of brightly clad tourists. He was wearing his usual outfit of black jeans, black T-shirt, and thick-soled black workboots. His sandy hair, receding at the temples, was pulled back into a little ponytail. He had a leather case for a laptop computer slung over one shoulder.

The Hardys threaded their way over to him. He put his hands on their shoulders and turned to the little group around him. "Gang, meet Joe and Frank Hardy, superdetectives," he said. "I'm hoping they'll tell us about some of their cases later."

Frank had looked over the list of contestants during the flight down. As David introduced them, he tried to pin mental tags on them. He would get to know them better pretty quickly.

Elizabeth Wheelwright was a tall, slim, blond preppie from Virginia. She was standing a small but noticeable distance apart from the others. She gave Frank and Joe a cool nod. She seemed to take it for granted that David would introduce her first.

Cesar Ariosto, standing next to her, noticed this and gave her a mocking grin. He was about five nine, with long black hair and the shadow of a mustache on his upper lip. He wore a silver-and-turquoise bracelet on his left wrist and had a bad case of nail biting.

"Cesar's from Albuquerque," David said. "And this is Jason MacFarlane, from Fort Worth."

"Yo, what's happening, dudes?" Jason said. He was wearing baggy jeans and a sleeveless T-shirt with the picture of a hot heavy-metal group. His dark hair was cut very short on top and long in back.

A boy of about ten in shorts and a long green

3

soccer shirt tugged at David's elbow. "Hey, what about me?" he demanded.

David smiled. "This is my son, Evan. Evan is currently in the doghouse," he added, with a pretend scowl.

"Oh? Why?" Joe asked.

"A little matter of some black plastic bugs," David replied. "On the flight down, they somehow found their way into our salads. The flight attendants were not amused."

"They were so," Evan said. "They laughed like anything when you couldn't see them."

"Evan—no more practical jokes. Is that clear?" David said.

Evan nodded. His expression made Frank wonder if his fingers were crossed behind his back.

"And these are our remaining finalists, Sylvie de Carabas and Boris Lebidof," David continued. "Sylvie is from near Montreal. Boris was born in Russia and now lives in Brooklyn."

"'Allo," Sylvie said, with a charming accent. Her blue eyes twinkled at them. "We will have much fun, no?"

Boris nodded to them. He had a narrow face topped by unruly blond hair. From the look of his shoulders and upper arms, Frank guessed that working out was a major hobby of his.

"Hold it," someone called. A light flashed. When the spots cleared from Frank's eyes, he saw a guy of about seventeen with straight black hair and almond eyes. He had two fancy cameras slung around his neck. He was wearing jeans and a khaki photographer's vest over a Day-Glo orange *Teenway* T-shirt.

"Meet Kenneth Lee," David said. "He'll be part of our band, too. He and Lisa are working as interns at the mag."

"Hi, Kenneth," Frank said. He looked over at Kenneth's companion. Lisa was also about seventeen, with pixie-cut light brown hair. Her brown eyes were partly hidden behind thick black-framed glasses. In one hand she held a slender black microcassette recorder.

"Lisa Burnham," she said. "I'll be covering this event for the magazine. Tell me, Joe, Frank—you guys have tackled real crimes. How does it feel to be part of the *Teenway* teen detective contest?"

She pointed the recorder at Joe.

"Great!" Joe said, grinning.

When the recorder was swung around to Frank, he said, "Joe's our spokesperson."

"Come on, guys, loosen up," Lisa said. "You can do better than that."

"You'll have plenty of time to interview them later, Lisa," David told her. "Right now we have a plane to catch. Anyone see the sign for our gate?"

The group started down a corridor. David explained, "For this last leg, we're on a real puddle jumper," David told Frank and Joe. "We'll take it as far as St. Hilda, where we rendezvous with the *Colombe d'Or.*"

"The column door?" Jason asked. "That's a dumb name for a boat."

5

Sylvie giggled. "Don't be so silly," she said. "It is French. It means 'pigeon of gold.'"

"'Golden dove,'" Elizabeth remarked, just loud enough to be heard.

Sylvie gave her a sidelong look but didn't say anything.

Jason moved up next to Sylvie. "Will you teach me some French?" he asked. "It's such a beautiful language."

Elizabeth rolled her eyes. Frank grinned at Joe. This was starting to look like an interesting bunch.

The airplane was a small two-engine turboprop that seated about twenty passengers. Frank and Joe followed the others up the steps and down the narrow aisle to the rear half of the cabin. Frank grabbed a seat across from Lisa.

"So . . . how long have you worked at *Teenway*?" he asked her.

"Oh, I don't really work for the magazine," she replied, coloring. "I'm just there on a two-month internship. The lowest of the low." She laughed nervously.

"But you said you're covering the teen-detective contest," Frank reminded her. "That's a pretty important assignment, isn't it?"

"It's a terrific opportunity," Lisa said. "But there's no guarantee they'll print my article. One of their staff writers could whip something up out of my information."

The plane taxied to the foot of the runway, and Frank gave up trying to talk over the noise.

He enjoyed takeoffs, partly because of the thrill he got from the element of danger. The pilot released the brakes. The engines roared, pressing him back into his seat. Then the ground dropped away.

The plane banked steeply to the left, out over the water. Frank was looking almost straight down. The parallel lines of surf and the V-shaped wakes of powerboats seemed to spell mysterious messages on the blue sea. The plane leveled off before he could decode them.

It seemed only minutes later that the island of St. Hilda came into sight. It looked like three steep, wooded hills edged by cliffs and a narrow beach with a huddle of buildings clustered around a small bay. Nowhere could Frank spot a patch of level ground large enough for a plane to land.

David, in the seat behind him, leaned forward. "This island is a big hit with people who design flight simulator games," he remarked. "Players go nuts learning how to land here."

"How about our pilot?" Frank asked.

David laughed. "He must have been nuts in the first place even to take the job! The nice thing is, the difficulty of flying in has kept the place unspoiled. There's no way to bring in anything much bigger than this. Oops, hold on. White-knuckle time!"

As the plane banked, Frank saw a short, narrow landing strip cupped by a curving hillside and bordered by the sea. The pilot coasted over the near hilltop and abruptly put the plane into a steep descent. Across the aisle, Lisa gasped loudly.

An instant later the wheels touched down. The propellers screamed in reverse pitch, bringing the plane to a quick stop. The passengers in the front of the cabin started to clap.

"If I were the pilot," David said, "I'd pass the hat after every landing here. I bet I'd make out like a bandit!"

The plane taxied to the terminal, a small building with white stucco walls and a red-tiled roof. The group climbed off the plane and walked across the landing strip.

Frank noticed an outdoor café on one side of the building. A slanted roof of palm fronds shaded the tables from the tropical sun. He nudged Joe. "I don't think we're in Bayport anymore," he murmured.

Joe grinned and put on his sunglasses.

Inside, the terminal was one big, airy room. Near the entrance, in a roped-off area, an official checked the travel documents of the arriving passengers. After David explained to the man who the group was, he waved them through.

A young woman came over. Her polo shirt was embroidered with a palm tree and sun. "We're unloading your luggage now," she told David. "We'll bring it straight to your van."

"Thanks," David said. "We may as well wait outside, then."

He led the group out to the curb. Just then two

shiny taxis pulled up with suitcases strapped to their roof racks. While half a dozen passengers got out and started inside the terminal, the drivers lifted down the baggage and stacked it on a nearby wheeled cart. A uniformed porter whistled as he waited next to the cart.

A man with thinning gray hair and a bright Hawaiian print shirt met David's eye. "Hi there," he said. "Just arrive?"

"Right," David replied. "Good stay?"

"Fantastic," the man said. "We hate to leave. You kids will have the time of your life!"

His wife was juggling two straw baskets and a big yellow gourd. "Come on, Charles," she said. "We don't want to miss our plane."

He smiled. "That's not going to happen, Nora. I bet we're the only group flying out right now."

With a nod and a wave, the couple went inside.

A dusty white van turned into the drive and stopped. The driver leaned out to ask, "You are for the yacht club?"

"That's us," David said. He started to bend down, then frowned and looked around sharply.

"Hey!" he exclaimed. "Where's my laptop? It's not here!"

2 A Warm Welcome Aboard

Joe quickly scanned the sidewalk from the curb to the wall of the terminal. He saw nothing that looked like a laptop case.

"What was it in?" he asked David.

"A black leather attaché," David replied. "This isn't funny. All the information about the contest is on my hard drive."

"Maybe you left it on the plane," Boris suggested.

"I'm sure I didn't," David said. "I had it on my shoulder when we came out here. Then I set it down."

He looked around. "Evan?" he continued. "Do you know anything about this?"

The boy looked scared. "No, Daddy, uh-uh," he said. "Not a thing. Really."

"No one in our group has wandered away since we came out here," Frank pointed out. "And no one who *isn't* in our group has come close enough to us to steal something."

"Frank, are you saying this is an impossible crime?" Lisa asked, pointing her recorder at him.

"There's no such thing," Frank retorted. "If it's really impossible, it can't happen."

"I read a story once . . ." Boris began.

"Whoop-de-do," Jason muttered.

Boris ignored him. "This thief had a suitcase with a trick bottom. All he had to do was set the suitcase down on top of whatever he wanted to steal, and *whoosh!* the object vanished."

"I've heard of that gimmick, too," Joe told him. "It sounds pretty clever. But as Frank said, no one came over here with a suitcase. And as for us, we don't even have our suitcases yet. It's probably just some mix-up."

"Here comes our luggage now," Elizabeth said. "It's about time. The workers must all think they're on vacation or something."

"You guys don't seem to understand," David said tensely. "If I've lost all the files on my laptop, that's it for the contest. *Finito!* Kaput!"

Everyone crowded around him and started protesting. Lisa thrust her recorder into the center of the group. Kenneth circled around them, taking one shot after another.

Joe glanced at Frank. "We'd better do something, quick," he said.

11

"Yeah . . . like find that attaché case," Frank replied. "It couldn't have just walked away."

Joe glanced at the approaching luggage cart. His jaw dropped. "No," he said tautly. "But it might have *rolled* away. I'll be right back."

Joe sprinted into the terminal and across to the runway side. A little cluster of departing passengers was walking across the concrete apron toward the plane. The cart with their baggage was sitting next to the open cargo hatch.

Joe started through the door. A police officer in a light blue uniform, white helmet, and white gun-belt blocked the way. His name tag read L. Mallet.

"Excuse me, sir," he said in a soft, Caribbean-accented voice. "Are you cleared to board this aircraft?"

"No, officer. I just came in on it a few minutes ago," Joe replied. "But I think my friend's computer case got put on that cart by mistake. Do you think you could check for me, please? His name is David Wildman."

Mallet glanced over his shoulder at the plane. Then he said, "Please wait here, sir."

He went over and spoke to the luggage handler. Together they checked the tags on the twenty or so suitcases. Mallet picked up a black leather case and showed it to the group of passengers. They all shook their heads. He returned to Joe, carrying the case.

"Your friend will have to identify this as his property, sir," Mallet said.

"Believe me, he'll be happy to," Joe promised. "I'll go get him."

Joe hurried out and came back with David. After showing Mallet his passport, David unzipped the attaché case to check the contents.

"It doesn't look as if anything's been disturbed," he told Joe. As they started across the waiting room, he added, "What a weird thing. I guess the porter saw my case and thought it belonged to those people who were leaving."

"It could be," Joe said doubtfully. "The way I remember it, though, the porter didn't load the cart. He just stood by. It was the drivers who carried the suitcases from their taxis to the cart. I guess one of them must have picked up your case by mistake."

"Well, however it happened," David said, "I owe you one. If it hadn't been for your quick thinking, my computer and all the contest plans would be on their way back to San Juan by now. I'm tempted to complain to the airport authorities. But we don't know who's responsible. Maybe it's better to let it go."

The moment they returned to the group, the others crowded around. "Oh, good," Elizabeth said. "You found it. An airline lost my bag once in London. I was devastated. I had nothing to wear for four entire days."

"What happened?" Cesar asked Joe. "Where was it?"

Joe laughed. "About to be loaded for a return flight to San Juan."

"So you won't have to call off the contest?" Jason said. "Cool. Let's get going."

"Wait a minute," Boris said. "This is a serious matter. Somebody's dirty trick almost ruined everything for us. We must discover who stole David's computer."

That did it. Five minutes later Joe was seething with frustration. Everyone in the group was a wannabe detective. Each one had his or her far-fetched theory about what had happened, who had done it, and why.

Boris was the worst. After explaining that one of the departing passengers must be in the pay of *Teenway*'s competition, he repeatedly demanded, "It is possible, isn't it? Isn't it?"

Finally Frank told him, "Anything is *possible,* but it just isn't very likely."

For a moment Joe had the feeling that Boris was about to throw a punch at Frank, but then thought better of it. A good thing for him, thought Joe. Boris might have spent a lot of time in the weight room, but Joe could tell by the way he moved that he didn't have Frank's martial arts skills. If attacked, Frank would have decked him.

"We're running late," David said after glancing at his wrist. "We'd better put this off until later. Personally, I think one of the taxi drivers probably made a mistake. But if any of you was responsible for this stunt, I hope you'll have the guts to admit it to me privately. It won't affect your chances in the contest if you do. That's a promise. If *I* find

14

out that one of you did it, that'll be another matter."

Joe met Frank's eyes and saw that he was thinking the same thing. David's threat was pretty empty. Unless one of the group suddenly recalled some crucial fact, the guilty party—if there was one—was not likely to be unmasked.

Everyone crowded into the dusty van for the short ride to the yacht club. The clubhouse was a white wooden building with a shady veranda around all four sides. White wicker tables and chairs were scattered across the lush green lawn.

The yacht club faced a sparkling blue bay, crowded with luxurious boats. As he climbed out of the van, Joe fell in love with a sleek fifty-foot sloop. It looked ready to sail around the world. He decided to sign on as a deckhand . . . once he had talked his dad into giving him permission.

Frank nudged him. "Ground control to Major Joe," he said. "Come in, please."

Joe indicated the sloop. "What do you say we swap *Sleuth* for something along those lines?" *Sleuth* was the name of the Hardys' little outboard runabout.

"Great idea," Frank said with a grin. "We could probably swing it if we threw in three or four hundred thousand bucks on the side."

Cesar joined them. "Can you believe this place?" he said. "There must be millions and millions of dollars' worth of boats out there . . . and this is just one island. Talk about loaded!"

"Successful people are always the targets of envy and jealousy," Elizabeth remarked from a few feet away. She did not look at anyone as she said it, but Joe saw the color rise in Cesar's cheeks. Cesar pressed his lips together as if holding back a retort.

A taxi pulled up next to the van. The woman who got out looked as if she had stepped out of the pages of a fashion magazine's resort issue. She went over to David and pushed her designer sunglasses up on her forehead.

"I was so *determined* to be here to greet you," she said. "Am I hopelessly late? Have you been waiting for me forever?"

David shook his head. "We just arrived," he said. "Gang, I'd like you to meet our hostess on this voyage, the editor of *Teenway*, Bettina Dunn."

He went around the circle, introducing everyone. Bettina had been very well briefed. She seemed to recognize each person and know a little something personal about him or her.

When David came to Joe and said his name, Bettina smiled. "Ah yes—one of the celebrated Hardy brothers. I've met your father. I can see the resemblance. He must be very proud of you. And, of course, this is your brother and partner, Frank."

Joe could not help feeling a warm glow.

When the introductions were finished, Bettina said, "We'll have a more formal welcome after we board the *Colombe d'Or*. For now, I'll just say how pleased all of us at *Teenway* are that you could take

16

part in this thrilling and challenging—and rewarding—contest."

Everybody clapped.

One of the staff started piling the group's luggage on a wheelbarrow. David kept a tight grip on his computer case.

Bettina led the way into the yacht club. Just inside the door, Joe noticed her stop to say hello to a white-haired man in white slacks and a blue blazer. The man turned away, pretending not to hear her. Bettina reddened and kept walking.

David was a couple of steps ahead. Joe caught up to him. In a low voice, he asked, "You see the elderly man in the blazer? Do you know who he is?"

David raised an eyebrow. "You caught that little exchange, did you? That is Walter Mares. He founded *Teenway*. A few years ago he was forced into retirement after a corporate takeover."

"And Bettina?" Joe asked. "What was her part in the story?"

"She was his discovery," David explained. "His crown princess, I guess you'd say. But when he was kicked out, she stayed on and rose to the top. He took it pretty hard. I doubt if they've spoken to each other since. I hear he's retired now and living down here full-time."

"Are you going to put them in one of your plays?" Joe asked as they stepped onto the veranda and Frank joined them.

David laughed. "I wish I could!"

17

Frank gave Joe a questioning look. "I'll fill you in later," Joe said.

Evan came running up. "Daddy? Which one is our boat?"

Good question, thought Joe. At least three dozen big motor cruisers and ocean sailers were berthed in the yacht club marina, gleaming in the tropical sunlight.

"That one, son," David said. He pointed toward the end of the finger pier. "The one with the blue smokestack. That's the *Colombe d'Or*."

Joe's eyes widened. The yacht David indicated dwarfed all the others in the harbor. It was easily half the length of a football field, with two full decks above the water line.

Frank gave a soft whistle.

"Quite an impressive barge, isn't she," David said with a grin. "Some Greek shipping tycoon had her built back in the fifties for his French girl-friend. Then they broke up. After lots of ups and downs, the *Colombe* ended up here in the Caribbean as a charter craft."

Some of the others stopped to listen to David. When he finished, Sylvie said, "I have heard something else about this boat. I have heard that it is under a curse. Terrible things happen to people who sail on it."

3 Along Came a Spider

Sylvie's startling statement was followed by a moment of silence. Then several people spoke at once.

"A curse?" Jason said. "Cool! Are there ghosts, too?"

"What nonsense!" Elizabeth said. Frank thought she sounded a little uneasy.

"Where did you hear this, Sylvie?" asked David.

"It is true, isn't it?" she demanded. "The Greek millionaire who built it disappeared overboard one night. His body was never found. Others, too, have died mysterious deaths."

David raised both hands like a symphony conductor. "Now hold on," he said. "It's true that the boat's first owner vanished at sea. He'd been having some serious money problems. A lot of people thought he must have jumped overboard."

"What about the other deaths?" Lisa asked. Frank saw that she was holding her tape recorder at waist level, where it wasn't so obvious.

David rolled his eyes. "People don't always die in hospitals," he said. "Sometimes they die in houses or apartments or hotels or airplanes . . . or aboard yachts. That doesn't mean there's anything sinister or mysterious about their deaths. Sylvie, where did you get all this curse nonsense?"

Sylvie looked away. "There was a magazine article," she muttered.

"Huh!" David exclaimed. "If it's the same one I'm thinking of, it appeared about four years ago, in a supermarket tabloid. How did you stumble across it?"

Frank had to listen hard to hear her reply. "It came by mail last week. A photocopy. There was no name or message."

"Did you notice the postmark?" Frank asked.

Sylvie shook her head. "No, but I'm pretty sure the stamps were U.S., not Canadian."

"Anybody else get a copy of this article?" asked Joe, glancing around the circle of listeners. No one responded.

"Some friend who knew you were going on this cruise must have sent it to you," Jason said.

"Some friend," Frank murmured to Joe. "With friends like that, who needs an enemy?"

"Okay, listen, people," David said. "We're going to have a great time and solve some great puzzles. And if any ghosts or curses try to stop us, they are going to be in major trouble. Right?"

"Right!" the group responded. Boris pumped his fist in the air and cheered.

"Then let's go on board," David concluded. "Find your cabins and settle in. We'll assemble on the afterdeck in half an hour for the official welcome and kickoff."

As they walked out along the pier, Joe leaned close to Frank. "I hope no one takes the word *kickoff* too seriously," he said.

The guest cabins were one level down from the main deck, along either side of a central corridor. Frank and Joe carried their packs down and studied the name tags on the doors.

Their cabin was partway along the corridor on the port side. David and Evan were on one side of them, and Elizabeth and Sylvie on the other. The cabins on the starboard side were assigned to Cesar and Jason, Boris and Kenneth, and Lisa, who somehow rated a single. Apparently Bettina was elsewhere on the boat, probably in the owner's cabin.

Once inside, Frank pushed the polished wooden door closed and dropped his bag on one of the two bunk beds. Joe wandered over to gaze out one of the two round portholes.

Frank examined the room. In one corner was a closet—in the other a bathroom, complete with a shower that was not much larger than the closet. Instead of dressers, there were latched drawers fitted under each of the beds. A table and two chairs completed the furnishings. Everything was solid and

comfortable, but the decor didn't have the showi-
ness he would have expected on a fancy yacht.

As they unpacked and stowed their clothes in the
drawers, Frank and Joe talked over the day so far.
Frank was curious about the encounter between
Bettina and her old boss. Joe was more interested in
the article about the curse on the boat. Who had
sent it to Sylvie, and why? *If* someone had sent it.
She could have invented that part of her story.
Maybe she had found the article herself by searching a database. But if so, why would she want to
hide it from the others?

Frank glanced at his watch. "We're due upstairs.
Oops—I mean, on deck."

Bettina was already on the aft deck chatting with
Elizabeth and Lisa. The *Teenway* editor had
changed into bell-bottom jeans washed almost
white, a striped fisherman's jersey, and boating
shoes. Near her was a table loaded with platters of
snacks and ice buckets of soft drinks. A big chocolate cake formed the centerpiece.

As the others arrived, they hovered awkwardly
around the refreshment table. Frank grinned to see
Evan sneak a cookie. No one else had the nerve to
take something first.

Finally Bettina said, "Are we all here? Wonderful! You are a very special group, you know. You
have been selected as the finest, most talented teen
detectives in the country. Sherlock Holmes and
Sam Spade should be happy they don't have to
compete with you!"

Frank found it hard to keep a straight face. From the expressions of the listeners, most of them had no idea who the fictional detective Sam Spade was.

"Over the next few days," Bettina continued, "as we get to know these beautiful islands and one another, you'll have a chance to use your talents. I know you will find it a challenge, and I hope you will find it fun as well. So, on behalf of *Teenway* magazine, I should like to welcome all of you and wish you bon voyage and the best of luck in the contest."

As the group clapped, Bettina moved over to the table and picked up a cake knife. "Now," she said. "Who would like to be the first—"

She let out a scream and jumped back. The cake knife clattered to the deck.

Frank was the first to reach her side. "What is it?" he demanded. "Did you hurt yourself?"

Bettina pointed at the cake. Frowning, Frank moved closer.

Trapped in the chocolate frosting were four black spiders.

Gingerly, Frank picked one out. It was plastic.

"May I see that?" David asked. Frank handed it to him. David took one look and growled, "*Evan!* Front and center, on the double!"

"I didn't do anything!" Evan wailed.

"Is this yours?" his father asked.

"Maybe. It looks like one of mine," the boy admitted. "But I didn't put it on the cake. Honest."

"Did you touch the cake?" David asked.

"Well . . ." Evan licked a corner of his mouth. Frank grinned to himself. A small smudge of chocolate still showed on the boy's cheek. "I tried a little of the frosting. Just to make sure it was okay. But I did it where it wouldn't show. And I *never* put spiders on the cake. That's not funny."

"I agree," Bettina said. "It's not funny at all. Who played this unfunny joke?"

In the silence that followed, Frank heard seabirds calling and feet shuffling uneasily on the deck. Somewhere on the island, a car horn tooted.

After a long moment David said, "I believe Evan. And I want to say that to pull a stunt like this is pretty childish. But to let it be pinned on a kid— that's really low."

Bettina took a deep breath. She said, "Well—we shouldn't let some twisted soul with bad taste in jokes spoil our welcoming celebration. Who would like a piece of cake . . . with or without spiders?"

Everybody laughed, more from relief than because it was funny. David picked up the cake knife, carefully wiped it, and handed it to Bettina. She began passing out slices.

Frank didn't feel like cake. He took a plate and piled on some veggies and dip, two bite-size sandwiches, and a few cold shrimp. He paused, then added a small wedge of creamy cheese.

He was pouring a cup of soda when he noticed a man with bushy sideburns and a deep tan move down from the upper deck. The newcomer was wearing white shorts, a white short-sleeved shirt with epaulets, and a blue baseball cap. He approached Bettina and murmured a few words to her.

She nodded. Then she took his arm and said, "Everyone—this is our captain, Bruce Mathieson. He tells me we'll be sailing in a few minutes. That won't break up the party, though. In fact, it gives us an additional reason to celebrate."

Mathieson returned to the upper deck. A young crew member in cutoff jeans and a Key West T-shirt came aft and took up a position near the stern mooring line. While waiting for the signal to cast off, he gazed around at the little gathering. His eyes met Frank's. Frank nodded and smiled. The crew member did not smile back or even seem to notice.

Frank had the odd impression that the guy lived in another world that just happened to run side by side with the one the *Teenway* contestants inhabited. An invisible barrier separated the two worlds. Or maybe it was just that the crew had orders not to fraternize with the passengers.

The ship's horn let out a mournful bellow. The deck began to vibrate as the huge diesel engines came to life. The crewman untied the mooring line, then looped it twice around the bollard and gripped the loose end.

The note of the engines mounted the scale. As the vibration spread and intensified, the crewman nodded to someone on the pier below. A moment later he reeled in the looped end of the mooring line. It left a sparkle of water drops on the deck.

Bettina and David left to join the captain on the bridge. David took Evan with him. Everyone else gathered by the stern rail to watch the pier and the island recede. The *Colombe d'Or* was under way.

As the boat left the sheltering arms of the bay and met the waves of the open sea, the deck began to move gently up and down and side to side. Sylvie clutched the rail and gave a small, uncomfortable laugh. "Ooo, this is fun . . . I think. Does the floor move like this always?"

"Oh, sure, always," Lisa said, giving Frank a wink. "Usually it's a lot worse than this. Don't worry, though. You'll get used to it after a few days."

"We're going to be on the boat for only a few days," Kenneth pointed out.

Lisa shrugged. "After that we can get used to being on land again."

As the laughter died down, Frank heard Elizabeth say, "I saw you hanging around the cake." He glanced over quickly. She was speaking to Cesar.

Joe had also overheard. "Is that right, Cesar?" he asked.

Cesar glared at Joe, then at Elizabeth. "None of your business," he said.

"That's original," Elizabeth said. "And it is our business. Stupid stunts like those spiders could ruin the trip for everybody."

"Okay, okay," Cesar said loudly. "Yeah, I was hanging out near the cake. I've got a thing for chocolate, all right? I was tempted to try the frosting. But I didn't do it. *And* I didn't put those dopy spiders on the cake."

"Did you notice the spiders?" Frank asked.

Cesar shook his head. "Nope. But maybe I wouldn't have. I'm a little farsighted."

"You would have noticed somebody leaning over the cake and pressing the spiders into it, wouldn't you?" Jason asked. "And you didn't, did you?"

"What's your point?" Cesar demanded.

"My point is, none of us could have put the spiders on the cake," Jason said. "The only time any of us was close enough to do it, we were all standing around looking at the refreshment table. Even a magician couldn't have sneaked those spiders past us and onto the cake."

Boris shouldered his way into the little circle and said, "They got there, though."

"Exactly," Jason said triumphantly. "Which means the solution is obvious. One of the crew put them there."

"Oh, brilliant," Boris said sarcastically. "You mean, 'The butler did it.' You've been watching too many old movies—*bad* old movies."

Jason reddened. "I suppose you've got a better solution, wise guy?"

Boris snorted loudly. "You don't have to be a cow to know when the milk tastes sour," he replied.

"Funny you should mention cows," Jason said. "After the way you horned in on this conversation."

Boris gave him a mocking smile. "At least I'm not

trying to give everyone a bum steer," he said. "I guess that's because I don't come from Cowtown."

Frank admired Boris's ready wit. How had he managed to recollect that Jason's home was Fort Worth, Texas, popularly known as Cowtown?

Jason was obviously infuriated by being topped this way. He let out a growl, lowered his head, and charged at Boris. Boris sidestepped out of his path and shouted, "Olé!"

Maddened by this additional barb, Jason swerved after Boris, but his foot slipped and he crashed into Lisa.

Lisa stumbled backward and started to topple over the rail. She let out a shriek of terror. More than a dozen feet below her was the water, churned into white foam by the powerful twin propellers.

4 Let the Games Begin!

Joe saw Lisa stumble against the rail, and he sprang into motion. Even before she began to topple over, he had narrowed the distance that separated them. With all the strength and grace he would have put into reaching out for a long pass, he grabbed her arm just above the elbow and tugged her to safety.

"You're okay," he assured her as she began to sob with mixed fright and relief. "Relax, you're fine."

Meanwhile, Frank moved quickly to Jason's side and put a friendly but warning arm around his shoulders. At first Jason seemed too shocked to react to Lisa's near fall, which he had caused. At Frank's touch, he snapped to attention. He shrugged off the arm and took a step away.

"Leave me alone," he barked.

"Hey, take it easy, fella," Frank said, moving between Jason and Boris. "We're all friends here."

"Think so?" Jason demanded. He took a couple of deep breaths and straightened his shoulders. "We'll see about that."

Not meeting anyone's eyes, he spun on one heel and stalked inside.

Lisa threw her arms around Joe's neck. "Joe Hardy, you saved my life!" she exclaimed.

Joe felt his cheeks grow warm with embarrassment. "Hey, that's okay," he muttered. He disentangled himself from her grasp. "No big deal."

"No big deal?" Lisa said. "I could have drowned or been eaten by sharks. You're a hero . . . and I'm going to make sure that every kid who reads *Teenway* knows it."

Looking past her, Joe saw that Frank was grinning. Joe's cheeks burned even more. He made a private vow. If Frank teased him about this, he was going to short-sheet Frank's bunk.

Sylvie seemed miffed by all the attention that was going to Lisa. "Are there really sharks here?" she asked with a dainty shiver.

"Sure, lots of them," Cesar said cheerfully. "But you don't have to worry about sharks as much as the jellyfish and electric eels and giant clams. Just let one of those clams get you inside its shell, and you're history!"

Elizabeth gave him a cold look. "Were you left back in tenth grade?" she asked in a haughty tone. "Or is it just your humor that's sophomoric?"

"Brrr!" Cesar said with a shiver. "I think I just hit an iceberg. Somebody get me a blanket, quick. Or better yet, a lifeboat."

Everybody laughed—everybody but Elizabeth.

Sylvie stretched and said, "It's been a long day. I think I'll rest before dinner."

"Good idea," Lisa said. "Me, too."

The two girls walked off. Boris asked, "Anybody for a game of chess? There's a board in the salon."

"Sure," Kenneth said. "I'll give it a shot."

Cesar gave Elizabeth a cheeky grin. "How about a hot game of checkers? Or maybe you know how to play fish? That kinda fits with being on a boat."

"I take back my remark about being sophomoric," Elizabeth said. "You're obviously stuck in fourth grade. Excuse me. I need to catch up on my reading."

As the girl from Virginia stalked off, Cesar looked over at Frank and Joe and rolled his eyes. "I hate stuffed shirts," he said. "Don't you?"

He didn't wait for an answer. He, too, went inside. The Hardys were left alone on deck.

"We should go have a talk with David," Joe suggested. "I'd like to make sure everything is set for tonight's crime."

"I hope there's only one," Frank replied. "The way some of these guys are getting along, we may have a murder to deal with."

Half an hour later Frank and Joe were on the sundeck near the bow with David, going over the details of that evening's puzzle. The notes of a triple chime resounded through the boat.

"That must be the signal for dinner," David said, getting to his feet. "You fellows go ahead. I'd better find my kid and make sure he washes his hands."

The dark, glossy table in the forward section of the main salon glittered with china and silver for twelve. The flames of two candelabra wavered in the light breeze from the deck.

Everyone waited near the entrance for somebody to go in first.

Bettina came in and stood near the head of the table. She had changed again—this time into a light green dress decorated with sea horses and anchors. "Please sit anywhere you like," she said. "We're going to be quite informal."

Cesar eyed the table. In a loud whisper he said, "If this is 'quite informal,' I sure hope she doesn't decide to get formal. I left my white tie and tails back in Albuquerque."

Sylvie went to a seat halfway along the far side of the table. Jason and Boris rushed over to grab the chairs on either side of her, then glared at each other.

Lisa came up to Joe. "May I sit next to you?" she asked sweetly. "I want to hear all about the mysteries you've solved."

Frank gave Joe an amused look. Joe wrinkled his nose at him.

Elizabeth took the seat next to David and asked him his views on the future of the American theater. From his expression, David would probably have rather been discussing the NCAA Final Four.

The first course was a salad with asparagus stalks and orange slices. The look Evan gave it cracked Joe up.

Everyone ate the salad in a tense and uneasy silence. Joe decided the problem was mostly the formality of the dinner table, but the tensions between some of the contestants didn't help the atmosphere.

The only one who seemed totally unaffected by the atmosphere was Evan. After eating his orange slices and sliding his asparagus under a convenient lettuce leaf, he looked around and said, "I know a riddle."

"Evan . . ." David said in a warning tone.

"What's your riddle?" Joe asked.

Evan took a deep breath. "Why did the boy throw his alarm clock out the window?"

Joe put on a very thoughtful expression. "Um, let's see . . . Because it went off too early and he didn't want to wake up yet?" he suggested.

Before Evan could respond to this, Elizabeth said, "Don't be ridiculous. Because he wanted to make time fly, of course."

"That's right," Evan said, crestfallen. "Wait, wait—I've got another one. How many balls of string would it take to reach to the moon?"

Not allowing enough time for anyone to speak, he said, "Give up? One, if it's big enough."

That got a chorus of groans from around the

table. Encouraged by the response, Evan continued. "Here's a good one. Where did Napoleon keep his armies?"

"In France?" Jason said.

"No, no," Boris cut in. "In Russia. You know what happened to Napoleon. Once his armies went to Russia, they never returned."

"You're both wrong." Evan chortled. "You know where Napoleon kept his armies? *In his sleevies!*"

After dinner Frank and David went to put the final touches on the first mystery. Joe stayed with the contestants in the salon. No one talked. Sylvie sat on the couch with a magazine open on her lap, never turning a single page. Boris paced around the room, pausing now and then to stare out at the darkness. The others simply sat, gazing vacantly into space. Joe decided they must be psyching themselves for the contest.

David and Frank returned. David was holding a baseball cap upside down.

"I've put five numbered slips of paper in here," he announced. "You'll each take one to determine the order of play."

He went around the room. Jason drew number one, followed by Cesar, Sylvie, Boris, and Elizabeth.

"Joe will take each of you in turn to the scene of the crime," David continued. "You'll have five minutes to look around. Don't touch anything. Afterward you'll fill out a report explaining your interpretation of the crime, the culprit or culprits,

34

and the evidence. Your score will be based on how close you come to the official version . . . in other words, mine."

That drew a slight, nervous laugh from everyone.

"Okay, let's go," David concluded. "And may the best detective win!"

Joe led Jason out of the salon and up a flight of stairs to a door marked Private.

"This is the captain's cabin," he explained. "As background, you should know that the yacht's owner asked the captain to keep a file of securities in his safe. Their value is over a million dollars."

"I can guess what comes next," Jason said.

Joe didn't reply. He pushed the door open and stood aside. He glanced at his watch. Then he followed Jason into the cabin.

The first thing he noticed was a body sprawled on the floor in front of the open safe. It was dressed in oil-stained khakis and work boots. A length of electric cord was knotted around the neck.

"That's a dummy, right?" Jason asked. His voice quavered.

"Right," Joe said. "And that is the only question I'm allowed to answer. Your five minutes started fifteen seconds ago."

Jason set to work. He studied the dummy from head to foot, then peered into the safe. The papers spilled on the rug occupied him for a minute or more. Then he moved around the cabin. He looked closely at the files on the desk and the overturned glass on the end table. A wrench half-tucked into a chair cushion didn't seem to interest him. He spent what was left of his five minutes getting down on his hands and knees to sniff the barrel of a snub-nosed .38 revolver peeping out from under the dummy's leg.

"Time," Joe announced. He escorted Jason back to the salon and returned with Cesar. Unlike Jason, Cesar kept up a running stream of comments as he examined the crime scene. Some of them were to the point. Others were so wacky that Joe had to work not to laugh.

Each of the other contestants also had a different style. Sylvie acted like an airhead, but she noticed as many important details as anyone else. Boris spent the first half of his time posed just inside the doorway. Only his eyes moved. Then he went around the cabin counterclockwise, pausing to check each clue in turn. As for Elizabeth, she stood as if she were there for a social engagement with the captain. Joe half expected her to send him off for tea and pastries.

After all the contestants had had their turns, they were given half an hour to complete their crime reports. Frank and Joe collected the five papers and took them to their cabin. Frank stuck the folder inside his suitcase for safekeeping. Then they returned to the salon. They expected that the others would want to party on their first night at sea, but the only one still there was Lisa.

"Everybody pooped out," Lisa told them. "It *has* been a pretty long day. But how could anyone give up the chance to watch the moon rise over the water?"

"When does it rise tonight?" Joe asked.

"Oh, I don't know," Lisa admitted. "But it has to come up sooner or later. Why don't we just go out on deck and wait for it?"

Pointedly, Frank picked up a magazine and sat down on one of the two leather sofas.

"You promised to tell me about some of your cases," Lisa added. "For my *Teenway* story."

Joe didn't recall making such a promise, but it was a reasonable request. He went out on the afterdeck with Lisa and told her about the time he and Frank had gone undercover as actors in a Broadway musical. It took a while. When he finished, he looked around. The moon still wasn't up. Or had it already set?

"I'd better turn in," he said, getting to his feet. "Big day tomorrow."

He said good night to Lisa and collected Frank from the salon. As they went down to their cabin, Joe noticed a line of light across the floor coming from the door to their cabin.

"Frank!" Joe whispered urgently. He grabbed his brother's arm. "We didn't leave the door open or the light on. Somebody has been in our cabin!"

5 Shutting the Barn Door

Frank instantly flattened himself against the wall on the near side of the door. Wordlessly he pointed to the far side of the door. Joe nodded and moved silently into position.

Frank took a deep breath and held up his left hand with three fingers showing. As he folded them, he counted down under his breath.

Three . . . two . . . one . . .

On zero, he shoved the door open, darted through the opening, and dodged to the right. He finished in a martial crouch, hands poised for either offense or defense.

At the same time Joe sprinted inside and took up a position to the left of the door.

Frank quickly scanned the room. No one was there. He jerked open the closet door. At the same moment, Joe pulled open the door to the bathroom and peered inside.

Frank straightened up. "All clear," he said, shutting the closet. He stepped over and eased the door to the corridor closed.

"Frank, look at this," Joe said. He pointed to Frank's suitcase. It was unzipped. The folder of questionnaires lay on the floor next to it.

Frank started to bend down to retrieve the folder. Then he stopped himself.

"This doesn't make sense," he said.

"Sure it does," Joe said. "One of the contestants decided to improve his or her chances by changing their entry . . . or by changing other people's entries."

"That's what we're supposed to think," Frank replied. "But if that's so, why was the folder left where we'd see it and know that someone had fiddled with it? Why were the lights on and the door open?"

"Nervousness?" Joe suggested. "Somebody came along before the intruder could put things back?"

Frank considered that and nodded slowly. "It's possible," he said. "I'm not sold. I have a strong hunch this is some kind of setup. But what kind, and why? See if you spot anything else."

While Joe circled the cabin, Frank checked the crime reports. Had any been altered? Each of the contestants had made some changes in what he or she had written. As far as Frank could see, however, the insertions and crossings out were done in the same ink as the rest of the entry. There were no obvious signs of tampering.

"Frank?" Joe said. "Come here a sec."

Frank stood up and crossed the cabin to where Joe was standing.

"Sniff," Joe told him.

Frank sniffed. "I smell something flowery," he reported. "Perfume?"

"I think so," Joe replied. "And I think I smelled it before, earlier today. Sylvie was wearing it. She must be the one who came in here."

Frank frowned. The thought of Sylvie playing burglar surprised him. His experience as a detective had taught him not to rule out suspects simply because they "weren't the type." Still, some people were more likely to carry out certain kinds of actions than others. Sylvie did not strike him as being very adventurous or daring.

Frank looked around. Set into the wall above Joe's bunk was the rectangular metal grill of a ventilator. On the other side of that wall was the cabin shared by Elizabeth and Sylvie. Could the scent have seeped in through the duct? And if so, what about sound? Could the girls hear what he and Joe said?

They had better be more careful about where they discussed anything sensitive. Frank tapped Joe on the shoulder, put a finger to his lips, and pointed up at the ventilator. Joe nodded grimly. Grabbing a pen and a piece of paper, he scribbled, "Tell David? Bettina?"

Frank glanced at his watch and shook his head. "Not now, it's too late," he said in a low voice. "We'll catch them first thing in the morning. This isn't news they'll want to hear."

Frank's prediction was right. Early the next morning he and Joe knocked on the door to David's cabin. Still in pajamas, he listened to their account of the intrusion. His expression grew more and more unhappy.

When the Hardys finished, David said, "We'd better let Bettina in on this. Just a minute while I throw some clothes on."

Once dressed, David took Frank and Joe up to the main deck, to the owner's cabin. It ran the full width of the yacht, with big windows facing the bow and both sides. There they repeated their story to Bettina.

She looked over the folder of entries. "Let me be sure I understand," she said. "Someone may have altered one or more of these, but you can't tell whether or not, or which one. Is that it?"

"'Fraid so," Frank said. "If only we'd looked at the papers when the contestants turned them in . . ."

"Spilt milk," Bettina said, with a wave of the hand. "So—what do we do about last night's mystery? Keep it? Scrub it?"

"I looked over the entries last night," Frank said. "They're all pretty good, but I didn't see any that seemed outstandingly good . . . or bad. My

41

guess is that they would all earn roughly the same score."

"In other words," Joe added, "whether we keep the first puzzle or drop it won't make that much difference to the final result."

"Hmm . . . I'd rather not cloud the contest with unnecessary controversy," Bettina remarked. "David? Any thoughts?"

"I see two possibilities," David said slowly. "One, somebody improved his own entry. Two, somebody sabotaged someone else's entry. Or both possibilities, of course."

"Okay," Bettina said. "What then?"

"I'm not sure how we could prove or disprove the first possibility," David continued. "But the second should be easy to check. We post all the entries for the contestants to look over. Then we listen for anyone's complaining that someone changed his entry. If we get any complaints, we decide then whether to honor the results. If we don't, we let it ride."

"And we'll be a lot more careful from now on," Frank said.

"Good point, Frank," Bettina said. "How are we going to secure the contest materials in the future?"

"How about the captain's safe?" Joe suggested. "I hear he's in the habit of keeping millions in securities there. A few contest entries should be a cinch."

After a startled moment, the others laughed.

"Sorry, you can't use that safe," Bettina said. "The combination was lost years ago. Any other ideas?"

"I have a file box in my cabin that locks," David offered. "You'd need a certain degree of skill to open it, and I doubt if anybody would have the nerve to make off with the whole file box."

Bettina gave a decisive nod. "All right, then," she said. "David, take these entries and score them. We're scheduled to reach Fort William early this afternoon. While we're docked, have someone make a couple of sets of photocopies. Then keep the originals locked in that file box of yours."

"Will do," David responded. "Should we announce the scores this morning, as scheduled?"

"We should do everything as normally as possible," Bettina told him. She stood up. "If someone hopes to disrupt our contest, we should make it obvious that it isn't working. That may drive him or her to make a mistake."

The Hardys returned to David's cabin with him. He showed them the file box, and Frank checked the lock. It seemed pretty sturdy.

"I'm going up to the sundeck to do the scoring," David announced. "It's very private at this time of day. Don't worry, I won't let the entries blow away. And the minute I finish—it shouldn't take long—I'll bring them back down here until we post them later. They'll be safe, I guarantee it."

The three left together. As Frank and Joe walked down the corridor to their cabin, Joe was startled to see the door to David's cabin start to open.

Evan walked out. "Oh, hi, Joe," the boy said. "Is it time to eat yet? I'm starved."

"Er—just about," Joe replied. His thoughts whirled. Evan had obviously been inside the room earlier, too. Where, in the shower? Had he overheard their conversation with his dad? And if so, should Joe warn him not to mention anything he'd heard to anyone else?

Maybe not—that might put ideas in the kid's head.

"You want to wait for us?" Joe added. "We're about to go up, too."

A breakfast buffet was set up in the dining area. Boris, Jason, and Lisa were already eating. Sylvie was waiting for Cesar to finish filling his plate. Frank, Joe, and Evan lined up behind her.

"We are all arguing about last night's mystery puzzle," Sylvie told Joe and Frank. "Will you end our suspense? Please?"

"That's David's job," Frank replied. "Don't worry—he'll be along pretty soon."

Sylvie poured a glass of orange juice and fixed a bowl of granola with fresh tropical fruit on top. Evan was more interested in the miniature pastries. He took three and reached for another,

44

then glanced up at Joe and took a glass of milk instead.

Joe and Frank each took a slice of fresh mango, scrambled eggs, and portions of an unusual looking sausage. They joined the others at the table.

Jason looked over at them. "The guy was the robber's inside man, right?" he said. "He and his boss got into an argument and the boss offed him."

"No comment," Joe replied.

"That's totally dumb," Cesar told Jason. He noticed Kenneth aiming his camera at him and paused to put on a big smile. Kenneth did not snap the shutter. After a moment Cesar dropped the smile and continued. "What about the ransom note? How do you explain that?"

"What ransom note?" Boris demanded. "There was no kidnapping."

Cesar stuck one finger in the air. "Aha!" he said. "No kidnapping—but there *was* a ransom note."

From the entrance, Elizabeth remarked, "These airs of mystery are so tiresome and passé. Not to mention childish."

With a wide grin, Cesar held his thumbs to his ears and waggled his fingers at her. Elizabeth put her nose in the air and sniffed loudly. Kenneth's flash went off.

"Oh!" Elizabeth exploded. "You had better not print that picture in the magazine! If my daddy saw it, he'd sue you and *Teenway* for all you're worth."

"Quick, somebody hold me," Cesar cried. "I'm trembling so much I can't stand up."

"You're sitting down," Boris pointed out.

"You see? That's how bad it is!" Cesar replied.

Joe noticed that Lisa was holding her tape recorder just below the level of the table. She pointed the built-in mike at each speaker in turn.

As Elizabeth came nearer the table, she spotted Lisa's recorder. "Is that thing on?" she demanded. "I want that tape!"

"You can order a copy from me when I get back to New York," Lisa said coolly. "My rates are pretty reasonable."

"I don't know anything worse than a dirty little snoop!" Elizabeth declared.

"Ooo—major diss!" Cesar said, snickering.

Lisa reddened. "I know something a lot worse than a snoop, and that's a snob!"

"Hey, come on, people," Frank said. "Lighten up."

He might as well have saved his breath.

"I refuse to be called names!" Elizabeth cried.

"Who started calling names?" Lisa retorted. She shoved her chair back and sprang to her feet. "Who started it?"

"Are we doing more riddles?" Evan asked eagerly. "'Cause I remembered some good ones."

Joe patted him on the arm. "Not now, Evan," he said in an undertone. "Eat your breakfast."

Elizabeth put her hands on her hips and glared at

Lisa. She opened her mouth to make another remark. Before she got a word out, she was interrupted by a distant, startled cry. Elizabeth looked over her shoulder toward the companionway, or stairway, to the cabin deck. At that moment there was a loud crash from below.

6 Slipping and Sliding

Frank jumped up from the table and darted toward the stairs. Joe was close behind him. As they zoomed down the steps, Frank saw one of the crew running along the corridor. The door to David's cabin was open wide. The crew member started inside.

"Wha—" he yelled. His feet flew out from under him. He landed flat on his back with a crash that shook the deck.

Frank stopped and held out his arm to warn Joe. They approached the doorway slowly and cautiously.

David was sitting on the floor of the cabin, just inside the door. He had a blue-and-white marble in his hand. Frank saw dozens more marbles scattered across the polished planks.

The crew member sat up. Frank recognized him.

He had handled the mooring line during their departure the day before. "Woo!" he said, rubbing the back of his head. "What hit me?"

"You slipped on a marble," David told him. "Sorry about that, ah—what was your name again?"

"Chuck . . . Chuck Arneson," the guy replied. "We'd better pick these up before somebody cracks their skull. How'd they spill anyway?"

"I can make a pretty good guess," David said. He got to his feet and massaged his hip.

From behind Frank and Joe, a tiny voice said, "Daddy? I have something to tell you."

David sighed. "Yes, Evan? What is it?"

Evan slipped past Frank and Joe. "Well . . . I heard you and Frank and Joe talking about robbers," he said. "And I was afraid a bad guy would come in our room. So I put my marbles on the floor to make him fall."

"It worked," David said with grim humor.

"I would have told you," Evan continued. "But I didn't know where you were. And then I went up to breakfast and I sort of forgot. I'm sorry. Are you okay?"

"I'm fine," David said. He reached over and tousled his son's hair. "But next time, check with me before you set any traps for bad guys. Okay?"

Evan grinned with relief. "You bet!"

Frank and Joe helped pick up the marbles. Then they returned to the salon with David and Evan. David carried an envelope in his hand. The room fell silent as they went in.

49

"I've looked over your solutions to last night's crime," David announced. "They are all worthy tries. I'm going to post them on the bulletin board next to the stairs for you to read. Then, in ten or fifteen minutes, we'll come together again to talk about the results."

The five finalists barely waited for David to tack up the entries before they clustered around to read them. Meanwhile, Lisa cornered Joe. She wanted to know what the commotion had been about earlier. He told her about Evan's marbles. She asked for a preview of the scores in the contest. Joe admitted he had no idea.

Lisa wanted his general reactions to the voyage so far. Joe talked about the boat, the sea, the weather, and the great group of contestants. He aimed his words at Lisa's tape recorder. In his head, however, he was focused on the mystery of the intruder from the night before. Finally he muttered an excuse and went to look for Frank. He found him on the afterdeck.

"Notice anything?" Frank murmured. "No anguished cries from anyone whose entry was altered."

"So either nothing was changed or our visitor last night came to touch up his own entry," Joe replied.

Frank nodded. "That's what it looks like. Unless . . . I can't stop thinking we were *meant* to notice that someone had fiddled with the entries. But why?"

Joe had the feeling an answer to Frank's question was lurking just out of sight. Suddenly he snapped his fingers. "How about this? One of the contestants was sure he'd messed up. So he decided to push us into throwing out the results. That way his poor showing wouldn't hurt him. Or her, of course."

"That fits," Frank said slowly. "The funny part is, from what David said, everybody did about the same. So breaking into our cabin was wasted effort."

"But whoever did it couldn't have known that." Joe glanced inside. "Speaking of David, it looks like he's ready to start."

Joe and Frank returned to the salon. David gave them a nod and a smile. Then he said, "The setup last night was meant to suggest that one of the crew, an engineer, interrupted a burglar who killed him to stop him from raising an alarm. That was a false trail. None of you fell for it."

"The knot was toward the front," Boris said. "The victim must have been facing his attacker. How do you get a cord around somebody's neck from the front unless he knows you?"

"And the gun," Sylvie said. "If I were the criminal and somebody discovered me, I would shoot him. I would not hope to find a piece of electrical cord to strangle him with."

Joe was tempted to point out that guns make more noise than strangling cords. He restrained himself. This was David's show.

"A quarrel among thieves," Cesar remarked. "But what about the ransom note? I spotted it under the chair. It offered to return the bonds for a quarter of a million dollars. Why would thieves do that?"

"Maybe the bonds are too hard to cash," Jason suggested. "You know—like counterfeiters who sell their phony bills for a few cents on the dollar."

"Cesar is the only one who mentioned the ransom note," David announced. "There's another detail none of you picked up on—the victim's hands."

"What about them?" Sylvie asked, puzzled.

"Wait, wait!" Cesar shouted. He slapped the table. "Of course! The hands were clean, and the nails were manicured. That was no engineer. An engineer would have oily hands and cracked nails. I bet that was the owner of the yacht. He was planning to steal his own bonds, then rip off the insurance company for the ransom! He probably gave the crew the evening off, to get them out of the way. But one of them suspected something and stayed behind."

"Bravo, Cesar," David said. "You got it."

"Yeah," Cesar groaned. "I got it today—but not last night, when it would have done me some good."

"Then the killer was the real engineer, right?" Boris asked. "He changed clothes with the victim to confuse the authorities while he made his escape."

"He certainly confused me." Sylvie laughed.

A general discussion broke out. Joe and Frank joined in. So did Lisa and even Kenneth. The only one who kept out of it was Elizabeth. Her expression and body language said she found the whole business childish. Joe wondered why she had entered the contest if that was how she felt. Here was still another puzzle to be solved.

The second part of the detective contest took place toward the end of the morning. It was a test of observational skills. Everyone gathered around the TV to watch a tape.

Like the contestants, Frank and Joe watched intently. On the screen, a man and two women met on a street corner. They chatted for a few moments. Two other men approached from opposite directions. One of them bumped into the woman on the left. He muttered an apology and walked away.

A moment later the woman he had collided with groped in her purse and let out a shriek. The man who was talking with her ran after the one who had bumped her. At that, the tape ended.

David stood up and passed out questionnaires to the contestants. "Okay," he said. "No conversation until all of you have finished your responses."

Joe took a spare questionnaire from David and gave it a shot. It was not easy. The questions included the clothing and personal appearance of all five people in the scene, what each had said, and exactly what had happened.

David collected the completed questionnaires and put them in a manila envelope. "Okay—any remarks?"

"This is kid stuff," Elizabeth said. "I'm not saying I remembered all those stupid details. Who could? But the important part was simply babyish."

"Wa-a-ah!" Cesar said with a grin. Elizabeth sniffed loudly and looked in the other direction.

"The important part being . . . ?" David asked, looking around the circle.

"The guy stole her wallet when he shoved her," Jason said. "That's an old stunt. Some dude tried it on me once when I was getting off a bus. I gave him a swift elbow below the belt. Boy, did he look surprised."

"What do you think happened after the tape ended?" David asked.

Boris shrugged. "The other guy—the woman's friend—probably caught him. He was pretty fast off the mark."

"And then?" David continued.

"The police put the pickpocket in jail," Sylvie said.

"Maybe it works that way in Canada," Cesar said. "My bet is he got himself a terrific lawyer and walked."

"So, Sylvie, you think the perpetrator was arrested. What about the rest of you? Everybody agree?" David asked, giving another look around the circle. The contestants nodded.

"Joe? Frank?" David added.

"Well . . ." Frank said. He glanced over at Joe, who gave him a grin. "Tell them."

"Even if the pickpocket got caught," Joe said, "I doubt if the cops could arrest him. No evidence."

"What about the wallet?" Elizabeth demanded. "Even if he threw it down on the sidewalk, it would still tell against him."

"He didn't have the wallet," Frank said. "Right after he took it, he passed it to his accomplice, who strolled off in the other direction. Right, David?"

"I *knew* there was something about that other guy," Cesar said. He slapped his palm against his forehead.

"You tricked us!" Elizabeth declared crossly.

David smiled. "Good," he said. "I was hoping to. Just remember, the bad guys aren't out to make it easy for crime solvers."

Lunch was assorted sandwiches and chips, served on the afterdeck. No one would have wanted to stay inside and miss the view. The *Colombe d'Or* was approaching its next port of call. Ahead, a green island loomed up out of the blue sea. Frank thought its steep slopes and peak looked like a child's drawing of a volcano.

David confirmed this. "That's Mount Orange," he told the group. "It's still active. The last major eruption was about fifty years ago. It buried one of the towns on the island under superheated gas and ash. Over ten thousand people died."

Sylvie shivered. "That's terrible! What if it explodes while we are there?"

"There's usually some warning before a big eruption," Frank assured her. "Sort of like clearing your throat before you sing."

"In any case," David added, "we'll dock at Fort William. The volcano has never touched it. The town that was destroyed was on the opposite side of the island. If we had more time, we could go over and explore the ruins."

"Spooky-y-y," Cesar said in a hollow voice. He waved his open hands in Sylvie's direction.

"Ooo, don't!" Sylvie exclaimed. Cesar grinned.

"Let her alone," Boris said gruffly.

"Yeah, stop playing the clown," Jason added.

Cesar's grin flickered. "At least I know when I act like a clown," he retorted. "Unlike some people I could name who don't know it and can't help it."

Sylvie smiled at him. "It's all right, Cesar," she said. "I know you were just trying to be funny. I think you're cute."

Cesar beamed. Frank glanced at Jason and Boris. Both were trying to look unconcerned.

"How long will we be stuck on this island?" Elizabeth asked in a bored voice. "Is there anything to do on it?"

"The old part of the city is very picturesque," David replied. "I like to just wander. There are also some very elegant boutiques and shops around the square."

Elizabeth's face brightened.

The boat docked alongside a palm-lined boule-

56

vard. Nearby, Frank spotted the colorful umbrellas of an outdoor café. From the harbor, the old town rose in level after level of white-stone buildings with lacy iron balconies and red-tile roofs. The green slopes of Mount Orange supplied a lush backdrop.

Frank and Joe stood at the rail admiring the view. "Do you think they have a college here?" Joe wondered out loud. "I could handle four years in a place like this."

"Huh," Frank replied. "You'd probably spend your four years lying on the beach waiting for a nice ripe guava to plop into your mouth."

Joe smiled. "You could do worse. But I like mangoes better." He lowered his voice and added, "We should try to keep an eye on everyone while we're ashore this afternoon. Why don't I concentrate on Sylvie? That was her perfume in our room last night."

"Good idea," Frank said. "And I'll watch Elizabeth. There's something I don't get about her attitude."

"*Attitude*'s the word," Joe said, rolling his eyes. "That girl is nothing *but* attitude!"

As the teens left the boat, David warned them to be back by four o'clock. "Have a great time," he added. "If you need to get in touch, you have the telephone number here. Bettina and I will both be on board."

The group stayed together just long enough to

reach the first corner. Sylvie eyed the narrow cobbled street that twisted its way uphill under lines hung with brightly colored wash.

"Let's go this way," she eagerly urged. "I bet we'll find some awesome views up the hill."

Elizabeth sniffed. "A slum's a slum," she said. "Even in the Caribbean. I'd rather find the square and check out the shops."

"Okay. Have fun," Sylvie said with a touch of sarcasm in her tone. She started up the little street. After a moment's hesitation the others followed. Only Frank stayed behind. Elizabeth bit her lower lip as she watched the group walk away. Then she tossed her blond hair in a way that was meant to say, "Why should I care about *them?*"

"I detest sight-seeing," Elizabeth told Frank. "It's so boring. Our place in Virginia is just a mile from a Civil War battleground. One of my daddy's relatives commanded a battalion there. But I've never visited. I can't stand all those noisy, smelly charter buses. And the people with their camcorders! Sometimes they walk right up to our house and take each other's pictures on our front porch. Can you imagine?"

Frank started to say, "Maybe you should charge admission." He thought better of it.

Elizabeth didn't notice. "I really thought there would be more people like me on this cruise. After all, a yacht in the Caribbean . . . I didn't stop to think that a magazine like *Teenway* has to appeal to a pretty mixed bag. I do wish the others didn't resent me for my advantages, though. I can't help who I am or who my ancestors were, can I?"

Frank was tempted to say that she might try not acting so stuck-up. He decided to keep his mouth shut. After all, he was a detective, not an advice columnist.

By three-thirty Joe was ready to bang his head against a wall. While sticking close to Sylvie, he was also trying to keep track of everyone else in his group. But how could he? All afternoon they kept wandering off, hanging back, dawdling in shops, hurrying ahead. It was as if they had all secretly decided to drive him bonkers!

Now he was in a tiny square where five alleys— they were too narrow to be called streets—met. Against one of the house walls, a stone fountain burbled. Cesar held his cupped hands under the stream of water.

"Don't drink that," Sylvie warned. "You might catch something."

Instead of drinking, Cesar poured the water over his head. "Ah! That's better," he said. He looked around. "Where is everybody?"

"Off," Sylvie replied with a vague wave of the hand. "It's late. We should get back to the yacht."

"How? Jason's the only one who can find his way around this place," Cesar said. "He's amazing."

As if summoned, Jason appeared. "We're late,"

he said. He pointed down one of the alleys. To Joe it looked no different from the others. "That should be the shortest way back."

As they walked downhill, the others joined them. Soon they emerged from the clustered houses at the seafront boulevard, just across from where the yacht was moored. At that moment Frank and Elizabeth came along. Elizabeth was carrying a shopping bag with the linked initials of a famous French designer. Joe caught Frank's eye. Frank shrugged.

The group started across the boulevard. Suddenly four motorbikes sped out of a side street and cut right in front of them. Each motorbike had a big metal box on the back, emblazoned with the words "All-Island Pizza. We D-liver, You D-light." The riders halted next to the gangplank of the *Colombe d'Or*.

"Hey, hey, hey," Boris said. "Looks like we eat pizza tonight. That's a nice surprise."

The four riders took stacks of cardboard boxes from the carriers and started toward the boat. A man in a double-breasted white chef's jacket met them and kept them from going aboard.

"NO!" he shouted as the teens drew closer. "No one ordered pizzas. If we want pizza, *I* make pizza!"

"Somebody ordered fifteen pies," one of the riders insisted. He held out a slip of paper. "Here, see? The name of the boat, fifteen pies, plain, mushrooms, extra cheese . . . it's all here."

"It must be a joke," the chef said. "I tell you, we did not order pizza."

"Some joke! What do we do with fifteen pies?" the deliveryman demanded.

From the upper deck, Bettina said, "It's all right. We'll accept them. Arnie, pay him—and be sure to include a generous tip."

"Yes, ma'am," the chef said in a grumpy tone.

"The prankster strikes again," Joe murmured to Frank. "We'd better—"

Nearby, voices were suddenly raised. "Come on, admit it!" Jason said to Boris. "I saw you sneak into that shop and make a phone call. And I overheard you say the name of the yacht."

"Big deal," Boris said. "That proves nothing."

Jason stuck out his chin. "You want proof? I heard more than that. I heard you when you said *mushrooms* and *cheese!*"

61

7 A Telltale Chime

Everyone clustered around Boris and Jason. From her position on the boat, Bettina heard Jason's accusation and came ashore to join the group.

"What about it, Boris?" Cesar asked. "Did you really call in that order for pizza?"

"It is not a very funny joke," Sylvie said.

Frank studied Boris's expression. He did not look flustered by the pressure. If anything, there was a hint of secret amusement. What was the joke—if not the pizzas themselves?

"Yes, I made a phone call," Boris announced.

"Really, **Boris**, this sort of prank—" Bettina started to say.

Boris interrupted her. "But I did not call a pizzeria. I called a friend back home. Her name is

Christina. If you want to check with her, I will give you her number."

"I heard you say the *Colombe d'Or*," Jason repeated.

Boris shrugged. "I was bragging about being on a fancy yacht. I told her the name of the yacht."

"Okay, but what about the mushrooms and cheese?" Joe asked.

"I told Christina that tensions were mushrooming among us," Boris replied. He smiled. "And—please excuse it, Bettina—I think I called you the Big Cheese."

"I don't mind," Bettina said. "As an editor, I've been called a lot worse."

Boris turned to Jason. "Satisfied?" he demanded belligerently. "Or did you maybe also hear me say something about anchovies?"

Everybody cracked up, except Jason, who turned away with a resentful expression.

"Hey, everybody, let's get with it," Cesar said. "All those pizzas are getting cold!"

The group boarded the yacht. Arnie, the chef and steward, had already set up a table on the afterdeck with plates, napkins, and cold drinks. As they filed back, he and Chuck, the crew member who had slipped on Evan's marbles that morning, appeared with four steaming pizzas, two plain and two with mushrooms. No anchovies, as Boris pointed out.

Frank and Joe each took a slice of pizza. Frank chose plain and Joe chose mushroom. They went to a corner of the deck where they couldn't be overheard.

"Our prankster seems to be getting more ambitious," Frank said. "First it's plastic spiders in the cake, now a lifetime supply of pizzas."

"Don't forget David's runaway laptop," Joe replied. "Not to mention entering our room and rifling the contest entries."

Frank nodded. "The thing is, we had no real leads until now. This is different. There's a good chance the trickster left a trail. Let's check it out. What was the name of that pizzeria?"

"All-Island, I think," Joe told him. "Anyway, how many can there be in a town this size?"

When the boat was at sea, the telephone for passengers worked via a satellite dish, but when the boat docked, the phone was hooked up to a landline.

Frank got the number of the pizzeria and dialed. A man answered. When Frank explained what he wanted, the man passed the phone to a woman with a Caribbean lilt in her voice.

"Oh, yes, I remember," she said. "I will not so easily forget an order for fifteen pies, and that a false one, too!"

"What can you tell me about the person who called?" Frank asked.

"Not so very much," she replied. "The voice was muffled. It was high for a man but low for a woman. A Yankee accent, I think. Like yours."

"Didn't it surprise you, getting such a big order

from a stranger? Weren't you suspicious?" Frank wondered.

"From now on I will be," the woman said with a musical laugh. "But we are used to orders from yachts for delivery to dockside. This is the first time we have a problem."

"I see," Frank said. "Do you happen to know what time the call came in?"

"Oh, yes, just before three-thirty," the woman told him.

"How sure are you?" Frank probed. "Did you write down the time?"

"No, but the caller asked us to deliver at precisely four," she replied. "I checked my watch to see if we could do it. Just then I heard a clock chime the half hour."

Puzzled, Frank asked, "A clock chimed? From a building near you, you mean?"

"No, no, I heard the sound over the telephone," the woman explained.

Frank glanced around. A few feet away, hanging on the wall, was an old-fashioned chiming clock. The hands indicated four forty-four. The second hand was just passing the halfway point.

Quickly, Frank said into the phone, "Please listen." He pointed the handset at the clock.

Bing bang bing bong . . .

The sound died away. He put the receiver to his ear. "Well?" he asked.

"That is exactly the same sound," the woman said. "But another clock might sound the same, too.

My auntie has one with chimes like that. I'm sorry. I wish I could help more."

"You've helped a lot," Frank assured her. "Thank you."

He hung up and told Joe what he had learned.

Joe stared at him. "But, Frank . . . you see what that means? If she heard this clock, then whoever made the call had to be on the boat at three-thirty."

"Right," Frank said.

Joe frowned. "I couldn't keep everyone in sight the whole time," he admitted. "But I don't see how anyone could have made it back here, placed the call, and got back up the hill without me noticing."

"And I was with Elizabeth the whole time," Frank said. "I think I deserve a bonus for that, by the way. Talk about a hardship assignment. So in other words, we can eliminate everyone . . . except David, Bettina, and the crew."

"And Evan," Joe pointed out. "Joke. Wait a minute, though. Kenneth *did* come back to the boat. He needed to get more film. Do you suppose he . . . ?"

"He's the most unlikely suspect," Frank pointed out. "But it's only in books that the most unlikely suspect is always the one who did it. In real life, it's usually the most *likely* suspect who's guilty. Still, maybe Kenneth saw something while he was here. We should ask him."

"Sure," Joe said. "But I think we should focus more on motive. Somebody wants to mess up this voyage. That's pretty clear. But why? How much do we really know about any of these people?"

"Not enough, obviously," Frank replied. "Let's go mingle and find out more."

The others were still on the afterdeck, enjoying the late afternoon sun and the fresh breeze from the sea. Lisa was seated near the rail with a can of soda in her hand. She saw Joe arrive and waved. He hesitated, then went over to join her. As a writer, she might have noticed something useful.

"Hey, Joe. Have you unmasked the pizza maniac?" Lisa asked.

Joe dragged over a chair and sat down. "Not yet. Any helpful hints?"

Lisa looked thoughtful. "Boris ate three slices with mushrooms," she said. "I'd call that a clue, wouldn't you?"

"A clue to his appetite, sure," Joe replied with a grin. "No, seriously—any idea why somebody would want to wreck the contest?"

Lisa stared out over the water. "It's a mystery," she said at last. "This contest means a lot to them. Not just getting to spend a few days living like a millionaire. Though I'm not putting that down. I like it. I could get used to it."

"Me, too," Joe assured her.

"Take Cesar," Lisa continued. "His grandparents immigrated from Mexico. His dad is an auto mechanic and his mom works in a dry cleaner's. He's got an older sister and two younger brothers. Winning this contest is his one big chance to be able to go away to a really good college. Do you think he's going to ruin that with some dumb stunts?"

"I see your point," Joe said. "How do you know so much about Cesar?"

Lisa smiled. "I asked. Most people love to talk about themselves. I love to listen to them. It's a perfect match."

It's different with me, Joe thought ruefully. When people know they're talking to a detective, they always watch what they say, even the ones who don't have anything to hide.

"Boris, too," Lisa said. "Back in Russia, his mother was a doctor and his father was an engineer. Now they run a little grocery store in Brooklyn. Boris will do okay whatever happens, but winning the *Teenway* scholarship would give him a big head start. Why would he want to blow that?"

"What about Elizabeth?" Joe asked. "She doesn't act as if she needs a college scholarship."

Lisa rolled her eyes. "Elizabeth's really not so bad when she forgets she's one of the Virginia Wheelwrights," she said. "The problem is, that doesn't happen very often."

Joe chuckled. "So who's left? Jason and Sylvie."

"I can't figure Jason," Lisa said, shaking her head. "One minute I think he's really sharp. The next minute I can't believe there's anything in his mind more complicated than deciding which side of his nose to pierce next. As for Sylvie, don't get me started. Either she's exactly the bubblehead she appears to be, or she is so deep it's scary."

"Whatever, it's hard to see what their motives might be," Joe said.

"Maybe we're looking too hard," Lisa suggested. "What if these stunts are just pure malicious mischief? What if somebody simply likes to watch the rest of us scurrying around, eyeing each other suspiciously?"

"Sort of like stirring an anthill with a stick?" Joe replied. "Could be. The trouble is, sooner or later one of the stunts may go too far. And when that happens, somebody could get hurt."

The yacht sailed from Fort William just after six. By sunset, only the peak of Mount Orange still showed above the horizon. As darkness fell, the sea became rougher. The boat rose and fell like a restless elevator. At the same time, it rolled noticeably from side to side.

The dinner gong sounded while Frank and Joe were on the afterdeck, talking over the day's events. When they stood up to go inside, the unexpected motion of the deck made Frank stumble.

"Oops," he said, grabbing the rail for support. "We're going to need our sea legs tonight."

Joe grinned. "Not to mention strong stomachs," he said. "I wonder who'll show up for dinner."

"After all that pizza, who needs dinner anyway?" Frank replied.

As it turned out, everyone showed up. Sylvie even changed for the occasion. She walked in wearing a navy skirt and gauzy white blouse, with a deep blue scarf loosely knotted at her neck. The gesture earned her a smile of appreciation from Bettina and a carefully composed portrait by Kenneth.

The main course was a delicate, very fresh poached fish in caper sauce, accompanied by tiny new potatoes decorated with sprigs of parsley. Frank thought it was sensationally good and polished his plate. However, whether because of that afternoon's pizzafest or the motion of the boat, most everyone else picked at the food without much interest.

The table was cleared. Arnie carried in the dessert. It was a big glass bowl filled with slices of colorful tropical fruit, topped with scoops of lemon, lime, and orange sorbet. There was a chorus of ooohs and ahs.

"I think I just found more room in my stomach," Boris announced.

"Me, too," Lisa said.

"It looks wonderful," David said. "But I'm going to have to pass."

Several more people said yes to dessert. Arnie had barely finished serving them when Boris clapped a hand over his mouth and jumped to his feet.

"What is it?" Bettina asked in an alarmed voice. "Do you feel ill?"

Boris didn't answer. He ran for the door to the deck.

"I—I don't . . ." Jason started to say. His face

70

suddenly went pale. He, too, jumped up and ran outside to lean over the rail, Lisa close behind.

Elizabeth sprang to her feet. Her chair clattered to the floor.

"You fools!" she screamed. "Don't you see? We've all been poisoned!"

8 Throwing Up Clues

At Elizabeth's alarmed cry, everyone jumped up from the table.

"Please stay calm," Bettina said, in a voice that cut through the hubbub. "There's no cause for panic."

"Bettina's right," David said. "Some people get seasick more easily, that's all. It's nothing to be nervous about."

"It's poison, I tell you!" Elizabeth wailed, clutching her middle.

Joe was on her left. He took her arm and said in a soothing voice, "Hey, it's okay. Calm down. We'll take care of it."

Elizabeth blinked a few times. She looked at Joe as if she had never seen him before. Then she turned to Bettina. "Please excuse me," she said. "I think I need to rest."

"Do that, dear," Bettina replied.

"You want me to come with you?" Joe asked.

Elizabeth straightened up and returned her nose to its usual airborne position. "Certainly not!" she said. "I am quite in control of myself . . . unlike some people I could name."

She left, taking the door that led upstairs.

"Did you notice something?" Frank murmured to Joe. "For all her talk about poison, she didn't leave in much of a hurry. I don't think she was actually nauseated."

"Daddy?" Evan said, tugging at David's shirt. "I don't feel so good. I think I'm going to be sick."

"Okay, take it easy, son," David said. "You'll be all right. Take deep breaths." He hurried the boy out of the salon. Just then Boris came back in, his face white and drawn.

"Oof!" he said, dropping onto his chair. "Whatever I ate, I hope never to eat it again!"

Arnie was still standing by the buffet, horrified. "Ms. Dunn," he said. "There was nothing wrong with the food, I swear it. All the ingredients were bought fresh this afternoon, from the most reliable sources."

"No one's accusing you or your food," Bettina said.

This diplomatic lie seemed to serve its purpose. Arnie calmed down.

Joe studied the table. It was just as he thought.

"Frank," he said in an undertone. "Everybody who got sick ate dessert. And nobody who skipped dessert got sick."

Frank, too, scanned the table. "You're right," he replied. Aloud, he said, "Arnie? Would you mind if we take a closer look at the fruit compote?"

Arnie's hysteria started to mount again. "There is *nothing* wrong with it!" he declared.

"Then it doesn't matter if we check it out," Joe said. "If we want to waste our time, so what?"

Bettina caught Arnie's eye and nodded. He gave the Hardys an irate look, but he stepped aside.

Joe leaned over the bowl and sniffed deeply. Then he moved back to give Frank room. Frank, too, sniffed the dessert.

"There's something," Frank said.

"Sort of like cough syrup?" Joe replied. "That's what I thought."

Arnie was listening. "This dish is perfectly fine," he said. "I had a portion myself. It was delicious."

"Smell," Joe suggested.

Arnie looked at him suspiciously before lowering his head over the bowl. When he raised it, his expression had changed to one of fury.

"Okay, what clown messed with my *coupe royale des fruits tropicales?*" he shouted, glaring around the table. "Come on, admit it!"

There was an awkward silence. During it, Jason and Lisa came back inside, both pale. Joe hid a smile. Even attacked by nausea, Lisa had kept her miniature tape recorder in her hand.

"Arnie—when did you last taste the fruit cup?" asked Frank.

"Why . . . this afternoon, not long after I made it," the chef told him. "I remember I had just rinsed my bowl when those pizzas arrived."

"And there was nothing wrong with it then?" Frank pursued.

"Nothing!" Arnie declared.

"What then?" Joe asked.

"Then I put it in the galley fridge to chill," Arnie said. "I took it out a little while ago to top it with the sorbets."

"But you didn't try it then?" Cesar asked.

Arnie shook his head. "No. If I had, I would have known something was wrong. I certainly wouldn't have served it. I would have fed it to the fishes."

"I have the feeling anybody can go into the fridge," Frank said. "Right?"

"Sure," Arnie replied. "We keep a shelf loaded with juices, bottled waters, and sodas just for the passengers."

"So if somebody wanted to put something in the fruit, it wouldn't have been hard to do without getting caught," Joe said.

"I guess not," Arnie admitted. "Put that way, we come out sounding pretty careless. Maybe we should change the way we do things. But we're not used to having poisoners as passengers."

"Look, everybody!" Boris shouted from the doorway. "I found it!"

He rushed into the room. In his right hand, held high, was a small brown bottle.

"*What* did you find?" Bettina demanded.

"And where?" Jason added.

Boris handed the bottle to Joe. As soon as Joe saw the label, he understood. "It's ipecacuanha— syrup of ipecac," he said to Frank. "Remember? From that first-aid course?"

Frank snapped his fingers. "I should have guessed!" To the others, he said, "Syrup of ipecac is a powerful emetic. In other words, it makes you throw up. It's used when somebody's swallowed a noncaustic poison and you need to get it out of their system fast."

"You mean somebody put a powerful medication in our food?" Sylvie said. "How could they dare? What if one of us died from it? That would be murder!"

Joe studied the label. "The usual adult dose is a tablespoonful," he reported. "And this whole bottle holds only two tablespoonfuls. Spread across a dozen portions of fruit, there wasn't much chance that anybody would even come close to a normal dose. It must have worked so well because people were already feeling queasy from the rough seas."

"Boris, good job finding this," Frank said. "Where was it?"

Boris beamed. "There is a wastebasket in the rest room next to the galley," he explained. "I found it under some paper towels."

76

"What made you look there?" Lisa asked.

"I was sure something had been put in the food," Boris replied. "I didn't think the trickster would risk leaving evidence in the galley. But I didn't think whoever it was would want to carry it very far either. So I looked near the galley, and there it was."

"That was very bright," Sylvie burbled.

"And very convenient," Jason said sourly. "It's almost as if you knew where to look."

"What's that supposed to mean?" Boris demanded, clenching his fists, his biceps bulging.

"Oh, nothing," Jason said. "So you spotted it in the wastebasket and you just reached in and picked it up. Didn't you ever hear of fingerprints?"

"Sure I have, wiseguy," Boris retorted. He gave Jason a narrow-eyed stare. "Everybody has. Including whoever put that stuff in the dessert. I figured he must have taken precautions."

"And in case he didn't," Jason pursued, "you made sure that *your* fingerprints were all over the bottle. Not to mention Joe's and Frank's."

Boris gave a low growl and started around the table toward Jason.

Joe quickly blocked his way. "Take it easy," he said. "Don't let him get to you."

"He'd better not let *me* get to *him*," Boris threatened. "When I'm done with him, he'll look like a pretzel!"

Bettina rapped her spoon against the table. "Stop it right now, all of you," she commanded. "I want no more taunts. Joe, Frank—you were starting to ask some very good questions. Please go on."

"Well . . ." Frank said. "There's one obvious question. *Why* did Boris find that bottle?"

Boris let out another growl. Frank held up a hand and said, "No, wait. What I'm getting at is this. There are thousands of square miles of open sea around us. If I wanted to get rid of something, I'd toss it over the side. Poof—gone forever. Why throw it in a wastebasket, where somebody might—where somebody *did*—find it?"

Cesar spoke up. "Simple as A-B-C. Because you want it to be found."

"And for a simple, twisted reason," Sylvie said. Her voice trembled with emotion. "This person wants us to know he is playing tricks on us. He wants us to believe he will play more and worse tricks. He wants to shake us up so we will not do so well in the contest."

For the last twenty minutes, Kenneth had been prowling the room, snapping candid shots of everyone. Now, to Joe's surprise, he spoke. "You're saying it's one of the other contestants?"

For a moment Sylvie looked confused. "I'm not accusing anyone," she insisted. "I don't know who's in back of this. But whoever it is, I think he gets a kick out of seeing us puzzled and upset. And I think that is really nasty!"

"I thoroughly agree, Sylvie," Bettina said. "Ordering those pizzas I can excuse as a juvenile prank. But jeopardizing people's health, even slightly, is another matter. You are all the guests of *Teenway*. If anything happens to you, the good name of *Teenway* is in danger. I won't have that. If these tricks do not stop at once, I shall have to think very seriously about canceling the contest and sending you all home early."

A shocked silence followed this declaration. Bettina looked around the table at each of the teens. Then she walked out of the room.

After that no one was in the mood to socialize. One by one, the contest finalists mumbled good night and drifted away. The Hardys were left with Lisa, Kenneth, and Arnie.

Arnie picked up the big glass bowl. "That compote was primo," he said regretfully. He started toward the door to the galley. "Why couldn't he have put that gunk in something like clam dip instead?"

Arnie left. "Let's go outside," Lisa said. "Maybe there's a moon."

The four went to the aft deck. The sky was lit with stars, but no moon. Joe recalled that he wanted to ask Kenneth about that afternoon. "You came back to the boat early, didn't you?" he said.

"Yes. I hadn't carried enough film into town," Kenneth replied. "I came back for more. Why?"

"You know the phone in the foyer?" Joe continued. "Did you notice anybody using it?"

Kenneth thought. "No. But I was just here for as long as it took to run down to my cabin, grab more film, and split."

Lisa lifted her recorder a little higher as she asked, "Well, Joe and Frank Hardy, do you have a lead as to the identity of the pizza maniac?"

Joe rolled his eyes. "No comment, as usual," he said. "Don't you ever put that thing away?"

"Sure." Lisa grinned. "When I've got my story!"

Joe and Frank kept at Kenneth, but they soon decided he probably didn't know anything relevant. A little later the crew anchored the boat for the night in the lee of a small island. Frank and Joe watched, then went down to their cabin to turn in.

Some time later Joe suddenly woke up. He lay on his bunk in the darkness, listening intently. Something had disturbed him. What?

After a few moments he heard furtive scraping sounds. His mental map told him they were coming from the corridor just outside the door to their cabin. Could it be the burglar returning? Or paying a visit to one of the other cabins?

Stealthily Joe pushed back the covers and stood up. He tiptoed across the dark cabin, felt his way along the wall to the door, and opened it a crack. The light in the corridor, which was left on all the time, was off. A bad sign—someone must have unscrewed a bulb.

A faint, almost indetectable glimmer of light came down the companionway from the main deck. Joe walked silently along the corridor toward it. Suddenly a shape loomed up in front of him, cutting off the light. He sensed, more than saw, two hands reaching out to grab him.

9 In the Bag

The instant he realized that he was under attack, Joe tucked his chin into his chest and dropped into a crouch. Reaching up, he closed both hands around one of his attacker's wrists. Then he did a half spin on the ball of one foot. His opponent's extended arm was now trapped against the fulcrum of his right shoulder. He took a deep breath and prepared to use the power of his thigh muscles to execute a full shoulder throw. Even as he did, he wondered why the other guy was hanging limp instead of resisting.

"Joe, hold on, it's me!" a familiar voice said in his ear. At the same time a hand grabbed the waistband of his pajamas at the back. This was a standard counter to his move. If he went ahead with the throw, he would find himself being pulled along with his opponent.

"Frank? What are you doing here?" Joe asked softly. He released his brother's wrist and straightened up.

"I heard a suspicious noise and got up to check it out," Frank replied, keeping his voice pitched low. "I saw a flickering light up on the main deck, near the head of the stairs. I went to see who it was, but by the time I got there the person had disappeared. What about you?"

"Same as you," Joe said. "But in my case the suspicious noise was you. Did you turn out the hall light?"

"No, it was like that when I came out of our room," Frank said. "I tried the switch. No go. The bulb must be unscrewed."

"So we're not dealing with somebody who just decided to get a midnight snack," Joe remarked.

"No way," Frank told him. "Do you remember where we put the flashlight? I want a closer look at the area near the head of the stairs."

The Hardys found their flashlight and climbed up to the main deck. They searched the foyer and the passage that led to the salon and dining area. They checked the washroom where Boris had found the ipecac bottle. They peered into the galley. Nothing seemed out of place anywhere.

They returned to the head of the companionway.

"Maybe it was just an insomniac after all," Joe said, disgusted.

"An insomniac with a phobia about lightbulbs?" Frank replied. "I don't think so."

"Well, whatever he or she was up to, no traces were left," Joe said. "Let's take another look in the morning."

"I guess you're right," Frank said. He waved the flashlight around for one last look. His voice changed. "Joe—look!"

He had stopped the circle of light on the bulletin board. Crudely painted in black on the white cork surface was a skull and crossbones.

A superstitious thrill touched the back of Joe's neck and ran down his spine. After a moment he recovered his cool. He stepped forward and touched a fingertip to the bulletin board. It felt dry, but when he sniffed his finger there was a faint odor of paint solvent.

"It's pretty fresh," he reported.

"It has to be," Frank replied. "We would have noticed if it had been there when we went to bed."

"A skull and crossbones," Joe mused. "The symbol for poison. And this evening ipecac, stuff that's used in poisoning cases, turned up in the dessert."

Joe paused and stared at the sinister drawing. It seemed to expand to fill his field of vision.

"You know what, Frank?" he continued. "Maybe whoever painted this is the same person who doctored the dessert. I bet this is meant as a threat. It's a warning. The message is, next time they'll use something more harmful than ipecac syrup. Something really poisonous."

"Could be," Frank said. "I can think of another

explanation, though. And it's one I like even less than yours."

"What's that?" Joe asked.

Frank cleared his throat. "A couple of hundred years ago this area we're cruising around was infested with bloodthirsty pirates. People like Blackbeard and Captain Kidd, who preyed on innocent sailors and travelers, plundering and killing them. And what was the flag the pirates used? The Skull and Crossbones!"

There was a tense silence. Joe turned his face away from the menacing symbol. As he did, something on the deck caught his eye. It was small and black. He bent down to pick it up. Then he held it out to show to Frank. It was a plastic spider.

"I remember back in grade school," Joe said, "I spent a lot of time drawing a skull and crossbones on the cover of my looseleaf notebook. I must have been about the same age as Evan is now."

"I probably did the same," Frank admitted. "Lots of kids do. But there's a difference between drawing something on your own notebook and painting it on somebody else's wall. Can you really see a kid like Evan sneaking out of his cabin in the middle of the night to spray a pirate symbol on the bulletin board?"

"Well, no, I guess not," Joe said. "And I can't see how he would reach the lightbulbs to unscrew them, either. So maybe Evan dropped a spider here at some other time. Or maybe the prankster deliberately left the spider near the drawing to try to pin the blame on Evan. That would be a really dirty trick."

"Or the prankster could have dropped it by accident," Frank pointed out. "But let's say the same person who painted this put the ipecac in the fruit. Finding this spider here makes it look pretty likely that he stuck the spiders on the cake yesterday, too. And if that's so, it means that once we've solved one puzzle, we'll have solved them all."

Joe held back a yawn. "The sooner the better," he said. "I wouldn't mind having a little time to enjoy the cruise."

Morning came quickly. Just after dawn the boat weighed anchor and started toward its next destination. When the Hardys passed the bulletin board on the way to breakfast, Joe saw that the skull and crossbones had vanished under a fresh coat of white paint. Captain Mathieson obviously ran a tight ship.

After breakfast everyone gathered in the salon. It was time for the second round of the teen-detective contest. David walked to the center of the room. He had a stack of booklets under one arm.

"This morning's trial is a little different," he announced. "For one thing, we haven't attempted to stage it, not even on tape. For another, the focus is on the testimony of witnesses rather than physical evidence. In fact, what I've tried to do is give you something like a classic 'fair play' detective story."

"Oh no," Sylvie groaned. "You mean with timetables? Who did what when? I always skip over those chapters. They just confuse me."

"I don't skip those chapters, I skip the whole book," Jason bragged. "Action, excitement, that's what counts. Not all this intellectual hoo-ha."

Joe saw David's smile flicker.

"I do not agree," Boris said. "The clash of witnesses is exciting. The moment when you see how to prove that someone is lying—that is a thrill."

"I hope you'll find this morning thrilling," David said, cutting short the discussion. "Here is the situation. A famous museum has just held a reception for its most important contributors. Afterward the director discovers that a small but priceless sculpture is missing. She asks you to figure out who took it, without disturbing any innocent contributors or causing a scandal."

Cesar laughed. "I get it. The title of this story is 'Don't Dog the Fat Cats.'"

David ignored Cesar's joke. He held up one of the booklets. "In here you'll find a floor plan of the exhibit and a series of statements by people who were at the reception. You have one hour to read the material, think it over, and decide who the thief is. Guessing won't do the job. You have to say how you identified the guilty party, citing evidence from the booklet. Any questions?"

"Can we use reference materials?" Boris asked.

"All the information you need is in the booklet," David told him. "Anything else? All right. Good luck."

The five finalists took their booklets and fanned out to different parts of the boat. Joe and Frank used this free period to make notes about all the incidents on the voyage so far.

They also found time to talk with Evan. They dropped casual mentions of pirates, poisons, and skulls into the conversation. Evan did not show even a flicker of fear or self-consciousness. Frank looked over at Joe and gave a slight shake of his head. Whoever had defaced the bulletin board, it was clearly not Evan.

Soon the hour was up. While Kenneth took one photograph after another, the contestants handed David their entries. He promised to score them right away and asked them not to discuss their solutions until he had finished.

"Very well," Sylvie said as David went off to his room. "But I have another mystery. Has anyone seen my scarf? I know I wore it last night, and now I do not know where it is. It is blue with green parrots. My favorite uncle brought it back from Paris for me, and I would hate to lose it."

No one had seen it since the night before.

"Hey, Joe," Evan said. "I bet we can find it. Will you look with me?"

"Sure, why not," Joe replied. "Where should we start?"

"How about under the furniture?" Evan suggested. "Whenever I lose something, that's where it always is."

Joe played along. While the others grinned at

them, he and Evan got down on hands and knees. They crawled around the salon, peering under the easy chairs and couches. Joe wondered if he'd get a sneezing fit from the dust, but the carpet was spotless. It had obviously been vacuumed very recently.

Evan looked under a pale green loveseat. Suddenly he crowed, "I see it. There it is!"

He lay down on his stomach, stretched his arm under the loveseat, and pulled out a blue scarf.

"Evan, you found my scarf for me," Sylvie cried. "Oh, thank you!"

"Wait, there's something else," Evan said. He reached again. This time he produced a crumpled brown paper bag. He wrinkled his nose in comic disappointment and tossed the bag away. As he did, a slip of paper fell out.

Joe retrieved it and gave it a casual glance. Then he looked more closely. It was a cash register receipt from a pharmacy in Fort William for a bottle of syrup of ipecac.

10 If the Frame Fits . . .

Frank was talking to Cesar about ancient ruins in New Mexico and Colorado when he heard Evan give a yell. He glanced across the room. Evan and Joe were sitting back on their heels, staring down at a small slip of paper. Frank recognized the concentration in his brother's posture. Joe had just found something important.

There was no point in attracting any extra attention. Without seeming to hurry, Frank stood up and crossed the room. He got down on one knee next to Joe. "What have you got?" he asked softly.

Wordlessly Joe handed him the paper. A quick scan was enough to tell him what it was.

He sensed someone looking over his shoulder. He tried to block the person's view of the register receipt. Too late.

"So!" Elizabeth exclaimed. "It was Sylvie who bought that disgusting stuff and poisoned the fruit. I should have guessed!"

"What are you saying?" Sylvie demanded.

Elizabeth pointed to the receipt. "There's the proof," she said. "You dropped it when you lost your scarf. So that's why you didn't eat dessert last night!"

Frank stood up. "Somebody on the boat bought ipecac in Fort William yesterday afternoon," he said. "We suspected that already. Now we know. Here's the proof of purchase. But we still don't know *who* bought it."

"The receipt was found with Sylvie's scarf," Elizabeth repeated stubbornly. "There's your proof."

"A childishly obvious frame," Boris said. "I wonder, Elizabeth, why you're trying so hard to convince us that Sylvie is guilty? Did you construct this frame yourself?"

"Don't be ridiculous," Elizabeth said, tossing her head. "And why are you so sure it's a frame? Even clever criminals make mistakes."

Sylvie reddened at Elizabeth's hint that she was not only a criminal but an unclever one.

"Sylvie could not have bought the stuff," Boris insisted. "She went nowhere near the drugstore. I can testify to that. We were together the whole time we were in town."

"Er . . ." Sylvie began. "I'm sorry, Boris, but that's not true. I did go to the drugstore. I needed to buy hair conditioner. Remember? You wanted to look at postcards, so I left you at the souvenir store."

Now it was Boris who turned red.

Frank stepped in. "Sylvie, do you still have the receipt for the conditioner?"

She opened her eyes wide, raised her eyebrows and made a little popping sound with her lips. "I do not know," she said. "I will look."

She ran out of the room.

Frank took Joe aside. "We've got to find some way of calming everybody down," he said. "Everybody's at one another's throats, which is probably just what the trickster wants. The sooner we find out who's responsible, the better. Any ideas?"

"Here's one," Joe replied. "I noticed the carpet is really clean, even under the furniture. It must have been vacuumed very recently."

"I get it," Frank said. "The scarf and the paper bag must have been put there *after* the last vacuuming. Why don't you go find one of the crew and ask when that was? I'll hold down the fort here."

"Aye, aye, sir," Joe responded. He headed toward the door to the galley.

Sylvie rushed in with a slip of paper. "I found it!" she declared. "You see—herbal conditioner. It is much more expensive here than in Quebec."

Frank studied the two receipts. The time on the one for conditioner was half an hour earlier than on the one for syrup of ipecac. Had Sylvie gone into the pharmacy twice? It was possible, but was it likely? If she wanted to hide what she was doing, would she do something so likely to draw attention to her? It did not make much sense.

"You see?" Boris said to Elizabeth. "I told you this is a frame. Now you see."

"I see something," Cesar said. "I see that when you gave Sylvie an alibi that turned out to be false, you gave yourself a false alibi, too. Why? Did you feel you needed one?"

"Yeah, dude, what say you now?" Jason demanded.

It looked to Frank as if Boris was about to express himself with his fists. Frank was getting ready to step in when Joe reappeared.

"Hey, everybody," Joe said. "Listen up. I just checked with one of the crew. This room was dusted and vacuumed at six-thirty this morning. And there wasn't anything under any of the furniture at that time. No scarf, no paper bag . . . and no receipt for ipecac."

"Ha!" Boris said. He thrust his chin in Cesar's direction. "What did I say? An obvious frame!"

Sylvie put an arm through his. "You defended me!" she said, looking at him with big eyes.

Jason looked away. Elizabeth rolled her eyes.

Lisa went over to Elizabeth. "I'd like to hear more of your ideas about what's been going on," she said, readying her tape recorder. "Can we talk?"

Elizabeth looked as if she had just discovered a

93

drowned bug in her cup after drinking half the tea. She turned her back on Lisa and walked away.

David came back. He immediately sensed the change in the atmosphere. He joined Frank and Joe. "What's going on?" he asked.

The Hardys filled him in on the discovery of the pharmacy receipt and the argument that followed. His face grew longer.

"Having the contest on a yacht in the Caribbean was supposed to make it more fun," he complained. "Instead, all we have are quarrels and backbiting. This won't do *Teenway* any good. It wouldn't surprise me if Bettina carries out her threat to cancel the contest and send us home."

"What if we find out who's responsible for the trouble?" Joe asked.

"Obviously that would help," David told him. "But we don't have much time. That stunt with the ipecac was not funny. Next time, we may be faced with something really dangerous. Now I'd better end the suspense about this morning's problem."

He walked to the center of the salon. The finalists gathered around.

"The museum director stole the statue, disguised as a janitor," Jason called out in a mocking tone.

Cesar said, "You missed the most important point, Jason. The museum director *was* the statue."

David raised a hand. "Okay, guys, settle down. You all did good jobs with this morning's puzzle. Congratulations. Still, one entry was clearly superior. That was Cesar's."

Cesar grinned, pumped his fist in the air, and said, "Yes-s-s-s!"

The others looked disappointed, except for Elizabeth, who as usual seemed uninvolved.

"Cesar, will you summarize your conclusions about the robbery?" David asked.

"Yikes," Cesar said. "Well . . . two different witnesses said that the statuette was there before the speeches. Mr. Banks said he noticed right after the speeches that the statuette was gone. Colonel Fortune confirmed that. As for Mrs. Bond and Mr. Diamond, they alibied each other. They said that they were together during the speeches, when the lights were down, and the whole time afterward, until the alarm was raised."

"The robbery obviously happened during the speeches," Boris said.

"And the alibis of Bond and Diamond for that time are not so hot," Jason added. "The lights were low. One of them could have slipped away. I think Mrs. Bond did it. *Cherchez la femme.*"

Jason's attempt to pronounce French made Sylvie giggle. Then she said, "The lights were low, but they were not out. If I was standing with a man at a party, I would notice if he left. And he would notice if I left."

"That's for sure," Elizabeth drawled.

David stepped in quickly. "So, Cesar—who took the sculpture?"

"It must have been Banks," Cesar said. Over muttered questions and protests, he explained. "In her statement, Mrs. Bond mentioned that Banks was with them from the time the speeches ended. They were standing on the opposite side of the hall from the statuette. So how did Banks know it was missing . . . unless he was the one who took it?"

Boris slapped his forehead. "I saw that!" he declared. "I saw it, and I did not see what it meant. Smart work, Cesar. Do you play chess?"

"I know how the pieces move," Cesar said cautiously. "I'm no expert."

"Let's have a game," Boris said. "Maybe I beat you and I don't feel so stupid anymore."

Just before noon the *Colombe d'Or* anchored near an island with a half-moon-shaped beach of glistening white sand. Arnie and Chuck used the yacht's motorboat to take a charcoal grill and boxes of picnic supplies ashore. Then, while Arnie got the fire going, Chuck returned to ferry the passengers to the beach.

"Watch yourselves," Chuck warned as he nosed the boat onto the sand. "This is the Atlantic side. It looks pretty calm now, but the surf can kick up without warning."

"Doesn't anybody live here?" asked Sylvie.

"Oh sure," Chuck said. "There's a town and harbor just a couple of miles away as the crow flies, on the other side of the island. But this is the nicest beach, and we have it to ourselves."

Jason was the first one out of the boat. With his bright orange jams, whitewater sandals, and portable CD player, he reminded Frank of an ad for a spring weekend at a seaside resort. In contrast, Elizabeth was hidden under an ankle-length cover-up, big sunglasses, and a straw sombrero with a wide, wide brim. A band of lime green sunblock streaked her nose and cheekbones.

"Who wants to jump waves with me?" Evan asked.

Frank glanced over toward the grill and serving table. The hamburgers, hot dogs, and skewers of veggies wouldn't be ready for at least twenty minutes. Plenty of time to splash around. "Sure, let's go," he said.

The beach shelved steeply. A few steps took Frank in up to his thighs and Evan up to his chest. "This is far enough," Frank said as a wave curling with white foam swept in toward them. He grabbed Evan's arm and hoisted him up as the wave passed.

"Whee!" Evan shouted. "Watch—I'm going to jump the next one all by myself!"

A few seconds later he laughed and sputtered as a whitecap casually slapped him in the face.

"Let's jump together," Frank suggested.

Nearby Lisa, Jason, Cesar, and Boris were standing in the surf, tossing around a volleyball. Lisa was in barely up to her knees. Jason and Cesar were up to their waists. For Boris, opposite Lisa in the circle, the water almost reached his armpits. He had to leap high to catch the ball or to avoid being dunked by each passing wave.

The surf obviously got in the way of Boris's

throwing, too. Once the volleyball sailed by a few inches from Frank's nose. Evan dived after it and tossed it back to the circle.

A gust of wind caught Boris's next throw and took it out to sea. The ball landed twenty yards offshore. Boris swam out to retrieve it. When he returned, he threw to Cesar. His throw was short. It hit the surface, splashing salt water in Cesar's face.

"Hey, cut it out!" Cesar yelled. He grabbed the volleyball and hurled it full force at Boris.

Hampered by the deep water, Boris couldn't bring his hands up fast enough to catch it. The ball struck the side of his head, just over the temple. He groaned and slipped beneath the surface.

11 Fitting Out

Joe was standing on the beach talking to Kenneth about cameras and lenses. Out of the corner of his eye, he saw the volleyball hit Boris in the head. Even before Boris's face went under, Joe was sprinting down the sand toward the water. A few steps into the surf he launched himself into a racing dive over an incoming breaker. His powerful crawl strokes carried him quickly close to the spot where Boris had been standing. He found his footing and scanned the area.

Boris was floating facedown a few yards away. Joe splashed over to him, lifted him by the shoulders, and turned him over so his nose and mouth were out of the water. Boris revived just enough to reach up and get a stranglehold on Joe's neck. Joe had not realized how strong Boris was until he felt himself being choked and pulled down into the water.

Urgently Joe pushed his clasped hands up between Boris's arms, then used them as a fulcrum to pry himself loose. The instant his neck was free, he moved behind Boris's head, out of reach of those grappling arms. He cupped one hand under Boris's chin and started towing him toward the beach.

Every step was difficult, and Joe felt his legs begin to tremble. Then he heard Frank say, "It's okay, Joe, we've got him. We'll take it from here."

Joe blinked the water from his eyes. Frank and Cesar had taken up positions on either side of Boris and were holding him up by the arms. With a sigh of relief, Joe released his grip and staggered up onto the beach, where he sprawled on the sand.

"That was terrific, Joe," Kenneth said, pausing between shots of the ongoing rescue. "Wait till you see the pix I got!"

"You were magnificent!" Lisa added, her eyes glistening. "I was so scared!"

Joe took a deep breath, then sat up and brushed the sand off his arms. "I didn't do anything so special," he said.

Frank and Cesar brought Boris out of the water. His eyes were open, and he seemed to be trying to walk by himself. Arnie and David rushed over to help him sit down and put a towel around his shoulders.

"Boris, I'm so sorry," Cesar kept repeating. His voice shook. "It was an accident, I swear!"

100

"It's—" Boris started to say. He was shaken by a series of racking coughs. When he could, he took a deep breath and continued. "It's all right, Cesar. One day I will learn not to use my head for stopping hard objects."

Once it was clear that Boris was okay, the beach party went on, but the near disaster continued to cloud the mood of the party. Even the aroma of grilling burgers, onions, peppers, and tomatoes didn't lift their spirits.

The only one who was having a good time was Evan. He obviously believed anything that was fun on land was even more fun if you were knee-deep in the surf. He had almost managed to convince Joe, too, when Joe's hot dog slipped out of its bun, fell in the water, and started to drift away. Before it got far, though, some underwater creature snapped it up.

"Did you see that?" Evan demanded, wide-eyed. "Do you think it was a shark?"

"A shark? No way," Joe said quickly. Inwardly, he was not so sure. Whatever had scarfed down his hot dog was hungry and liked meat!

When he went to the grill for a replacement hot dog, Joe told Arnie what had happened. "Are there sharks around here?" he asked.

"Sure," Arnie said cheerfully. "You generally don't find them in close to land, though. They like it better in open water. And even there, chances are they'll leave you alone unless you're thrashing around and bleeding."

"I'll try to keep that in mind," Joe promised.

Lisa came over to him. "I've been thinking," she began. "It's really important for you and Frank to find out who's behind all these dirty tricks. I'd like to help you."

"Uh, thanks," Joe said. He looked around. Frank was all the way at the other end of the beach, talking to Bettina and David. "I'll—"

"Here's my idea," Lisa continued, interrupting him. "I've got all these tapes I've been making, you know? Talks I've had with people, of course, and also tapes of them talking among themselves. At meals, sitting out on deck, whatever."

Joe smiled to himself. Lisa's microcassette recorder was in her hand, dangling inconspicuously at her side. He was pretty sure it was going. She was taping herself telling him about taping people!

"Anyway," Lisa continued, "I bet a talented detective like you would find tons of clues on the tapes. I can't promise that they'll lead you to the trickster, but it's worth a shot, isn't it? I need my recorder, of course, but I also have a tape player in my cabin that has a speaker. I don't have a roommate. You could listen without anybody bothering you. And if you find anything, I can write about it in my story for *Teenway*. What do you say?"

Joe found himself uneasy about listening to conversations that had been taped without people's knowledge. There was something else that Lisa had apparently overlooked. To listen to twenty hours of conversations, he would have to spend at least twenty hours in her cabin with his ear next to her machine!

"Thanks for the offer," Joe said. "I'll check with Frank and get back to you, okay? After dinner?"

"Yeah, right," Lisa said. It was clear she didn't believe him. Her back was stiff as she turned and walked away.

At four o'clock the motorboat took everyone back to the yacht. Frank went straight to his cabin. After an afternoon on the beach, he needed to rinse off. The mixture of salt, sand, and sunscreen made his skin feel like a dry-rubbed roast.

After his shower, Frank pulled on a pair of blue volleyball shorts and a Bayport Boosters T-shirt. Someone started pounding on the cabin door. When he opened the door, a white-faced Evan almost fell into the room.

"Frank, help!" Evan blurted. "Some bad guy's going to blow up the boat!"

"Hey, hey," Frank said. He put his arm around the frightened boy's shoulders. "It's okay. Whatever it is, we'll take care of it."

"I looked for my daddy," Evan continued. "He's not in our room. I don't know where he went. And I *had* to tell somebody right away. It couldn't wait!"

Frank pulled over a chair and said, "Here, sit down. Tell me all about it. Then we'll go find your dad and tell him."

Evan took a deep breath. "You know that walkway along the outside of the room where we eat?

103

I like to sit there and read. Nobody ever comes there, and I can look out at the water."

"Sounds nice," Frank said.

"When we came back from the beach, I got my book and went out there," Evan continued. "There's a door that goes inside, to the hall where the stairs and the telephone are. The door was open. I could hear whenever anybody went through, but they couldn't see me because I was sitting on the deck."

"Okay, I get the picture," Frank said, nodding. "What then?"

Evan's lower lip started to quiver. "I wasn't paying any attention. I was at an exciting place in my book. Then all of a sudden I heard a man talk about blowing up the boat. I scrunched down and listened hard. I was afraid he'd see me."

Frank considered what to do. He did not want to make Evan more nervous than he already was, but the boy had to understand how important this might be.

"Evan? Do you think you can remember any of the exact words you heard?" Frank asked.

Evan closed his eyes tight. "Something about sinking the project," he said. " 'I'll send it to the bottom.' And something about making a bomb, too."

" 'Making a bomb'?" Frank repeated. "Could he have said making *it* bomb?"

"That's it!" Evan said, opening his eyes. "I knew it didn't sound right. What does that mean?"

"It may mean you heard the person who's been playing all these dirty tricks," Frank told him. "Now think carefully, Evan. Whose voice was it?"

"I don't know!" Evan wailed. "It wasn't anybody I know, I'm sure of that. I wish I'd peeked, but I was too scared."

"You did just right, Evan," Frank assured him. "Come on, let's go find your dad."

David was in his favorite private spot, on the sundeck atop the bridge. Joe was with him. Frank quickly filled them in on Evan's discovery. David took Evan off for a comforting talk.

"If Evan didn't know the voice, the guy we're after must be one of the crew!" Joe exclaimed.

"Unless he was disguising his voice," Frank pointed out. "But why would he do that?" He countered his argument immediately. "He had no idea someone was overhearing him. I think we'd better hunt up Captain Mathieson."

The captain was in his office. The room looked different without a strangled dummy sprawled on the deck. When Frank explained what they wanted, Mathieson shook his head firmly.

"I know every member of the crew well," he said. "You're barking up the wrong tree."

"Do you know if any of them might have money problems?" Joe asked. "Someone might have bribed one of them."

"This whole region is devoted to the luxury trade," the captain said with a frosty smile. "Anybody who's trying to live around here on an ordinary salary has money problems. That doesn't mean we would agree to anything that might harm our passengers."

Frank scratched his head. "So all the crew have worked for you for a long time?" he asked.

"I didn't say that," Mathieson replied. "I said I know them well. In fact, there's one member of the crew who has never sailed with me before. But I've known him for years. He agreed to work this charter as a favor to me. One of my usual crew fell ill at the last moment. You probably met him. He was helping the chef at the picnic today—Chuck Arneson."

"What does Chuck do when he's not working for you?" Joe asked with mounting excitement.

"Why . . . he usually crews on a smaller private boat that's based at St. Hilda. A gorgeous fifty-foot sloop, the *Stet*. I don't know where the name comes from."

"I do," Frank said grimly. A few more pieces of the puzzle had just fallen into place. "It's a term used by proofreaders. It means roughly, 'Leave it the way it is.' Who is the owner?"

"A retired magazine publisher," the captain said. "Fellow named Mares."

The Hardys went in search of Chuck. "Mares— he's the guy who snubbed Bettina at the yacht club," Joe said. "I told you about that."

"I know," Frank said. "So Chuck's boss has a major grudge against Bettina and *Teenway*. It fits."

They went out on the afterdeck. The whole

group was there, including David and Evan. Chuck was standing behind a table to one side, mixing fruit drinks. He saw them coming and noticed their grim expressions. His shoulders hunched.

"Some juice?" he asked, picking up a pitcher.

"No, thanks," Frank said. "Tell me, Chuck—the captain tells me this is a temporary job for you. You usually work for Walter Mares, who used to own *Teenway*. Quite a coincidence, isn't it?"

Chuck's knuckles whitened. "What of it?" he growled.

"Your phone call this afternoon," Joe said. "Somebody overheard you bragging about the dirty tricks you've been doing."

Chuck's eyes blazed. He didn't waste time on denials. He raised the pitcher of papaya juice and flung the contents in Joe's face. Then he threw the pitcher itself at Frank. It struck him in the chest, crashed to the deck, and shattered.

Joe and Frank recoiled from the sudden attack. Chuck spun on one foot, took two running steps, and dived over the rail into the sea.

12 The Timetable's Tale

Everyone on the deck started yelling. Frank ran to the rail. Chuck was already twenty yards from the yacht and moving fast. He looked as if he was a strong swimmer. He would have no trouble making the beach.

Frank tore off his shirt and started to climb over the rail. Captain Mathieson appeared, drawn by the uproar, and grabbed his arm. "What's all this?" he demanded. "What are you doing?"

"Going after Chuck," Frank said, pointing to the dot in the water that was Chuck's head.

"I can't allow you to swim to shore from here," the captain declared. "You're my passenger. It's too risky."

"Then radio the cops," Joe said urgently, wiping the juice off his face. "Tell them to pick up Chuck."

The captain released Frank and spread his hands. "The nearest police station is two islands away," he said. "By the time we could get an officer here, a skilled sailor like Chuck would have found a boat and been long gone. In any case, what is it you're accusing him of?"

"He was the trickster," Frank said.

"Frank!" Joe shouted. "The motorboat!"

The yacht's motorboat was still tied up farther forward. Joe and Frank sprinted toward it and jumped down into the cockpit. While Joe went to the bow to handle the line, Frank took the wheel and reached for the starter button.

There wasn't one. Instead of a button, he found an ignition lock like one in a car—and no key.

"Hey!" someone shouted from the deck of the yacht. "What do you think you're doing?"

Frank looked up. A crew member was staring down angrily at him.

"We need the ignition key," Frank said. "Quick, where is it?"

The crew member gave them a nasty grin. "If it isn't there," he said, "maybe Chuck has it in his pocket. He was the last to use the boat."

"There has to be a spare somewhere," Joe said.

Frank gave a frustrated sigh. "Sure," he replied with a hint of bitterness. "But by the time one of the crew decides to cooperate and finds it for us, Chuck will be miles away."

David and Bettina came hurrying forward.

"Joe, Frank," Bettina called. "Please wait. Come back. We have to talk."

"Don't worry, we're not going anywhere," Joe said, scowling. "We can't."

Frank and Joe clambered up the rope ladder to the deck of the yacht.

"Let's go to my cabin," Bettina said, glancing over her shoulder at the little crowd of curious contestants and crew members.

One corner of the owner's cabin was furnished with a sofa and two club chairs. The Hardys took the sofa.

"You boys have done a remarkable job," Bettina began. "Congratulations."

"Thanks," Frank said. "But while we're sitting here shooting the breeze, the guilty party is getting away."

"That's what I wanted to talk to you about," Bettina said. "Is what David told me correct? One of the crew is actually employed by Walter Mares? And he is the one who has been sabotaging our cruise?"

"That's right," Joe said. "His name's Chuck Arneson, and right about now he's landing on the beach where we were this afternoon and getting ready for the next stage of his escape."

"Let him go," Bettina said.

"Let him go?" Frank repeated incredulously. "Just like that?"

Bettina gave a decisive nod. "Just like that. For

one thing, I still have a lot of respect and fondness for Walter. I don't want to drag him through the muck. For another, a public scandal of this sort would not do me or the shareholders of *Teenway* any good."

"And suppose you guys caught up with Chuck? What then?" David added. "Okay, we all know he's guilty. The way he ran shows that. But what about proof that would stand up in a courtroom? And what was it he did, anyway? Some tasteless pranks. The police would listen with polite faces and laugh at us behind their hands."

"Making people sick by putting a drug in their food is more serious than a prank," Joe pointed out. "It was bad enough for you to talk about canceling the contest and sending us home."

"You're quite right, Joe," Bettina said. "That was a very nasty thing to do. But as you and Frank said at the time, the amount of emetic Chuck put in the fruit came to much less than even an ordinary dose per person. Nasty, yes, but not actually dangerous. I was so concerned out of a fear that his next move *would* hurt someone. Fortunately, your detective skills kept that from happening."

"So call off the dogs and throw them a bone," Frank muttered resentfully.

"Frank, listen," David said. "I understand that the case feels incomplete to you. I share your sense of frustration. But there's nothing more to be done here. You and Joe should be satisfied with the fine work you've done. You unmasked Chuck and brought his campaign of dirty tricks to an end. Now we can put all that behind us and get on with the contest and the cruise."

"Fine," Joe said. "But how about we go ashore and try to catch Chuck? Even if the law can't touch him, we could at least get a confession from him. With that in our hands, we'd be sure that this Mares guy won't try anything else."

"I'm sorry," Bettina said stiffly. It was obvious that she wasn't accustomed to having people argue with her decisions. "We're on a tight timetable. There's nothing to be gained from pursuing this any further."

"Okay, we get the message," Frank said, getting to his feet. Joe stood also. "You're the boss."

Bettina stood up. "Thanks for being so understanding," she said. "Unless you object, I'd like to ask Arnie to prepare something special this evening as a sort of celebration."

"Sure, why not?" Frank said.

"As long as it isn't an ipecac sundae," Joe added, without cracking a smile.

As they left Bettina's cabin, Frank muttered, "We're not through yet."

"I didn't think so," Joe replied.

The Hardys found Captain Mathieson in his office once again. Frank asked him for permission to search Chuck's locker. The captain clearly did not like the idea, but he agreed.

The crew quarters were in the bow, on the same

deck as the passenger cabins. A locked door separated the two areas. Chuck had bunked in a two-person cabin on the port side. As the newcomer, he had been assigned the upper bunk.

Joe did a rapid search of the bunk. He looked under the thin mattress and felt along the edges. All he turned up was a cassette. Apparently Chuck liked reggae.

Meanwhile, Frank looked through the locker. He was careful not to disturb anything. This was still Chuck's personal property, after all.

"Nothing," he reported. "A couple of changes of clothes, a portable tape player, half a dozen cassettes, and a book called *Global Positioning System for Sailors*."

"I wouldn't mind taking a look at that," Joe remarked. "So—no coded messages? No copies of the secret plans?"

"Nothing," Frank repeated. "Zip."

Joe and Frank returned to the afterdeck. Everyone crowded around them, asking how they had solved the case.

"The credit really belongs to Evan," Frank declared. He explained how Evan had overheard Chuck's phone call and how they then found out Chuck's background from the captain.

"Who was Chuck talking to on the phone?" Cesar asked.

"Good question," Joe replied. "Offhand, I'd guess some friend who was in on his plans. We'll be able to pin it down better from the ship-to-shore telephone records."

"Have you searched Chuck's belongings?" asked Sylvie. "Maybe he left some clues behind."

"We can't comment on that," Frank answered.

"Has anyone put out an alarm on Chuck?" Boris wondered. "Will he be arrested?"

"No decision has been reached on that," Frank said, mentally crossing his fingers.

"How does it feel to break a case so fast?" Lisa asked.

"Great," Joe replied. "But we had luck on our side. Luck, and a very alert kid named Evan."

While Frank continued to answer questions about the mystery, Joe went to their cabin to wash his face. When he returned, he caught Frank's eye and made a gesture with his head.

Frank joined him at the rail. "What's up?" he asked.

"That call to the pizzeria was just before three-thirty, right?" Joe said in a low voice. "Look at this."

Frank looked. Joe was holding the receipt for the ipecac syrup. Next to the date was a time: 3:26 P.M.

"There is no way Chuck could have bought the ipecac in town at three twenty-six and been back on board in time to order those pizzas at three-thirty," Joe pointed out. "He must have been working with someone else . . . someone in the group who went ashore."

"Someone in our group, in other words," Frank

114

said. He tried to think. Had he noticed any of the others speaking to Chuck? He had to admit that, until an hour ago, he had barely noticed Chuck at all. The members of the crew became a little like the furniture, always there but not really seen.

"I've got an idea," Joe said.

"Let's hear it," Frank said.

"What if we set a trap?" Joe suggested. "Chuck's accomplice, whoever it is, won't be expecting that. We've all been talking as if Chuck was the one and only bad guy and the case is closed."

"Hmm, yes," Frank said. "Here's what we can do . . ."

A few minutes later the Hardys moved closer to the group around the snack table.

"We'd better lock all that stuff in the captain's safe," Joe declared. "It's important evidence."

"That's a total waste of time," Frank retorted. "Chuck split. Who's going to walk into our room and take that file? Besides, I want to spend some time on it tonight after dinner. There may be more to this case than we've realized."

"Well—okay," Joe said. He glanced around and seemed to notice the others for the first time. "What say we go up to the sundeck? We need to talk over a couple of things about the contest."

Joe and Frank climbed up past the captain's cabin to the top-level sundeck. Frank took up a position by the railing, in plain view of the people on the aft deck, and acted as if he were having a spirited conversation with Joe.

Joe, meanwhile, scrambled down to the pilot house, then down to the cabin deck. Once inside his and Frank's cabin, he placed a file folder in plain sight on the table. Then he ducked into the closet, closed the door to a crack, and settled down to wait.

It was a long wait. The stuffy air in the tiny closet and the gloom in the unlit cabin gave Joe an urgent wish to lie down and take a nap. From time to time he checked the nightglow dial of his watch. The hands did not seem to move at anything like normal speed.

To keep himself alert, he silently recited the lyrics of his favorite golden oldie songs. It worked, but he had to struggle not to hum along. He had just started trying to remember the words to yet another song when he heard a click from the latch of the cabin door. He eased the closet door open a little farther and put his left eye to the crack. A shadowy form was creeping across the cabin. The intruder picked up the file from the table and riffled through it, then started to turn to leave.

At that moment Joe felt a speck of something land in his eye. He blinked furiously, but the pain made his eye water more. Quickly he moved his head to put his other eye to the crack, but he was a split second too late. All he heard was the cabin door shutting.

Joe wanted to kick the wall, but he couldn't spare the time. He slammed the closet door open and dashed out of the cabin and into the corridor. To his left a shadow flitted across the wall going upstairs. Joe bounded over and ran up the steps as fast as the narrow space and sharp spiral twist allowed.

Joe had almost reached the top step when he sensed a movement to his left, from within the telephone niche. He started to turn. A long, dark object came swinging toward his head. He dodged right, taking the blow on his shoulder, but the impact pushed him off balance. He took a quick step to the rear, but his foot missed the next step down.

Joe felt himself start to topple backward. He grabbed for the handrail, but his fingers found only air. He pulled up his knees. If he could get his head tucked and convert the fall into a roll, he might be all right.

Too late. Joe's alarmed shout was cut short when his head slammed against the edge of one of the steps.

13 Joe Takes a Tumble

The sundeck on top of the bridge was an elongated oval with bench seats along each side. Toward the bow was a Ping-Pong table and a locker for sports equipment. The yacht's old-fashioned blue smokestack, decked like a Christmas tree with radar, radio, and navigational antennas, cast a gnarled shadow on the weathered teak decking.

Frank had the sundeck to himself. He paced up and down. Occasionally he paused to look down toward the afterdeck, two levels below. The only person still in sight was Lisa, who was sitting with an open notepad on her lap. Where were the contestants? Was Chuck's accomplice, whoever he or she was, about to take the bait? How long should Joe stay hidden in the cabin closet before he gave up and decided the trap hadn't worked?

Frank moved his lower jaw from side to side, trying to release some of the tension in his face. He understood the arguments Bettina and David had given for not pursuing Chuck. He even agreed with them, more or less. Even so, the decision to let Chuck escape irked him. Why go to all the trouble of finding out whodunnit if that person then thumbed his nose at you and walked away laughing?

A sudden shout from one of the lower decks broke into Frank's thoughts. The shout was immediately followed by a distant crash. What was that? He rushed to the side. Kneeling on the bench seat, he leaned over and searched for the source of the ruckus. All he could see was Lisa running along the narrow walkway that led to the foyer. Something had happened!

One powerful leap brought Frank to the head of the companionway. He grasped the two railings and let gravity carry him swiftly to the bridge deck, then down the next set of stairs to the main deck. He ran through the salon and dining area to the foyer. Lisa and several others were standing frozen at the head of the companionway to the cabin deck, staring down. Frank pushed past them.

At the base of the stairs, Joe was crouched on his hands and knees. He shook his head as if trying to

119

clear it. Frank darted down to his brother's side. Just then Boris and one of the crew appeared from different directions. The crew member took Joe's elbow and started to help him up.

"I'm okay," Joe muttered, shaking off the hand. He pushed himself to his feet, then gingerly touched a spot just above his left ear.

"Are you sure?" Frank demanded. "What happened?"

"I fell and hit my head," Joe replied with a glance at the crowd of eager listeners. "No big deal. I'm fine now."

He gave Frank a meaningful look and started back up the stairs. Frank followed. The people at the top drew back to let them through. Joe paused to scan the telephone niche—Frank, too. What was so interesting? The wooden stool next to the telephone table was lying on its side. Otherwise, everything was just as it always was.

"Let's go out on deck," Joe said. "I need some air."

As soon as they were out of earshot of the others, Frank said, "Okay, what's the real story?"

"Somebody came for the folder," Joe reported. "I couldn't see who it was. The person whomped me with something at the head of the stairs and got away."

"Probably the stool," Frank said. "You could have been badly hurt. Are you sure you're okay?"

"Yes, I'm sure," Joe said impatiently. He touched the side of his head again and winced.

"So our trap worked fine, but we didn't catch anything," Frank mused. "Too bad you didn't see who it was."

"I didn't see who it was," Joe replied. "But I can make a very good guess. I recognized the perfume."

The Hardys went looking for Sylvie. They found her sitting in the salon with a magazine open on her lap. She looked up when she heard them approaching. Frank could see her hands tighten on the pages.

"Joe? You are all right?" she asked.

Joe shrugged and didn't reply.

"He'll probably have the mother of all headaches tonight," Frank said. "But I don't think there's any lasting injury."

"That is very good," Sylvie said. She looked down at her magazine as if she thought the exchange was finished . . . or wanted it to be.

"Sylvie," Frank said, "Joe and I need to talk to you. Will you come with us?"

Her face pale, Sylvie followed them onto the deck. Joe dragged three chairs into a tight circle. The moment Sylvie sat down, she covered her face with both hands and started to weep.

Frank glanced around. Jason, Boris, and Cesar were all watching from a distance. When he glared at them, they slowly drifted away.

"I am so sorry," Sylvie sobbed. "I never meant for this to happen. Never!"

"What is your connection with Chuck?" Joe asked.

She dropped her hands to stare at him. "Chuck?" she said, wiping her cheeks. "I have no connection with Chuck. I do not even know this Chuck."

"You entered our cabin and took that file, didn't you?" Frank demanded.

"But of course I took the file," she replied. "I had to. I am sure Chuck was not working alone. Someone else on the boat is part of his scheme. When you talked about the evidence lying unguarded in your cabin, I was afraid. What if the unknown accomplice took it and destroyed it? We might never reach the truth."

"Hold it right there," Joe said. "Are you trying to tell us you took the file to protect it?"

Sylvie spread out her hands, palms upward. "But of course. To protect it and to use it. You must understand. I *know* I am a good detective. But I did not do so well on the puzzles yesterday or today. Winning the contest is very important to me. It is a chance that will not come again. I thought, if I solve a real mystery, one of importance to the people of *Teenway*, perhaps that will help me in the contest."

"In other words, you stole the file as a way of helping us," Joe said in a tone of disbelief.

"To help you and to help myself," Sylvie replied. "I see now that you set a trap. So you too have understood that the accomplice is still at large."

Joe rolled his eyes and made an incredulous noise. It sounded something like *phfuah!*

"And then, when Joe came after you, you beaned him with a stool and knocked him down a flight of stairs," Frank pointed out. "That's a funny way of helping us."

"I was afraid," Sylvie said with a shrug. "I heard someone chasing me. I thought it was the villain. I had to defend myself. So I hid in the alcove by the telephone and picked up the only weapon I could find. I did not see it was Joe until I was already swinging the stool at him. Then I tried not to hit so hard, but the boat rolled and he fell. I am very sorry. Are you sure you are all right?"

Frank and Joe went on questioning Sylvie for another ten minutes, but she stuck to her story. She had wanted to guard the file of evidence and use it to unmask Chuck's secret accomplice. She had hit Joe in self-defense. She was very, very sorry, but she was also happy Joe had such a thick skull.

"I'd say she took that round on points," Joe muttered, as he and Frank went down to their cabin. "Do you believe her?"

Frank put out his hand, palm down, and wobbled it from side to side. "As Sylvie would say, *comme ci, comme ça.* Or in plain American, six of one, half a dozen of the other."

While Frank made notes about the afternoon's events, Joe took a shower, then sat holding a cold washcloth to his head. Soon it was time for dinner. They reached the main deck just as Arnie stepped out of the galley. He was holding a wooden mallet and a set of chimes.

"Hey, if it isn't the men of the hour," he said. "Time to call everybody to dinner. Would you like to do the honors?"

"Sure," Frank said. He took the chimes and gave Joe the mallet. Joe whanged away, with more enthusiasm than musicality. Finally Arnie reached over and took back the mallet.

The day had been long and full of excitement. It had started with a round of the contest and continued through a picnic on a deserted tropical beach, a near drowning, the unmasking and successful escape of a dirty-tricks artist, a chase, and a dangerous tumble downstairs.

Frank had expected that everyone around the dinner table would be dying to talk about one or another—or all—of these events. Instead, over Cajun-style crawfish stew with dirty rice, they started swapping airport horror stories.

"National is the worst," Elizabeth claimed. "I swear it was built a hundred years ago for the Wright brothers."

"At least you can get there," David said. "Evan and I visited England last summer. We spent nearly as much time going from Manhattan to JFK as from JFK to London!"

Boris grinned. "In America we are lucky," he said. "Where I was born, before the plane takes off, the passengers have to get out and help wind up the rubber bands!"

The table exploded with laughter. When it died down, Sylvie said, "Montreal has a very good modern airport. I like it." She turned to Jason, who was sitting next to her. "What about your home?"

"What, Fort Worth?" Jason shrugged. "The airport's okay, I guess. It's nothing special."

"O'Hare," Kenneth said. "That's the real pits."

"I don't much like O'Hare either," Bettina said. "But landing at St. Hilda the other day was the first time an airport made me think seriously about writing my will."

When everyone finished the main course, Bettina announced that dessert would be served outside on the aft deck. She pretended not to hear when Boris muttered, "That is so we will be closer to the rail, in case there is something in the dessert again tonight."

They went outside. The sea was dark, but overhead the sky was still a pale blue. To the east, night crept up from the horizon. A few early stars glimmered. A cool breeze blew in.

"I think I'll get a sweater," Lisa said with a little shiver. "I'll be right back."

As she left, Arnie appeared carrying a cake with two lit sparklers in it. The frosting was chocolate. On the top, in white frosting, was the outline of a boat and the words *Teenway Detectives*.

"This cake is for everyone who is part of our cruise, but especially in honor of Joe and Frank

Hardy," Bettina announced. "They've shown us what it really means to be teen detectives."

Everyone applauded. Frank looked over at Joe and smiled. It was nice that what they had done so far was appreciated. Now, after a tribute like this, they had no choice but to finish solving the case as quickly as possible.

Arnie cut the cake. Bettina handed the first two pieces to Frank and Joe. Frank was taking his first bite when Lisa ran out onto the deck.

"My tapes!" she cried. "All my tapes are gone! They've been stolen!"

14 A Criminal Record

The rest of the group stared silently at Lisa. Her tapes? All those little cassettes she had so carefully recorded were missing?

Joe could tell that he and Frank were both thinking the same thing. Apparently Lisa had been right when she had suggested that there was important evidence on her tapes. Why else would anyone steal them?

Bettina stepped over to Lisa, put her hands on the girl's shoulders, and said, "How terrible for you. Are you sure? Could you have put them someplace different that slipped your mind?"

"They're gone, I tell you," Lisa repeated. "When I looked in the box where I keep them, all I found was this."

She held up a thick, dog-eared paperback.

"Hey, that's my book," Boris declared. "I left it on deck this morning before the picnic, while I went to get my swimsuit. When I came back, it was gone. I haven't finished it."

"Here," Lisa said. Joe heard an edge of hysteria in her voice. She tossed the book in Boris's direction. "I don't want your dopey book. I want my cassettes back. My whole story about the contest is on them."

She turned to Joe. "You'll find them for me, won't you, Joe?" she pleaded.

"We'll try," Joe promised. "Where was this box?"

"On the table in my cabin," Lisa replied. "I can't believe I was such a dodo, leaving it out like that. The first day I kept the box in the drawer under my bed. But it was too much of a hassle to get it out every time I wanted to put away another tape or listen to an earlier one."

"Was your cabin locked?" Frank asked.

Lisa's cheeks turned pink. "No. I . . . I have a thing about losing keys. I'm always getting locked out of places because I lose my key. So I don't lock up if I can help it. I know that sounds dumb."

"I guess I don't have to ask if the box was locked," Joe said. He gave Lisa a reassuring smile. "What does it look like?"

A confused expression crossed Lisa's face. "The box?" she said. "But it's not gone. Oh—you mean what is it like? It's a nice old wooden box with an attached lid. I guess it was meant as a jewelry box. It's just the right size for my recorder and a bunch of cassettes."

"Do you keep your recorder in there, too?" Joe asked.

"When I'm not using it, sure," Lisa replied. "Of course, I had it with me today."

"Of course," Elizabeth echoed in a snide tone.

"I can see why somebody might steal your tape recorder," Kenneth said. "That's an expensive piece of equipment. But why would anyone want a lot of used cassettes?"

"It's not the cassettes, Kenneth, it's what's on them," Cesar told him. "Look at the way Lisa's been snooping around ever since this trip began. Almost anybody might want to get rid of them."

Lisa's eyes blazed. "The only people who have something to fear are people who have something to hide," she retorted. "How about you, Cesar? What are *you* trying to hide?"

"My urge to pour a glass of lemonade over your head," Cesar promptly replied.

"This isn't getting us anywhere," Joe pointed out. "Lisa, when was the last time you saw the missing tapes?"

"I put a couple of cassettes in the box when we came back from the beach," Lisa replied. "Everything was okay then."

"Call it four o'clock," Frank mused. "And you realized just now the cassettes were missing. So

129

that's about a five-hour stretch when the theft could have happened. Were you in your cabin for any part of that time?"

"I took a nap," Lisa said. She sounded embarrassed, as if naps were only for little kids and old people. "From about four-thirty to five-thirty. Then I came out on deck. I got here a little while before you and Joe tangled with that guy."

"This is a waste of time," Cesar said. "Her room was wide open and the box was in plain sight. How long would it take somebody to duck inside, grab the cassettes, and split? She might as well have left them in the salon with a little sign that said Free—Take One."

"You sound as if you know all about it," Elizabeth remarked. "I wonder why."

"Listen, you—" Cesar growled.

"Don't you call me 'you,'" Elizabeth snapped.

"What am I supposed to call you? 'Him'?" Cesar retorted.

"That's quite enough," Bettina declared. "We're all overexcited and overtired. We're starting to say things we don't mean, things we'll regret in the morning. Let's enjoy this wonderful cake our chef has made for us. If Joe and Frank have questions to ask about Lisa's tapes, they can do it one on one."

Frank awoke very early the next morning. A faint gray light shone through the porthole over his bed. A slight vibration and a difference in the motion of the boat told him that they were under way again.

130

He sat up, slipped on shorts, a tank top, and a pair of boat mocs, and tiptoed out of the cabin without waking Joe.

Two levels up, he went out onto the walkway past the pilot house. Captain Mathieson, at the helm, waved and called, "Good morning." At the front of the pilot house, a companionway led down to the bow. This was a working area of the yacht, not meant for passengers. Instead of comfortable seats and teak coffee tables, there were two big coils of inch-thick rope and a grease-specked power winch used for hoisting the anchor.

Frank rested his arms on the metal rail. By leaning out, he could watch the wave of white foam cast up by the boat's bow. The individual lines of bubbles constantly changed form, but the general shape of the wave remained the same. Like this case. The details changed, but the basic questions remained the same. Who was Chuck's accomplice? What was on Lisa's cassettes that was so dangerous to the conspiracy?

A tiny island appeared off to starboard. A patch of grass no bigger than a tennis court, with a single wind-twisted tree ringed by a beach of white sand. Just beyond it, a thirty-foot sailboat swung at anchor. A man in the cockpit noticed Frank and waved. Frank waved back. Then he returned to his thoughts.

The investigation the night before had been a bust. Everyone had been down to the cabin deck at some point before dinner. Anyone could have slipped in and taken Lisa's cassettes. No one had seen anything suspicious. Finally, before turning in for the night, Frank and Joe had taken David and Bettina aside to propose a daring plan. The participants in the contest were all supposed to be talented teen detectives. Why not put them to work detecting?

After half an hour Frank went to the galley and cadged a mug of hot coffee and a freshly baked cinnamon roll from Arnie.

"I've been thinking," Arnie told him as he sliced bacon for breakfast. "About Chuck. He's not the guy who invented the wheel, if you get my drift. He must have had somebody else telling him what to do."

"You think so?" Frank replied, his tone casual. "Any idea who?"

Arnie paused with his knife in the air. "Not specifically," he said. "But I'd bet it was a guy. Chuck is a little backward in his thinking. He would have a problem taking orders from a girl."

"Did you notice him talking to any of the passengers?" Frank asked.

Arnie shook his head. "Nope. Sorry." He grinned. "We're not supposed to fraternize. Company policy."

Frank grinned back. "Is that what we're doing? Fraternizing? And I thought I was just stealing one of these awesome cinnamon buns . . . or two!"

Frank refilled his mug and went back to the bow.

An island was just peeping above the horizon, dead ahead. For the next twenty minutes or so, as it grew larger, he leaned on the rail and let his mind wander. Then he went in to make sure Joe was up and getting ready for breakfast.

After breakfast everyone gathered in the salon. David seemed ill at ease as he said, "We have decided to do something a little different for today's round in the teen-detective contest. In a minute I'll pass out a booklet with summaries of all the incidents that have marred our cruise these last few days."

"You mean that's the mystery we have to solve?" Elizabeth asked.

David nodded. "Right. Your assignment is to decide what Chuck's role was and whether he was working alone. If not, who was his accomplice? You should back up your opinions with reasoning and evidence."

Cesar raised his hand. "Are we limited to using the evidence in the booklet?"

David glanced quickly at Frank, who shook his head.

"No, you're not," David told Cesar. "Any information you have, you can use. But if it's not in the booklet, you have to explain how you know it. We'll reconvene in one hour."

Before the hour was up, the yacht arrived at its next port of call, Galleon Bay on the island of St. Mark. The town was built on three sides of the wide bay, which was thick with sailboats and motor cruisers. The *Colombe d'Or,* the biggest craft in port, was given a place of honor alongside a waterfront boulevard called the Embarcadero.

When the time expired, everyone reassembled in the salon. David collected the five entries. Then he said, "At this point I'm going to turn the chair over to the Hardys. Joe, Frank?"

"Who wants to go first?" Joe asked, looking around the circle.

After an awkward silence Boris said, "I will. Chuck did not have an accomplice. The odds are against finding two conspirators in such a small group."

"Pure guesswork." Elizabeth sniffed. "How could one person have done everything?"

"He didn't," Boris replied. "But he did not have an accomplice. Someone else was playing little jokes on his own . . . just as he did on the flight down, with his spiders. It was Evan who painted the skull and crossbones and hid Sylvie's scarf under the couch where he later found it."

David pressed his lips together. Joe could see that he was furious about this attack on his son.

"Aw, come on," Cesar protested. "Are you saying Evan bought the syrup of ipecac, too? He wasn't even ashore!"

"Hold it," Frank said. "Let's hear what everyone has to say before we start arguing. Who's next? Sylvie?"

Sylvie twisted her fingers together and stared at

the floor. "I think Chuck was working with one of us to wreck the contest," she said in a low voice. "Most of us want very much to win and want very much for the contest to be a success. We would not wreck it. But there is one who seems to care nothing about the contest. I do not know why she would want to wreck it, but that is the only answer I can see."

Everyone turned to look at Elizabeth. Her face turned red. "Ridiculous!" she exclaimed. "Totally lame!"

"What is your solution?" Joe asked her.

"Chuck was working alone," Elizabeth replied.

"What about the times on the drugstore receipt and the pizza order?" Boris demanded. "How could he be in two places at once?"

"He wasn't," Elizabeth said. "The cash register at the pharmacy had the time wrong, that's all."

Boris gave a sarcastic laugh and said, "Talk about lame!"

Frank turned to Cesar. "What about you?" he asked.

Cesar was visibly troubled. "I don't think I want to say anything," he announced. "Solving mystery puzzles is fun. This is different. This involves real people. What if somebody accuses me? I will be very hurt, even though I know I am innocent. So how can I do this to someone else? I wrote down what I had to say. When David reads it, he can decide if it makes any sense."

There was a short silence. Then Jason said, "That

leaves me. Yeah, there's a conspiracy, all right. But Chuck has nothing to do with it."

Everybody started talking at once. Jason held up his hand. "Yo, let me say my piece! Okay, so Chuck ran away. What does that prove? Nada! You might do the same—if you figured out you were being framed by a couple of hotshot detectives."

"Oh, now, wait a minute," Lisa said. "Are you trying to tell us—"

"You got it, sister," Jason said. "All those stunts were pulled by none other than Frank and Joe Hardy! They set up the whole thing so they could solve it and get their faces on the cover of *Teenway*. We have all been had!"

"Any reaction to that?" David asked Frank.

"Sure," Frank said. "The best defense is a good offense."

"What is that supposed to mean?" Jason demanded.

"If Chuck had an accomplice among our group, it means that one of us is not who he or she seems to be," Frank said.

Joe picked up the thread. "We couldn't figure out who that might be . . . until the imposter blew his cover. Jason—last night you said the airport in your hometown is pretty ordinary."

"Yeah, so?" Jason replied. "It's an airport."

"In fact," Frank said, "the airport that serves Fort Worth is one of the two or three largest and most modern in the world. It's bigger than the whole island of Manhattan. Fort Worth shares it with Dallas. How is it you didn't know that?"

"Big deal," Jason sneered. "Did you ever look at a map of Texas? Dallas and Fort Worth are practically the same town."

"Now I know you're an imposter," Joe said. "Anyone who's really from Fort Worth would eat his boots and ten-gallon hat before saying his town has *anything* in common with Dallas . . . except that enormous airport you didn't seem to know about."

"Another thing," Frank said. "When we were in Fort William, you seemed to find your way awfully easily. Have you spent time around here before?"

"This is a load of garbage," Jason declared. "Why would I want to wreck the *Teenway* contest?"

"Maybe it has something to do with this," Frank said. He held up Jason's portable CD player. Unsnapping the flap of the leather case, he continued, "There's a name written on the inside. Your name. Your *full* name—Jason Mares MacFarlane."

15 Race to the Finish

"Give me that!" Jason shouted. He rushed Frank and grabbed the CD player. "You can't mess with my property!"

Bettina stared at him, openmouthed. "You're Walter's grandson," she said. "I thought you looked familiar. You're a lot like him. Didn't you spend a day at the office with him a couple of years ago?"

"That's right," Jason said, venom dripping from his voice. "That was just before you and your buddies stole his magazine and broke his heart."

"I can understand how it would seem that way to you," Bettina said in a steady voice. "There were a lot of considerations involved that the general public didn't know about."

Jason turned his back on her. To Frank and Joe he said, "Okay, gumshoes. What now? Are you going to have me arrested? For what—a couple of harmless practical jokes? That'll look great when it hits the papers."

Frank looked over at Joe. They both remembered the reasons David and Bettina had given for letting Chuck go. All their arguments applied even more strongly to Jason.

"What about my tapes?" Lisa demanded. "What did you do with them?"

"Get out of my face," Jason told her. "I wouldn't touch your tapes with a barge pole. There's nothing on them I care about anyway."

"Let's just clear up a few things," Joe said. "Were you the one who put David's computer on the outbound luggage cart the day we arrived?"

Jason laughed. "Sure! It nearly worked, too."

"And after the first puzzle, you broke into our cabin, didn't you?" Frank said. "What were you after?"

"Nothing in particular," Jason replied. "I figured it would raise questions about the results."

"And you sent me that terrible article about the boat?" Sylvie asked. "Why me?"

"No reason," Jason told her. "I jabbed my finger at the list of finalists and hit your name."

"And the spiders on the cake?" Frank asked. "I can't see how you did that."

"Simple—I didn't." Jason smirked. "On the plane I held on to some of Evan's spiders, just in case I found a use for them. Then I passed them to Chuck. He's the one who put them on the cake."

139

"And then he accidentally dropped one while he was painting that skull and crossbones," Joe said. "And the ipecac—you bought it, he put it in the fruit. Then one of you shoved the paper bag, the receipt, and Sylvie's scarf under the sofa for us to find."

"That was *not* nice!" Sylvie hissed.

Jason spread his hands. "Hey, nothing personal. I saw the scarf lying there and I used it, that's all. I didn't even know whether it was yours or Miss Snobbo's. Besides, that turned out to be a major goof. The receipt tipped off our heroes here that Chuck was working with somebody else. If they hadn't found it, they'd never have figured it out."

"Don't be so sure," Frank said. "By the way, how did you swing getting chosen as a finalist in the contest? Did you have help from somebody on the *Teenway* staff who still feels loyal to your grandfather?"

"That's enough," Jason said coldly. "Here's the program. I'm going to go get my pack and I'm going to walk off this tub without anybody hassling me. I'll make it back to St. Hilda on my own. Got it?"

Frank glanced at Bettina, then at David. Both nodded grimly.

"Got it," Frank said. Then, on his own, he added, "But you might not get the welcome you're expecting. We're going to call your grandfather and tell him exactly what you've been up to."

"Yeah," Joe said. "You think he'll jump for joy when he finds out you've been trying to wreck the magazine he founded and spent years making into a success? You think he'll like it when he finds out his grandson is a little sneak?"

"*Shut up!*" Jason twisted at the waist and cocked his right fist, ready to punch Joe in the face. Joe waited calmly. He wasn't about to pick a fight with Jason, but he certainly wasn't going to back away from one, either.

Boris stepped forward and grabbed Jason's wrist. Jason tried to pull loose, but Boris was much stronger than he.

"If you're going, you had better go now," Boris said in his ear. "If you stay, we may prove to you how unpopular you have just become."

"I'm going," Jason muttered. Boris released him, and he walked off toward the stairs without another word. What he had meant to make a triumphant escape had turned into a crushing retreat.

Elizabeth turned to Sylvie. "I can't believe you thought I was the one!" she declared.

"I'm sorry," Sylvie said. "It's just—"

"Don't be sorry," Elizabeth said, cutting her off. "It's rather . . . exciting. I never saw myself as the adventurous sort. Maybe I should try it."

Boris went over to David. "Where is Evan?" he asked. "I want to apologize."

"The chef is giving him a fishing lesson," David replied. "Since he didn't hear you accuse him, there's no need to apologize. Forget it."

"I will try," Boris said. "It will not be easy. I do not like seeing myself be made a fool."

141

Lisa came running in. Frank had not noticed her leaving. "Hey, everybody," she shouted. "I've got it!"

"You found the cassettes?" Kenneth asked. "Where were they?"

"No, I didn't find them," Lisa told him. "But I figured it out. If Jason didn't take them, it must have been Chuck. But he didn't have them with him when he jumped off the boat. So they must still be here somewhere. He must have hidden them."

"Okay," Boris said. "The boat is only a hundred and sixty feet long and twenty-five feet wide, with four or five levels. If we start searching now . . ."

"Cut it out. I *know* where to look," Lisa said. "Once I figured out he'd taken them, I asked one of the other crew members a few questions. Guess what? After Chuck brought us back from the picnic, he volunteered to reorganize the supply closet in the galley. He must have hidden my cassettes there!"

Everybody trooped into the galley. It was a tight fit. There was only enough room for one person in the supply closet. The others delegated Frank to do the search. The closet had shelves from floor to ceiling. Each shelf had an elastic cord across the front to keep things from sliding off in rough seas.

Frank started at the bottom left and worked his way up and around. The third shelf held half a dozen boxes of fancy English crackers to serve with cheese. When he tilted one box forward, he saw a plastic freezer bag behind it. The bag was filled with tiny cassettes. They were not dated, but each one was numbered. Before announcing his discovery, Frank pawed through the bag, took out the cassette with the highest number, and hid it in his pocket.

Lisa was overjoyed. "I told you we'd find them here!" she crowed. "You see, Joe? You're not the only detective on this boat!"

"Far from it," Joe said with a glance at the four remaining contest finalists.

Frank took David aside. "Am I right that you brought a microcassette recorder with you? May I borrow it for a few minutes?"

"Sure, it's in my cabin," David replied. "I'll go get it. Do you want to come along?"

Frank got the recorder, then collected Joe. They went to the top-level sundeck. As usual, it was deserted. Frank put the cassette in the recorder. "Assuming Lisa numbered them in order," he explained, "this should be the most recent."

He pressed the Play button. The person speaking was in the middle of a sentence.

". . . *Chuck talking to on the phone?*"

"That's Cesar's voice," Joe said.

"Shhh!" Frank hissed.

"*Good question,*" Joe's voice answered. "*Offhand, I'd guess some friend who was in on his plans. . . .*"

Frank pressed the Stop button.

"You see what this means, don't you?" he asked.

Joe nodded. "I sure do."

Two decks below, the lunch chimes sounded.

The Hardys were the last to come to the table. As they sat down, Evan was asking, "Are we going to be here long?"

"Why?" David replied.

"We could go horseback riding," Evan said. "Arnie says the trails are totally awesome. You can swim under a waterfall."

"With your horse?" Boris asked.

"No, silly." Evan laughed. "You get off the horse to go swimming. Can we, Daddy? It's really fun here, but there's not many places to go when you're on a boat."

"We'll see," David said.

There was a short silence while bowls of mussel salad and cracked crab legs were placed on the table. As people began to serve themselves, Frank said, "Lisa? When I found your cassettes, I took one of them out of the bag."

He handed it to her. She glanced at the label. Her face went white. "Did you listen to this?" she asked breathlessly.

Frank nodded. "Is there anything you want to tell us?" he asked.

Lisa coughed twice, then said, "Uh . . . Listen, people—I have to say something. Something important."

Everyone stopped talking to listen.

"The thing is . . ." She stopped to swallow. "Nobody stole my cassettes. I made it up. Then I hid them and pretended to find them."

In the silence that followed, Bettina asked, "Why, Lisa?"

"I wanted to write about it in my article," Lisa told her. "I figured if I was the victim of a crime and I solved it myself, my article would be so hot that you'd have to run it in *Teenway*. I'd be on my way to becoming a rich and famous writer, just as I've always dreamed."

"Not many writers become rich and famous, Lisa," Bettina said. "But if what they write is true and honest, they have other satisfactions. If they write lies, they have to live with those. And sooner or later their lies catch up with them."

"I'm sorry I tried to fool everybody," Lisa said. Her eyes glistened. "I'm still going to write an article about the cruise. But in it I'm going to explain how I was tempted to do something dishonest. And I'm going to explain how my plan was foiled by two brilliant detectives, Joe and Frank Hardy."

"Hey," Boris called. "How did you foil her plan anyway?"

"We listened to the last cassette in the series," Frank said. "It was from yesterday afternoon, when all of us were talking about Chuck's escape. But how could he have stolen a tape of a conversation that happened after he'd jumped ship?"

Boris laughed. "Brilliant! And simple, like many brilliant ideas."

"Speaking of brilliant," David said, "I have an

145

important announcement. As you all know, the *Teenway* teen detective contest is scheduled to continue through two more puzzles. Given everything that's happened—"

"Oh, you're not cancelling it!" Sylvie wailed. "You can't, not now!"

"We're not," David assured her. "However, having only four finalists still in the contest does make a difference."

"I know—you're going to cut back on the number of prizes," Boris said gloomily.

"Not at all," Bettina assured him. "I just got off a call with my publisher, giving some advance warning of today's startling developments. We discussed what to do about the prize situation. Our decision was to add a special grand prize to the three awards already offered."

The four teen finalists looked at one another. It seemed to Frank that they found it hard to believe what they were hearing.

"In other words," David added, "you are all sure to win an award."

"*Yes-s-ss!*" Boris shouted, and turned to give Cesar a high-five. Elizabeth grabbed Sylvie and gave her a big hug. Sylvie was so surprised by Elizabeth's gesture that she started talking rapidly in French. Kenneth was taking so many pictures that his camera almost smoked.

"By the way, who's ahead?" Boris wondered, when the excitement died down.

"The first puzzle, the body in the captain's

office, was pretty much a wash," Frank reported. "No outstandingly good—or bad—performances."

"And no one spotted the wallet being handed off in the second puzzle," Joe added. "However, Cesar finished that one ahead on points. He remembered the most details. Sylvie was second."

"And as you know," David said, "Cesar's solution to the museum caper was clearly the most on target."

"I start to detect a pattern," Boris said. Frank did not think he sounded displeased.

"But what about real life?" Sylvie said. "This morning, all of us told our solutions to the dirty tricks, and all of us were wrong. But Cesar never said what he had written."

"True," David said. "Cesar, what did you write about this morning's problem?"

Cesar shrugged. "Albuquerque is not that far from Fort Worth," he said. "To fly to New York, I had to change planes at Dallas–Fort Worth. So I knew when Jason made that remark about the airport that he was not who he pretended to be. From that, I assumed that he might be Chuck's accomplice, who could not have done everything. But unlike Frank and Joe, I did not take the next steps and figure out who he really is and why he did what he did."

"Perhaps not, but you did a magnificent job," Bettina declared. "And you already had a substantial lead in the scores. I'm not going to prejudge the contest—"

"No, no, please don't!" David exclaimed. "Frank and Joe and I still have a couple of great puzzles to spring on everyone."

"So I won't say any more," Bettina concluded. "Except to wish all of the contestants continued good luck."

Cesar slapped Frank and Joe on the shoulder. "With these guys on the case," he said, "solving mysteries is never a matter of luck!"

DAREDEVILS

Contents

1 Hollywood or Bust

Fire. There was fire everywhere. Frank Hardy stole a furtive glance at his younger brother, Joe. Frank, the dark-haired older son of Laura and Fenton Hardy, was sweating, wishing he could be safe at home instead of trapped like a rat. Joe, who was seventeen and a year younger than Frank, looked completely cool.

He's drinking this in, Frank thought. He looks as if he's in seventh heaven.

Frank stared into the flames. Are we ever going to get out of here? he thought. Is this ordeal ever going to end?

Then a lone figure emerged from the flames.

The man—tall, with a rugged face apparent despite a coating of ash and soot—headed straight for the brothers. He paused to glance back over his shoulder at the raging inferno. Holding his hand out, he uttered the words Frank Hardy had longed to hear since he had become trapped in this building nearly two hours earlier.

"I've had enough of this heat," the man said with a toothy grin. "Let's get out of here and into someplace cool."

"I'll second that," Frank whispered. He stood up and stretched his back. "Come on, Joe."

"Wait a minute," Joe replied. "I want to see the credits."

Frank stared for a heartbeat at his brother. Then, knowing that protest would be futile, he sat back down. When the lights finally came on inside the Bayport Multiplex, Frank offered up a prayer of thanks.

"Now can we go?" he asked his brother.

"I take it you didn't like the movie," Joe said as he stood up.

"What was there to like?" Frank asked. He reached down to the floor and retrieved an empty popcorn bag. *Flame Broiled* was definitely half-baked."

"I admit the movie wasn't great," Joe replied,

"but it was just an action flick. And some of the action was really good."

"It did have some awesome stunts," Frank said as he stood. "But the plot was so thin you could see right through it." He glanced at the floor around him. "Did we pick up all our garbage?"

"Got it all," Joe said.

"I especially liked the stunt where Michael Shannon used the emergency fire hose to swing from one ledge to the other to rescue the cat," Frank said as they emerged onto the street. "But a stunt should not be the only likable part of a whole movie."

It was a hot summer day in Bayport, and though he had wished to be out of the theater only moments before, he now regretted leaving the building's air conditioning.

"Actually, that wasn't Michael Shannon in that scene," Joe said as he rooted in his pockets for the keys to the brothers' van. "At least I don't think it was."

"What do you mean? I thought Michael Shannon was one of those actors who always did his own stunts," Frank asked.

"He used to," Joe responded. "But I read in a review that the studio had brought in a stuntman be-

3

cause of the difficulty and danger of some of the action."

"You read a review of this movie and we still went to see it? Just for that, you ride and I'll drive."

Joe handed his brother the keys. "Ah, who listens to reviews these days?" Joe got into the van. "Anyway," he added, "that's why I wanted to see the movie credits. I wanted to see who did the primary stunts."

"Like you know one stuntman from another," Frank said with a laugh.

"Hey, some guy's job is to jump into fires, drive in high-speed chases, and fall from a cliff, I figure the least I can do is show him some respect by learning his name."

"And?" Frank asked after a moment of silence.

"And what?"

"And what was his name?"

"Oh," Joe said. "Terrence. Terrence McCauley."

Twenty minutes later Frank and Joe were standing in the living room of their home. Fenton Hardy was on the phone, and by the former police officer's somber tone, his sons could tell that something was seriously wrong.

"You're right, Brian," Mr. Hardy said into the

4

mouthpiece. He sat next to the coffee table, looking down at some notes he had hastily scribbled on a small pad.

Rope—cut?
Window—glass
Empty extinguisher!

"When did you get the last call?" Mr. Hardy asked. "Yesterday?" he inquired as he jotted down the words. "Two on Tuesday."

Frank and Joe gave each other questioning looks, but neither had any idea why their father was so concerned. Since retiring from the police force, their dad had been a private detective. Obviously, the conversation had something to do with a case, but what they were hearing didn't seem to fit what the two knew about the cases their father was currently working to solve.

"I see, Brian," Mr. Hardy said. "Not a problem. I owe you one anyway. I'll make the arrangements and get back to you with the details. Until then, keep your eyes peeled and keep him safe."

Mr. Hardy hung up the phone.

"Keep who safe?" Laura Hardy asked as she entered the living room. Frank and Joe's mother had become accustomed to the occasional danger the men in her life found themselves in.

"Brian McCauley's son," Mr. Hardy replied. "You remember him, don't you?"

"Little Terrence?" Mrs. Hardy was surprised. "What kind of trouble has he gotten himself into?"

"Terrence McCauley!" Frank shouted. "What a coincidence."

Mr. Hardy looked at his older son. "What do you mean?" he asked.

"We just saw *Flame Broiled*," Frank answered. "And Terrence McCauley was the stunt double for the star, Michael Shannon."

"Stunt double," the boys' mom said. "So he followed in his father's footsteps."

"You sure have a memory for details, dear," Mr. Hardy said with a smile.

"Speaking of details, Dad," Joe said, "how about filling us in. What kind of trouble has this Terrence McCauley gotten into?"

"Well, first of all, it's not so much trouble that he got himself into," Mr. Hardy started. "It's more the trouble that somebody else wants to put him in."

Mr. Hardy sat on an armchair across from his two sons. Mrs. Hardy sat next to her husband on another chair.

"Let me start at the beginning," Mr. Hardy continued. "I know how you two like to get all the background details on a case."

Frank reached over and took the writing pad and pen from the coffee table. "Shoot, Dad," he said when he was ready to take notes.

"I met Terrence's father some twenty-two years ago while he was in New York making a movie. I was working as a detective with the NYPD. There had been a robbery near the movie set. I was chasing down the thief on foot, and without knowing it, we both ran into a building that had been rigged with explosives for a stunt in the movie. Brian saved me and the thief when the building began to crumble."

"So that's how you two became friends?" Frank asked.

"Yes," Mr. Hardy said. "We kept in touch over the years. Your mom and I even went out to visit Brian and his family in California once. We were there when . . ."

Mr. Hardy's voice trailed off. His wife reached over and gave his knee a loving squeeze.

"We were there when his wife died in a car accident," Laura finished for her husband.

There was a moment of awkward silence.

"So what's going on now?" Joe asked.

"Well, Brian raised Terrence alone since the boy was three. The first thing Brian did was quit being a stuntman. He didn't want to risk his life anymore because his death would leave Terrence an orphan."

"So what did he do?" Frank asked.

"Brian stayed in the movie business," Mr. Hardy continued. "He became a stunt coordinator."

"So Terrence grew up around action movie sets?" Joe inquired.

"Exactly," Mr. Hardy responded. "And when the boy turned sixteen just five years ago, he became a stuntman—against his dad's better wishes, I might add."

"Why didn't Brian McCauley want his son to become a stuntman?" Joe asked. "Because of the danger?"

"Brian had so convinced himself that stunt work was deadly dangerous, probably as a way to rationalize giving up the work himself, that he didn't want Terrence to be a stuntman," Mr. Hardy answered.

"So what happened?" Frank asked.

"In the end Brian gave in. Terrence threatened to move out and do it anyway. Brian realized it was better to keep the boy close at hand and try to be the stunt coordinator on some of his jobs so he could watch out for him."

Mr. Hardy stood up. "Now it seems that somebody besides his father wants Terrence to give up stunt work. He's received several threatening calls and anonymous notes telling him that his days are numbered. And there have been a few odd accidents on the sets where he's worked. Yesterday, a rope he was using snapped and he nearly fell twenty stories. Luckily, another stuntman was there to save him."

"So, where do we fit in?" Joe asked.

"*We* don't fit in. I fit in."

"Aw, come on, Dad," Joe protested. "We want to help on this case. Don't we, Frank?"

"It has been a while since we've been to California," Frank said in support of his brother. "And anyway, what is Terrence, twenty-one? We're closer in age to him than you are. We'd blend in with his crowd better, so we could keep an eye on him."

Mr. Hardy slowly shook his head at his wife. "How is it that our sons always have a good point?"

"Now, if you three think you're going off to Hollywood and leaving me here alone," Laura scolded, "you've got another think coming."

"Mom!" Joe and Frank shouted in unison.

9

Laura stared her sons straight in the eyes. "If Terrence McCauley is as stubborn as you two, he's going to need all the people he knows looking out for him."

"All the people, dear?"

"Yes, Fenton, all the people. I haven't seen that boy or his father in a lot of years. Plus, a summer vacation in Hollywood could be a lot of fun!"

Forty-two hours later the Hardys arrived in what was usually known as sunny southern California. This particular Thursday, however, the normally clear summer sky was filled with thick clouds as a rare rainstorm blew in from the Pacific Ocean.

The Hardys piled into the two cars they had rented and made their way to the Curtis Hotel. Brian McCauley had wanted them to stay at his house, but Mrs. Hardy insisted that six people would be a crowd and that she was looking forward to staying in a hotel.

The Hardy-McCauley reunion was not delayed, though. Terrence and his father were waiting in the hotel lobby when Frank, Joe, and their parents arrived. After the introductions were made, the McCauleys and Hardys retired to their suite so the Hardys could freshen up.

"You folks picked a good night to arrive," Brian McCauley said. "There's a big Hollywood party tonight, and we're all going."

"What party?" Joe asked.

"Mad Alliance Studios, the makers of *Flame Broiled*, are throwing a party to give the movie some more heat," Terrence said. "Have you guys seen it?"

"Yeah," Frank said unenthusiastically. Then he added, "Loved the stunt with the cat. Was that you?"

"Yup," Terrence said. "In fact, it was my cat!"

The group split into two to head for the party. Frank and Joe wanted to shower, so Brian McCauley took Mr. and Mrs. Hardy in his car to the party. About twenty minutes later, well after sunset, the younger men exited the hotel.

"I called to have my car brought around," Terrence said.

Joe's eyes lit up when the valet attendant pulled up in a beautiful silver sports car.

Under the hotel awning, Joe admired the car's sleek lines, playing his fingers across the gleaming silver exterior.

"You want to drive?" Terrence asked.

"Does he want to drive?" Frank laughed.

Twenty minutes later Joe opened the car up as

11

he guided it into the Hollywood hills. The rain was pouring down, making the roadway treacherously slick, but the sports car hugged the asphalt.

"Supreme handling," Joe said, beaming.

"Uh, Joe," Frank said from the car's cramped backseat, "are you slowing down?"

"Haven't touched the brakes," Joe replied. "Not going fast enough for you?"

"Not me," Frank responded, "but that truck behind us is sure coming up fast!"

2 Life of the Party

Joe looked in the rearview mirror. Through the pouring rain, he could see the bright headlights of a pickup truck. Joe fixed his eyes in front of him. He was rapidly approaching a sharp curve and knew he would have to slow down a little to negotiate the bend.

"Brace yourselves!" Frank warned just as the sports car entered the curve. There was nobody ahead of them, so Joe chose not to slow down as much as he should have. Still, the car's own speed did not prevent the impact, though it did lessen its force.

The pickup truck smacked into the rear bumper of the sports car.

"Hey!" Terrence yelled, even though the driver behind them could not hear.

The force of the impact was enough to make the car swerve as it rounded the bend. Joe fought the wheel to stay in his own lane. He didn't want to risk a collision with any cars that might be coming around the bend from the opposite direction. The tires gripped the slick road just enough to keep the car from careening into an oncoming station wagon.

As the sports car exited the curve, the pickup truck smacked into the rear bumper again, this time with even more force. Terrence McCauley's expensive dream machine began to fishtail toward the edge of the cliff, protected only by a metal guardrail.

Joe worked the brake and then the accelerator to keep the car from spinning into the barrier. The pickup truck drove up next to them.

The truck smacked the sports car on the driver's side, sending it toward the railing once again.

"Right rear!" Joe shouted in warning, calling out the spot on the car he knew would hit against the barrier. He successfully fought the steering wheel to lessen the impact. The car kissed off the guardrail exactly where Joe had planned. Unfortunately, the kiss was strong enough to catapult the car back into the lane at a forty-five degree angle, allowing the truck to sideswipe it again.

This time the impact was on the driver's side fender. Terrence groaned at the sickening crunch.

"Straight, brakes!" Frank shouted from the backseat. His shout warned his brother that he needed to stay in his lane and slow down a bit. As the pickup truck swerved into the lane just ahead of the sports car, Joe realized why Frank had called out the instructions. There was traffic coming in the other lane and Joe needed to give the pickup truck a chance to squeeze in front of them.

The two vehicles rounded another bend. Joe wanted to stop, but there was no place to pull over. As they entered another narrow straightaway, the pickup swerved into the now-empty left lane. It decelerated a bit and rammed its fender into the sports car's driver's-side door. Terrence's car began a treacherous spin as the pickup truck accelerated and sped away.

Time seemed to slow down for the three young men in the silver sports car. Joe struggled with the steering wheel. He used both feet to work the accelerator and brake, subtly changing speed to try to bring the car under control. He managed to stop the spin just enough to keep the car from hitting the guardrail with too much force. The metal rail bent out over the cliff and the front of the car crumpled, but Joe had succeeded in keeping the car from breaking through the railing, thus saving them from a deadly plunge.

"Is everybody okay?" Frank asked from the backseat.

"My shoulder hurts a little, but it's just a bruise," Terrence replied.

"My knuckles are sore from gripping the steering wheel, but otherwise I'm just peachy," Joe answered. "Steamed, but peachy."

"Man, that was some great driving, Joe," Terrence said as he unbuckled his seat belt. "You could be a professional stunt driver."

"Thanks," Joe replied. "In our line of work, it's a requirement."

"Yeah," Frank added. "But the car insurance payments end up setting us back a bundle."

"Hey, this is California," Terrence said. "My insurance rates are going to be higher than a mortgage payment after this."

Terrence and the Hardys got out of the car. "I just wish I could haul that maniac in the truck into court to make him pay for this."

Frank watched the sparse traffic whiz by.

Though every driver slowed down to peer at the scene, not one of them stopped to help. They all just went on, leaving the three of them standing in the rain next to the heavily damaged sports car.

"You'll get your chance," Frank said. "I got the truck's plate number."

"During all that mayhem?" Terrence was surprised. "Boy, you guys really are good. We'll just tell the police and let them go arrest that lunatic."

"Nope," Frank said. "We keep this info to ourselves and tell the police some truck bumped us twice and we spun out on the wet road. If the cops haul him in for this, we get him on reckless driving and your life is still in danger. We need to nail him for more than a traffic incident."

More than an hour after the "accident," the three young men arrived at the *Flame Broiled* Light-the-Fire Party. A passing motorist had finally stopped to help. The good Samaritan used his cell phone to call the police. After giving their statements concerning the incident to the authorities, Frank, Joe, and Terrence were free to go. They asked the police to phone for a cab, which took them to the Mad Alliance Studios event.

The Hollywood party was being held at Clemen's Terrace, a favorite facility of movie stu-

17

dio executives. Clemen's Terrace was a huge renovated warehouse, and the studios could decorate it any way they wanted. In this instance, the facility had been transformed into several scenes from *Flame Broiled*, each depicting one of the many fiery locations where the movie's primary action took place.

"Terrence McCauley!" a sweet voice called out almost immediately after the three men entered the party. "I was beginning to think that you would never arrive."

The techno-rock party music was loud, yet Frank and Joe instantly locked in on where the voice had come from. Joe tapped Terrence's arm to point his attention in the proper direction.

"Pam Sydney," Terrence muttered under his breath before the woman was in range. Joe could see that Terrence instantly became uncomfortable as the woman approached, but he wasn't sure why. Pam Sydney was pretty. She had short, raven black hair, and her round face was very animated. By the way the woman's eyes glittered as they took in Terrence McCauley, it was obvious that she was attracted to the handsome stuntman.

Pam tucked her arm in Terrence's as soon as she was within reach.

"My, I can tell by your expression that something is wrong," Pam said to Terrence. She reached up with her free hand and straightened his hair. Terrence shook his head at her touch, a bit too strongly Frank thought.

"Nothing's wrong, Ms. Sydney," Terrence said. "Nothing some body work won't fix."

Pam looked confused.

"We had an accident on the way here," Joe said as he offered his hand to the attractive woman.

"Uh, do I . . ." Pam began to say.

Terrence cut her off. "Pam Sydney, meet Joe and Frank Hardy. Guys, this is Pam Sydney. She runs Mad Alliance Studios."

"Friends of yours?" Pam asked. "A bit young for you, perhaps?"

"Good friends of mine," Terrence said.

Pam shook Frank's and Joe's hands. The handshakes were brief, and Pam quickly rehooked her arm in Terrence's.

"Your accent," Frank said. "Australian?"

"Very good," Pam replied. "Pam Sydney, from Sydney."

"Oh, look," Terrence said. He wiggled his arm free from Pam. "It's our folks," he said, pointing across the room at nobody in particular.

19

Frank immediately followed Terrence's lead. It was obvious to him that Terrence was trying to extricate himself from the woman.

"Oh, yeah," Frank said. "We should check in with them and tell them about the car."

"I don't see your dad," Pam said as she quickly glanced around. "You should stay in one spot so he can find you." Pam put a hand on Terrence's shoulder.

Joe could see that Pam wanted Terrence right where she had him, and Terrence, though he was attempting to mask his true feelings, wanted to put some distance between himself and the studio executive.

"Well, I see my dad," Joe said as he looked in the general direction that Terrence had pointed. "And he came with Brian McCauley, so we should report to him."

"Oh, all right," Pam said. "We'll go find your parents." She slipped her hand around Terrence's closed palm.

"Perhaps you should mingle with the press and the other guests," Terrence said. "You know, make yourself available to the media." He began to walk away from Pam.

"I guess you're right," Pam said halfheartedly. Then she recovered her smile and perked up. "I am the voice of Mad Alliance, after all." Pam headed off in the opposite direction.

When they were out of earshot, Frank gave a gentle shoulder bump to Terrence. "Using the old I-see-my-dad trick, I see."

Terrence laughed.

"What I don't get," Joe said as the three meandered toward the center of the room, "is why you wanted to ditch her. She's very pretty, and it's obvious that she likes you."

"No kidding," Terrence responded. "But I'm not interested."

"Why?" Frank asked.

"She's a spoiled rich kid," Terrence said. "She came here a few years ago from Australia with her daddy's checkbook, opened a studio, and declared herself a movie mogul."

"But you work for her," Joe said.

"Lots of people work for her," Terrence replied. "The studio produces several movies a year. She's even made some money for her dad. Not that he would care. Kyper Sydney would do anything for his daughter."

"The guy must be loaded," Joe said.

"Very," Terrence said. "He owns Mad Alliance International. They're a huge corporation with interests mainly in shipping, airlines, and construction. He gets what he wants, and Pam thinks she can have anything *she* wants."

Frank scanned the room. He had yet to spot his parents or Brian McCauley. Before he even had time to wonder if they had arrived, though, the partygoers began to applaud.

"Our illustrious guest of honor has arrived," Terrence said. Frank noted the sarcasm in the young stuntman's voice.

Blinking his eyes against the flashes of light, Frank zeroed in on the center of attention.

"Michael Shannon," Joe said as he spotted the movie star. Shannon made his way toward the front of the room, putting him just a few feet from the three young men. The star of *Flame Broiled* ascended three steps onto the raised dais at the front of Clemen's Terrace.

"Thank you everyone, thank you," he said, raising his hands in mock modesty. Camera flashes filled the air with spots of light.

"It's great to be on fire!" Shannon shouted in reference to his movie. The crowd laughed. "Now, I know I haven't done many interviews for the press lately, but with a hot movie like this, I'm willing to field a few questions."

"He's one big image, huh?" Joe whispered to Terrence.

"All image," Terrence replied as Michael Shannon answered a question concerning his next project.

As the actor quipped for the press, a tall, lanky man with bleached blond hair pushed his way past Frank.

"I have a question," the man shouted at Michael Shannon. The actor gave the man a quizzical look.

"Ian Edrich, *Slow Motion* magazine," the man said. The actor nodded his head, indicating that he would field the question.

"Thanks," Edrich said. "First, we all know that *Flame Broiled* is a turkey at the box office. Care to take the blame for this one, or are you going to pass responsibility off onto somebody else like you did with your last failure?"

The crowd became silent.

"I'd say the only turkeys are the ones in the audience who couldn't grasp the subtleties of a masterful story," Shannon replied abruptly.

"Heh, yeah," Edrich mocked. "One more thing. When are you going to give your stunt double top billing? After all, he does all the hard work."

Michael Shannon's face flushed with anger. "Why you dirty . . ." the actor snarled as he leaped off the stage.

3 Bad Press

Michael Shannon's hands were around the reporter's throat before his feet even touched the ground. He squeezed the man's neck and shook him hard.

"You filthy little liar!" he shouted in Ian Edrich's face.

Frank, who was the closest person to them, grabbed Michael's right wrist and applied pressure until the actor was forced to release his stranglehold. Michael whirled on Frank and took a swing. Frank easily blocked the wild punch.

"Who do you think you are?" Michael shouted as he readied another punch. Before the actor could aim a blow at Frank, Terrence McCauley grabbed the enraged movie star from behind.

"Michael, Michael," Terrence said. "Get a hold of yourself."

"Let me go, you wannabe," Michael spewed. He wriggled free from Terrence's grip and turned to face the stuntman. "If anyone's turned my movie into a turkey, it's you! Your easy-way-out stunts made me look bad."

"Michael, dear," Pam Sydney cooed as she stepped into the fray. She placed a calming hand on Michael's shoulder. "Manners, manners," she said. Then she cocked her head toward the crowd.

"You'll have to excuse my tired star," she said loudly. "He's been working himself very hard lately. All of us know how stress can make us act a bit silly."

Pam began to walk Michael away from the crowd. "Come on," she said, "let's get you something cool to drink." She pointed a hand at the DJ and nodded her head. "Come on, everybody," she shouted as the DJ cued up some music. "This is a party!"

As Pam Sydney led the seething actor away, Frank turned his attention to the man whom Michael Shannon had attacked. He saw that his brother was already helping the man, who rubbed his neck. The reporter was breathing heavily.

"Man," Ian Edrich said as he gasped for air, "that guy's grip is stronger than I thought it would be."

"You mean you figured he was going to attack you?" Joe asked.

"Uh, no," Ian said, glancing sideways at the teen. "I, uh, just figured that a guy who didn't do his own stunts wouldn't be all that strong."

"Stunts take skill, not just strength," Terrence said as he and Frank joined Joe and the reporter. "And I think you've overstayed your welcome." Terrence pointed a stern finger at the front door.

Ian Edrich straightened his clothes. Without a glance at the stuntman or the two teens, he began to walk toward the exit. However, Frank, Joe, and Terrence all wanted to see him out to the street. They had some questions for the reporter.

"You deliberately provoked Shannon," Joe said. "Why?"

"Hey, if he can't take a little heat, he shouldn't make movies like *Flame Broiled*. Criticism is the name of the game in Hollywood."

"True enough," Terrence said. "But you used me to set Michael Shannon off. I don't even know

26

you, and I thought I knew all the reporters at *Slow Motion* magazine."

"I'm new," Edrich said. "Looking to make a name for myself. And, hey, I'm the reporter—I'll ask the questions."

"Ask away," Frank said.

Edrich hesitated.

"You guys are nothing," he said after a moment. "I'm not wasting my time talking to you." The reporter began to walk toward the parking lot.

"Hey!" Joe shouted.

"Ah, let him go, Joe," Frank said. "There's nothing to get from him now."

Frank then turned to Terrence. "You, on the other hand—I think there's something we can get from you."

"What do you mean?" Terrence asked.

"What's the deal with you and Michael Shannon?" Frank asked. "He went rabid at just the mention of you, his stunt double. If somebody hates you enough to want you dead, I'd say he's suspect number one."

"Michael Shannon?" Terrence sounded incredulous. "Yeah, you can say the guy doesn't like me. But enough to try murder?"

"Why doesn't he like you?" Joe asked. "Anything specific?"

"We've known each other since we were kids," the stuntman replied. "If you know a bit about his career, you know he began acting when he was nine. I was around the movie sets a lot because of my dad. He was a spoiled rich kid, I was just a poor kid to him. You could say we never liked each other."

"You know a lot of spoiled rich kids." Joe laughed.

"Here in Hollywood money equals status," Terrence said. "People sometimes forget to take you for what you're worth instead of for what your house is worth."

"Did you guys ever fight?" Frank asked.

"Verbally most of the time—physically a couple of times."

"You win?" Joe asked.

"Win, lose." Terrence scuffed his feet. "Nobody wins a fight."

"Especially when it's kids who are fighting," came a voice from over Terrence's shoulder. Brian McCauley put a hand on his son's arm. "It's not about who's stronger, it's about right and wrong."

"You taught your son well," Mrs. Hardy said as she and Mr. Hardy joined the group.

"But you and Michael Shannon are enemies,"

Mr. Hardy said. "At least in his eyes I'd say after that display of temper. I think we have to give that young actor a hard look. He has a motive, if that scene inside was any indication. To me it looks like he's blaming you for his flagging career."

"Now we need to prove opportunity," Joe said.

"Right," Frank added. "He did come to the party late. That would give him plenty of time to ditch the truck."

"What truck?" Mr. Hardy asked.

"It's a long story," Frank answered.

"Well, tell it to us back at the hotel," Mrs. Hardy said. She turned to both Brian and her husband. "Shall we?"

"Uh, could we have some cab money?" Frank asked.

Mr. Hardy gave his sons a wry smile. "I think Terrence should ride back with you and his dad," he said to Laura. "I'll go in the cab, and these two can fill me in on what happened."

The next morning the bright sun had returned, and Joe woke his brother early and hurried him through breakfast.

"Get a move on, Frank. Terrence told me if we're at the set by ten o'clock, we'll catch him filming some stunts."

"It's pretty cool of him to get us onto a movie set," Frank said.

"True, but it's part of our job," Joe replied. "After all, we are here to protect him."

"Where are Mom and Dad?" Frank asked.

"They already left for the set. They gave me keys to one of the rental cars," Joe answered.

"Great," Frank said. "You bring the car around and I'll meet you out front. I want to grab my laptop."

"Why do you need a computer on a movie set?" Joe asked.

"You'll see," Frank responded.

At nine forty-five Frank and Joe drove onto the Mad Alliance lot. After parking the car, they were directed to the set where Terrence McCauley was working on *Major Miners,* Mad Alliance's latest action flick. The two brothers took up a spot next to Brian McCauley and their father.

"Where's Mom?" Frank whispered.

"She went shopping. For her, this is a vacation."

"Quiet on the set!" the director yelled, signaling that they were ready to begin filming.

All their attention was directed to a fifty-foot-high scaffold. At the top of the metal tower stood a well-dressed woman and a burly guy dressed as a construction worker. The worker had one hairy arm wrapped around the woman's throat.

"Action!" the director screamed.

From his spot on the ground, it looked to Joe as if the woman had bit the construction worker's arm. Then, seeming to be startled by the pain, he pushed the woman away. She fell off the scaffolding backward and plunged toward the ground, where she landed safely on a huge inflated airbag.

"Cut! Perfect stunt." The director beamed.

"Boy, it's a good thing I knew they were acting," Joe said. "My first instinct was to race to the rescue."

"Then your instincts are way off." Frank laughed. He pointed to the woman as she began to walk toward the spot where the brothers and the two fathers were standing.

"What the—" Joe began, his eyes wide.

"Hey, good-looking," the woman said as she removed her wig.

"Terrence?" Joe was shocked. "When you were up there, I could have sworn you were a woman."

"The magic of makeup," Brian McCauley said. "Good fall, guy."

"Thanks, Dad," Terrence replied. "And speaking of makeup, I'm going to go to my trailer to clean this stuff off. You guys coming with me?"

"Sure," Frank said. "What about you, Dad?"

"Nope," Mr. Hardy responded. "I want to snoop around, maybe ask some questions. The accidents that hit Terrence last week all happened here. With Brian escorting me, I should get access to most everywhere."

"Sounds good," Joe said. "We'll hook up with you later."

The two fathers headed off in one direction while their sons headed for the stuntman's trailer.

"Wow, this is the life!" Joe exclaimed when the three young men entered the trailer. "I wish I worked in a place like this."

"Ah, this is nothing," Terrence replied. "Hey, Joe, could you unhook me?" The stuntman pointed to the back of the dress he was wearing.

"Sure," Joe said.

"Do you have your cell phone here?" Frank asked while Terrence began to change into some jeans.

"On the table," he replied. "What for?"

Frank hoisted his laptop onto a small wooden dining table. "I'm going to tap into the Department of Motor Vehicles' registration files so I can track down that license plate from last night."

"My brother, the boy genius," Joe said. He watched Frank connect a wire from his computer

32

to Terrence's portable telephone. Frank then switched on the system and began dialing an Internet access number.

"That's odd," Frank said after a moment.

"What?" Terrence asked as he finished removing his makeup.

"I keep getting a connection," Frank answered, "but it won't hold for more than a couple of seconds."

Frank hit Redial on the cell phone. The familiar modem sounds echoed in the trailer, but after just a few pings and chirps, the phone's dial tone cut in.

"That makes four tries now," Frank said. He hit Redial once more.

"Hey, while Frank diddles with that," Joe said, "do you mind if I raid your fridge?"

"Help yourself," Terrence said. "There's some fruit and cold drinks in there. I'll take an apple, please."

"I don't get it," Frank said as his brother squeezed past the table and headed for the kitchenette. "According to my computer diagnostic program, there's some sort of interference that keeps me from getting a clear Internet signal over the cell phone."

Frank hit Redial at the same time that Joe

poked his head into the refrigerator. Again, the modem made a connection, chirps and beeps filled the air for a few seconds, and then the dial tone cut in.

"I give up," Frank said. He started to reach to disconnect the modem wire from the computer.

"Don't do that!" Joe shouted.

4 Dial E for Explosive

Experience made Frank stop. He recognized the urgent tone in his brother's voice and knew instantly what Joe wanted. Frank left the modem connected to the cell phone, and he hit Redial for good measure, somehow knowing that action was important, too.

"Talk to me, Joe," Frank said desperately. "What do you have?"

"A messy fridge," Joe replied. He opened the refrigerator door wide enough for both his brother and Terrence to see inside.

"That's a—" Terrence McCauley began. He

35

pointed to the top shelf, right next to a container of orange juice.

"Yup," Frank said. He hit Redial on the cell phone once more. "A bomb. A remote-controlled one, I would guess, by the way that blinking red light on the front keeps coming on and off in time with the noise from my modem."

"Wow," Joe said in admiration. "This is some setup."

"How so?" Frank asked. Suddenly the modem stopped chirping. From his vantage point at the table, he could see the red light on the front of the bomb click off and then on. Frank hit Redial on the phone, and the bomb light went dark.

"Remote control, about two pounds of explosive, and if I know my bombs, a tamper-proof fail-safe," Joe replied. "I won't be able to disarm it."

"Why hasn't it gone off?" Terrence asked. The stuntman, no stranger to danger but out of his element now, was frozen with fear.

"I figure the remote control's incoming signal is being blocked by the Internet connection," Frank explained. "The two radio signals keep blocking each other. It's pure luck that the two are tuned to the same frequency."

"Well," Joe said as he backed away from the refrigerator, leaving the door open, "our luck won't hold forever."

Frank hit Redial again. "We'd better get out of here. Terrence, open the front door. Joe come here and carry the laptop while I carry the cell phone. We need to keep the connection going."

Terrence moved swiftly to the trailer door. He twisted the knob and tugged. "It's stuck!"

"Probably barred from the outside," Joe said, scanning the room.

"That window above the bed," he said, pointing to it with his chin. "It's the only one big enough for us to crawl through."

"Well, crawl fast," Frank instructed Terrence.

The young stuntman climbed on the bed. He opened the window. "It's not going to work," he said, frustration and worry thick in his voice. "It's a horizontal slide window. There's only one pane of glass that opens."

"Then break it," Joe yelled.

Joe's tone of voice made Terrence regain his composure. Danger was a part of his everyday existence. Instinct took its place above fear, and Terrence acted accordingly.

With a lightning-fast, thunderously powerful karate strike, Terrence thrust his arm against the window, shattering the glass and opening a route to safety. He began to crawl through the narrow window.

"We can't make it through, holding the phone and computer," Joe said.

"Hand me the laptop," Frank ordered. Joe did as he was told. Frank carried the machine back to the table, hitting Redial as he did so. "Now out," he commanded.

Joe hopped on the bed and climbed through the window. Terrence helped him to the ground on the other side.

Inside the trailer, Frank hit Redial one last time. Then he sprinted the two strides between the table and the bed, jumped as if the cushion were a trampoline, and hurtled through the window. A piece of glass still stuck in the window frame cut his arm, but Frank wasn't going to let that slow his momentum. He wriggled through the window, Joe and Terrence pulling him out and to the ground.

"Run!" Frank yelled.

The three young men bolted from the trailer, but only a few feet separated them and the trailer when it exploded. Frank, Joe, and Terrence were thrown to the ground by the force of the blast, debris showering down on them.

To Joe, the rain of metal and wood seemed to

last for an eternity, though the last pieces clattered to the ground less than forty seconds after the explosion.

"Joe, Joe!" Joe felt a strong hand shake his body. He lay facedown on the pavement. The ringing in his ears muffled the voice of whoever was trying to rouse him.

"Joe, are you okay?" came the voice again, a little more clearly this time.

"Uh, a—a little dazed and confused," Joe stammered as he raised his head.

"Oh, then you're normal," Mr. Hardy said as he helped his younger son to his feet.

Joe looked around him. His older brother was sitting on the ground, dabbing at the blood that seeped through the cut on his left arm, but otherwise none the worse for wear.

Terrence McCauley was being tended to by his father. Joe could see that the elder McCauley was applying pressure to Terrence's shoulder.

"Injuries?" Mr. Hardy asked.

"I'm intact," Joe replied. He nodded toward his brother and the stuntman. "What's the damage?"

"Cut arm for Frank," Mr. Hardy replied. "A piece of wood hit his leg, and he'll just have a deep bruise. Terrence, however, is going to need his shoulder stitched up."

Mr. Hardy pointed to the burning husk of the trailer. The movie studio safety crew, a must on any action movie set, were putting out the fire with chemical extinguishers. "What happened in there?" he asked. "Gas leak?"

"Wrong number," Joe replied. His father gave him a puzzled stare. "Bomb," Joe added. "Whoever is after Terrence has really upped the ante."

"And then some," Mr. Hardy said. "You guys must have been pretty close to the blast."

"Less than twenty feet," Joe answered. He began walking toward his brother, who was just standing up. Though all three young men had been next to one another when they began to run, the force of the blast had thrown them several yards apart.

"How are you feeling?" Joe asked.

"Rattled, and my leg is throbbing," Frank answered. "The cut on my arm is actually from crawling through the window."

"How long was I out?" Joe asked.

"Four, maybe five minutes," Frank answered. "You sure you're okay?"

"I'm fine," Joe replied.

"We'll get him checked out just to make sure," Mr. Hardy said.

"If this all happened a few minutes ago, why

no cops?" Joe asked. "A boom like that is hard to miss."

"It's a movie lot," Mr. Hardy answered. "Stunt explosions happen all the time. Cops would only respond here if called."

The three Hardys walked over to Terrence and Brian McCauley.

"How are you doing, T?" Joe asked.

"I'll be good as new." Terrence smiled. "McCauley men are built tough."

"And thick headed," his father added. "Now maybe you'll ease off from stunt work for a while."

"I'm not letting some psycho scare me out of my life's work, or keep me from Daredevil Fest," Terrence said.

"Daredevil Fest?" Frank asked.

"It's a stunt competition. It starts tomorrow," Terrence replied. However, before he could explain any further, a purple convertible screeched to a halt a few feet away.

"What is going on here?" Pam Sydney's voice pierced the noise of the safety crew's fire-fighting efforts.

"There was a little extracurricular activity," Terrence McCauley said.

"Oh my gosh!" Pam cried. "Terrence, you're

41

hurt!" She pushed past Joe to get to Terrence's side. She stroked the stuntman's forehead.

"I'm fine, Ms. Sydney," Terrence said. "I've been hurt worse before."

Just then one of the safety crew members approached. "The fire's out, Brian."

"Thanks, Tast," Mr. McCauley replied. "Have the ambulette transport these three to the hospital."

"Hospital!" Pam Sydney screeched. "But we still have another stunt to shoot. I thought you said you were fine, Terrence."

"He'll need stitches," Brian growled.

"And they should all be checked out by a doctor," Mr. Hardy added a bit more soothingly.

"Maybe I can help," came a voice from over Pam's shoulder.

"Antonio Lawrence," Terrence said. Joe noted the veiled anger in his friend's tone.

The approaching man was about the same size and build as Terrence McCauley, no more than twenty-two years old, with short black hair and a square jaw, Joe noticed.

"A stunt get to be too much for you?" the newcomer quipped.

"Ease off, Antonio," Brian said. "You too, T."

"If you need a stunt, I'm your man," Antonio said to Pam.

"Just like you," Terrence said. "Always sniffing around other people's stuff."

"You're yesterday's side dish," Antonio said. "I'm today's main course." Antonio flashed a toothy grin at the movie studio exec.

Pam looked into the interloper's steel gray eyes. "I do need a man who's in good shape," she said.

"Then it's settled," Antonio said. "You go play doctor, Terrence, while I go help Pam."

Frank saw Terrence's body tense. He was certain that his friend was about to lunge at the sarcastic newcomer. He stepped in front of Terrence, stopping any rash action.

Antonio locked eyes with Frank for a heartbeat. Then he snorted out half a laugh.

"Let's go make some movies," Antonio said. He took Pam Sydney's hand, and the two walked away from the group.

"He's a real piece of work," Terrence began.

"Save it for later, boys," Mr. Hardy said. "Here's your ride to the hospital."

A small van pulled up to where the group stood. A paramedic—Stan, by the name patch on his blue uniform—exited the back of the vehicle.

"Won't need a stretcher," he commented. Stan pointed to the back of the ambulette. Joe went to climb in first but lost his balance and stumbled.

"You sure you're okay, Joe?" Frank asked as he reached out to steady his brother.

"Little wobbly, that's all," Joe replied.

"We'll order up a skull X ray, just to be safe," Mr. Hardy said, concerned.

"Well, we know that'll turn up empty." Frank laughed. He used his uninjured arm to help his brother into the back of the van.

"Ha, ha. Very funny," Joe mocked.

Frank climbed into the van and sat next to his brother. "Now we'll have proof that I got all the brains in the family."

Terrence climbed in behind Frank and Joe, being careful not to bump his injured shoulder.

"You two and all this brotherly love," Terrence said with a fake sniffle. "It's enough to make me cry."

The three young men broke out in laughter.

Ten minutes later the ambulette arrived at Gerlinsky General Hospital. It was a typically slow day in the emergency room. Gerlinsky was situated close to the posh neighborhoods surrounding the newer movie studios. Unlike inner city hospitals, which saw emergency rooms flooded with the victims of street violence, Gerlinsky General saw mostly bumps, bruises, and cuts.

Nonetheless, Gerlinsky was a well-staffed professional facility. Joe, Frank, and Terrence were attended to immediately.

Joe was sent to X-ray, and a call was put in to a neurologist to take a look at him to make sure he didn't suffer any lasting damage from having been knocked unconscious.

"I'm telling you, Doc," Frank said as Joe was led away, "you're not going to find anything!"

Later that evening the Hardys and the Mc-Cauleys relaxed at the Hollywood Hills home that Terrence shared with his father. The doctor at Gerlinsky General Hospital had confirmed that none of the young men had been seriously injured. Frank's cut had been bandaged, Joe had flirted with some nurses, and Terrence had had twenty-five stitches in his shoulder. Brian Mc-Cauley wanted the doctor to forbid his son from participating in Daredevil Fest, but Terrence protested and the doctor gave him the green light.

"So, what is this Daredevil Fest?" Frank asked. He sat on a chair across from Terrence, who was on the couch. Joe stood across the room scanning a bookshelf for something interesting to thumb through, and the adults were in the kitchen, cleaning up after dinner.

"It's this awesome stuntman competition," Terrence answered. "They hold it every year. It's a variety of tests of a stuntman's skills."

"It sounds pretty important to you," Joe said over his shoulder.

"It is," Terrence replied. "It sort of sets the pecking order among stuntmen. You know, whoever's the best gets the best jobs."

"And let me guess," Frank said. "You're the best."

"You'd better believe it," Terrence said.

"And this Antonio Lawrence wants to be the best," Frank added.

"He's a newcomer to Hollywood stunt work," Terrence answered. "He's done a lot of work in the foreign markets but not much since arriving in Hollywood last year."

"So if he wins Daredevil Fest," Joe said, still scanning the bookshelves, "he becomes top dog. Sounds like a suspect to me."

"Getting some theories together?" Mr. Hardy asked as he entered the room. He sat down on the couch.

"We have two good possibilities," Frank responded. "Michael Shannon and Antonio Lawrence. Both have a dislike for Terrence."

"Being a stuntman, Antonio probably has the knowledge and skill to pull off the attempts that have been made on T," Joe added. "And a highly

paid actor like Shannon could certainly hire someone with the skill."

Just then the phone rang.

"Could I get that for you," Frank asked, pointing at the phone on the small table across the
room.

"Sure," Terrence said.

"McCauley residence," Frank said into the
mouthpiece. Instantly, his face perked up. He hit
the button marked Speaker so everyone in the
room could hear.

"You hear me!" came the disembodied voice. "If
the stitches don't keep him out of action, maybe
this will!"

Suddenly there was a crash. The glass in the
bay window of the house shattered, and an object
came whizzing into the room.

5 Fall Down and Go Boom

"Explosive!" Frank yelled as the single three-inch stick of M-80 landed four feet from him, hissing as the fuse burned down.

The Hardy brothers sprang into action. Joe hurtled himself toward the sofa, while Frank ran toward the kitchen entrance.

Like the expert football tackle that he was, Joe Hardy dove at the couch as if he were tackling an opposing ball carrier. He hit the back of the sofa between where his father and Terrence were sitting, toppling the heavy piece of furniture backward.

Mr. Hardy and Terrence flew backward, too,

48

and when they landed on the floor, the large wooden frame and plush cushions of the couch fell over them, protecting them and Joe from the explosion.

Meanwhile, Frank ran to his mother and Brian McCauley, who were entering the living room from the kitchen, carrying trays of drinks. The glasses they carried, as well as their bodies, flew backward as Frank wrapped his arms around them and used his momentum to hurtle them back into the protection of the kitchen just as the M-80 exploded.

Frank and Joe's lightning-quick reflexes saved everybody from injury.

"What was that?" Laura Hardy wanted to know.

"That," Frank said, "was an M-80 firecracker, as much explosive in it as a quarter stick of dynamite."

"The damage isn't too bad—the bottom of the couch is singed, the carpet's burned, but the window is totally gone," Joe said, assessing the damage.

"That's it, enough is enough," bellowed the elder McCauley as he reentered the living room, wiping iced tea and coffee from his pants. "It's time we left California for a while and let the police sort this whole thing out."

"No way, Dad!" Terrence protested as he rose to his feet. "I will not be run off like some scared puppy dog. Daredevil Fest starts tomorrow, and I am going to compete."

"Besides," Frank added as he steadied his mom, "unless you leave forever, there's no guarantee that all this won't start again once you return home. For that matter, a determined killer might just follow you wherever you went."

"Frank's right," Mr. Hardy said. After hearing the distant police sirens move closer to the house, he added, "But in any case, we're going to have police involvement now, whether we want it or not. They're on their way. It would be hard to hide an explosion in a residential neighborhood."

"Does that mean we're off the case?" Joe asked.

"Since when has police involvement ever stopped you boys from completing a case?" Laura Hardy asked.

Frank and Joe both laughed. "Then we might as well decide what to do next before the police get here," Frank said.

"I'm still voting for leaving," Brian said.

"Vetoed," Terrence responded.

"Let's divide up the labor then," Mr. Hardy said.

"Right," Joe said. "I'll stick close to Terrence, so I can watch his back."

"How are you going to do that during Daredevil Fest?" Terrence asked.

"I'm going to enter."

"What?" Mrs. Hardy was shocked.

"I'm almost eighteen," Joe said. "That should put me in the same age category as T. And since Frank is injured, I'm the logical choice."

Knowing that arguing would do no good, Laura threw up her hands in frustrated defeat. "You'd better be more careful than you've ever been," she said to her son.

"I want to finish what I started today," Frank said. "Tracking down the truck from the other night."

"And Brian and I will be at the competition to help Joe watch Terrence's back," Mr. Hardy said. "Later I might want to ferret out leads around Mad Alliance Studios."

"Great, then that's settled," Joe said.

"Hey, you're forgetting about me," Mrs. Hardy stated.

"What do you mean?" Mr. Hardy asked his wife.

"Yeah," Joe said, "what do you plan to do?"

"I'm going to try to make a new friend during the competition." Laura Hardy smiled. "Pam Sydney. From what you've told me, she has a crush on Terrence and plenty of cash to make things happen. A woman who's been rejected, especially a rich one, can make a terrible enemy."

"We'll make a detective out of you yet, Mom," Frank said.

"Make me one?" Laura responded with a laugh. "Who do you think cracks all of your dad's tough cases?"

The next morning, after hours with the police, explaining to them that the M-80 was a prank, and with a carpenter who threw up some plywood to cover the blown-out window, everyone except Frank met at the site of Daredevil Fest's first event. Frank had taken one of the rental cars to the local library to use the computers to track down the truck that tried to run them off the road on the Thursday of the *Flame Broiled* media party. The competition's first event was skydiving. Terrence had used his influence with the competition supervisors to get Joe added as a last-minute entry.

Joe and Terrence were already dressed when the rest of the gang came to wish them luck. After all the "Be careful" 's and "Go get 'em" 's, the parents went to find seats in the grandstands.

"We'd better go pack our parachutes," Terrence

said. The seasoned stuntman led Joe toward the long table where several other competitors were working the silk chutes into the packs.

"Big T," one competitor said, extending a friendly hand. The rugged-looking young man had a blond Mohawk. "Ready to soar?"

"You bet, Caleb," Terrence responded, clasping hands with his exuberant competitor.

"Who's the kid?" Caleb asked, indicating Joe.

"Joe Hardy," Terrence said.

Caleb offered a hand to Joe. "A little wet behind the ears," he said. "You a rookie?"

"Oh, I have some experience doing stunts," Joe replied. "I just don't get paid to do them."

Caleb laughed. "Rock on, Little Joe." Caleb picked up his packed parachute and headed off toward the competitors' trailer.

"Friend of yours?" Joe asked Terrence.

"If you're asking as a detective, I give Caleb a zero on the suspect-meter. He's a joker with a heart of gold."

"Could just be a cover," Joe said. "I've come to learn that just about anybody, friend or foe, can have a motive to do another person harm. It's an unfortunate fact of life."

"Maybe," Terrence said. "But I'll cling a little longer to my instincts. Caleb's a good guy."

"Humor me," Joe said. "Fill me in on his background."

"Not much there," Terrence replied. "His father's a pastor at a local church. Let's see, he has an older brother named Severin who's a pretty good athlete from what I hear."

"Any rivalry there?" Joe asked. "You know, something that would maybe make Caleb want to make a bigger name for himself by becoming the number one stuntman?"

"I've known this guy for a while, Joe," Terrence answered. "When he competes, it's for fun only. He wins, he loses. It doesn't faze him. He's just a bass guitar–playing, loud-talking, fun-loving stuntman."

"Ever compete for jobs against him?" Joe asked.

"Not really," Terrence said after a moment's thought. "He does a lot of key stunt work on small-budget films, stuff I don't usually touch."

"Being number one and all," Joe laughed.

"Yeah." Terrence smiled. "Being number one and all. And Caleb's a good number two or three man on big films. In fact, we worked together on *Flame Broiled*."

"You really giving him a zero on the suspect-meter?"

"Yeah, Joe," Terrence said seriously. "An absolute zero."

Just then a short, balding man with a round face and wide eyes came trotting up to the table.

"Terrence, Terrence," he said, stepping between Joe and the stuntman, "I can't believe you're going through with this."

"What do you mean 'going through with this'?" Joe asked abruptly. If Caleb wasn't supposed to set off Joe's suspect instincts, this older man certainly was ringing the bell.

The man ignored Joe.

"I heard about yesterday," the man said to Terrence. "The explosion. I know it landed you in Gerlinsky General."

"I'm fine, Mr. Silver," Terrence said. "Thank you for your concern."

"Forget my concern," Mr. Silver said. "But how about my offer? Come on, give up this behind-the-scenes, stuntman anonymity junk. Step out in front of the camera. It pays better, and it's safer."

"Terrence," Joe said. "Mind introducing me to your friend?"

Mr. Silver glanced sideways at Joe, annoyed by his interruption. However, Terrence followed Joe's lead, sensing that he wanted to question the man.

"Joe Hardy, meet Mr. Phil Silver, head of Silver

Lining Productions. Mr. Silver, Joe's a friend of mine from the East Coast. Perhaps you might want to take a look at him if you're hoping to build up your talent pool."

"Oh, are you an agent?" Joe asked.

"Agent?" Silver seemed shocked. "Most certainly not. I'm putting together a new studio, and I need young talent with long-term potential," Silver explained.

The studio executive took a moment to stare at Joe. Joe felt as if he were being sized up.

"I like what I see, young man," Silver said. "Your good looks, obvious charm, athleticism, and your friendship with Terrence—I could use someone like you.

"As I've already offered to Terrence," Silver continued with a new smile, "I'm willing to sign a four-picture leading-man deal with him so he can give up stunt work for good. And I'm sure something can be worked out for the person who helps me convince Terrence to take the offer."

"A four-picture deal? I thought the days of studios signing actors to multimovie contracts went out in the fifties."

"They did," Silver explained. "But in Hollywood, everything old is new again. I'm looking to establish Silver Lining as a studio with longevity, not just some fly-by-night operation. To do that, I'm going to use a name-brand approach. You know, build a stable of talent that financial backers and movie patrons alike can have confidence in."

Silver turned his attention back to Terrence. "And I'm willing to make you one of my cornerstones," he said.

"Oh, no, you don't!" shouted a voice with a familiar Australian accent. Pam Sydney stormed up to the gathering at the parachute-packing table. "I want you to take twenty paces away from my man. He still has a picture to finish for Mad Alliance."

"He is not your personal property," Silver responded. "He can make your little movie the last time he has to be a nameless stuntman. I'll make him a star."

"Wow, such attention over a stuntman," Joe quipped.

"What can I say?" Terrence laughed. "Good looks and strong muscles are in these days."

"Oh, in that case," Antonio Lawrence said as he joined the group, "then they should be fighting over me."

Joe rolled his eyes.

"I was wondering where you were," Terrence said. "I was thinking you'd decided not to show."

"In your dreams, ex-champ," Antonio said.

"While you were jawing, I was strapping on my chute and posing for the cameras."

Antonio leaned in between Silver and Sydney. "You two should start bidding on me instead of yesterday's news."

Just then the verbal jabbing was interrupted by a voice booming over a loudspeaker.

"All right," the voice said, "we're ready to begin the Aerial Acrobatics Competition. The first three contestants will be Antonio Lawrence, Joe Hardy, and Terrence McCauley. Please report immediately to the airplane."

"But we haven't strapped on our chutes," Joe said.

"I guess you forfeit already," Antonio said with a laugh. The cocky stuntman turned and headed for the small prop plane that was revving its engines a dozen yards away.

"No way," Terrence said as he grabbed his parachute pack. "We'll strap in while we're climbing to the jump-point."

Terrence began to jog to the plane. "Come on, Joe," he shouted over his shoulder.

Joe grabbed his parachute and followed Terrence. He saw Antonio climb into the plane. Then Terrence handed his parachute pack to a tall, thin man inside the plane, and he, too, climbed aboard.

Joe held up his chute, thinking that somebody would grab it as Terrence's had been. However, no one reached down to take the pack. Frustrated, Joe held the pack in his left hand and reached up to the airplane's entryway with his right. He began to pull himself into the aircraft but slipped. The skydiving gear he wore was very slick, and he could not gain any leverage.

Joe tried again, and this time somebody gripped him around his arm. The grip was strong but felt weird. Joe couldn't figure out why, but he did note that the hand holding him applied a strange sort of pressure. As Joe was pulled into the airplane, he looked at the person who had aided him. It was the same thin man who had grabbed Terrence's pack. The man wore a helmet, headset microphone, and sunglasses. Joe couldn't make out his face, but he could see that the guy was the pilot.

Joe put his parachute pack down. He turned to help Terrence put on his pack, but he saw that it was already on. Joe gave the stuntman a quizzical look, but he couldn't question him over the drone of the plane's twin engines. He assumed that either the pilot or Antonio had helped Terrence into his pack.

Joe picked up his chute and handed it to Terrence, who helped him get strapped in and ready to skydive.

After the three competitors took their seats, the pilot throttled up the airplane and taxied down the runway. Ten minutes later the man signaled that they were at the jump-point. All three competitors lined up at the doorway.

Antonio was the first to jump. His wildly colored green, purple, yellow, and red outfit billowed around him as he tumbled into his first set of aerial maneuvers.

Joe was the second to exit the airplane. As soon as he cleared the wing, he twisted and turned, using aerodynamic changes in his posture to execute a variety of acrobatics. Out of the corner of his eye, he observed Antonio, still flipping and flopping like a falling peacock.

6 Terrence Drops a Load

Joe twisted his body to get a look at Terrence, who had just jumped. Terrence was in trouble. His chute was gone—the whole chute. He was holding out the silk of his skydiving outfit to add a bit of resistance, but it wouldn't be enough to keep him from reaching terminal velocity and being crushed on the ground below.

I need to time this just right to save him, Joe thought. And me without a calculator.

He turned his back to his falling friend and faced the ground. He gripped his ripcord and pulled. A colorful flow of silk billowed out from his pack, catching the wind and slowing Joe's descent. When the parachute was fully deployed, Joe's downward momentum was momentarily reversed. The shift in velocity brought him close to Terrence.

"Need a lift?" Joe joked, even though he knew his friend could not hear him.

Joe grabbed Terrence around the waist, and the stuntman wrapped his arms around Joe's chest. The two gave each other weak smiles.

Terrence cocked his head to the side and pointed, indicating a bull's-eye target painted on the field of grass below them.

Might as well land with flair, Joe mused. He worked the cords of the parachute, mindful to compensate for the extra weight he was carrying. Several minutes later, Joe put both himself and his package down in the center of the bull's-eye.

Their parents met them at the drop zone.

"What happened up there?" Laura Hardy shouted as Brian McCauley began to help Joe out of his chute pack.

Terrence removed his helmet. "As soon as I went into my first tumble, my pack just tore away from my body." Terrence hugged his father, and then he tried to hug Joe but couldn't, because Laura Hardy was there before him.

"Thanks for the save, man."

"That's what I'm here for, T."

"Was the pack buckled properly?" Mr. Hardy asked.

"Snapped it on myself," Terrence replied.

"Could it have had a faulty strap?" Joe asked.

"Or a cut one," Brian McCauley offered.

"I'd like to take a look at the pack," Mr. Hardy said.

"Good luck finding it," Joe stated flatly. "It could have fallen just about anywhere."

"Well, as far as I'm concerned, this competition is over for you, son," Brian McCauley said.

"Not by a long shot," Terrence said, refusing his dad's advice. "It was bad luck, that's all."

"I'm serious," Brian said.

"So am I, Dad. I'm finishing what I started."

Before the senior McCauley could argue further, Antonio Lawrence came strutting up.

"Didn't you boys know this was a singles competition?" he joked. "What's the matter, Terrence? Can't 'air dance' on your own?"

"Shut up," Terrence spat at Antonio. "I lost my parachute. While you were air dancing, Joe was busy being a hero."

"Oh," Antonio mocked, "a hero. Hey, you can blame your equipment if you want. It'll give you something to cry about when I run away with the prize."

Terrence lost his cool and lunged at Antonio. Mr. Hardy and Brian grabbed him before he could attack his rival.

Joe stepped between Antonio and Terrence. "Listen, wise guy," he said. "This is far from over. And before it's done, the only prize you'll walk away with is egg on your face, if not a whole mess of trouble on the side."

Antonio stared at Joe. Then he cracked a wide smile. "Whatever you say, little hero," he said, and turned to walk away.

Daredevil Fest was delayed for an hour while the competition's organizers discussed the skydiving "accident." At Terrence's insistence, however, and with no evidence that the problem with the parachute pack was anything more than faulty equipment, Daredevil Fest resumed.

The other competitors prepared for the skydiving competition, while Joe and Terrence ate a light brunch. The two competitors were joined by Frank. Fenton and Laura Hardy and Brian McCauley decided to go watch the remaining skydivers.

"I hope you had better luck than we did," Joe said to his brother.

"Compared to you," Frank replied, "I had the easy job."

"So what did you find out?" Terrence asked.

"I hacked into the Department of Motor Vehicles' database. The license plate number for the truck that almost sent us over the cliff is registered to a company—Silver Lining Productions. Ring any bells?"

"Bells?" Joe said excitedly. "It sets off a whole fireworks display."

"How so?" Frank asked.

"I had a little run-in with Phil Silver, owner of Silver Lining Productions," Joe said. "He had 'suspect' written all over him."

Joe went on to explain his earlier encounter with the slick businessman.

"So he left you with the impression that he could be trying to harm Terrence?" Frank asked.

"I don't think he'd want to kill me," Terrence said.

"Maybe not kill you," Joe said. "But he might be trying to put a scare into you so you'll leave stunt work and sign with him."

"Well, I'd say his scares are pretty risky," Frank said. "An M-80 at home and a bomb in a trailer are definitely enough to kill Terrence and a whole crowd."

"He might have an if-I-can't-have-him-nobody-will attitude," Joe offered.

"Could be," Frank conceded. "Although it's a little sick. In any case, he definitely bears a closer look, and I'm going to head over to his offices now."

"Great," Joe said.

"Yeah," Terrence agreed. "Joe and I have to get to our next event."

The next event was a hang glider race. Joe and Terrence rode in a van with Caleb and a couple of the event coordinators up to Aceto-Zimmer Bluff, where the race would begin.

"The bluff is an awesome place for a race," Caleb said. "Have you ever glided there, T?"

"Yeah, I filmed a stunt for the movie *Rhonda and Roseanne* there."

"You did the car-off-the-cliff stunt?" Joe asked. "I loved that movie. Hey, that was a Michael Shannon flick, right?"

"Yeah," Terrence said. "When he was younger."

"And could act at least a little," Caleb added.

The three young men laughed. Joe was getting to like Caleb.

"So fill me in on Aceto-Zimmer Bluff," Joe said.

Caleb unfolded a detailed map of the area. He showed Joe the high oceanside cliff that would mark the start of the race. He traced his finger along the route.

"There are pylons along the beach," Caleb said, "that anchor helium balloons. Those are your markers. You need to fly around the first two markers and then make a sharp turn toward this cove."

"Be careful at the cove," Terrence warned. "The updrafts there are treacherous."

"Believe it, Little Joe," Caleb added. "You'll dive through the cove and fly under a rock outcropping that sort of looks like a bridge. Hit that spot with too much air under your wings and you'll be cliff-pizza on the huge rocks below."

Joe examined the map, locking the stunt flyers' advice in his mind. He noted where all the turn markers were, three on the beach and one offshore. He didn't think he could win the race, but he certainly wanted to be in the competition.

When the van arrived at Aceto-Zimmer Bluff, Joe and Terrence took some extra time to examine their hang gliders. After the parachute incident, Joe wanted to be sure that the hang gliders had not been touched.

Satisfied that the equipment was not sabotaged, Joe and Terrence mounted their hang gliders.

The two were matched against each other in the second qualifying heat. Caleb and Antonio had just completed their race, and though the conceited Lawrence had just barely edged out the fun-loving stuntman, both competitors posted very impressive times. Joe and Terrence would be hard-pressed to fly fast enough to qualify for the next round.

"Good luck, Joe," Terrence said.

"I'm here to watch your back," Joe replied, "but I'll give you a run for your money."

The race began. Terrence vaulted into the air, and used his superior skill to gain an early lead. Aceto-Zimmer Bluff dropped away behind them, and the two flyers dove toward the first set of beach markers. Joe had a bit of trouble making the sharp turn toward the cove, so he lost sight of Terrence for a moment.

Joe tightened his legs to streamline his profile a bit more as he entered the cove. He glanced down at the rocks below him. The ocean waves crashed against the rocks, splashing water high into the air. Joe jigged his body to the side to keep the water from glancing off his wings.

Joe avoided the sea spray, but raising the glider

allowed too much air to get under his wings. He exited the cove on an updraft that propelled him at a steep angle. He had too much altitude and knew that he wouldn't be able to make the sharp turn around the marker fifty yards down the beach from the rocky cove. Still, he headed toward the marker to finish the race even if he wouldn't post a good time.

As Joe angled toward the marker, he spotted Terrence a dozen yards ahead and below him. The seasoned stunt flyer had already made the turn and would quickly head out toward the ocean for the final turn marker. Joe admired how Terrence handled his glider, floating effortlessly just above the treacherous rock outcroppings.

Suddenly something else came into Joe's field of vision. It was small and moving fast, and it was coming up from behind Terrence. At first Joe couldn't make out what the object was, but he was certain where it was aimed.

Then Joe realized that the object was a remote-controlled model airplane. He felt helpless as he watched the plane fly straight through the wing of Terrence's hang glider, ripping the fabric. The wing collapsed, and Terrence went plummeting toward the jagged rocks below.

7 Cut and Run

Joe twisted his body. Thanks to his accidental altitude gain, he had a chance of saving his friend.

A chance, he thought, but only one.

Joe pointed the nose of his hang glider down, and the craft immediately began to lose altitude. As it descended, the hang glider gained speed, closing the gap between Joe and Terrence.

The stuntman struggled to keep his own craft together. The hole in the wing forced Terrence to let go of the guide bar so that he could stretch out his arms to bolster both wings.

To Joe, Terrence looked like a wounded bird. With his arms spread out as they were, Terrence could not steer his craft. The hang glider went into a slow spin as it lost altitude. Joe broke into a sweat. He was gaining on Terrence but not fast enough.

He'll hit the rocks, Joe thought. I have to knock him clear.

Joe was still slightly above and a few yards away from Terrence. He knew that in just a few moments Terrence would smash into the rocks in the shallow water below.

"I hope the water's warm," Joe said out loud. He let go of his guide bar. Doing so caused Joe's feet to swing forward with a violent jerk. As his body's momentum shifted, he grabbed hold of the emergency strap release on his harness. He pulled the release, and his body began to fall away from his glider.

As soon as his feet were clear of the glider, Joe pulled his knees up to his chest. He arched his back as his legs came up, thus putting his body into a sort of backward somersault.

He rotated twice, and as he came out of the second revolution, Joe kicked his legs away from his body.

"Contact!" Joe shouted, hoping that he had calculated the maneuver correctly. His feet flailed outward, smashing into the side of Terrence's collapsed hang glider.

71

The force of the blow had the desired effect. Terrence was violently pushed a few yards to the side. He hit the water, missing the jagged rocks by no more than four feet. Joe's own momentum splashed him into the water nearly on top of Terrence. Buoyed by the fabric of Terrence's demolished hang glider, the two young men floated in the Pacific Ocean.

"You—?" Joe struggled to gain his breath.

Terrence nodded his head, indicating that he was okay. Joe smiled.

Three minutes later a Daredevil Fest safety crew motored up to the two exhausted competitors. Veteran stuntwoman Donna Roman, along with lifeguard Justin Stanfield, fished Terrence and Joe out of the bobbing waves.

"Oxygen?" Stanfield offered a mask to Terrence and Joe, who were both having a little trouble catching their breath. Both took a long drag from the oxygen tank.

"What happened out there?" Donna asked.

"You wouldn't believe me if I told you," Terrence replied.

Both Roman and Stanfield gave Terrence a quizzical look.

"Equipment failure," Joe stated flatly as he watched the remains of Terrence's hang glider sink beneath the surface of the water. He glanced at Terrence to indicate that no more information than that should be shared with the rescue team.

"That's twice now," Donna commented as she put the boat into gear.

"You've got a dark cloud over you," Stanfield added as he draped warm blankets around both wet young men.

Joe and Terrence just nodded.

Twenty minutes later, as Terrence and Joe changed into dry clothes, their parents came bursting into the competitors' trailer.

"What was it this time?" Brian McCauley asked. "Sniper?"

"Low-flying aircraft," Terrence said.

"What?" Mr. Hardy asked.

"It was one of those remote-controlled model airplanes," Joe explained. "It came swooping in on T and cut straight through his wing."

"Did you see what direction it came from?" Mr. Hardy asked.

"It came from the direction of Aceto-Zimmer Bluff," Joe said. "And then it spiraled into the ocean after shredding the wing of the hang glider."

"Well, that finishes it," Brian said. "Someone's definitely trying to knock you out of this competition—if not permanently—and I say we give him what he wants."

"Dad!" Terrence protested.

"Mr. McCauley," Joe cut in, "if we take T out of visible circulation, we may lose our best opportunity to flush his attacker into the open."

"But that means my son is nothing but bait," Brian said.

"Joe's right," Mr. Hardy offered. "Whoever is behind this appears to be willing to come after Terrence wherever he is or whatever he's doing. I'm not keen on exposing T to any danger, but Daredevil Fest may be our best forum to trip up this villain."

"But that puts a bull's-eye on my son's chest."

"It is my chest, Dad," Terrence said. "And we McCauleys don't live in fear."

"All right, we can see where this is heading," Mr. Hardy said. "Let's just let Terrence stay in the games. And the assignments stay the same. Joe, you make that target on Terrence's chest harder to hit. Meanwhile, Brian and I are going to hunt up some scuba equipment. I want to do a little late-night Pacific Ocean diving to see if we can recover that model plane. That could be a good clue."

*　*　*

While Joe and Terrence had been gliding above the ocean, Frank was doing some legwork on the ground. Knowing that the truck that played bumper cars with them the other night was registered to Silver Lining Productions, Frank drove over to their offices.

Seeing the building, Frank got the distinct impression that Phil Silver was a very conservative and shrewd businessman. His office was one of a few in a small Santa Monica four-story office building. Unlike most people who try to set themselves up as Hollywood high rollers, Silver had spent his money wisely. Modest office, probably a lean staff, and as his DMV search had revealed, only one company truck and one company car.

Being a smart money manager didn't put him above attempted murder though, Frank thought. He scanned the parking lot for the truck. If he could find the vehicle with any damage on it, it could be key evidence.

There were very few cars in the lot on a Saturday afternoon, and the pickup truck was not among them.

He probably took it to a body shop to cover himself, Frank thought.

Frank made his way into the building. Inside the lobby, there was a cleaning woman sweeping the floor and a little boy, probably her son, playing with action figures. Neither one so much as glanced up at Frank.

Frank scanned the directory and saw that the complex held only seven businesses. Silver Lining shared the second floor with the law offices of Drake & Zaccheo.

"Well, if he's guilty," Frank mused, "Silver won't have far to travel to get legal counsel."

Frank made his way across the lobby to the stairwell. He walked up to the second floor. After making sure the hallway was empty, Frank left the stairwell. The door to Drake & Zaccheo was closed.

He made his way down the hall to Silver Lining Productions. The office door was closed and locked, but there was no indication of any sophisticated security system.

Low rent probably means low security, Frank thought. He took out his lockpick set and examined the two locks on the Silver Lining door. He selected one small and one oversize pick and within a matter of seconds was inside the office.

Frank was right about Silver's business savvy—the man had a spartan office. The reception area had a few chairs for waiting visitors and a desk for a secretary. The workstation was kept neat, Frank noticed.

What I want is probably through there, Frank thought as he quietly closed the main door behind him. He headed for the door to an inner office. Once inside the office, Frank scanned for places to begin his search.

I'll start with the filing cabinet, he thought.

The first two drawers of the cabinet offered little to tie Phil Silver to any attempts on Terrence's life. There were several movie scripts with notes written in the margins. The only indication that Silver even had an interest in Terrence was a penciled reference on one script that it might make a good first film if the stuntman decided to turn actor with Silver Lining.

The third file drawer also bore little fruit. There were lists of contact names—scriptwriters, production crews, agents—but little else.

Frank turned his attention to Silver's desk. He turned on the computer and began to go through the desk drawers while he waited for the machine to boot up.

"Pay dirt," Frank said triumphantly. On top of some papers inside Phil Silver's drawer, there was a third-party life insurance policy quote. The quote was for a $1 million–dollar accidental death policy, and the name of the potential insuree was none other than Terrence McCauley.

Frank began to flip through the insurance paperwork, looking for the beneficiary and any official signatures. Just then, however, a telephone ring broke his concentration.

Frank stared at the phone. After two rings, the answering machine picked up. The volume was turned up rather loud, and Frank was forced to listen to Silver's businesslike greeting.

After the tone, Frank was riveted to the voice that left Phil Silver a message.

"Mr. Silver," came the recognizable voice, "Ian Edrich here. I have something I think you'd be interested in seeing. I'm going to ring your mobile phone, but just in case I don't catch you, call me back as soon as you can. I won't sit on this for long."

"That's an interesting message," came a voice from behind Frank. "But not as interesting as finding you here."

8 Strange Partners

"So," the stranger asked Frank, "who are you and what are you doing here?"

For a split second Frank thought about trying to bluff the stranger who had surprised him in Phil Silver's office, but instead he decided to be evasive.

"I should be asking you that question," Frank said boldly. "What are you doing in Phil Silver's office on a Saturday?"

"Well, seeing as I am Phil Silver," the man replied, "I can come to my office whenever I want."

"Phil Silver, huh," Frank said. "Prove it."

The man held up a set of keys.

"I have the keys," he said. "I didn't have to break in."

Frank knew he could no longer bluff or be evasive. He was caught red-handed, but he still had one trick left—direct confrontation.

"Well, Mr. Silver—if that's who you really are—then you have a lot to answer for."

"Answer for? To some teenager who obviously broke into my office?"

Frank kept his cool. "I'm part of a team hired to investigate the recent attempts on Terrence McCauley's life," Frank said. "And I have to say, you're looking pretty good as a suspect."

"If I'm a murderer," Silver replied, "you just took a big chance being caught alone with me in my office."

"Who said I'm alone?" Frank asked. "I said I'm part of a team. Expect my backup to be close by."

"Don't worry," Silver responded. "You have nothing to fear from me. If you're really here to protect Terrence McCauley, then you can expect full cooperation from me."

"Really?" Frank was surprised. "Given the evidence against you, I would think you'd be bolting for the exit."

"What evidence?"

"Well, let's start with the truck registered to Silver Lining Productions," Frank began, "the truck that tried to run Terrence McCauley off the road the night of the *Flame Broiled* party."

"How do you know it was my truck?"

"I'm pretty good with license plates," Frank replied.

"Did you get a look at the driver?"

"Can't say that I did. The windows are tinted, as you know. But I'm sure once I put my hands on the truck, I'll have all the evidence I need to prove you tried to run us off the road."

"It wasn't me, uh—what is your name?"

"Frank."

"It wasn't me, Frank," Silver began again. "The truck was stolen. I filed a police report Friday morning."

"But the 'accident' happened Thursday night," Frank stated. "So a Friday morning police report gives you plenty of time to ditch the truck."

"I didn't know the truck was missing until I got to work Friday morning," Silver explained. "And, anyway, I have witnesses who can verify that I was elsewhere Thursday night. Check it out if it makes you feel better."

"Oh, I'll check it out," Frank said. "You can be sure of that."

"Look, Frank," Silver said, "I'm not trying to hurt Terrence. In fact, if you ask him, I've been trying to get him to quit stunt work and become an actor for me."

"Maybe you are," Frank responded. "But he has refused to sign with you, so maybe you're looking for revenge."

"Revenge isn't my game," Silver said.

"But maybe insurance scams are," Frank accused. He held up the million-dollar life insurance quote he had found on the desk.

"Good try," Silver said. "But that piece of paper proves nothing."

"Then why have you been looking into accidental death policies on Terrence McCauley?"

"I'm a businessman trying to launch a movie studio. I want Terrence to sign a long-term contract with me as a way to entice investors. That means that people want to know that their investments are protected. Given that Terrence might want to do his own stunts in Silver Lining films, it makes sense for me to see how much it would cost to insure him. If you dig deeper into my desk, you'll find policy quotes on half a dozen people."

"That still doesn't make you any less a suspect,"

Frank said. "You might be looking to get Terrence insured, kill him, and collect."

"Look at the policy you're holding. It's unsigned and is only in effect if Terrence is under contract with Silver Lining. If money was my goal, I wouldn't be trying to hurt him before he was on my payroll."

Frank flipped the pages of the policy. After a moment, he spoke again.

"Okay," he said, "I think you're on the level. But I do have one more question."

"If it'll help keep Terrence safe, you can ask me anything."

"What was that message from Ian Edrich all about? The one I was listening to when you came in."

"That Edrich is some character," Silver said. "He keeps telling me he's going to be the next kingmaker here in Hollywood. Says the press can make or break anybody. He keeps offering me dirt on actors, but I keep turning him down."

"Why?" Frank asked.

"Why does he offer it? Because he's trying to position himself as a man of importance."

"No," Frank said. "I meant, why have you turned him down?"

"I don't do business the same way the rest of

Hollywood does. Movies are an important part of America's past, and the world's future. Movies can be so much more than moneymakers or status symbols. I'm trying to build a company based on principles here. Buying dirt from a weasel like Ian Edrich will just make me as dirty as the other producers here in Hollywood."

"A man of integrity," Frank said. "The world sure needs more of those."

"Thanks," Silver said. "Now get out of my office and go protect Terrence."

It was late afternoon when Frank returned to the Curtis Hotel. The sun was still visible in the western sky, even through the thick haze of pollution that hung over the Los Angeles basin.

Frank had the valet park the rental car, then made his way up to the hotel suite he shared with Joe and his parents. He was surprised to find everyone in the room, including the McCauleys.

"I didn't figure to see you guys back here yet," Frank said. "Wasn't there supposed to be another event after hang gliding?"

"It was canceled," Joe said. "The whole competition might be shut down."

"What happened?" Frank asked.

Terrence and Joe filled Frank in on the details of what occurred over the Pacific Ocean.

"So you're saying that the remote-controlled airplane was timed to hit the wing to make Terrence smash into the rocks," Frank stated. "We've got to be dealing with an expert who can get his hands on some good equipment. The bomb, the plane. What's next?"

"I don't want there to be a next," Brian McCauley interjected.

"None of us do," Mrs. Hardy said comfortingly.

"So what's our next move?" Frank asked.

"Dad's going swimming," Joe replied.

His brother gave him a puzzled look.

"Brian and I are going to do some diving off the cove while we still have some light, to see if we can find the plane. It might yield something."

"What about the rest of us?" Joe asked.

"The rest of you are going to rest, have a good dinner, long showers, and stay safe for one night here at the hotel," Mrs. Hardy said. "No need to put you into any further danger by having you traipse around Hollywood."

"But, Mom—" Joe began to protest.

"Let it go, Joe," Frank said. "I've seen that look in Mom's eyes before. There's no use arguing."

* * *

It wasn't until after ten that Fenton Hardy and Brian McCauley returned to the Curtis Hotel. Their dive had been a success. Mr. Hardy held a damaged model airplane in one hand.

"A model of a jet fighter plane?" Joe was surprised. "I thought most models were of classic aircraft."

"They usually are," Brian said. "But this one is a custom design. It's a pusher model. The propeller is in back. We couldn't find the nose section, but I'm betting it was sharpened to a point to rip through the hang glider fabric."

"Pretty ingenious," Frank said. "How do we find the person who was flying it?"

"Well, Daredevil Fest is closed tomorrow while the officials decide the fate of the contest," Joe said. "We could check out where this plane may have come from."

"Sounds good," Mr. Hardy said.

"But let's not all get caught up in that," Frank suggested. "Even with Phil Silver off the suspect list, there're still plenty of other people to check out."

"So we'll split up," Joe said. "Assignment?"

"I've got a lunch date with Pam Sydney," Mrs. Hardy stated. "I convinced her yesterday that I'd be a good way to get to Terrence."

86

"Way to go, Mom!" Joe said proudly. "Okay, I'll take Antonio. Any ideas on where to pick up his trail, T?"

"Yeah, there's a church over on Pulaski Road that he goes to on Sundays. He never misses. Even refuses to do stunts before noon on Sundays."

"Great," Frank said. "And I'll set up surveillance on Michael Shannon. We haven't given him much thought since he tried to choke that reporter, Ian Edrich, two nights ago."

"That leaves checking out the hobby shops to Brian, Terrence, and me," Mr. Hardy said. "A rig like this, even a custom-built one, had to get its parts from somewhere."

After getting a good night's sleep, Frank awoke Sunday morning before five. He showered, dressed, and ate a light breakfast before heading off into the Hollywood Hills. Terrence had given him directions to Michael Shannon's home.

Frank arrived just after sunrise and spent a few minutes surveying the area. Shannon's house occupied a corner lot in a very posh neighborhood. A seven-foot-high wall blocked Frank's view of the house. However, Frank discovered that if he climbed a tree at the edge of the woods across the street from the house, he could see into the actor's large backyard. Plus, this particular spot allowed Frank to remain hidden while observing Shannon.

His early morning arrival quickly paid dividends. Only ten minutes after settling into his perch, Frank saw the actor exit the patio door and jump into his swimming pool. Frank became bored, however, watching Shannon swim laps for over thirty minutes.

Well, it's a good way to stay in shape, Frank thought as Shannon finally stepped out of the pool. Frank watched the actor towel off, then saw that something had suddenly drawn the man's attention. Shannon picked up a cordless phone from the poolside table and spoke into it for only a minute.

Frank watched the whole scene, but lost sight of Shannon when he went back into his house.

I've probably seen all his backyard activity today, Frank thought. An early morning call like that might have been a summons to go somewhere.

Playing on his hunch, Frank climbed down from the tree and went to his car. He had parked the car in a spot that gave him a good view of Shannon's front gate.

When the actor left his house, Frank was ready. He followed Michael Shannon's green sports car at a discreet distance.

Frank was led farther up into the Hollywood Hills. Here the homes were farther apart and the woods thicker. Finally, Shannon left the road and turned his car into a forest.

Frank pulled off the road and entered the woods on foot. He used a pair of binoculars to watch the actor, who had parked his car and gotten out.

Frank saw Shannon approach another car, a Jeep. Unfortunately, the bushes and the open door of the vehicle blocked Frank's view of the person with Shannon. Frank could see, however, that the person the actor had met had given him a large manila envelope. Frank watched as the actor pulled what looked like a set of enlarged photographs from the envelope. Frank couldn't make out what the pictures were, but they made Shannon very happy. Frank could see him smile widely as he handed the pictures and envelope back to the other person.

The mystery person got into the Jeep, but Frank still could not see who it was. He made a quick decision: following the Jeep might yield better results than watching Shannon go through his Sunday routine.

Frank raced back to his car and was in position to follow the Jeep when it left the woods. After a forty-five-minute drive, the Jeep finally stopped in front of a low-rent apartment complex. Frank parked across the street.

"Well, I'll be . . ." Frank said to himself as he saw the driver of the Jeep get out of the vehicle.

Without hesitating, Frank jumped out of his car and raced across the street. The person had just entered the door of a first-floor apartment. Before he could close the door, Frank had put his shoulder against the wood and muscled his way into the apartment.

"Sort of strange, don't you think," Frank said gruffly, "that you and Michael Shannon would have a friendly get-together?"

9 Spin City

"Who . . . what?" The person Frank was confronting began to stammer.

Frank was not about to let his suspect regain his composure. "Don't play dumb, Edrich," he said.

Frank could see that the lanky reporter was scared. It must have been the element of surprise, but whatever it was, Frank decided to press his advantage.

"I just saw you with Michael Shannon," Frank said. "You guys must have made up pretty fast, seeing as the last time you were together he tried to choke the life out of you."

"I, he—" Edrich started to say.

Frank kept the heat turned up. "So, are you blackmailing him? I saw you show him some pictures."

The reporter put his hands and the manila envelope behind his back.

"You might as well let me see them," Frank said. "Or I can call the police and you can show what's inside that envelope to them."

"Okay, okay," Edrich said, holding out the envelope to Frank, who took the pictures out. He studied them for a second.

"What's this all about?" Frank asked. "All I see here are a bunch of photos of Michael Shannon in a dark bar with some woman I don't recognize. You really are trying to blackmail him."

"No, it's not that," Edrich replied.

"Out with it," Frank said, "or I call the police."

"We're, well, sort of working together," Edrich stammered.

Frank shook his head in disbelief. "Start explaining," he said.

"Shannon's career is flagging," the reporter began. "He's too clean-cut for today's Hollywood. People today like to see a bad boy up on the screen. It's the day of the antihero, and Michael

Shannon is trying to remold himself. Without a new image, his career is sunk."

"So a couple of fistfights, attacking a reporter, a mystery woman in a seedy club, and he figures he can get a new lease on his career?" Frank asked.

"Exactly. We tarnish his name, sling a little mud on his pearly white image, generate some heat around him, and *boom*, he's headlines again." Edrich smiled at the beauty of his plan.

"Where do you fit in?" Frank was more than curious.

"I know Shannon's cousin," Edrich explained. "I got to Hollywood hoping to make a name for myself as an entertainment reporter. The cousin hooked me up with Shannon, and we concocted this plot to light a fire under both of our careers. Two stars for the price of one."

"Does your plot include trying to kill Terrence McCauley?" Frank asked.

"No," Edrich nearly shouted. "No way. McCauley was only a convenient tool the night of the *Flame Broiled* thing. He was standing there, so Shannon ad-libbed a little. The whole town knows they've never liked each other."

"That's a convenient and unconvincing response," Frank said flatly. "You're going to have to do better than that."

"Look, I'm being straight here," Edrich pleaded. He ran his long skinny fingers through his bleached blond hair.

"Think about it," he continued. "What quicker way to tank an already-sinking career than by being tossed in jail for murder? You can't do much acting from behind bars. Kill McCauley and get caught, and Shannon's doing himself in as well. The guy's only trying to remake his image. He's an actor. The only thing he could kill is a good script. He's not looking to do any harm to that stuntman."

"Makes sense," Frank said. He turned to leave the reporter's apartment.

"Oh," Frank added, turning to face Edrich once more, "don't think I won't let it out what you two are up to if you tell anyone about our talk. Then you'd have to start looking for a new job," Frank added. "I hear they need ghostwriters for kids' books."

While Frank was with Ian Edrich, Joe was across town sitting outside a church on Pulaski Road in the other rental car.

After an hour, with only occasional bursts of music from inside the building to break the monotony of the wait, the service ended. Joe immediately caught sight of Antonio Lawrence. The stuntman exited the church and spent a few minutes talking to some people. After exchanging a few hugs, he got into his blue convertible sports car.

Does everybody here have a nice car? Joe mused. Maybe we should move.

Antonio pulled his car out of the church parking lot and zipped down Pulaski Road. Joe put his car in gear. He lay back a bit and followed just close enough to keep Lawrence in view.

I hope I don't do anything to tip him off, Joe thought as he decelerated a bit and fell even farther back.

Joe saw Lawrence make a sudden, unsignaled turn and guessed he'd been spotted. His guess was confirmed when Antonio made two more unsignaled turns in rapid succession.

Joe tried to close the gap between the two cars, but he couldn't risk speeding or causing an accident.

Now that he knew he was being tailed, Antonio made more sharp turns and played tricks with traffic to try to shake Joe. The younger Hardy hung tough and kept his prey in sight.

When Antonio led Joe out of the downtown area and up into the hills, it gave Joe an opportunity to open up the car a bit. He pressed down on the gas pedal as he watched the blue convertible careen around a bend in the road.

As Joe rounded the same bend, however, his eyes widened in horror. The road narrowed suddenly and Joe watched Antonio pull a maneuver that only a stunt driver could accomplish in such a confined space: the man hit his brakes and whirled the car around one hundred and eighty degrees. He came speeding straight at Joe!

10 Driver's Ed

Joe slammed on the brakes and jerked the wheel to the right, bringing the car to a skidding halt. The rental car was turned sideways, straddling both lanes of the road.

Antonio also slammed on his brakes and turned his wheel. When his blue convertible came to a complete stop, his driver's-side door was less than a foot from the driver's-side door of the rental.

With unbelievable speed, Antonio was out of his car and in Joe's face. The stuntman had left his car door open, which brought it to rest against Joe's door, trapping him inside his car.

"What do you think you're doing?" Antonio

yelled at Joe through the open window. He leaned into the car and grabbed Joe by the shirt collar.

Joe quickly outlined his options. There were none. The way the cars were positioned, he was trapped. The rear of the vehicle was too close to the rocky cliffside wall to use reverse as an escape route. And to drive forward could mean plunging over the cliff if he did it too quickly.

"What am I doing?" Joe questioned. "You're the one who drove down the hill in the wrong lane aimed directly at me."

"I'll ask again. Why are you following me?"

"It's what I do," Joe replied. "I always keep an eye on anyone who might be trying to kill a friend of mine."

Antonio laughed and released his grip on Joe.

"You're funny," he said, and patted Joe's chest once. "I could demolish you at any time, and you just get right in my face. You have guts."

"And brains," Joe said. "Brains enough to know that you'd love to see Terrence go down so you could win Daredevil Fest and be the top stuntman in town."

"Oh, I'll be the top dog in this town," Antonio said with confidence. "And I'd love to see that pretty boy knocked low. But try to hurt him? No way."

"You're just covering up," Joe said.

"Covering up what? When I beat Terrence for the top spot, I don't want him saying it was a tainted victory. If I don't beat him cleanly, then people won't take me seriously."

"But any victory you'd get now will be suspicious," Joe replied. "With two attempts on his life occurring in the first two events, the lead you have now means nothing."

"First of all, there are a lot more events to go, so no lead is safe. And second, those so-called attempts on his life were probably caused by incompetence," Antonio said.

"Of course you'd have to say all this if you were trying to kill him. I don't buy that what's happened to Terrence in the past couple of weeks, especially during the competition, was because of incompetence. And you certainly have motive, opportunity, and expertise to pull all of this off."

"Sure," Antonio answered. "I could pull any of it off. But I'm not."

"Can you prove it?" Joe asked.

"I don't have to. I'm innocent until proven guilty."

"So all I have is your word."

"Yeah," Antonio said, "that's all you have."

"So where does that leave us?" Joe asked.

"It leaves *you*, man," Antonio responded. "You investigate anything you want. Me, I'm going to visit my mother."

Antonio returned to his sports car. Without a backward glance, he put the convertible in gear and sped away.

When Joe returned to the Curtis Hotel, he found a message from Frank to meet at Terrence's house. After a quick shower, Joe got back in the rental car and went to hook up with his brother.

"What's all this?" Joe asked as he entered the McCauleys'. He pointed to two large boxes in the entryway.

"Check it out," Frank said as he led his brother into the den.

"So he's got you hooked?" Joe asked Terrence, nodding at the brand-new computer that sat on an oak desk.

"Welcome to the Information Age." Frank smiled.

"Your brother convinced me that I shouldn't live without one of these," Terrence said. "So he went with me and helped me pick out some equipment."

"I didn't want to go to the library again to do research," Frank admitted.

"So, what are we researching?" Joe asked.

"Depends on what you came up with," Frank stated.

"You first," Joe said. He slumped into a chair.

"Okay," Frank started. "The short version is that I don't think Michael Shannon is the one trying to kill T."

"What brought you to that conclusion?"

"Well, I did find out he was up to something—something to jump-start his career. It turns out that he's trying to cultivate a Hollywood bad boy image. Killing Terrence is not the sort of scandal he'd need to boost his career."

"I took him for all bark anyway," Joe said. "Antonio, on the other hand—that guy might have plenty of bite."

Joe filled Frank and Terrence in on his run-in with the cocky stuntman.

"So, where does that leave us?" Terrence asked.

"Pretty much with nothing," Frank answered. "He could have you in his sights, or he could be telling the truth."

"T," Joe asked, "do you know much about Antonio?"

"Just what he lets people know," Terrence said. "Which is nothing but what's in his bio. That, and the church he likes to go to."

"Maybe we can check out his past, his background," Frank offered.

"How?" Terrence asked.

Frank smiled at the computer.

For the next two hours Frank wielded the machine's keyboard as if it were a sword. He made his way through the World Wide Web, searching for information on Antonio Lawrence. Frank looked into the local records of the various places Antonio had lived, but came up with nothing other than previous addresses, paid parking tickets, and one arrest for disorderly conduct with charges dropped.

"We have nothing more than we did before," Terrence said.

"Research doesn't always yield the results you want," Frank stated.

"You can say that again," Mr. Hardy commented as he entered the den.

"So, the sweep of the hobby stores came up empty?" Joe asked.

"Yeah," Mr. Hardy replied. "There are just too many suppliers and too many buyers of radio-controlled equipment. After talking with some shop owners, we realized that pretty much any skilled hobbyist could have made the modifications to that plane that took out the hang glider."

"But the trip wasn't a total loss," said Brian Mc-Cauley as he entered the den carrying a large red-and-white box. "I see I'm not the only one who did some shopping. Nice computer."

"What do you have there, Dad?"

"A remote-controlled replica of flying champ Scott Pellegrino's Zano 2000."

"A what?" Frank asked.

"A Zano 2000!" Joe was excited.

"The very one flown by Pellegrino when he won the world championship. You like airplane racing, Joe?"

"I love it," Joe responded as he gazed at the pictures on the model's box. "This is one fast, sleek aircraft. First time I saw it in action, I couldn't believe the kind of acceleration and speed a propeller plane could generate."

Just then everyone heard the front door open.

"Where is everybody?" Mrs. Hardy called from the hallway. The men all exited the den and joined her as she made her way to the kitchen.

"Ah, the last of our investigators," Mr. Hardy beamed. "Come up with anything?"

"More than you, from the sound of that question," Laura replied. She sat down at the kitchen table.

"So spill, Mom," Frank said. "Is Pam good for the crime?"

"Most certainly not!" Laura exclaimed. "The only thing that girl is good for is a broken heart. Her own, most likely. She's head over heels in love with Terrence. But she doesn't know how to express herself in any other way than with noise and flash. She loves him—she doesn't want to kill him."

Mrs. Hardy looked at Terrence. "You don't have to date Pam if you don't want to," she said, "but be her friend. There's more to her than you see."

"Unfortunately, that 'more' doesn't get us any closer to who's behind all this," Brian McCauley said.

"So what next?" Joe asked.

Just then the phone rang. Terrence picked it up, and after listening for a few seconds hung up.

"Good news or a threat?" Mr. Hardy asked.

"Great news," Terrence said. "Daredevil Fest is back on for tomorrow!"

The next morning the contestants gathered on the back lot of Mad Alliance Studios. There was a spectators' grandstand set up at one end of the lot. The rest of it was set up as an obstacle course, complete with pylons, small ramps, gates, oil slicks, and speed bumps.

"Wow, that's some course," Joe said to Terrence. "We're driving sports cars?"

"Better than that," Terrence replied. He pointed to a warehouse at the far end of the course. The warehouse doors opened and two eighteen-wheel semi-trucks came rolling out.

"Awesome!" Joe shouted.

The first Daredevil Fest contestant to drive was Antonio. Both trucks were kept idling, but only one was driven at a time. This way the second truck could start immediately while the first truck was being refueled so that each racer would drive a vehicle with the same fuel weight, making race results more accurate.

Antonio made a decent run, but his time was not spectacular. He missed one of the gates and was penalized, opening the door for the other contestants to move up in the standings.

Terrence was up next. He began his run while Joe mounted the semi that Antonio had just used. He watched Terrence start out fabulously. Then he lost sight of the truck as it rounded the warehouse. That part of the course took the semi out of Joe's sight for a minute.

When the truck came into view, it was moving much faster than Antonio had been.

Joe realized in a flash that the truck was moving too fast. Then he heard the semi's airhorn blast. He couldn't make out Terrence's face inside the cab, but from the way the stuntman was laying on the horn, Joe knew that something was wrong. Very wrong, Joe realized, as the truck gained speed and headed straight for the grandstands!

11 Smash-Up Derby

"All right," Joe said out loud. "Now even I want Terrence to quit Daredevil Fest!" Joe squinted so he could bring the stuntman's face into focus.

No steering, Joe guessed, and no brakes.

Terrence's eighteen-wheeler was still on a course headed straight for the grandstand.

"Clear out!" Frank Hardy yelled. He began to scramble off the grandstand, prompting other spectators to leave their seats as well.

"Come on! Move, move, move!" Mr. Hardy yelled, taking up his son's call. The spectators all began to move. Some ran from the grandstands.

Others leaped off the side, not even worrying about the short drop to the ground.

Confident that everyone was clear, Mr. Hardy and Frank ran, just as Terrence's truck smashed through the iron and aluminum structure and veered off away from the grandstand.

Meanwhile, Joe Hardy had thrown his eighteen-wheeler into gear. The semi lurched forward, slowly picking up speed as Joe worked the truck's gears.

As he had done with the hang glider, Joe quickly figured a possible intercept angle from where he was to where he could deflect Terrence's truck. Still, crashing two eighteen-wheel trucks together was not what Joe had in mind.

I need to be more subtle, Joe thought as he swung his truck parallel to Terrence's vehicle.

Joe jerked the wheel and bumped Terrence's truck. He did it again and again, using the gentle nudging to cut the out-of-control semi's speed.

This isn't working fast enough, Joe said to himself. He shot a glance at Terrence, hoping the stuntman had a fresh idea.

Terrence pointed. Joe followed his finger and saw that Terrence was indicating a large concrete building dead ahead.

Well, crashing his truck into the concrete would

stop it, Joe thought. Probably kill T, but it would stop the truck.

"I hope there's a second part to your plan!" Joe shouted even though he knew Terrence couldn't hear him over the roaring engines.

With both trucks traveling over forty miles per hour, Joe violently jerked the wheel of his vehicle and smashed it into the other semi. The jolt was insufficient to alter Terrence's course. He was still angled straight at the building.

Joe knew how desperate Terrence was when he saw him open the driver's-side door of his speeding truck and climb out of the cab.

Where is he going? Joe thought in disbelief. Then he caught on to Terrence's plan.

Joe sped up and closed the distance between the two vehicles once more. He maneuvered his truck so that his front end was just short of Terrence's driver's-side door as the semis ran parallel to each other.

"Now would be good!" Joe shouted. He wasn't certain that Terrence heard him, but at that precise moment Terrence did propel himself away from his eighteen-wheeler.

The stuntman landed with a thud on the front hood of Joe's truck.

"Hang on!" Joe screamed. He violently jerked

the wheel just in time to veer away from the concrete building. In his sideview mirror, Joe saw the now-empty semi smash into the concrete building. Both the truck and the wall crumpled, but at least the rampaging eighteen-wheeler had come to a complete stop and hadn't burst into flames.

Joe eased his truck to a stop. Terrence smiled at him through the windshield, and Joe smiled back. As they both got to the ground, Frank, Mr. Hardy, and Brian McCauley came jogging up.

"What the Evel Knievel happened out there!" Brian McCauley shouted.

"I'm not sure," Terrence replied. "The run was going great when all of a sudden—*pop*—she jerked up from the ground a bit, like she'd hit something in the road."

"Did you hit something?" Frank asked.

"Not that I saw," Terrence replied. "But I was concentrating on the obstacles, so there could have been something in the road. In any case, after the jolt, I had no steering and no brakes! I couldn't even downshift to cut speed."

"We figured as much," Joe said.

"I want to get a look at the truck," Frank said. The older Hardy brother jogged over to the concrete building that had ended the eighteen-wheeler's joyride.

When he got to the scene, somebody else was already poking around under the vehicle.

"Hey, what are you doing!" Frank asked.

The man, startled by Frank, nearly bumped his head against the bottom of the truck as he stood up. He turned around and glared at Frank. The stranger was tall and painfully thin, and by Frank's guess probably in his midforties. Frank immediately noticed a long thick scar that ran along the man's cheek from his left eye to his jawbone. It was a glaring disfigurement, and Frank tried not to stare.

"I should be asking you that question," the man replied in a deceptively smooth voice. Frank was surprised that such a melodic voice came from such a hard-looking face.

"I came to see what happened," Frank said. "I work with the driver."

"So do I," the man said. "I'm William Thompson, safety consultant for Daredevil Fest."

"Frank Hardy," Frank said. He extended his hand in greeting, but Thompson did not remove either of his own hands from the pockets of the overalls he wore.

"Well, Frank Hardy," he said, "you have no reason to be here, so run along."

With no official reason to remain, Frank simply walked away.

"Who's that William Thompson guy," he asked as he rejoined the group.

"Slim Billy Thompson," Brian McCauley said with a shake of his head. "Now, there's a tragedy."

Frank, Joe, and Mr. Hardy gave the senior McCauley a questioning look, but he just cast his eyes down and stared at the ground deep in thought.

"William 'Slim Billy' Thompson," Terrence said, filling the silence. "He's the safety consultant for this whole event."

"Well, he's not doing all that great a job," Joe stated flatly.

"What's his story?" Frank asked.

"It's a tough one," Terrence began. Before he could say any more, though, he stifled himself.

Slim Billy was approaching. The thin man gave the entire group a steely glare. He obviously had something serious on his mind.

"Terrence," he said tersely as he joined the gathering, "I've got some troubling news."

12 Safety First

"What do you mean, 'troubling news'?" Mr. Hardy asked. "What did you discover?"

"I haven't discovered much of anything yet," Slim Billy replied.

"But . . ." Brian McCauley quizzed.

"But I think enough has happened to warrant a full investigation. I hate to do it, but as safety consultant, I'm hereby shutting Daredevil Fest down."

"What!" Terrence immediately complained. "You can't do that."

"I certainly can," Slim Billy replied calmly in his singsong voice. "And you're the reason why."

"What are you saying?" Joe asked.

"I'm saying that all of these mishaps have happened to Terrence," Slim Billy said. "They could be coincidence, they could be sabotage. . . ."

"Or they could be his incompetence," Antonio said as he joined the gathering.

"You wish!" Terrence shot back at his competition.

"Look," Antonio said, "you're the only one who can't get it together. No reason for all of the competitors to suffer because of you."

"I thought you wanted to win this tournament with Terrence in it," Joe said.

"Sure, I'd like to," Antonio answered. "And I know I can. But I don't want to see the whole thing go down the drain just because T here has lost his edge."

Terrence pressed his angry face into Antonio's. The two were nearly touching noses.

"I have my edge, boy," Terrence said, steamed. "Edge enough to take you down."

Brian McCauley pushed his body between the two hotheads.

"Enough!" he shouted. "This is about more than Daredevil Fest. Somebody wants my son dead, and this has gone way past any game."

"Well, I don't know if anybody is trying to kill

your boy," Thompson said. "But if that is the case, my investigation will uncover any sabotage."

"Can't you investigate while the competition continues?" Terrence asked. He eased a few inches away from Antonio.

"No, and that's final," Slim Billy replied. "I'm concerned for your safety, Terrence," he stated. "Frankly, I'm concerned for all of the competitors' safety."

"Aw, man, this is bogus," Antonio spat out as he flung his hands above his head. He walked away in a huff.

"Well, we appreciate your concern," Joe said. "It's getting tiring, hauling T out of danger. Just please let us know what you find." Joe held out his hand in a gesture of friendship to Slim Billy. The haggard-looking safety consultant absentmindedly took Joe's hand and gave it a weak, very abrupt shake.

Joe immediately noticed that Slim Billy's grip was very strange. Then Joe realized it not only felt weird but oddly familiar. Joe was certain he had encountered the man—or at least his hand—in the past few days.

The skydiving airplane, Joe realized, when the pilot grabbed my shoulder.

Perhaps a bit too obviously, he looked at the

man's right hand as Billy pulled it away and jammed it in his pocket.

"Uh, well," Joe stammered, "I guess we should go get cleaned up."

"Good idea," Brian said. "Thanks again, Billy."

"No problem," Thompson replied. He turned and walked back toward the wrecked eighteen-wheeler. Frank noted that Slim Billy had a serious limp. His left leg was extremely stiff.

"I guess we'll head on back to the house," Mr. Hardy said. "You coming, Frank?"

"Nah, I'm going to stick with Joe and T. We'll see you back there."

Brian and Mr. Hardy said goodbye and left for home.

"Let's hit the trailer and change," Terrence suggested. The three young men began to walk.

"Spill it," Frank said to Joe. "I saw something on your face while you were talking to William Thompson."

"His hand, man. Didn't you notice it?"

"What about it?" Frank asked.

"He has only two fingers and a thumb on his right hand," Joe said. "His middle finger and his pinky are missing. I wonder how he could fly a plane with such a damaged hand."

"What do you mean, 'fly a plane'?" Terrence asked.

"I recognized his strange grip," Joe responded. "He was the one who helped me get into the airplane when we went skydiving."

"So?" Terrence said. "He's the safety coordinator for this show. Plus, he's actually a great pilot. It's not odd that he would pilot the skydiving event."

The three entered the changing trailer. No other competitors were in there, so they had privacy.

"There are no restrictions given his handicap?" Frank asked.

"I'd fly with him," Terrence said.

"You seem to have a lot of respect for the guy," Joe said. He took off his sweaty shirt.

"I guess I do," Terrence said. He got himself a bottle of water from the refrigerator. "He was a great stuntman in his day. He could have been the best."

"I hear a *but* in your voice," Frank said.

"But," Terrence continued, "he was very reckless. He was a big risk taker when he did a stunt. Always pushing the envelope. Studio execs had a love-hate relationship with Slim Billy. He always delivered the most action-packed stunts, but he was a killer on their insurance premiums. Studio accountants used to joke that they needed to take out a 'Slim Billy rider' on the insurance policies if he was working the film."

"So one of his stunts finally caught up with him," Joe said as he put on some fresh shorts.

"I'll say," Terrence said. "I was there when it happened." He slumped down to the couch, obviously depressed by the story he was about to relate.

"It was two years ago," Terrence began. "On the set of *The Bridges of Rodriguez Ridge.*"

"The World War II movie?" Frank asked.

Terrence nodded and continued.

"Anyway, by that time, it was difficult to get other stuntmen to work with Thompson. He was too reckless. But the studio needed a blockbuster, so they went with him as the lead stuntman. I was young and wanted work, so I signed on as well."

Terrence took a drink and stared at the floor.

"We were doing a stunt on a mountainside," he finally said. "There were a lot of explosions as we charged up what was something like a twenty-percent grade. *Boom, bam, bang!* Explosives were detonating all around us. I was in the lead. Then, *boom,* a charge goes off close to me and I lose my footing. Some rocks start to slide. One bounces and hits Slim Billy square . . ."

Terrence choked on his words.

"Hit him square . . ." he started again, but could not proceed.

Frank sat down next to the emotional stunt-man. He put a reassuring hand on his leg.

Terrence never stopped staring at the floor.

"The rock hit him right in the face," Terrence said. Frank and Joe could see that there were tears welling up in their friend's eyes. "Slim Billy fell backward, right onto one of the buried explosive charges just as it detonated. He took shrapnel in his leg and face. It blew off the two fingers from his right hand."

The room fell silent for a minute.

"It wasn't your fault," Joe said reassuringly.

"Actually, that's what the investigation revealed," Terrence replied. "Turns out that there were twice as many charges planted on that hill as there should have been. It was never discovered who planted the extra explosives, but the prevailing theory was that Thompson had done it himself. All in the name of realism. For a better stunt, the man almost killed us both."

Terrence got up from the couch and finished changing into fresh clothes.

"Still," he said, "I can't help feeling I was responsible. Even though Slim Billy has gone out of his way to show that he knows it wasn't my fault."

"Maybe that's why he called off Daredevil Fest," Joe said as they left the trailer. "He probably doesn't want any tragedies happening to the people he feels responsible for."

"You're probably right," Terrence said. "He could never work as a stuntman again after the accident, but he stayed in the business as a coordinator and consultant. In fact, movies he works on these days have the best safety rating in the industry."

Frank looked at the sun as it crawled across the western sky.

"Let's catch an early dinner before heading to your house," he said.

Ninety minutes later the three friends arrived at the McCauley home.

"Looks like everybody's here," Terrence said as they pulled up in front of the house. He pointed at the rental car and his father's truck. The three young men had the other rental car at their disposal while Terrence's beloved sports car was being repaired.

When they got into the house, however, there was nobody there.

"That's odd," Frank said. "Where are the parental units?"

"Beats me," Terrence said.

"Uh, T," Joe said, "did you buy a new tape player when we weren't looking?"

"No," Terrence replied. "Why?"

Joe pointed to a small tape recorder on the living room coffee table.

"I've never seen that before," Terrence said.

All three cautiously approached the tape player. Taped to the front of the device was a note: Let's play.

13 Where Have All the Parents Gone?

" 'Let's play'?" Terrence said. He reached for the Play button on the unfamiliar tape machine. "Maybe my dad's come up with a new way to make sure I don't miss his messages."

"No! Wait!" Frank screamed. He quickly slapped Terrence's hand away from the tape machine.

"What was that for?" Terrence asked, rubbing his wrist.

"It could be booby-trapped," Frank said. "We have no idea who put that machine here. I'd say with all that's gone on lately, it's better to err on the side of caution."

Terrence nodded his head in agreement.

"I'll go check out the rest of the house," Joe said. He headed up the stairs.

Frank crouched down beside the coffee table to get a closer look at the machine.

He scanned the device from every angle without actually touching it.

"I don't see anything unusual," he said softly. He then reached into his back pocket and took out his lockpick set. He chose the longest tool in the kit. With the pick, he gently prodded the machine, moving it ever so gently.

"So far so good," Terrence said, relieved that nothing had exploded.

Frank gently picked up the tape player. He turned it over and examined the battery compartment.

"Four double As," he said. "No special wires or signs that the machine has been modified."

"I guess we should press Play, then," Joe said as he returned to the living room. "The house is clear. No sign of any forced entry."

"Okay, here goes," Frank said. He put the machine back down and pressed Play.

An electronically disguised voice emanated from the machine's tiny speaker.

"No more games," the voice said. "I've given

Terrence a fighting chance to stay alive, but even so, he should be dead by now. And he would be if it wasn't for the meddling Hardy brothers. You two kids think you're so good at this? Let's see how you do with a real challenge. By now you know that your parents aren't around. That's because I have them. I wonder if you two can save their lives and still keep me from killing Terrence. You'll get further instructions by phone at nine P.M. Standard kidnapping rules apply: alert the police and I'll kill my hostages."

The tape machine went silent. Frank pressed the Off button.

"No options," Joe said flatly.

"Not so," Frank interjected. "We may not be able to pick up anything from the voice on the tape. It could have been male or female for all we know, but we still have some suspects we can check out."

"What suspects?" Terrence asked. "Everybody you've checked out on this case has an excuse why it isn't them."

"Then we start by checking out everybody again," Frank stated.

"No time," Joe said. "We could call around to each of our suspects, but if we call the actual culprit, he or she might panic and harm our folks."

"Well, what do we do?" Terrence asked.

"We go with our gut and check out our prime suspect in person."

"Who would be?" Frank asked.

"I'm voting on Antonio Lawrence," Joe said. "I don't like the guy, and I don't trust him."

"If that's your best guess," Frank said, "let's go for it."

"I'll let you know what I find," Joe said, heading for the door.

"No, I'll let you know," Frank said, cutting off his brother. "You and Antonio don't like each other even a little bit. You won't get anything out of him if there's a confrontation."

Joe had to agree with his brother's logic. It was decided that Frank would check out their prime suspect, and Joe would keep a watch on Terrence to make sure the kidnapper didn't try a double-cross by coming back to the house instead of phoning.

As the hour approached nine Joe began to get worried. "Frank should have been back by now," he said. "I hope he hasn't run into any trouble."

"Maybe we should go to Antonio's," Terrence stated.

Just then the telephone rang.

"I guess we'll know something now anyway," Joe

said. He reached for the phone and hit the speaker button so both of them could hear the instructions.

"Glad to see you can follow instructions," came the disguised voice through the telephone's speaker. "I want the three of you to drive into the hills. There's a cliff exactly three and seven-tenths miles farther up the hill from where we played bumper cars last week. It's secluded, so we won't get interrupted as this all plays out. And don't take any side trips getting up here. My patience is wearing thin."

The line went dead.

"Well, I get the feeling that our bad guy doesn't know that Frank isn't here," Joe said. "I don't know if that's good news or bad news." Joe picked up a pen from the coffee table and scribbled his brother a note.

"In any case," he said as he wrote, "we can't wait for him to return. We'll have to do this with just the two of us."

"I'm up for it," Terrence said. "Let me gather some stuff from my room. You go get some rope, flashlights, and whatever else you think we might need from the basement."

"Good thinking," Joe said. He stood up and headed for the basement. "We'll make a detective out of you yet," he called.

Joe opened the door to the basement and flicked on the light switch. He was only halfway down the stairs when he heard the door slam shut behind him. The distinctive sound of a deadbolt lock being thrown filled the musty silence.

"What's going on!" Joe shouted as he ran back up the stairs.

He grabbed the door handle and gave it a twist.

"Locked!" he grunted. Joe banged on the door.

"Terrence!" he shouted. "Terrence, let me out of here."

"Sorry, Joe," came the stuntman's voice from the other side of the door. "No can do."

Joe banged on the door again.

"What are you up to, Terrence?" he asked.

"I can't put you in any more danger," Terrence replied. "I have to finish this myself."

"Come on, T. This is no time to go solo on me."

Joe's shout was greeted by silence.

"I'm pleading with you here," Joe continued. "Don't do anything foolish."

Again, only silence.

"T?" Joe yelled. "Oh, man," Joe said. He slumped to sit on the top stair. "He's gonna get himself and our parents killed."

14 All Locked Up with Someplace to Go

Forty minutes before Joe found himself locked in the McCauleys' basement, Frank arrived at Antonio Lawrence's home. He parked his car down the block from the house and quietly approached the building on foot.

Frank used a row of hedges that divided Antonio's lawn from that of the neighbors to hide his approach. Certain that he could not be seen by anybody who might be inside Antonio's place, Frank made his way on all fours to a large bush just outside Antonio's living room window. He cautiously peeked through the window. The lights were off, and with the sun now beyond the western horizon, Frank was left with little illumination.

Just then Frank was grabbed from behind. A set of powerful arms had him in a full nelson, and Frank was pulled to his feet.

"What . . . uh . . . ow," Frank grunted as he struggled with his unknown assailant. Frank felt his head being pushed into his chest by the force of the wrestling hold. With practiced smoothness, the older Hardy brother shifted his weight, moved his hip into the body of his attacker, and flipped the man over his shoulder and down to the ground.

Whoever Frank's attacker was, the person was a very skilled fighter. Before Frank could focus his eyes to see his assailant, the figure on the ground kicked out with both legs and tripped Frank. A powerful punch then struck Frank on the back.

Sensing another blow was on its way, Frank rolled away from his attacker and sprang to his feet. His opponent also sprang to his feet and threw a punch straight at Frank's face. Just then Frank made out who his attacker was.

"Enough!" Frank shouted, and blocked the incoming punch. With one fluid motion, Frank turned the block into a wristlock. He twisted, applying enough pressure to force his attacker to his knees.

"I have the advantage now, Antonio," Frank huffed tiredly.

"Hardy?" Uncertainty echoed in Antonio's voice.

"Yeah," Frank replied. "Wait, you didn't know it was me when you grabbed me?" Frank eased the pressure on the stuntman's wrist enough so he could get to his feet.

"No," Antonio replied. "I was stretching after my evening run, and I saw somebody snooping around my house. With all the weird stuff that's been going down lately, I thought maybe somebody was after me."

"You mean, you saw me and thought it was somebody out to get you? I came here thinking you were the one who was trying to harm Terrence."

"For the last time, I am not trying to kill Terrence. Yeah, I want to be top stuntman, but not enough to hurt somebody. That's why I attacked you. I'm beginning to think somebody hates all stuntmen, and I may be the next target."

Frank released his hold on Antonio's wrist.

"Man, that leaves us at square one," Frank said.

"What do you mean?"

"I mean," Frank said, "that now we have no idea who's after Terrence. I can assure you that you are not a target. Whoever wants T dead is definitely doing it for personal reasons."

"Well, I hope you find the guy," Antonio offered. "I may not like the dude, but with Terrence around, I know I always have to be on top of my game."

Antonio held out his hand to Frank. "Just do me a favor," he said. "Terrence is competition enough for me. When this is done, could you and your brother move back to wherever it is you came from? With the way you fight and your brother drives, you'd probably have me and T both flipping burgers while you two carve up all the stunt work."

Frank shook Antonio's hand. "Don't worry," he said. "Joe and I would probably find stunt work too tame compared to what we usually go through, but thanks for the good word."

Frank turned to leave.

"Good luck," Antonio called. "I hope you take this villain down."

It was just after nine when Frank returned to the McCauley house. The first thing he noticed was that Brian McCauley's truck was gone.

Joe and Terrence must have already gotten the call and left, he realized. Frank ran into the house, hoping they'd left a note.

Immediately Frank's attention was grabbed by the sound of his brother's shouting.

"Hello! Frank! Is that you?" came Joe's voice.

"Joe?" Frank shouted. He followed Joe's voice to the basement door and unlocked it. Joe came shooting into the kitchen.

"What's going on?" Frank asked.

"We got the call," Joe replied. "I went into the basement to get some supplies. Terrence locked me in."

"Terrence locked you in! Why did he do that?"

"He said he didn't want to put anybody else in danger," Joe answered. "He said he wants to finish this himself. I pleaded with him to let me out, but to tell you the truth, I don't think he heard a word I said."

"Any idea where he went?" Frank asked.

"Oh, yeah," Joe replied, "I know where he went. And I know who he's going to find when he gets there."

15 One Last Stunt

"If you figure on finding Antonio Lawrence there," Frank said, "then you figure wrong. I just tangled with him, and I'm convinced he's innocent."

"Innocent," Joe said. "That I don't know about. But I do know he's not the one trying to kill Terrence. That honor goes to William 'Slim Billy' Thompson."

"Slim Billy!" Frank was shocked. "How do you figure that?"

"Some clues, some hunches," Joe said, "but I'm sure I'm right. I figure he has motive: the accident during filming on *The Bridges of Rodriguez*

Ridge. Opportunity for sure: he's the safety consultant for Daredevil Fest, so he's had full access to the events. Plus I'm certain he was the pilot for the skydiving event. Terrence handed him his parachute pack. Thompson could have slit the harness while he was helping T into the pack. The skill factor is a no-brainer: he's handy with explosives, and besides being a stuntman, he was also a stunt designer, stunt coordinator, and probably a technical expert."

"So, where do we find Slim Billy?" Frank asked.

"That's the final clue," Joe replied. He described the cliff where they were to meet Thompson. "Tie this location back to the scene where his career was ended, and it says William Thompson all over it. Cliffs hold a special place in the relationship between Terrence and Thompson."

"Good work," Frank said. "But at this point, knowing who our opponent is does little to bring this to a close. He's got hostages, he's probably got Terrence by now, and he's had a whole lot of time to prepare whatever trap he's going to spring on us. This has gone from being a mystery to being a rescue operation."

"Then let's get prepared," Joe stated flatly. He jogged down the stairs to the basement. When he came back into the kitchen he was holding a long coil of rope, a grappling hook, and a lantern.

"Put these in the car," Joe said as he handed the equipment to his brother. "I've got to get one more thing."

When Joe got into the car, Frank was examining a map.

"What did you just toss in the trunk?" Frank asked.

"A little surprise," Joe replied with a grin.

"I figure we should take a different approach to the cliffs," Frank said as he traced his finger along the map. "Maybe cut down Slim Billy's advantage a bit by reaching the spot unexpectedly."

Joe took the map from his brother so Frank could start the car. "Good thinking," he said. "At this point, any little thing that shifts the initiative away from Thompson may give us the room we need to bring him down."

Frank put the car into gear. "Just remember, the stakes here are high," he said. "This lunatic has our parents and may have our friend. Don't get reckless, but if you see an opportunity to take him out, there's no need to be gentle."

"Trust me, making nice with this guy is not in the program," Joe said.

Twenty minutes later Frank eased the car to a

stop on a deserted dirt road at the base of the Hollywood Hills.

"The way I figure it," he said to Joe, "the spot where he wants us to meet is a ten-minute walk."

"Yeah, except he'll be at the top of the cliff and we'll be at the bottom."

"If I remember correctly, the hills aren't that high at the spot he wants us to meet him. Plus, we won't both be at the base of the cliff if you stick to the plan."

"I'll be in position," Joe assured his brother. "You just keep him focused on you."

The two brothers split up. Frank walked along the base of the cliff while Joe made his way up the rocks to the top. It was rough going for Joe. He was holding a large box, and Frank had purposely kept the rope and grappling hook. For their plan to work, it would be a matter of both precise timing and well-honed skill.

Frank walked for ten minutes through the darkness. He had considered using a flashlight, but decided that every step he got closer to Slim Billy without alerting the man would be precious.

Unfortunately, Slim Billy was not about to oblige Frank's wishes. Without warning, a gunshot rang out and a bullet kicked up the dirt at Frank's feet.

He must be wearing night goggles, Frank thought. He can see me, but I can't see him.

As if in answer to Frank's unspoken request, Slim Billy fired up a powerful electric lantern. He shone the beam around the top of the hill.

In silhouette Frank could see Slim Billy standing over the still body of Terrence McCauley. He could also see that the young stuntman was bound at his wrists and ankles.

As if that weren't bad enough, what Frank saw next caused him to shudder. Bound and gagged and standing shoulder to shoulder on a narrow six-inch ledge with their backs flattened against the cliff face were the three missing parents. The drop to the rocks below was only about thirty feet. But tied up as they were, if they fell they would be seriously injured if not killed outright.

"Kids today just do not listen," Slim Billy shouted. "You were all supposed to come together. Instead this joker shows up all alone," he said as he jabbed Terrence with his boot. "And now we're still one Hardy short."

"Sorry to disappoint you," Frank said.

"Well, I'll just change my plans," Slim Billy said. "First, drop that rope you're holding," he said, indicating with his revolver the equipment that Frank was carrying.

137

Frank let the rope drop to the ground. However, as he did so, he surreptitiously gave some slack to the end with the grappling hook.

"So what's your new plan?" Frank asked Slim Billy. If he had calculated correctly, Joe was still probably out of position. He needed to buy his brother a little time.

"Nothing too elaborate," Thompson responded. "Nothing like the traps I set up before. I think I'll just shoot poor Terrence here and then I'll trigger some explosions that'll send your folks to their graves. I'll leave you and your brother to pick up the pieces while I escape out of the country. That'll teach you to meddle in my business."

"So how did you set up your stunts?" Frank asked. "Some were absolutely brilliant." He needed to keep Thompson's attention riveted on him. An ego stroke or two could do the trick.

"Come on, none of them were all that tough," Slim Billy said.

"Humor a stupid kid like me," Frank added.

"Remote-control stuff, mostly," Slim Billy explained. "I love explosives. Bomb in the trailer refrigerator—expensive but not that hard to acquire. M-80 through the window—no problem. Okay, so trying to run you off the road in that truck I stole from Silver Lining may be a bit too straightforward, but, hey, you work with what you got.

"I cut the strap on Terrence's parachute pack and hitched small explosives to the steering and brake lines on the semi," Slim Billy continued. "The trickiest part was shooting him out of the sky with that remote-controlled airplane."

"Speaking of airplanes," Frank said. A loud buzzing sound suddenly filled the sky. Instinctively, Slim Billy took his eyes off Frank to locate the noise.

His eyes locked on Brian McCauley's model Zano 2000 just in time. Slim Billy ducked as a large, sleek model airplane came buzzing straight at his head.

Frank used the distraction to make his move. He dropped to the ground and with one fluid motion grabbed the grappling hook, rolled to his feet, and threw the steel object with pinpoint accuracy. The hook flew to the top of the cliff. One of its sharp tines cut into Slim Billy's left leg. With a mighty tug, Frank jerked the rope attached to the hook, sending Slim Billy tumbling to the ground with a shout of pain.

The injured man struggled to get to his feet. At the same time, he tried to raise his gun. However, the model airplane buzzed him once more, keeping him pinned to the ground and knocking the gun from his hand.

After using the remote control one last time to make the Zano 2000 plummet to Slim Billy's chest, Joe dropped the unit and ran up to where the villain lay. He kicked the gun out of Thompson's reach.

"Don't you just hate it when one of your own traps comes back to bite you?" Joe said, beaming as he dropped down beside Thompson. He rolled him over and put a knee into the small of the man's back. Then he used the rope that was attached to the grappling hook to bind Thompson's arms and legs together.

"Just like in the rodeo," Terrence murmured as he regained consciousness.

"How you feeling?" Joe asked as he untied his friend.

"Groggy and bruised, but I'll be okay."

"Good," Frank said as he came panting up the hill, "because this isn't over by a long shot."

16 One Last Bang

"Bad guy caught, case closed," Terrence said.

"Nope," Frank responded.

"I heard him say something about explosives," Joe added.

Terrence shook his head. "Our folks!"

"Bound and gagged on a narrow ledge with dynamite strapped to them," Frank said. "And with a perfectionist like Slim Billy, I'm betting there's a timer attached to the explosives, just in case his remote control failed."

The three young men went to the edge of the cliff and peered down into the darkness at the tops of their parents' heads.

"Get some light," Frank ordered.

Joe retrieved the flashlight that Terrence had dropped when Slim Billy knocked him out. He returned to the cliff edge and shone the beam down.

"You guys okay?" Frank asked.

"Are they okay?" Joe chuckled nervously. "They've got dynamite strapped to them."

"I meant, are they all conscious," Frank explained. He looked down at the three parents.

Each adult nodded.

"Good," Frank said. "We won't have to haul dead weight up here."

"So you have a plan?" Terrence asked.

"Yeah," Frank replied. "What you'll have to do is lower me down the side of the cliff so I have both hands free."

"You!" Terrence protested. "I'm the stuntman here. I'm going over the side."

"Nope, me," Joe said. "Terrence is too heavy."

"You're stronger than I am," Frank said to his brother. "I'd feel better if both you and Terrence held the line." Frank began to wind the rope around his waist. "Plus, there's no time to argue," he said as he tied the rope into a reliable knot.

"First thing when I'm down there, I'll disarm the explosives and then we can haul our folks up."

"Slim Billy is a genius when it comes to rigging explosives," Terrence said.

"I sure am," Thompson said from the ground. He seemed amused at the young men's predicament.

"Never mind him," Frank said. "We're going to do this just fine."

"When we lower you down," Terrence suggested, "ungag my dad first. He should be able to talk you through the process."

"Good idea," Frank said.

The three friends peered over the cliff edge once more.

"Let's do it," Frank said.

Joe and Terrence took a firm grip on the rope and braced their legs against giant boulders. "Good luck," they both said as they slowly lowered Frank over the side.

"How are you doing?" Frank asked, hanging next to Brian McCauley as he undid the gag around his mouth.

"Just dandy," the man replied, moving his jaw back and forth to get the circulation going. "Okay, let's not waste time. Work fast but carefully."

The first person Frank was to release was Mrs. Hardy. Bracing his feet against the ledge his mom was standing on, Frank removed her gag and waited for Brian McCauley's instructions.

"You see the green wire that runs from the first stick of dynamite into the timer?" he asked.

"Yeah, I see it," Frank answered.

"Good. What you need to do is lift the wire gently, but don't break it."

Frank reached for the wire.

"Wait!" Brian exclaimed. "Did you bring something to cut it with?"

Frank squeezed his hand into his back pocket. He removed his Swiss army knife and opened the wire-cutter tool.

"Good," Brian McCauley said.

"Hurry up down there," Joe shouted from atop the cliff. "Our arms are giving out."

"After I release Mom and you haul her up, I'll have a ledge to stand on."

"Get back to work," Brian directed.

Once more Frank gently lifted the green wire.

"Okay, now strip off the covering very carefully. Don't cut through the wire."

Frank did as he was instructed. When he had removed the green plastic covering he saw that the wire inside consisted of several twisted strands of copper.

"Now what?" Frank asked.

"Put the knife in your mouth," McCauley said. "You'll need two hands for this next step."

When both of Frank's hands were free, McCauley continued.

"Carefully separate the strands from one another. There should be five. Untwist them very carefully. Now cut the one in the middle," Brian McCauley instructed.

Frank took the knife from his mouth. He positioned it around the center wire and neatly snipped it.

Immediately, there was a noise like a clock winding down.

"Booby trap!" Brian McCauley screamed.

Frank's instincts took over. Realizing that Thompson had rigged the timer to wind down to zero if the device was tampered with, Frank simply tore the dynamite from his mom and threw it toward the rocks below.

It exploded mere feet away, the force of the blast throwing Frank into his mother and against the cliff wall.

"I'm losing my grip!" Joe screamed.

Joe and Terrence struggled to maintain their hold. Terrence swiftly wrapped the slipping rope twice around his own arm.

"Ahhh!" he screamed as the rope bit into his skin.

"I'm solid again," Joe said as he recovered his hold on the rope.

"What happened?" Frank asked Brian.

"He's got this wired up so strangely," Brian replied.

"Or he changed the wire casing colors so we'd have trouble disarming them," Frank suggested. "Why don't I just rip all of the explosives free?"

"Too dangerous," McCauley answered. "Carefully untie my hands, get topside, and then toss the rope down so your mom can be hauled up. I'll examine the device strapped to me so when you come back down to disarm it I'll know a little more."

Frank did as he was told. After his mom was safe on top of the cliff, he tied the rope back on his own waist and was once again lowered over the cliff.

"We'll need to work fast," Brian McCauley said. "We're almost out of time."

"Do his dynamite first, son," Mr. Hardy instructed after Frank removed his father's gag.

Frank knew better than to argue with his dad.

"I have this one figured out," Brian McCauley stated. "After you disarm it, get up top and send the rope back down. I'll free your dad."

Frank worked swiftly, following Brian Mc-

Cauley's instructions. The stunt coordinator was soon free from his trap.

Ten minutes later all three parents stood beside their sons and the trussed-up Slim Billy Thompson. They all sat down and rested while Joe walked out to the highway to flag down help.

Thirty minutes later, Joe returned.

"I got a passing motorist to put in a call to the police."

"Uh, could somebody at least turn me on my back?" Slim Billy asked sheepishly. "All the blood is pooling in my forehead."

"I should just throw you over the edge," Brian McCauley spat into the face of the former stuntman.

"Not necessary, Brian," Mr. Hardy said. He put a restraining hand on his friend's shoulder.

"With more than a dozen counts of attempted murder hanging over his head, I think Slim Billy will be spending the rest of his days in jail," Frank added.

"He'd better be," Terrence said. "If he thinks he was somehow paying me back for the accident that ended his stunt career, he doesn't even want to know what I'll do to him for putting our parents in danger."

"Speaking of danger," Joe said, "do you think

they'll redo Daredevil Fest now that the accidents have been cleared up?"

"I hope so," Terrence said. "If for no other reason than I won't have to hear Antonio Lawrence whine for a whole year about how he got cheated out of a chance to beat me."

"Beat *you?*" Joe laughed. "Hey, if the tournament is back on, you'll both have to worry about beating me!"

SKIN & BONES

Contents

1 A Nasty Surprise

A hollow *click-clack* sounded above Frank Hardy as he pushed open the door to the shop. Eighteen-year-old Frank, who was six feet, one inch tall, felt something brush the top of his dark brown hair.

"Cody doesn't miss a trick," Frank's brother, Joe, said with a grin. His blue eyes focused on the bones hanging over Frank's head. Joe was an inch shorter and a year younger than his brother.

Frank reached up and tapped the mobile hanging above the doorway. Narrow white bones dangled on clear plastic cords from a small skull with hollow eye sockets.

The Hardys stepped inside the San Francisco shop called Skin & Bones and put down their travel bags.

"Hey, guys, you made it." Cody Chang strode across the room to greet the Hardys. He was twenty-four years old, with black spiky hair. He had a wide smile, and his dark brown eyes flashed with pride as he swung an arm in a wide sweeping motion. "So what do you think? Pretty cool, eh?"

"Who buys this stuff, anyway?" Joe asked as he pushed his blond hair back and leaned over a display case. Through the glass he saw bird claws curved into deadly points, twisting tubes of shed snake skin, and shiny, bright-colored fish fins.

"Artists, teachers, doctors," Cody answered, looking around the shop. Several people were poring over displays in cases and on the walls. "Some people use them for decorations and crafts. You'd be amazed. Excuse me for a minute." He stepped away to help a customer.

A couple of minutes later the *click-clack* of the bones mobile announced another visitor to the shop.

"Hey, Dad," Cody said, raising a hand in greeting to his father. Frank noticed the affectionate smiles that the Changs exchanged. He knew that Cody and his father had become very close after Cody's mother had died, ten years ago.

"Sergeant Chang," Frank said, walking over with Cody to greet the short stocky man. "Great to see you.

Our dad was really sorry he couldn't make this trip with us."

"Not as sorry as I am, I'm sure," Thomas Chang said, greeting the Hardys. "It would have been great to talk over old times with Fenton. The last time you were here Cody hadn't opened Skin and Bones, had he? Isn't it something?"

"It sure is," Joe said. He was examining one of the skeletons hanging behind the counter.

"Wait till you see the rest of this place," Cody said. "I live on the second floor, but the real fun's up on the third. That's where my lab is." Cody's eyes sparkled as if he had a wonderful secret.

"You're still planning to stay at my house, I trust," Sergeant Chang said to the Hardys. "The guest room and refrigerator are waiting for you."

"You bet," Frank said. "And thanks for the invitation."

"Did you rent a car?" Cody asked.

"No," Joe answered, coming over to shake hands with Mr. Chang. "We took the Airporter into town and cabbed over here."

"Exactly why I stopped by," Mr. Chang said. "I just got a new car, but I haven't sold my van yet. You can use it while you're here—if you want. I figured you two might like some wheels while you're in town."

3

"Totally cool," Joe said, taking the keys for the house and van.

The four chatted until Sergeant Chang's partner picked him up, and Frank and Joe decided to take off to get settled in, clean up, and change clothes.

"Okay, get out of here," Cody said, walking them to the door. "Say, would you guys like to meet me at the zoo? Two-thirty at the snack bar. I have to pick up a package there."

The boys agreed, and after getting directions to the zoo, took off for Sergeant Chang's in the van. "This reminds me of our van," Joe said, turning to check it out. "Except it's red, of course."

The Hardys had stayed at Mr. Chang's comfortable small home on the west side of town in the Sunset District before. They changed into jeans, T-shirts, and sweaters before heading out to meet Cody.

At about two-thirty Frank had parked the van and was wandering with Joe through the zoo toward the snack bar. Cody was waiting for them at one of the small tables. His brow was wrinkled as he gazed into the distance.

"Hey, guys," Cody greeted them. "It's about time. I'm starved. I haven't had lunch yet." The three walked up to the snack bar window. "So, did you get all settled in?" Cody asked as he ordered a burger and fries. The Hardys ordered a shake each because they'd already eaten.

"Sure did," Joe said. "And it's great to have the van."

"We have some time to kill," Cody said as he gathered up his lunch. "My package won't be ready until four or so. Let's hang out for a while."

The young men took seats on a bench in front of the orangutans. The male orang lolled in a hammock, his huge body practically dragging on the dusty ground below. A rust red baby orang darted out from behind a tree, batting a ball around the play yard.

"So, what's in this mysterious package you're picking up?" Joe asked.

Cody didn't answer.

"Earth to Cody," Joe said. "Come in."

"Hmm? What?" Cody said. "Oh, sorry. Did you say something?"

"I asked what's in the package you're picking up," Joe said.

"Stuff for the store," Cody answered in a matter-of-fact way. "An ostrich skeleton, a couple of anaconda skins, a zebra skull, and the real prize—anteater claws."

"Do you get all your merchandise from zoos?" Frank wondered, shooing a sea gull away from Cody's fries.

"Not all of it," Cody answered. "Some comes

5

from game wardens at preserves and parks, some from farmers and ranchers, some from fishermen. I've got a whole network of suppliers all over the world."

The three finished up and dumped their trash in a bin. Then they wandered around the zoo until Cody's crates were ready. The Hardys helped him load the stuff into his SUV. "You're coming back to my place, right?" Cody asked.

"Yep," Joe answered. "I want the full tour of your building, especially the mysterious third-floor lab you mentioned."

"Okay," Cody said, climbing into his SUV.

"Say, is that pizza place near Fourth and Irving still in business?" Frank asked. "I remember it from the last time we were here. They had the best pepperoni I ever tasted."

"It sure is," Cody said, nodding.

"Great," Frank said, heading for the van. "We'll stop to pick up some stuff we can reheat later—if that's okay with you," he called back. Cody agreed enthusiastically.

Frank watched Cody pull away before guiding the van into the traffic on Sloat Boulevard. About fifteen minutes later, he was parking the car a few yards from Alma's Pizzatorium. The Hardys strolled around the neighborhood while their pizzas and ravioli were being baked. Wisps of fog floated in from the ocean, and the temperature seemed to drop ten degrees.

By the time they gathered up the food and headed back to Skin & Bones, the fog had become a dense watery veil, making everything appear dim and blurry.

Frank parked around the corner from Cody's, in the only space available. "I don't think he's here yet," Joe said as they made their way toward the front. "He didn't mention stopping anywhere, did he?"

"No," Frank said. He slowed down instinctively. "But you're right. There's only one light on in the whole building. It sure doesn't look like anyone's in there. Let's check the garage—see if the SUV's there."

Joe peered in through the garage door window. It was dark inside, but he could see the hulking outline of Cody's vehicle. "It's there. He must be inside somewhere."

After Frank tried the front door and found it locked, Joe pulled on the handle of the old-fashioned garage door. To his surprise, it started to lift up. He put the bag of ravioli on top of the pizza boxes Frank was holding and continued pulling on the garage door handle.

The wooden door creaked as it moved out and up.

Fringes of fog darted in through the opening, and Joe squinted his eyes a little to get a better look.

A shot of adrenaline slammed through him as the floor next to the SUV slowly came into view. There was no mistaking the crumpled form lying next to the driver's side door. It was Cody Chang!

2 Roof Rage

"Frank!" Joe said. "It's Cody. And he doesn't look good."

Frank dropped the food on the ground and followed Joe into the garage. As Frank knelt next to Cody's still body, Joe flicked on the light.

"Cody!" Frank called, carefully lifting Cody's arm to check his pulse.

"I'd better call nine-one-one," Joe said.

"No!" Cody mumbled, rolling his head from side to side. "No, don't call anybody. I'm okay." He pushed himself up to a sitting position and rubbed the side of his head.

"You've got a lump," Frank said, examining Cody's head. "And the skin's all scraped away. You might have a concussion. Are you sure you don't want to see a doctor?"

"Yes, I'm sure," Cody said firmly. "No doctor. I just got knocked out. It's not the first time. Don't worry, if I think I'm in trouble, I'll let you know."

Frank knew he couldn't make his friend go to a doctor, so he resolved to keep an eye on him for a few hours, just in case. "What happened?" he asked, leaning down to help Cody to his feet.

"Somebody must have been waiting for me when I got back," Cody responded. "As soon as I stepped out of the car, I got hammered." He shook his head. "The bones!"

Joe and Frank lunged for the SUV. "There's one crate missing," Joe reported.

Cody checked each crate, reading the codes on the outside. "Oh, man," he said with a moan. "The ostrich skeleton. They took the ostrich skeleton and the anteater claws."

"They?" Frank said. "More than one?"

Cody thought for a minute, then sighed. "I don't know. I just said that. I never really saw anyone. I wonder why they left the rest," he added, staring at the other two crates.

"Are you sure you're feeling okay?" Joe asked Cody. "How about an ice pack?"

"Yeah, I'm fine. But ice sounds good. Let's go inside." Cody led the way out of the garage and into his office behind the shop.

While Frank picked up the packages from Alma's Pizzatorium, Joe checked the garage door lock. "The lock is pretty rusted out, but it might have been jimmied," he told Frank as they made their way into Cody's office.

"Wow," Joe said when Cody flipped on the light. The office was a mess, with papers and files flung around the room.

Frank reached down and picked up one piece of paper with mud caked on it.

"Is that a footprint?" Joe asked, tilting his head for a different angle of the smudged shape.

"Might be," Frank said, "but it's not very clear. We could probably narrow it down to size but I can't make out a sole design. It would be pretty hard to trace."

"What's this stuff?" Joe asked, picking off a reddish brown crumb. "There seem to be dozens of these stuck in that mud. It's soft, kind of spongy."

"I think I know what it is," Cody said, taking the speck and slipping it under a microscope on the table behind his desk. "Yeah, I was right. It's redwood bark and it's fresh."

"Fresh? What do you mean?" Joe asked.

11

"I mean it's untreated—it actually came from a tree," Cody answered. "It's not a piece of a weatherproofed deck or some chip that's been treated to be garden mulch."

"So are there actually giant redwood trees in San Francisco?" Joe asked.

"There sure are—very special ones. The coast redwood grows only in a very narrow strip of Pacific coast in northern California and southern Oregon," Cody answered. "The largest concentration around here is in Muir Woods National Monument, about twelve miles north of the city. There's a small grove in the city in Golden Gate Park."

"That doesn't really help us pinpoint a suspect," Joe said, picking up more loose files. Frank pitched in, and soon they had everything stacked neatly on Cody's desk.

Cody slumped into a large carved chair and leaned his elbow on the desk. With a sigh, he propped his head on his hand.

"Do you have any idea who did this, Cody?" Frank asked, pulling up another chair.

"Not exactly," Cody said quietly. "I mean I don't know who it is, but it's probably the same person or people who've been causing other trouble lately."

"Tell us what's up," Joe said, perching on the corner of the huge desk. "Maybe we can help."

"Man, the last several months have been tough," Cody began. "I've had a couple of other burglaries. The first time they just took stuff from the shop while I was at a police benefit Dad had organized. I figured it was a routine burglary—you know, B and E—breaking and entering."

"How about the next time?" Frank asked.

"That was different. They stole a shipment that had just arrived. Wasn't even uncrated. I'll bet they were surprised when they opened one of the crates. It was full of skulls and jawbones. Not what the run-of-the-mill burglar wants to try to unload." Cody gave the Hardys a weak smile.

"Any money taken? Safe robbed?" Frank asked.

"Nope," Cody replied. "Just merchandise. And this is the first time I've ever been hurt or there's been any vandalism," he added.

"I'm not sure this was just vandalism," Frank suggested. "Whoever did this might have been looking for something specific. You need to go through your files and papers to try to figure out whether anything's missing."

"Are those the only problems you've had?" Joe asked.

"No," Cody said. "At first I didn't think this other deal was related, but now I'm not so sure."

13

"What other deal?" Frank asked, jotting a few notes in a small pocket notebook.

"I've had trouble with shipments not arriving. Stuff mysteriously getting lost—some of it very special merchandise from faraway suppliers. That's been a real problem."

Cody stood up and began pacing behind his desk. "My business is different. I can't just order things the way a traditional store owner does and have them delivered by a certain date. I have to take what's available from my suppliers or wait until nature takes its course."

"What do you mean?" Joe asked.

"Say someone wants a mountain lion skeleton for a museum," Cody explained. "I can't just go out and shoot one or have someone shoot one for me. I never kill animals or have them killed. I have to wait until one dies from natural causes."

"The orders that were lost in transit were special orders for the same guy," Cody continued. "One I'd been waiting for for a couple of years. So I lost not only the shipment, but one of my best customers."

"And you think the lost shipments weren't really lost?" Joe asked. "You think they were stolen or something?"

"I sure do," Cody said firmly. He stopped pacing

14

and glared. "One shipment lost, maybe two. But three in five months? I don't think so."

"What did the freight carrier say about it?" Frank asked.

"Just what you'd expect: 'Sorry—file a claim.' Each time the order was changed to a pickup instead of a delivery. Not a pickup here in San Francisco, but one somewhere between the point of origin and here."

"Who changed these orders?" Joe asked.

"No one knows. It was all done on computer. The crates were signed for by someone using my name—I have copies of the receipts." Cody rummaged around in a desk drawer and pulled out three orders with his signature at the bottom.

Frank studied them. "Do these look like your signature?"

"One of them is kind of close," Cody said, "but it doesn't really matter. I'm talking about someone picking up one of my orders on a dock in Indonesia or a village in Nairobi. I sent the freight company my signature and asked them to send a copy to everyone along the shipping route, so signatures could be checked against it. But it didn't do any good. And it probably wasn't too smart, anyway. Now my signature is floating around the world, so anyone can copy it."

Frank scanned the receipt. He had the feeling

Cody was holding something back, that he had more to tell.

"Um, there's one more thing," Cody said as if reading Frank's mind. "Someone's been hacking into my computer and leaving threatening messages."

"Whoa," Joe said. "Like what?"

"I've got some printouts upstairs," Cody said. "I'll show them to you."

The three went up to Cody's apartment. A large living room stretched across the street side, over Skin & Bones. Behind the living room was a kitchen with an eating area at one end. A short hallway led to a bedroom and a large bathroom.

Frank and Joe settled at the dining table while Cody got the printouts of the threatening messages. Over heated pizza and sodas, the three looked at the pages. "As you can see, they're pretty standard stuff," Cody said.

"I'm watching you" was written on one. Others said, "You can't escape" and "Close Skin & Bones or you'll be sorry."

"Boy, there aren't any clues on these at all," Joe said.

"They're hacked in, so there's no originating address or number or anything," Frank pointed out.

"You guys met Dave Cloud the last time you were

16

out here, didn't you?" Cody asked. He waited while Frank and Joe nodded. "He and I used to be partners. He's started an online computer supply and equipment auction site."

"I remember him," Joe said. "He was a pilot and a technical wizard."

"That's him," Cody said. "I told him all about this. He's going to try to trace the hacker."

"What does your dad say?" Frank asked.

Cody gulped a big slug of soda and shrugged his shoulders. "I haven't told him. Look, he seems okay with everything now, but he was totally against the store at first. He wanted me to be a cop or a government agent or something like that—follow in his footsteps, you know? He was afraid I'd go bust with the store. If I tell him what's happening, all his worry genes will kick right in."

"But you've reported the burglaries to the police, right?" Frank asked.

"Sure," Cody answered. "Dad knows about them, but we both thought they were standard breaking and entering, like I said. That was before the other stuff happened. I haven't told him about the intercepted shipments or the computer hacking. I want to be able to handle it myself."

"We'd be glad to help," Frank offered.

17

"I was hoping you'd say that," Cody said. "Your being here is great timing."

"Hey, three heads are better than one," Joe said, grabbing another slice of pizza. As he took a bite, he heard a noise outside.

He sat up, his ears straining. "Shhh," he cautioned the others. "I heard something."

The three sat still. Then Joe heard it again, an odd grating, like metal rubbing against metal. He put a hand up, gesturing to the others to stay put. Carefully, he inched his chair back and walked to the kitchen window. It was very dark outside.

Joe quickly made his way down the stairs to the first floor and into Cody's office. His ears tuned to all outside noises, he quietly unlocked a door at the side of Cody's office. The door opened onto a narrow passageway between Cody's building and the one next door.

There was a wooded lot behind Cody's building—a dark area of trees and large bushes. Joe stood still, listening. This time he heard something from above. Stepping away from the house, he looked up. Someone was moving on Cody's roof.

Joe watched the shadowy form darting back and forth. He strained to see who it was, but it was too dark. He sprinted down the narrow passage to Cody's fire escape at the rear of the building. He lowered the

18

bottom ladder inch by inch, trying to keep the metal from scraping.

At last it was down and he was able to scale the ladder. He climbed up until he could see over the edge of the roof. Through the darkness, he could make out the back of someone kneeling in the shadow of the chimney at the far end of the roof.

Joe felt all his muscles tighten as he boosted himself up onto the roof. Crouching, he crept toward the kneeling figure. He held his breath as he moved nearer.

"Joe! What are you doing up there?"

When he heard Cody's voice from below, Joe felt as if his heart had stopped beating. He was distracted for just a second, but that was one second too long. In a single fluid movement, the person beside the chimney stood up, wheeled around, and kicked.

Pain washed over Joe as the kick landed in his stomach. Unable to catch his breath, he crumpled to the roof.

3 An Enemy Is Loose!

Joe gasped for air, each breath causing a new ripple of pain through his body. He shook his head and pushed himself to his feet. I've got to stop that guy, he told himself.

As Joe sprinted to the end of the roof, he called out to Frank to stop his attacker. He was too late. The person had already scrambled down the fire escape and disappeared into the bushy woods behind the house.

Joe walked to the chimney and checked out the area where the person had been kneeling. He found nothing but a small mirror, which he put in his pocket, and climbed down the fire escape to join Frank and Cody. They agreed the mirror wasn't much of a clue.

The three went up to Cody's apartment and into the kitchen. "I'm feeling a little woozy," Cody said, pouring a glass of soda.

"It's time to get you to the doctor," Frank said. "No more arguments."

"We'll see," Cody said noncommittally. "Joe, can you give me a description of the guy who kicked you?"

"Well, I keep saying 'the guy,' but you know, it could have been a woman, I guess," Joe answered. "I didn't get much of a look at the person—dark pants and sweater, hair under a knit cap. I never saw the face at all. You might be able to get a toe print from my stomach, though," he added with a half-smile. He could still feel the spot where he'd been kicked.

"Cody, I get the feeling you have a suspect in mind—for *everything* that's happened to you," Frank said. "Have you got a name for us?"

"Mike Brando," Cody declared.

"Who's Mike Brando?" Joe asked. "And could he be the guy who got me on the roof?"

"Nope, not on the roof, but everything else maybe. When I first opened Skin and Bones," Cody explained, "Brando was one of my best suppliers. He told me he was a former game warden and had worked in animal parks and game preserves in Australia, Africa, and Brazil."

Cody put down his soda, then leaned back in his chair. The expression on his face showed that he was still angry. "He had the whole package—career records, references, a list of terrific contacts all over the world."

"That sounds pretty impressive," Frank said. "Did his references check out?"

"Yep," Cody said. "He'd started his own search business and offered to serve as my middleman to line up the best specimens."

"He'd be sort of a bones broker," Joe concluded with a chuckle.

"Exactly," Cody agreed with a lopsided smile. He ran a hand through his thick dark brown hair. "He—" Cody was interrupted by the sound of the door buzzer.

Cody checked his watch as he stood up. "Yikes, I almost forgot—Deb was going to drop by tonight to meet you guys."

"I'll get it," Joe said.

Joe went down and unlocked the shop door. Waiting outside was a pretty young woman in a long skirt and jeans jacket. Thick wavy blond hair cascaded around her face. "Hi, I'm Deborah Lynne."

"I'm Joe Hardy. Come on in."

He led her through the store and back up to Cody's kitchen. Cody introduced her to Frank, saying that

Deb was his new business manager and also helped out in the store. He quickly filled her in on what had happened earlier.

"So, what did the doctor say?" Deb asked, helping herself to a piece of now cold pizza.

"I haven't seen one yet," Cody said with a sheepish glance toward Frank and Joe. "I'm okay."

"Come on, Chang," Deb said. She took the pizza out of Cody's hand and slapped it onto his plate. "I'll take you to Dad's. At least he can check you out. My dad's a doctor," she told the Hardys.

"All right, all right, I'll go," Cody said with a grin. "I can't fight all three of you."

Deb drove Cody to her father's, and the Hardys headed back to Sergeant Chang's. As the brothers were getting ready for bed, Deb called to say her father had given Cody a clean bill of health, and Cody was already back home. They agreed to meet at Cody's for brunch at ten o'clock the next morning.

Tuesday morning was cool and damp, and the city was cloaked in thick fog. Deb arrived shortly after the Hardys. In his kitchen Cody was fixing a big platter of burritos and eggs, and Frank was relieved to see that he looked well and rested.

Over breakfast Frank got right down to business.

"So, let's finish our conversation from last night," he said. "Why do you suspect Mike Brando?"

"Mike's first deliveries were great," Cody explained. "He got stuff I'd had trouble locating because I didn't have his contacts. But then he offered to get things that I knew were illegal," he said, his expression troubled.

"Internationally restricted bones and skins," Deb added. "No one can buy or sell them."

"But at that point it was just my word against his," Cody pointed out. "Dad organized a sting, and Brando walked right into it. Man, was he mad. He swore he'd make us pay."

"Oh," Joe said, "so that's why you said he couldn't be the guy on the roof. He's in prison."

"Yes," Deb said. "But we figure he could have someone on the outside helping him."

"He definitely could be behind the computer messages," Frank pointed out. "He's not in for a violent crime. He'd probably be a good candidate for computer privileges."

"If it's not Brando, then I haven't a clue who it could be," Cody said, finishing his third burrito.

"Great breakfast, Cody," Joe said, leaning back in his chair.

"Agreed," Frank stated. "So, how about that tour of

your lab you've been promising, Cody. I want to see how your business works."

"That's right!" Cody said. "You've never seen Bug Central. C'mon—let's go."

"I'll open the shop," Deb said, and went down to welcome the morning's customers.

Cody led the Hardys up to the lab, which took up nearly the entire third floor. "Over here is all my media stuff," Cody said proudly. A wall of floor-to-ceiling bookcases was crammed with tapes, books, and CDs. "I've got videos and books about nearly every animal, fish, and bird in the world. Plus prehistoric life and fossils." More shelves held boxes and albums of photographs, neatly cataloged, filed, and labeled.

A second wall looked like one in an artist's studio. Shelves, pegboards, and tables were covered with brushes, wire scrapers, scissors, rulers, colored pencils, compasses, tubes of paint, display stands and easels, frames, and rolls of tape and wire.

"Here's where I do a lot of the final work," Cody said, seating himself on the stool in front of his drafting table. "This is my favorite part, really—doing custom work for a client or getting a display ready for the store."

A third area of the room looked like a science lab. A worktable with two sinks anchored the wall. Bunsen burners, cleaning fluids, microscopes, and other para-phernalia stood waiting for Cody.

The fourth wall was nearly covered floor to ceiling by stacks of crates and boxes. In the corner was a door with a hand-lettered sign: Bug Central—Do NOT Open!

"So, this is Bug Central?" Frank said.

"Yep," Cody said, chuckling. "My specimens arrive in different conditions. They're not always clean, white, and ready to go. Sometimes they still have bits—or even a lot—of flesh on them."

With a wide grin, Cody opened the door to a large closet. On one wall were shelves of fiberglass bins of different sizes. Four old refrigerators lined the other wall.

Cody led the Hardys to one of the larger fiberglass bins, which was clear and gave them a view of what was going on inside. A large skull lay on a bed of cotton batting. Swarming over it were thousands of tiny caterpillars.

"Meet my assistants," Cody said with a flourish. "The dermestid beetle colony."

"You're kidding!" Joe said. "This is amazing."

"Lots of museums around the world have used dermestids since the eighteenth century—sometimes whole rooms of them," Cody explained. "Nothing cleans a bone faster. Adult beetles lay eggs in the flesh on the bone. The larvae—the little caterpillars—hatch and eat the meat. Then they burrow into the cotton at the bottom of the bin as pupae, emerge as adults, and the cycle begins again."

"Totally cool," Frank said, watching the dermestids in action. "What kind of skull is this?"

"That's the zebra skull we picked up at the zoo yesterday," Cody said. "It was pretty clean. I put my buddies to work on it last night when I got back from Dr. Lynne's."

"And the refrigerators?" Joe asked.

"I have colonies in them, too," Cody answered. "I pick up old refrigerators. Hey, the price is right—and they're really secure. See, the trick is to keep the dermestids from 'bugging' out on their own."

Frank and Joe groaned at the bad joke.

"They'll eat anything organic," Cody continued, "so they're very destructive. They eat wood, so this room has paint that's toxic to them. In case any of the little critters get away, they won't be able to eat through the wood."

Cody and the Hardys left Bug Central and went back into the lab. "This is really great," Frank said. "Looks like you have everything you'd ever need here."

"And I love it," Cody said, his eyes sparkling.

"Sometimes I wish I could afford to hire all the help I needed to run the business. Then I could just stay up here and play."

Frank and Joe followed Cody down the two flights of stairs to the shop. A pretty young woman in her late twenties stood at one of the display counters, talking to Deb.

"I know you," Cody said. "You recently bought Reflections, the club next door. Sorry I haven't been over to welcome you to the neighborhood."

"Yes, I'm Jennifer Payton," the young woman answered. She was tall and looked as though she worked out regularly. Her golden brown hair was pulled back off her face, and she had a huge friendly smile. "And you can make it up by doing me a favor," she added. "I'm in charge of a fund-raiser for the Children's Shelter."

"That's this weekend, isn't it?" Cody said, nodding. "You're doing a haunted house at the Soxx Mansion. You've done a good job promoting it."

"Except I'm in a real jam," Jennifer said, "and if you don't help me out, we may have to cancel."

A frantic look came over Jennifer's face, and for a minute Frank thought she was going to cry. "What happened?" he asked.

"There was a plumbing disaster at the mansion over

28

the weekend," Jennifer answered. "There was a lot of water damage, and it can't be cleaned up by this weekend. Plus I lost most of my haunted house decorations. I'm sunk." She sighed. "Unless . . ." She looked at Cody with a pleading expression.

"I don't get it," Cody said. "What can I do?"

"Well, I had only two choices, really," Jennifer said. "Cancel or relocate the whole thing to Reflections. I decided to relocate. And that's where you come in. . . ."

"I think I get it," Frank said. "You need to borrow some things from Skin and Bones to replace your decorations."

"Very good deduction," Jennifer said. "Say, you'd make a great detective!"

Frank and Joe grinned at each other.

"So, will you?" Jennifer pleaded. "Will you lend me some skeletons and shark jaws and other scary stuff? Please? It's for a good cause."

"Of course," Cody said. "Glad to help. We'll even help you set the stuff up."

"Thanks," Jennifer said, looking around the shop. "Some of this will be perfect."

"A haunted house, hmm?" Joe said. "Do you need any help *during* the event?" he asked. "Ticket-taker? Monster? Ghost?"

"Always room for more volunteers," Jennifer answered with a grin. "I've got the perfect costumes for all four of you. You can pick them up when you bring over the bones."

Jennifer bustled out the door, and Deb returned to tending to Skin & Bones customers.

"I want to take a look at the records of your transactions with Mike Brando," Frank told Cody.

"Last night when I got back from Deb's dad's, I sorted through all that stuff we picked up last night. So everything's better organized than usual. I can easily get the Brando stuff."

"Could you tell whether anything was missing?" Frank asked. "Records, receipts, whatever?"

"Nothing that I could tell," Cody said. "Maybe it *was* just vandalism."

"I don't know," Frank said. "One target was obviously the packages from the zoo. The lab wasn't touched, but it looks like the person wanted something from your office." Frank found it hard to hide his frustration. "Did Brando have an associate or anyone working with him when he was legitimate?" Frank asked as they shuffled through the papers.

The phone rang before Cody could answer. "Dave, what's up?" he said into the phone. "You're kidding! When?" Cody started pacing. Frank could see that Cody was getting angrier by the second. "I don't believe it," Cody said. "He had two more years. Okay, see you then. Thanks for calling."

Cody clicked off and turned to the Hardys. His dark brown eyes seemed to be shot through with darts of anger. "That was Dave Cloud. He's about three minutes away," he said. Cody's voice was very low, and his lips were pulled into a thin line over his mouth.

"It's making sense now," he continued almost to himself. Then he remembered Joe and Frank. "Mike Brando's out. He was released yesterday morning."

4 Clang, Clang . . . Crunch!

"Mike Brando's out," Joe repeated. "He had to be the one who decked you last night. He probably came here straight from prison."

"I wonder if your father knows he's out," Frank said. "He might be able to find out what his plans were for after prison."

"I'll talk to him later," Cody said. "Boy, it's all coming together now. It's no coincidence that I'm attacked the day Brando is released from prison."

"And you think the person who kicked Joe on the roof was also Brando, right?" Frank asked.

"I sure do," Cody answered.

"Who are we talking about?" came a strong voice from the door into the office.

"Hey, Dave," Cody said with a broad smile. Cody turned to the Hardys. "Guys, you remember Dave."

Dave greeted the Hardys while Cody got everyone a soda from the small refrigerator in the corner. Dave took a seat next to Cody's desk. He was tall and slim, with long legs, and moved loosely, like a basketball player.

"So, who are we talking about?" Dave repeated with a friendly smile.

"Mike Brando," Frank answered.

"That loser," Dave said, his smile vanishing. "Imagine letting him out for good behavior. He doesn't know the meaning of the term."

The four talked a while longer about Brando and his past crimes. When Dave finished his drink, he announced he was ready to go to work. "Let me at that computer, Cody. I'll see what I can find out about those e-mails." He pulled a computer disk from his pocket. "I wrote a program for you, which I'll load while I'm here. If you get any more threats, this will make them easier to track down."

While Dave worked on Cody's desktop computer in the office, Frank and Joe took the records of the interrupted merchandise orders and the files of the suppliers involved up to the lab and went over them with Cody. Frank also checked out the suppliers through the Internet, in case there was any information about them that would lead him to the person who had ripped Cody off. He ran into one dead end after another.

Joe concentrated on learning how Cody developed his vendor leads to see whether there was a pattern that might allow someone access to the orders.

Cody went back and forth, from learning the new software from Dave, to helping Deb with customers in the shop, to answering questions for the Hardys. Dave poked his head in the lab at about four o'clock to say goodbye and agreed to return the next evening to go out for dinner. Deb left, and Cody closed the shop around six o'clock.

"I'd like to head back to your father's," Frank told Cody. "With the news about Brando getting released, this would be a good time to ask him a few questions."

"Okay," Cody said. "But remember, you promised not to tell Dad everything that's been happening around here. When we solve the case, then we'll tell him."

"You know, Cody, he could be a big help to us," Joe pointed out.

"I know, I know," Cody said. "But I'm not ready to confide in him yet. Let's give it another day or two—see what we can figure out."

"When to tell your father will be your decision," Frank agreed.

"Good. Say, I'll pick up something for dinner and meet you at Dad's."

As they drove to Sergeant Chang's, Joe and Frank talked about the person on the roof. "I know Cody thinks it was Mike Brando," Frank said. "But what would he be doing up there? Especially if he'd just clobbered Cody and ripped off those packages."

"Well, if he was interrupted when we came on the scene, maybe the roof was just a handy place to hide." Joe was silent for a minute. "No, that doesn't make sense. It would have been easier to hide in that wooded lot behind the shop."

"It would have been even easier to just get out of there," Frank said as he pulled into Mr. Chang's driveway. "I mean, why hang around at all? It doesn't make sense."

The Hardys and Cody's father talked about Mike Brando while they waited for Cody to arrive with dinner. Frank and Joe were both careful to keep their promise not to tell Mr. Chang specifics about the problems his son had been having.

After talking about Cody's business dealings with Brando, Frank steered the conversation to the prisoner's release the day before. "Cody was surprised that Brando was released so soon," he said.

"Well, I was, too," Sergeant Chang replied. "But that's the way things work nowadays. He apparently was a model prisoner, so he got time off for that. And they counted his time served while waiting for trial. He didn't make bail because the judge set it too high. The court figured that with all his international contacts, Brando could have easily skipped the country. I agreed with that."

"Are you worried about the threats he made when he was sentenced?" Joe asked. "Cody told us Brando said he'd make both of you pay for catching him in that sting."

"Well, it's always wise to be cautious about any threats," Sergeant Chang said.

"About any what?" Cody asked as he walked in with sacks full of dinner for the four of them.

"We were talking about Mike Brando making good on his threats," Frank said.

"That's right, son," Mr. Chang agreed. "I've talked to several people, and the consensus is that Brando'll head north to his sister's in Seattle."

The Hardys helped Cody lay out the white paper cartons of steamed buns, aromatic chicken, beef with garlic almonds, sticky rice, and sweet-and-sour ribs.

"Brando behaved himself in prison," Mr. Chang added, taking his seat at the dining room table. "Even took some computer training."

Frank and Joe exchanged glances as Cody changed the subject. "I showed the guys Bug Central today," he told his father.

"That's really something, isn't it?" Cody's dad said, chuckling.

"Unbelievably cool," Joe said. "Sort of like the ant farm I had when I was a kid—only on a galactic scale!"

"There's something weird when you think about all those fuzzy little guys, crawling over bones, munching away," Frank said.

"I know," Cody said. "Don't you love it? Some museums have used them to clean off whole elephants or giraffes. One Canadian museum's beetle colony specialized in whale carcasses."

Frank, Joe, and Cody told Sergeant Chang about Jennifer Payton's request and the upcoming haunted house fund-raiser.

After dinner Sergeant Chang told them he was having trouble with the starter on his new car. Joe offered to take a look at it, so Cody's father and he went out to the garage. Frank and Cody cleared off the dining table.

"My dad's one of the best detectives around," Cody told Frank. "But he didn't know Mike Brando as well as I did, and I can't believe that Mike has changed that much. That man seemed to be born without a conscience."

The Hardys, Cody, and Mr. Chang stayed up late talking so Cody decided to stay over at his dad's that night.

Wednesday morning Sergeant Chang's car wouldn't start at all. He said he'd take a bus to work, but Frank insisted he use his van. Sergeant Chang agreed, saying he'd get his car fixed and the van over to Skin & Bones later that afternoon.

Joe drove Cody's SUV away from Sergeant Chang's, with Cody in the front passenger seat as navigator and Frank in the back. "I've got a couple of stops to make on the way back to the shop," Cody said. "I need to pick up my new flyers and some skeleton chains. Take the next left."

"Hey, guys," Joe said as he turned on to Geary. "Looks like we may have picked up a tail."

"Someone's following us?" Frank said, sneaking a peek out the back window.

"The dark green sedan," Joe said, periodically checking his rearview mirror. "He's been with us since we left."

Joe carefully wove in and out of a couple of lanes and drove completely around one block. He watched the green car follow each move at a distance.

"There's the printer's," Cody said, pointing to a storefront on the right. "You can stop in the loading zone for a few minutes while I get my stuff."

Joe pulled into the loading zone. They all watched as the dark green car slowed down, then suddenly sped up, cruising past them.

"Did you see the driver?" Cody asked. "He went by so fast, I didn't get much."

"Dark nylon jacket—black or maybe navy blue," Joe said. "Wraparound shades, black knit ski cap pulled down over the ears, gloves."

"I couldn't tell whether it was a man or woman," Frank said. "Could it have been the person on the roof, Joe?"

"Yeah," Joe said. "It could have been. Let's split up," he added suddenly. "I want to go after that guy. See you back at the shop."

Frank and Cody jumped out of the SUV, and Joe took off after the green car.

After they had picked up the flyers, Frank and Cody headed for the metal craftsman's studio to get some of the special chains that held up the skeletons at Skin & Bones.

Frank and Cody walked a few blocks to a cable car stop. Within minutes they were climbing a series of very steep hills in the rumbling, clanging car.

When they reached the top of the third hill, at a very busy, noisy intersection full of cars and pedestrians, the cable car stopped. A lot of passengers got off and even more got on before it started the steep descent down the other side of the hill.

Frank was sitting at the front end of one of the open benches that ran along the outside of the cable car. He could see far down the hill to Fisherman's Wharf. In the distance, the prison Alcatraz sat on an island in the bright bay.

The cable car gripman clanged the familiar bell, alerting everyone that the car was about to move. There was a final flurry as last-minute passengers hopped aboard, elbowing one another.

Frank and the others already on the car were jostled in the frantic rush. Suddenly, someone inside the car shoved Frank's shoulders forward so he was leaning out over the street. He started to turn around to complain, but he was rammed again from behind—this time in the middle of his back.

Before Frank could get his balance, he lurched out of his seat. He flew forward until his forehead scraped the ground. He realized that he was only half on the street—the rest of his torso and legs were hanging over the cable car footboard.

He tried to roll off completely, but a sharp pain in his ankle stopped him. With a sickening feeling, he realized his foot was caught in the vertical handrail attached to the front corner of the cable car.

In the din of the traffic, he heard Cody call his name. He doesn't see me, Frank realized. He can't see where I am!

Frank twisted and turned, trying to get free, but each move inched him farther around the front of the cable car and closer to danger. He called back, but the noisy intersection swallowed up his yells. He felt the cool slickness of metal against his cheek and realized his head was resting on one of the tracks. His pulse seemed to tear through his throat as he heard the grinding scrape of the grip lever.

Clang-clang. Frank's heart seemed to stop as the loud bell noisily announced that the cable car was about to move.

5 The Suspect Slips

Clang-clang, clang-clang. The sound of the cable car bell cut through the air again. The busy intersection was crowded with cars and pedestrians. Over the din, Frank could hear Cody calling his name. He could also hear a few people yelling at the gripman.

Either the gripman couldn't hear or it was too late because Frank could feel the rumbling vibration of the car as it began to move downhill.

Twisting and sliding, Frank struggled to pull his body up so he could free his leg with his hands. The vertical handrail that had his foot trapped was nearly within reach. Calling on all his strength, he strained to raise his shoulders and head until he was almost sitting. With a great gulp of breath, he flung his arm out and grabbed for the handrail.

The feel of the cool steel rod in his palm renewed his energy and determination. "Cody!" he yelled. "Down here!"

"Frank!" Cody saw him at last. So did others on the cable car. Frank heard the grinding of the ratcheted lever as the gripman pulled it partway back. The jaws of the cable grip released its tight hold, and the cable car vibrated to a humming idle.

Frank and Cody worked Frank's foot out of its trap, and Frank hoisted himself back up on to the footboard of the cable car. He was bombarded with questions from the gripman and a few of the passengers.

"Are you really okay?" Cody asked after Frank had assured the others he was fine.

"Yes," Frank said, reaching down to rub his ankle. "Thanks for the assist."

"No problem," Cody said. "What happened, anyway?"

"I was pushed," Frank said in a low voice. "I'll tell you about it later."

Clang-clang. As the gripman prepared to close the grip jaws on the underground cable, Frank noticed a man in the shadows of an alley straight ahead. The man seemed to be staring at him. He was tall and built like a football receiver, solid and muscular. He wore sunglasses and a baseball cap pulled low over his face.

When Frank caught his eye, the man turned and quickly darted back down the narrow gap between two buildings.

"Looks like this is our stop after all," Frank said to Cody as he jumped off the cable car.

Frank's ankle complained painfully, but he kept running after the mysterious man.

"What's happening?" Cody called from behind, panting.

Frank didn't take time to answer his friend. His whole concentration was focused on ignoring his throbbing ankle and catching up with the man. At last the man was cornered in a courtyard. There was no way out of the courtyard except the way they had entered.

The man turned to face Frank, who watched carefully to see whether the man was carrying a weapon. He seemed to be unarmed. Still, Frank stayed on his guard.

As Frank and the man faced off, Cody ran into the courtyard. "Mike Brando!" Cody yelled.

Frank's nerves tingled—even more on alert.

"So?" Brando grunted. "It's me. So what?" His voice was deep and throaty. It sounded like faraway rolling thunder. He glared defiantly at Frank and Cody. It seemed as if he was daring them to take him on.

Cody took the bait. He started toward Brando, but Frank's arm shot out to hold Cody back. "Why are you following us?" Cody asked. "And why did you push Frank off the cable car?"

"What are you talking about?" Brando sputtered. "*I'm* the one being followed here. I'm standing around minding my own business and you two take off after me."

"Were you on the cable car back at that intersection?" Frank asked.

"And what about last night?" Cody asked. "Where's my ostrich?"

"Give me a break," Brando said. "What's happened to you while I was away? Sounds like you've gone a little crazy, Chang. I'd watch that if I were you. They might lock *you* up." Brando grinned at Cody.

Cody flew toward Brando again, but Frank managed to catch him before he got too far. "Don't do it, Cody," Frank warned. "Don't let him get to you."

"You're right," Cody agreed. "But let's call the police—or my dad. We'll get to the truth then."

Brando's grin turned to a scowl. "Pay attention to your pal here, Chang, and back off," he snarled. "In fact, I think I'll give the cops a call myself. Seems to me *I'm* the one being bugged here."

Frank turned to Cody. "He's right," Frank said quietly. "We have no proof that he's done anything."

As Frank and Cody retraced their steps out of the courtyard, Cody couldn't resist a final jab. "Don't think you're getting away with anything, Mike," he called over his shoulder. Frank turned and walked backward, so he could keep an eye on Brando.

"You'll slip up," Cody yelled as they left the courtyard, "just like you did the last time."

"We've got to get that guy, Frank," Cody said as the two walked back to the cable car stop. "He's been out of prison two days, and he's already managed to attack us both."

"I agree that it's probably more than coincidence that he was standing a few yards from where I was pushed," Frank said. "But coincidence won't cut it. We need proof, Cody."

"But how are we going to get that?"

"Our best bet is to find out who interrupted your shipments and who's sending the threatening

46

e-mails," Frank answered. "You know, it might be time to tell your father about your suspicions."

"Maybe you're right," Cody said. "I want you and Joe to help, but it's not fair to put you in such danger."

"That's not what I mean," Frank said. "It's just that your father has contacts who could help. For example, he knew that Brando took some computer training. Your dad could contact the prison where Brando served time. Maybe they could check the hard drives of the computer he worked on. Even when you delete files, they're still in there somewhere. If Brando sent the messages to you from a computer in the prison, a trained technician might be able to pull them out."

"That sounds good, Frank," Cody said. "I see your point, but just give me a little more time. I'd like to see what we can find out first. Dave's been working on the e-mails. He might have something for us by the time we get back."

While Frank and Cody waited for the next cable car, Frank saw Mike Brando emerge from the alley and slink off into the crowd. Brando probably pushed me, Frank thought, but we've got to get some proof. I wonder how Joe's doing.

* * *

47

While Frank and Cody were narrowly escaping danger on the cable car and then confronting Mike Brando, Joe was pursuing his own lead.

When the brothers split up, Joe sped quickly after the dark green car he was sure had been tailing them. It took him a few blocks, but he finally spotted the car. Within minutes he settled in a few cars back, so the other driver wouldn't spot him.

Is this the same guy who nearly kicked me off Cody's roof? Joe wondered. Looks like the same kind of hat and jacket. Of course a lot of people wear that style.

"So why did you follow us from Sergeant Chang's," he muttered. "What do you want?"

Joe expertly wove Cody's car through the lanes of traffic, keeping his quarry in sight. He watched the dark green car pull into Golden Gate Park. Then the cars in front of Joe slowed as the light at the intersection ahead turned yellow, then red.

Joe pounded the steering wheel once in frustration. He watched the green car take the first left inside the park. Joe waited impatiently for the light to turn green again.

At last he was able to continue. He pulled into the park and turned left.

There were no cars on the street ahead of him. From the high seat of the SUV, he was able to scan over and around the cars parked along the street and within scattered parking areas. But nothing looked like the car he'd been following.

Finally he did spot the dark green sedan parked at the Polo Field. The area was very crowded, with lots of pedestrians ringing the track and filing into the Polo Field stands.

Joe drove around the area, searching for someone dressed in a dark jacket, wraparound sunglasses, dark knit cap, and gloves.

"Nothing," he muttered. Then suddenly Joe saw his quarry. The driver of the green car was headed for the stands along the side of the track.

One thing's sure, Joe thought as he parked the SUV and took up the chase on foot. This guy followed us from Sergeant Chang's, and I'm going to find out why.

But once again his target slipped away. Joe searched the polo stands for fifteen minutes but couldn't find the person. "I don't give up this easily," Joe muttered. "If I can't get you, I'll settle for the car."

He headed back toward the green sedan. He knew he'd have no trouble finding it if it was still there. It was parked at a sloppy angle, and Joe figured the driver had been in a big hurry.

As he walked toward the parking area, Joe felt a whoosh of air behind him. He turned just in time to see the person in the dark windsuit and knit cap drive by.

Only this time the person wasn't in the green car. The person was behind the wheel of Cody's SUV!

6 Ride to the Rescue

Frustration spilled into anger as Joe watched the man he'd been tailing drive off in Cody's car. "He must have hotwired it," Joe muttered, feeling Cody's keys in his pocket. He whipped around, looking for a police officer or a guard, but saw no one.

"Yes!" he finally said, spotting the large complex of buildings making up the Golden Gate Stables. Within minutes he had rented a horse and was saddled up and on the bridle trail.

The trail was nearly empty, so Joe made up time by galloping along in the direction that Cody's SUV had gone. When he met up with slower riders, he left the trail and carefully made his way along the street.

At last he spotted Cody's vehicle a block ahead,

weaving in and out of traffic, working its way toward the west end of the park. In the distance Joe saw the white foam of ocean waves beyond the park. A honking horn behind him drew his attention away for a second. He skillfully moved the horse back on to the bridle trail.

When he glanced back at the street again, he saw Cody's vehicle ahead. It was parked on the grass under a grove of cypress trees near the oceanside entrance to the park.

Joe rode slowly toward the car. He could see no one inside, so he guided the horse to a halt under the cypress grove. He dismounted and tied the horse to a small tree. Across the street a full-size windmill stood in a small garden. Its sails turned in the breeze from the ocean.

Cautiously, Joe approached Cody's car. It had been abandoned, the driver's door slightly open.

"What's this?" Joe mumbled, reaching inside the car. A set of keys on a simple brass chain protruded from the ignition.

Joe opened the glove compartment and found the owner's manual. Without touching either key, he pulled on the brass chain. The ignition key came out, and he dropped the two keys between pages of the owner's manual. Then he put the manual in his jeans pocket and closed the car door, locking it.

He ran quickly through the cypress grove, searching for the man who had stolen Cody's car. There was no one there.

Joe doubled back to the car and hurried out of the park to the open area stretching to the oceanfront.

A wide stretch of concrete, crisscrossed with parking lines, connected the park to the oceanfront street known as the Great Highway. A short cement wall separated the street and sidewalk from the low grassy dunes, the sandy shore, and the Pacific Ocean. The wind blew across the water, swirling sand up from the dunes and depositing it on the street and in Joe's eyes.

There were no cars on the street, and as Joe walked toward the beach, he noticed a sign. The street would be closed that afternoon, the sign said, so that the city could sweep.

Joe knew there would be no swimmers in the water. Posted warnings forbidding swimming warned of a dangerous current. But a few people were scattered along the wide beach. A mother and two children were building sand castles, a boy was walking his dog, several young women were sunbathing, a couple of older men were fishing, and a girl was pacing the sand with a metal detector.

Nobody in a dark windsuit, Joe thought as he gazed

down the beach in both directions. Sea gulls swooped and called, watching for their lunch to appear.

Joe ran back across the highway, uncomfortable about leaving the horse alone much longer. On his way he passed a hot dog vendor stirring a steaming bin with a long-handled spoon. Joe walked up to the vendor's cart.

"How ya doin', young fella—what can I getcha?" The vendor greeted Joe with a big smile topped by a bushy mustache.

"Some information, I hope," Joe said. "Did you see anyone run out of the park in the last few minutes?"

"Sure did," the vendor said. "You."

"Besides me," Joe answered. "Before I did. Dressed in a dark windsuit."

"Don't think so," the vendor said, looking around. He took off his hat and seemed to be thinking hard. "Nope. I had some customers about ten minutes ago. I was pretty busy with them, so I might have missed him."

Next Joe raced into the glassfront restaurant just outside the park entrance and asked the cashier the questions he'd asked the hot dog vendor.

"You know, I might have seen who you're talking about," the young woman said. "Was it a man or a woman you're looking for?"

"I'm not sure," Joe said. "Could be either one."

54

"That's what I'm thinking, too," the cashier said, nodding her head. "This person came tearing out of the park, looked around for a minute, then turned and raced back in. Seemed to be heading toward the windmill. But I couldn't tell you much more than that. I sure couldn't give you any kind of ID, if that's what you need."

"Thanks a lot," Joe said. "You've been a help." He sped back into the park. Glad I took Cody's keys, he told himself. Whoever it was must have realized there was no place to hide out here and ran back in to grab the SUV again.

Cody's car was still parked where it had been, and the horse was still tied to the cypress tree. From behind him, Joe heard the sails of the windmill creaking in the wind. Joe crossed over to the small garden of purple and orange flowers that surrounded the windmill.

The structure was fifty to sixty feet high, and each of the two crisscrossed sails looked as if it was nearly that long. As the sails came down, they missed the deck by only a couple of feet. As they climbed back up, the wind from the ocean wrapped them in greenish gray fingers of fog.

A third of the way up, a large overhanging deck with a railing encircled the stone-block building. A plaque near the windmill said that it had been built in

1902 to pump water to a reservoir and had been restored in 1981.

Joe walked around the sidewalk that circled the base of the windmill. A much smaller building stood at the end of a path in a wooded area. Joe reasoned that was probably a pumphouse or maintenance shed.

There were several window openings in the wall, some round and some rectangular. From where Joe stood, they all had been closed off with brick or cement, although his line of sight was partially blocked by the large deck above his head.

A few concrete steps led down to large double doors made of rusted steel in the base of the windmill. In the doors were two holes about four inches square. Joe looked through one and saw only a round dark room. A few paper cups and some leaves littered the floor. There were small piles of trash either blown in or thrown through the square holes.

Joe thought he heard a noise from inside but couldn't be sure what it was. Probably an animal or bird, he thought. But the twitch he felt at the back of his neck told him he ought to make sure.

He checked to see if he was alone. There was no one in sight. At this end of the park it was still damp and foggy—not ideal conditions for strolling.

Then he heard another sound. It was a woman's

voice, and it sounded as if it was coming from inside the windmill. He couldn't hear the words, but she seemed to be arguing with someone.

The double doors seemed to be held together by a rusted padlock. Joe glanced around again. Then when he checked out the padlock, he saw that it was attached only to the pin on the hasp of one door. Someone had gone in this way. He pushed on the door.

He held his breath and peered inside. It was very still within the dusty room. As he stepped inside, a waft of fog entered with him.

As Joe closed the door, the light was blocked out and he stepped into nearly total darkness. Only dim light filtering in through the two square holes and a sliver of light on the wall above gave him any bearings at all. A scratching scuttling noise above sent a wave of heat down the back of his neck.

His thoughts came quickly. There's a door or window up there to the deck. Whoever was in here heard me come in and stepped out onto the deck.

He heard the woman's voice again. It sounded as if she said "away," but then her voice was muffled.

I was right, Joe thought. She's out on the deck. But someone must be with her. And she doesn't sound too happy about that.

Joe squinted to get a clearer picture. He was very

cautious as he edged around the room, his back to the wall. He tried to remain calm, but his pulse beat faster and louder with each step. He knew he was an easy target. He looked around for something with which he could defend himself. This will have to do, I guess, he thought, reaching for a short plank of wood.

His eyes now used to the dark, he spotted something in the corner—a navy blue ski cap. He immediately thought of the driver of the green car. He picked up the cap and stuffed it into his back pocket. As he did, something slipped to the floor.

It was a small white cardboard disk, rimmed with metal, with the number 5773 printed on the front and the numbers 14-7-38-5-9 on the back. A small hole was punched through the top of the disk.

Joe scooped it up and jammed it into his front pocket. He inched on around until he reached a rough ladder made of wooden planks bolted into the wall.

Please don't creak, he thought as he stepped onto the lowest plank. There was no sound, so he continued climbing up toward the sliver of light coming from around the edge of the deck door.

Joe reached the last step and a landing next to the door. He could feel the chill of the fog as it wound in the opening and around him. Carefully, he scrambled up and onto the platform. With his back hugging the wall, he peered out through the narrow opening to the deck.

Outside, two people, both dressed in dark clothes, were struggling in a sort of slow-motion wrestling match. The whistling vibration of an approaching windmill sail penetrated the air. Joe strained to get a good view of what was happening before he took any action. Then he heard the young woman cry out. "Let go of me—now!"

Joe jumped into the action. "Hey," he yelled, slamming open the door. He stepped onto the deck, holding the plank high. He could see only the dark-jacketed back of one of the two people. That person whirled around. Joe's pounding heart nearly drowned out the sound of the approaching windmill sail.

The man facing Joe wore a ski mask. In an instant, he had lifted the young woman up and was holding her out, across the railing. He didn't speak, but his gaze dared Joe to come closer.

Joe looked at the woman in the dark purple windsuit. He was stunned when he recognized her. "Deb?" he said. "Is that you?"

Her reply caught in her throat and came out as half gasp, half sob.

Startled, the man glanced around. Then he suddenly dropped Deb and raced off.

When he let go of her, Deb was half sitting, half lying on the deck railing. The sudden release made her lose her balance. She flailed her arms, trying desperately to keep from rolling over the railing and onto the walkway below.

Joe rushed toward her, but he knew he couldn't make it in time. The adrenaline pumped through his veins as he yelled, "The sail . . . grab a sail."

Deb flung her arms toward the sail inches away. Her fingertips connected, and she hooked them through the gridwork that edged the wooden sail.

With a huge burst of energy, Joe lunged toward her, throwing himself at her toes as she was pulled up from the deck. Her slick leather shoes slid right through his fingers.

Deb stared down at Joe in terror as she disappeared into the misty cloud curling around the top of the windmill. Her scream seemed to blast the fog right into his face.

7 Busting Out

Deb's scream drilled into Joe's brain. His temples thundered as he saw her clinging to the windmill sail, rising higher and higher into the fog. As the sail moved, her legs swung wildly.

"Try to hold still, Deb!" Joe called. "And don't look down. Just hold tight. You'll be back around soon and I'll bring you in." In the distance he could see the man with the ski mask disappear into the woods.

The windmill sails were huge, but they creaked and shook as they carried their accidental passenger. They inched around, slowing to a crawl. For a moment Joe's breath stopped as he thought the windmill might halt completely, with Deb dangling far out of his reach.

But the crisscrossed wood kept moving, drawing its *X* in a huge circle.

"I'm still here, Deb," Joe called. "I'm waiting for you. You'll be off that thing soon. Just hold on."

As the sail moved, Deb's position changed. At first she was hanging off the bottom end of the sail, straight down. When it drew up so that it was horizontal to the ground, she dangled at a right angle to the sail.

"I can't do it," she yelled. She sounded very frightened. "I can't hang on."

"Yes, you can," Joe urged. "It's scariest right now, while the sail is horizontal. Soon you'll be hanging from the top of the sail, and you'll feel more support from it."

The sail carrying Deb moved toward the top of its arc. Joe could barely see her through the fog—she was so high, far above the treetops. The sails slowed to a crawl, then a stuttering halt. But with a shuddering tremor, they began moving again.

At last Deb was coming back down, moving around the circle. As she neared Joe, his pulse quickened. He knew he had only a few moments to rescue her. If he missed the opportunity, she'd have to go through the whole circuit again.

"I have to get her on the first try," he mumbled, pumping himself up with anticipation. "I don't think she can take another go-round."

"My fingers are numb," she called down to him. "I don't know how much longer I can hold on."

"Long enough," he yelled back. "You can hang on long enough to get back down here. I'll take it from there."

Joe went over the possibilities in his mind. He could have her start swinging her body toward the deck railing as soon as she got near enough. That way, he'd have several chances to grab her. He was bound to make good on one of them. But what if she didn't have the strength left to do her part?

He could wait until she was right in front of him, less than a couple of feet away. Then he could reach out, grab her under her arms, and hoist her inside the railing. But he'd have only one shot.

He could reach out for her legs as soon she came close enough, then, holding tight, fling her back across his shoulder like a large sack. But if she fell backward when he grabbed her instead of forward toward his shoulder, he could be pulled off balance and they would both crash to the ground.

None of the plans was perfect. Even worse, they all depended on Deb's trusting him enough to let go of the sail. Joe decided to try all three. One of them has to work, he told himself.

He tried to picture how the rescue would work.

As Deb approached, he'd ask her to swing toward him so he could catch her. If she didn't have the strength for that, he'd try to grab her legs and swing her over his shoulder. If that didn't work, he'd grab her under the arms when she was directly in front of him. And if that failed, he'd have one more chance to grab her legs as she started back up again.

"I'm slipping," Deb called, her voice shaky. Her anxious call brought him back to the present. "Here I come," she said. "Are you ready?"

"Absolutely," Joe answered. Deb's sail was horizontal and she dangled dangerously from the end. "I'm going to get you off there, Deb. Just do what I say, okay?"

"Whatever it takes," she said. She sounded determined. "Tell me what to do."

"When I give the word, you swing toward me. Give it everything you've got. I know you're tired, but try hard. We're almost there now." In spite of the adrenaline barreling through him, he managed a half smile in her direction.

As the sail carrying Deb grew nearer, Joe got ready. He planted his feet solidly on the deck and leaned against the railing for extra support. He watched for the perfect moment, then his voice exploded. "Now!" he yelled. "Swing toward me."

"Mmmmmmumph." Her breath came out in a whoosh. Still clinging tightly to the sail, she swung her body toward the railing. Joe reached out for her but grabbed only air.

"Again!" he yelled. "Now!" As Deb swung in, Joe reached out. With perfect timing, he caught her around the hips and held tightly. He felt the pull of the sail as it continued to move, still holding its cargo.

"Let go, Deb," Joe said, bracing himself. "Let go of the sail. I've got you."

With a "Yiiieee," Deb released her grip. The shift in momentum yanked Joe forward. But he was prepared. With a surge of strength, he pulled back, stumbling a little. He kept his balance and dropped Deb gently to her feet.

"Man, that was some ride," Joe said, smiling. Deb looked pale and shaky but otherwise okay.

"I don't recommend it," she said, her voice low. "Thanks," she said, flexing her fingers. "You saved my life—from the windmill and from the creep who forced me here in the first place."

"No problem," Joe said. "What happened exactly?"

"I got a call at the shop from someone who said he had information for Cody about Mike Brando. I was to tell Cody to meet this guy alone at the Polo Field."

"So did you?"

65

"Well, you know what Cody's been through over the last couple of days," Deb said with a small smile. "I figured he's just going to give him some information. Where's the danger?"

"So you decided to meet him yourself," Joe concluded. "I'm sure you didn't even mention it to Cody."

"You're right," Deb said, nodding.

"But how did you end up here?" Joe asked.

"I took a cab to the Polo Field and walked to the spot where we were to meet," Deb explained. "Someone came up behind me, stuck a gun in my back, and told me to walk to the parking lot."

"Did you see the gun?" Joe asked.

"Not really," Deb said, "but I felt something, and I didn't want to argue about it."

"Smart move, actually," Joe agreed. "Did you recognize the person's voice?"

"Not really," she said. "He talked in muffled grunts—didn't say much."

"How did you get to Cody's car?"

"It was weird," she said. "We were headed toward the parking lot when I spotted Cody's car. The guy told me to stop. I was really surprised to see Cody's car, so I was looking around for him. I don't know, maybe the guy was, too."

66

Joe remembered walking around the stands, trying to find the driver of the green car. "I must have been nearby," he said, "but I never saw you."

"Anyway," Deb continued, "he walked me over to Cody's car and ordered me to get in the backseat and put my head between my knees."

"I saw him pull away, but I didn't see you. No wonder," Joe said.

"He took me into the windmill and was going to tie me up, but I broke away. He was in front of the door, so I ran up the ladder to the deck. I figured I could yell for help, but he was right behind me."

"That must have been when I came in," Joe concluded.

"Yeah—you know the rest."

Joe pulled the cap he'd found out of his back pocket. "Was the man wearing this?"

"Not when I saw him, he wasn't," Deb answered. "I never saw him, really, until he came out on the deck. He was always behind me at the Polo Field. And it was so dark inside the windmill." She shuddered. "Let's get out of here."

In a few minutes they were out of the windmill and back in the garden. Deb looked up at the sails and shuddered again. "Wow," she whispered.

"There's Cody's car!" Deb exclaimed. She looked

across the drive as Joe followed her out of the windmill. "And a horse?"

"It's a long story," Joe said. "Are you really okay? Can you drive Cody's car back to the stables? I'll take the horse and meet you there."

"Sure," Deb answered. Joe handed her the keys. As she pulled out on to the street, he mounted the horse and followed.

When they got back to the stables, Joe returned the horse. Then he took the wheel of Cody's car. "Before we go, I'd like to check on something," he said, pulling away.

Joe drove back to the spot where the green car had been parked. "It's still there," he said when he spotted it. "I'm pretty sure that's the car your kidnapper abandoned to steal Cody's."

The green car was locked, but Joe could see from the papers lying on the front seat that it was a rental car. He wrote down the name and phone number of the car rental agency and a description of the car, including the license plate number.

Finally he and Deb left Golden Gate Park, and Joe drove them back to Skin & Bones. In his mind, he was going over his encounter with Deb's kidnapper, making sure he remembered every detail. "I haven't had any lunch," he finally said, "and it's nearly four

68

o'clock. Let's pick up some food." They stopped for burgers and fries—enough for everybody.

Cody greeted them when they arrived and turned the Skin & Bones customers over to his salesclerk. "Let's go," he said to Joe and Deb. "Frank's upstairs. Wait till you hear what happened to us."

"Looks like we're going to have some major show-and-tell," Joe said. They joined Frank, who was sitting at the kitchen table, resting his bandaged ankle on a chair. "We've got our own tale," Joe added, "one we need to tell the police."

Frank raised his eyebrows at Cody. "Okay," Cody said with a resigned sigh. "I guess it's time to let Dad in on all this. Let's call him."

Deb reported her kidnapping to Sergeant Chang. Then Joe talked to Cody's dad, telling him that he thought the driver of the green car had followed them from his house. He also reported that Cody's car was stolen near where the green car was parked. But he agreed with Sergeant Chang there was no proof the driver of the green car stole the SUV.

"You'll need to speak to the police and give a description to the police artist," Joe said to Deb when he hung up. "They're sending a cruiser for you now."

"Okay," she responded. "But then I'm going home to bed. Today was way more excitement than I

69

needed. Joe, you fill them in. I'll talk to you all later."
Cody walked her to the door and waited with her until
the cruiser arrived.

"Man, these smell good," Frank said, grabbing a
burger. "Cody was just talking about going out to pick
something up. We missed lunch."

"You, too?" Joe said. He reached for some fries,
brushing a fly away from the bag. "Okay, you heard
most of our story—all but the fun part about Deb and
the windmill. I'll tell you about that in a minute. First,
what happened to your ankle?" he asked Frank.

Frank told Joe about his encounter with Mike
Brando. Cody came back and chimed in with a few
angry additions.

"Whoa, that was close," Joe said when they'd finished. "It's a pretty big coincidence—you getting
pushed out of the cable car and Brando appearing a
few minutes later." He batted at another fly buzzing
around his head. "Is there a door open somewhere?"

"Must be," Frank said, swatting at his own fly. "We
seem to be sharing our meal with unexpected guests."

"No!" Cody yelled suddenly. He sprang up from his
chair so fast that it fell over behind him.

Joe looked at Cody, then at Frank. Then he more
closely studied the three small bugs crawling across
the kitchen table. When he moved his hand, the bugs

70

took to the air, joining a few others circling the counter.

Joe leaped up from his chair and headed for the stairs. Frank and Cody followed close behind. As they sprinted up to the lab, they were greeted by small swarms of flying insects.

The lab door was ajar. Joe pushed it open to see what looked like a scene from a horror movie.

The door to Bug Central stood open. Swarms of dermestid beetles darted from spot to spot, looking for leftover flesh on the bones and skins that were Cody's current lab projects. Uneven lines of small hairy caterpillars looped across the floor, inched up table legs, and hung from bookshelves.

8 The Clue in the Claw

There were bugs crawling and swarming everywhere.

"I'll get the door," Frank said.

"Yeah, close it. We can contain as many as possible in here for now. But it's really too late," Cody said sadly. "I'll have to call the fumigator. All my colonies are lost."

They left the lab, closing the door behind them. Cody went to the first floor to send the salesclerk home and close up the shop. Then he went back to his office to call the fumigator. Frank and Joe checked the doors and windows for signs of a break-in. The back door of the office looked as if it had been jimmied.

"Guys, you have to help me out," Cody said when he came back to the kitchen. "I have to stay here until the fumigator arrives. But I told Jennifer Payton I'd bring over the stuff for her haunted house today. Can you take it over for me? You've got to get out of here, anyway."

He ran his fingers through his hair. "Dad's car is fixed, and he had the van delivered for you. I saw it parked around the corner. Just take it whenever you want. I'm going to have to stick around here until the fumigator's finished gassing the place. I'll call you later at Dad's."

"Is this going to be some sort of plague unleashed on the city of San Francisco?" Joe asked.

"No, actually dermestid beetles are common in households all over North America," Cody said. "Just not in concentrated colonies in such large numbers. People aren't aware of them because they're so small. But now that mine have busted out of Bug Central, I've got to get them cleaned out. If I don't, they'll ruin my clothes, furniture, everything."

"They didn't just bust out," Joe said.

"No, they didn't," Cody said through clenched teeth. "Someone let them out."

"We were all at your dad's last night and didn't get back here till this afternoon," Frank pointed out. "Plenty of time to do the damage here."

"If Mike Brando was driving that green car this morning, it means he knew we were at Dad's," Cody said. "He could have known we were there last night, too, and broken in here then. He knew all about the bugs. I'd shown them to him when he was my broker."

Cody showed the Hardys a stack of boxes. Inside were the bones and other spooky specimens he had set aside to lend to Jennifer for her haunted house. "Thanks for taking these over," he said, his voice low. "See you later. Don't tell Dad about the bugs. I want to tell him myself."

"Before we go, I want to get this key thing figured out," Joe said. "Whoever stole your car had a key, Cody. How many sets of keys to your SUV?"

"My regular set, which was in the car when you took it over, Joe," Cody answered. "And an extra set in my file cabinet."

"Maybe they're there," Frank said, "maybe not."

Cody raced to the file cabinet and pulled open the second drawer. After rummaging noisily around the file folders, he turned back to face the others.

"They're gone," he said, his face drawn into a tight scowl. "Whoever trashed my office Monday night must have pocketed them!"

Joe opened the owner's manual and showed

Cody the small brass chain. "Do these look familiar?"

"Yeah, that's them," Cody said.

"We'll give them to your dad," Frank said. "Maybe he can get some prints off them."

"Didn't you say the driver wore gloves?" Cody asked.

"Yes," Joe said. "But you never know. He—or she—might have touched them sometime with bare fingers. It won't hurt to run a test." He slipped the owner's manual back into his jacket pocket.

"Okay, let's go," Frank said. He and Joe piled the boxes on a couple of dollies.

"Cody's really down," Frank said as they worked. "Losing the beetle colony is a pretty low blow. We've got to find out who's doing this. His business can't stand much more trouble."

When they got outside, Joe stopped Frank for a minute to talk. They sat on a bench outside Skin & Bones. "Hey, Frank, are you sure you're okay?" Joe asked, looking at Frank's ankle. "Maybe *you* should see a doctor."

"I'm fine," Frank said. "It's just a little sore. And it looks like Mike Brando moves to the top of our suspect list—with at least one accomplice. Remember—if he's behind the attacks on Cody, he had to have an accomplice while he was in prison."

"And you and I were attacked in separate areas of the city at the same time by two different people," Joe said.

"That means we've also been branded as targets," Frank said.

Joe showed Frank the ski cap he had found in the windmill and the small cardboard disk that had fallen out of it.

"That looks familiar," Frank said. "Cody had a disk like that in his desk drawer, but it had a different number printed across the center."

"What is it?" Joe asked.

"It's a tag for a locker at his mailing station. He gets so many weird packages—some of them really large—so he has many of them delivered to a mailing station over on Larkin. They rent him a refrigerated locker there. The number on the front of the tag is the locker number; the number on the back is the combination to the locker padlock."

"Good," Joe said. "Something else to check. We're finally getting somewhere."

"First, let's get this stuff next door," Frank said. "Jennifer's waiting for it."

"Before we leave, I want to take another look around Cody's roof," Joe said as they pushed the dollies up the sidewalk. "I didn't get enough time to do a good search. I'd like to have a little more to go on than that scrap of mirror."

Frank and Joe took the Skin & Bones merchandise into Reflections. Then Joe excused himself so he could pay a return visit to Cody's roof while it was still light.

Meanwhile, Jennifer took Frank on a quick tour of the club. The ceiling of the large room was draped in black, with occasional bursts of tiny red twinkle lights. The large room was divided into small cubicles.

"Each cubicle will have a separate scary scene," Jennifer explained.

"This is quite a place," Frank said.

"I inherited it from my grandmother about a year ago," Jennifer said. "What you see is just the beginning. I'm expanding it big-time. I want to add a restaurant, an outdoor café . . . maybe a small theater. I'd like to see this neighborhood move from basically retail shops to more of an entertainment area. You know . . . theaters, music and comedy clubs, restaurants."

Jennifer piled costumes on to Frank's outstretched arms. "I need to take care of some things," she announced. "Here are the outfits for all of you. We've got a short dress rehearsal Thursday evening and a party for all the volunteers afterward. Will you and the others come early and help me set up?"

"That'd be fun," Frank said. "See you then. Before I go, may I use your phone?"

"Sure," Jennifer said. "There's one in my office in the far corner.

Frank sat behind Jennifer's desk and checked the phone number for the mailing station Cody had mentioned. He dialed the number, and while he waited, he looked at the display of photographs on Jennifer's wall. She's a sports and fitness fanatic, he thought to himself. There were photos of Jennifer dressed in every conceivable sports uniform and receiving certificates and awards for every conceivable competition.

The taped recording told him that the mail stations were closed until seven o'clock the next morning. The room with private mailboxes and lockers was open twenty-four hours.

Joe was walking in as Frank was walking out. "Did you find anything?" Frank asked his brother as they got into Sergeant Chang's van.

"No," Joe said. "Nothing."

On the way back to Sergeant Chang's, Frank and Joe continued to compare notes. "I know I was pushed off that cable car," Frank said. "I can't prove it—but I felt two strong hands on my back."

"It can't be just a coincidence that Mike Brando was nearby," Joe pointed out.

"I might not have been the target," Frank said. "He could have been following Cody and meant to push him. Just when he started to shove, he could have been jostled, lost his balance, and I was the one in the street."

"How about the guy on the windmill deck?" Frank asked. "We're pretty sure it's the same guy who was driving the green car, right?"

"Seems likely," Joe agreed. "The car was parked right there."

"Could it be the same guy who kicked you on the roof?"

"I didn't get much of an idea about the one on the roof," Joe reminded him. "First he was crouching, then I was bent over, then he was gone. Actually, it's pretty much the same thing with the guy on the windmill deck. His back was to me most of the time. Then when he turned around, I was distracted by the danger facing Deb."

Frank told Joe about calling the mailing station. "We should get on that," he said. "That could lead to something."

"So how does the club look?" Joe asked. "Is it going to be pretty scary?"

"It's going to be cool. The kids should love it." Frank told Joe about Jennifer's plans for the neighborhood.

"Does Cody know about this?"

"He hasn't mentioned anything to me," Frank said.

"It doesn't sound like his shop will fit the image she has in mind."

The house was empty when they arrived at Sergeant Chang's. He had left them a note saying he wouldn't be home until later and to help themselves to anything in the kitchen. He also mentioned that a package had been left for them.

The bulky bundle lay on the table next to the note. It was wrapped in brown paper and tied with strong cord. There was no return name or address—just the delivery service stamp and the word *Hardys* typed on a small label taped to the brown paper.

Frank cut the string and pulled back the paper. Inside lay a deep wooden box with a sliding lid. Carefully, Frank slid the top of the box to one end and lifted it out of the groove. Pale yellow tissue paper concealed a lumpy package. Cautiously, Frank peeled the tissue off a gruesome sight.

"Whoa, it's some kind of a claw!" Joe said, his voice

hushed. An animal foot covered with long black hair lay on the paper. Projecting out from the top were very long gray nails which hooked around and under the hairy claw.

Joe pulled a piece of paper from under the claw. The message was neatly typed from a computer printer: "Stop following me or the next package of bones might be yours."

9 A Bloody Visit

Cautiously, using the tissue paper as a shield, Frank picked the hairy claw up out of the deep wooden box and examined it. There were no tags or identifying labels attached to the grisly object.

"I'm calling Cody," Joe said, reaching for the phone. Cody picked up after the first ring.

Joe quickly told Cody about the package.

"It's an anteater claw," Cody said, his voice sounding as if his jaw were clamped shut. Joe could tell he was furious. "Probably the one from the zoo packages that were stolen from me!"

"Here's something," Frank called to Joe. Carefully, he pulled back the hair from the underside of the claw. A tattoo marked the skin beneath the hair. "Ask

Cody if this means anything," Frank said. Then he read the tattoo. "X-3-7-C2."

Joe repeated the tattooed numbers to Cody.

"Just a second," Cody said through the phone receiver. "Let me check my order sheet."

Joe could hear paper rustling, and then Cody returned to the phone. "Yes," Cody said. "That's one of the anteater claws I picked up Monday. But how come he sent it to *you* and not me?"

"Don't forget, the driver of the green car followed us from your dad's," Joe pointed out. "So he's probably been staking the place out. He must know we're staying here and we're friends of yours."

"Mike Brando knows who my father is," Cody offered. "He could definitely be behind all this."

"Is he wondering why we got the package?" Frank asked. Joe nodded.

"Somebody's obviously been staking out your place, too," Frank called out, loud enough for Cody to hear. "He or she could have seen us coming and going. If the driver of the green car sent the package, it could be a warning after his run-in with Joe this afternoon."

"Man, we've got to get this guy," Cody said in Joe's ear.

"How are the beetles?" Joe asked. "Did the fumigator come yet?"

"The beetles are making their way from Bug Central to Bug Heaven," Cody said. "Did you get things set up with Jennifer okay?"

"Yes, we did," Joe answered. "How well do you know her?"

"Not at all," Cody said. "We just met the other day."

"Did you hear about her expansion plans?" Joe asked. "How she wants to change this neighborhood from retail to entertainment."

"No," Cody said. "What do you mean?"

Joe repeated what Jennifer had said. "She really wants to change the atmosphere of the neighborhood."

"I haven't heard a thing about it." Cody's voice got a little louder. "And speaking as a retailer, I'm not sure I like it."

Then Cody switched subjects. "Is Dad there?" he asked.

"Not yet," Joe answered. "He left us a note saying he'd be back later."

"Well, Dave called," Cody said. "We were supposed to meet him for dinner tonight, remember? I told him about the bugs. I'm going to meet him at Dad's in about an hour. I'll just pick up something for us to eat. I don't feel much like going out."

"Okay, great," Joe said. "See you soon."

After Joe hung up, he and Frank wrapped the

anteater claw back in the yellow tissue paper. Then Joe set it down in the shredded plastic foam it had been packed in. Frank fit the wooden lid into its groove, slid it closed, and put the box on the kitchen counter. Then he and Joe went to their room to clean up.

Frank showered first. He pulled on jeans and a blue sweater. Then, while Joe took his turn in the shower, Frank turned on Sergeant Chang's computer and searched the Internet for the mailing station company. He wanted to track down the locker that matched the disk Joe had found in the windmill.

"Yes," he said aloud, when he found that the company had a website. There was information about the company's services, branch offices and addresses, and other contact information.

The company had several branches, and each specialized in a specific type of mailing or storage facility. There was only one branch that featured large refrigerated lockers—the one where Cody had his account.

The website also featured layouts of each branch, showing different sizes of lockers and mailboxes. Each box and locker was numbered. Number 5773 was a large refrigerated box in the same branch as Cody's.

Then Frank called the courier service that had delivered the strange package.

"Listen to this," Frank reported when Joe emerged from the shower. "I just talked to the delivery service that brought us the anteater claw. It's an outfit that specializes in offbeat deliveries."

"I think ours certainly qualifies," Joe said. He pulled on jeans and a Forty-niners sweatshirt.

"They advertise that they will deliver anything, anywhere, anytime. The girl I talked to said they get a lot of unusual jobs. She took the order for our package by phone."

"No name, I'm sure," Joe said.

"Right."

"Could she tell if it was a man or a woman?" Joe asked.

"She thought it was a man, but she wasn't sure. No one ever saw the person who ordered the delivery. The weird part is where they had to pick up the package."

"Where?" Joe said.

"Muir Woods," Frank announced.

"The redwood forest? North of the city?" Joe asked.

"That's what the courier said," Frank answered. "He was directed to a hollow tree in a secluded area of the forest. The package was in there, along with an envelope of cash to pay for the delivery."

"No check, no credit card," Joe observed. "Nothing to trace back to the sender."

Frank grabbed the keys to the van and his beat-up leather jacket. "I'm going to the delivery service office. They're open twenty-four hours. The girl says the courier who brought us the claw is on a run right now, but should be back in about fifteen minutes."

"Okay, I'll stay here. Cody should be here soon— I'll try to save some food for you." Joe gave his brother a big grin.

While Joe was combing his hair, he thought he heard a sound in the driveway.

"Cody?" Joe called. "Sergeant Chang?"

Then it was quiet. He heard nothing.

Then another noise caught his attention. It was like a scraping or a scuffling outside.

"Is that you, Frank?" Joe called. "I'm just about—"

Joe's words were cut off by a thunderous pounding on the front door. It felt as if the whole house was vibrating.

"Boy, somebody definitely wants in," Joe said in a low voice, "or we're having one of San Francisco's famous earthquakes."

The pounding stopped and it was very quiet.

Joe moved soundlessly to the front door, every nerve alive and alert.

He looked through the peephole but saw nothing.

Slowly, he inched open the front door. A cool wash of foggy evening air sent a chill through him.

At first he saw nothing. Then from beside the door, a man took one step toward him and fell into Joe without a word. "Cody," the man whispered as he slid to the floor, his jacket smeared with streaks of blood.

10 Two Heads Are Better

Dave Cloud fell against Joe, who tried to catch him, but Dave slipped from his grasp and slumped to the floor. Joe's sweatshirt was streaked with blood where Dave had fallen against him.

Joe knelt next to Dave and took his wrist.

"What happened?" Frank asked, running up the front walk.

"It's Dave," Joe said. "His pulse seems okay."

Dave's head rolled from side to side, and his eyes opened. "Hey, Joe," he mumbled. "What's up?"

Dave sat up and took a deep breath, but before he could say anything, Cody burst up the front walk, too, his arms full of sacks.

Frank and Joe were helping Dave stand. "It's not as

bad as it looks," Dave said, brushing at his blood-stained jacket.

Cody put down the bags of food and helped the Hardys get Dave into the house and into a chair. "Here. Sit," he ordered Dave.

"Really, I'm not hurt that bad," Dave said with a slight smile. While he peeled off his jacket, his expression turned to anger. "It was Brando."

"Man, that guy is really getting around," Joe said.

"Look," Frank interrupted. "While you're talking, I'm going to take you to the hospital. You could be seriously injured."

Frank stood up and started toward Dave, but Dave stopped him. "Nah, I don't think so," he said. "I'll be okay. I'll get cleaned up and you'll see. It looks a lot worse than it is."

Dave rolled up his shirtsleeve to reveal a cut on his forearm. While he washed his wound in the bathroom, Dave told the others what had happened.

"I was getting ready to come over here," he began. "I thought I heard a noise outside my apartment, but I checked and didn't see anyone. I made a couple of calls, then left. Someone jumped me as I walked to the car."

"And you're sure it was Mike Brando?" Frank asked.

Dave had a small cut on his chin. He dabbed it with

an ice cube to stop the bleeding. "It was dark," he finally answered. "So I didn't get a good look at his face, but I'm sure it was Brando."

"Why?" Joe asked.

"His voice," Dave answered. "I'd know that sound anywhere."

Frank flashed back on his encounter with Brando. Dave was right. Brando's voice was different. It was deep and rumbly, like a wildcat's growl.

"What did he say?" Joe asked.

"Not much that made sense," Dave replied. He dried his hands and dropped the towel on the counter. "He mumbled something about payback and settling scores with old enemies. Oh, and he mentioned your name, Cody."

"Yeah?" Cody said. "Sent me his best wishes, I'll bet."

"Not exactly." Dave gave Cody a crooked smile. "He said to tell you that Skin and Bones is going down— and you and I are going with it. He's angry with me because I was your partner when he was caught."

"Sorry about that," Cody said. "You had nothing to do with Brando's troubles."

"Well, you've heard the old saying about the company you keep," Dave said with a weak smile. "Just kidding, of course. He still associates me with the business, I guess."

Cody handed Dave some antiseptic lotion.

"How'd you get that cut?" Frank asked. Dave's arm had stopped bleeding, but it was swollen and looked sore.

"Brando had a knife," Dave said. "He came right at me with it. I was able to deflect the blow, but he swiped my arm." Wincing, Dave dabbed some of the antiseptic on the cut, and Cody and Frank bandaged Dave's arm.

"Did you report your attack to the police?" Frank asked.

"Sure," Dave said. "I stopped at a station on my way over here. I was okay then, but by the time I got here, I was pretty shaky."

"You lost a lot of blood," Joe said, looking at Dave's jeans and shirt. "Your clothes are a mess."

"Come on," Cody said to Dave. "I'll get you some clean clothes. I've still got stuff here in my old room."

"No, I'm going home," Dave said. "This shook me pretty good. I'll talk to you later."

While Joe changed his blood-smeared sweatshirt for a sweater, Frank and Cody laid out their meal in the dining room—a feast of Mexican favorites.

The three eagerly dug into their dinner. "What a day," Joe said. "I am so hungry."

"What about tomorrow?" Cody asked. "I'm going to

have to stay here again tonight. In fact, I have to close the shop for twenty-four hours. The smell's pretty gross. So I'm available to help you dig into my case."

"We finally have some real leads," Frank said. He told Cody about what he'd learned from the delivery service. "In fact, that's where I was before Dave got here."

"Did the courier have any more information to offer?" Joe asked.

Frank reached into his pocket and pulled out a piece of paper. "I say we check this out," he said.

He laid the paper on the table. It was a rough-drawn map in an area of Muir Woods. He pointed to an X at the top. "I had the courier draw it for me. This is the tree where he picked up the anteater claw."

"Yeah, I sort of know where that is," Cody said. "I mountain bike up in that area." He hoisted himself up to sit on the counter.

"But isn't Muir Woods a public park?" Joe asked. "Wouldn't somebody see the package and rip it off?"

"There are regular trails," Cody said. "But there are some very secluded areas in the fringes of the forest, off the public trails. You're not supposed to go there, of course. Most people don't. But if you really know your way around, you could probably pull it off."

Frank could see that Cody was excited about the

prospect. "It's so dark in there," Cody added, "even during the daytime. The trees are enormous and block out most of the sunshine. It's still very primitive and wild. There's no real development except for the visitors' center and a few marked trails."

"We'll go tomorrow," Frank said.

"Sounds like a plan," Joe agreed.

"I've got more information," Frank said. "While I was out, I stopped at the mailing station. The private boxes and lockers are open twenty-four hours a day.

"And?" Cody urged.

"The good news is that I found the locker that matches the tag Joe found," Frank said.

"Did the combination work?" Joe asked.

"It did," Frank answered, taking a gulp from his soda.

Then Cody turned to Frank. "So what's the bad news?" he asked.

"There was nothing in the locker but a few scraps of brown paper," Frank said, dropping the fragments on the table.

Joe turned a couple of them over. They were blank on both sides. "No clues here," he agreed.

"I did get a look at the locker register," Frank said, "while the night clerk was busy on a personal phone call. There was no name matched to my locker—only the code b-two-g."

They all thought about what Frank had said. Finally Joe stood up. "I'm going for ice cubes," he said. "Speak now if you want anything."

Joe went to the kitchen. As he walked toward the refrigerator, a movement in the driveway caught his attention.

He walked to the back door and stared out the window. But he could see nothing but the shadowy forms of Sergeant Chang's trimmed hedges and bushes. As he turned toward the refrigerator, a faint noise outside pulled him back to the door.

Joe turned the doorknob on the back door slowly, so it wouldn't make any noise. Behind him he could hear Frank and Cody planning the Muir Woods excursion for the next day.

He stepped out into the cool night and moved toward the direction of the sound he'd heard. It was quiet now, except for the noisy yakking of a Steller's jay high in a eucalyptus tree.

Without making a sound, Joe crept toward the red van. He walked around the drive but saw and heard nothing. He opened the van and put one knee on the driver's seat, so he could lean in and look into the back. It all looked the same as when he and Frank had returned here.

He swung around and sat in the driver's seat. He

checked the visor and the dash. Then he reached for the glove compartment. As he did, a movement on the floor in front of the passenger seat caught the corner of his eye.

Joe froze. Holding his breath, he looked down. Coiled on the floor in a pretzel-like pile beneath his arm was a large, dark, thick snake. Its flat, blunt head rose up out of the pile and began a slow but threatening dance.

11 Another Suspect?

Don't move, Joe told himself. Don't even breathe. His eyes narrowed as he focused on the coil and the thick clublike end that wove its threats in the air.

As his gaze intensified, Joe made a startling discovery. This snake's head had no eyes, no mouth! Joe's breathing started to return in small sips. That's the tail, he realized. This snake is waving its tail!

Joe knew he still had to get his arm out of the way—and the sooner the better. With a gasp Joe raised his arm straight up until it hit the top of the van.

The snake convulsed along its whole coil, then disappeared beneath the passenger seat.

Joe was out of the van in an instant, locking the door behind him. As he raced up the sidewalk to the house, one of the shadowy forms that looked just like another bush began to run.

Joe changed directions immediately and angled off in pursuit. He ran the man down half a block away. With one giant dive, he hurled himself at the running figure, bringing the person down with a crunching thud.

"Aaaahhhh," the man yelled as Joe decked him. It was a strange, low, throaty rumble.

"You must be Mike Brando," Joe said, pinning the man's arms behind him. "I've been hearing a lot about you the last couple of days. You seem to be living up to your reputation."

With his free hand, Joe patted Brando down. "Well, look at this," Joe said, pulling a small revolver out of Brando's boot. "Another parole violation. Okay, come on." He pulled Brando up.

"Let go of me," Brando growled. "You don't have the right to hold me." He seemed to want to struggle, but Joe's slamming blow had apparently knocked the wind out of him.

"Well, let's just go back to the house and check that out with Sergeant Chang, shall we?" Joe said. Still holding Brando's wrists behind him, Joe pushed the man across the lawn and in the back door of Sergeant Chang's house.

"You asked us if we wanted you to bring us anything," Frank said with a surprised smile when Joe shoved Brando into the kitchen. "We didn't think to ask for Mike Brando." He went to the phone and called nine-one-one while Joe tied Brando to a chair with a rope he found in the cleaning closet.

"Brando!" Cody said, joining Frank in the kitchen. "Finally, we'll put an end to your sabotage and dirty tricks."

"You think this is the end of it?" Brando snarled. "It's just the beginning. Putting me away isn't going to stop me," he continued.

"Because you have help on the outside?" Frank suggested. "Was someone working with you while you were in prison?"

"And was it the same person attacking Deb and Joe in Golden Gate Park while you were stalking us on the cable car?" Cody added. "And what about stabbing Dave Cloud just a few hours ago? How long did it take you to plan all this, Mike?"

"What are you talking about?" Brando grumbled. "I don't know anything about anything in Golden Gate Park."

"That's okay," Joe said. "You don't have to tell us, but the police will have to hear about it."

Brando's chin jutted out as he glared at Cody.

"And how about the little present in the van," Joe said. "Don't tell us you don't know anything about that."

Brando's face broke out in a nasty grin. "The snake I'll admit to," he said.

"Snake!" Cody said. Joe told Frank and Cody about his encounter in the van.

"Sounds like a rubber boa," Cody said. "They're called the two-headed snake because both ends look alike. A rubber boa likes to stay hidden, but when it feels threatened, it winds up into a tight ball. Then it raises its tail up and waves it as if it's about to strike with it. They're pretty common around here because they like to hang out in forests."

"Just a little tidbit for your collection, Chang," Brando said. "Not quite dead yet, of course, but all things in time. Those crazy bugs of yours will make short work of it."

"My beetles," Cody said, heading for Brando, his fists clenched. "You ruined my colonies."

"Easy, Cody," Frank said. "We've got him now. He'll be going back to prison for sure."

"Yeah?" Brando barked. "Well, they can't keep me in there forever. I'll get out again. And when I do, you'd better be ready."

"You might be in a little longer this time," Joe

pointed out. "Attacking me with a snake and pushing my brother off a moving cable car could be interpreted as attempted murder."

"The cable car wasn't moving," Brando said, raising his voice. "And I wasn't after your brother, anyway," he added. "Somebody bumped me. I meant to push you—it should have been you!" He tried to jump at Cody, but the rope Joe had tied held him fast to the chair.

"So you did do it," Joe said, smiling at Cody. "You did push Frank."

Brando flashed a mean look at Joe, then sank into surly silence.

"Dad!" Cody called, looking gratefully toward the door as his father walked in with two uniformed officers.

"I picked up on the nine-one-one call," Sergeant Chang said. "Everybody okay?" He looked from Cody to Frank to Joe. They all nodded back to him.

"There's a rubber boa in the van," Cody said.

"Well, Mike, here we are again," Sergeant Chang said, shaking his head. "I thought you were headed for a quieter life up north."

"No lectures, Chang," Brando said. "Just get me out of here so I can talk to my attorney in private."

"You take him to the station and the snake to Animal Control," Sergeant Chang told the officers. "I'll get the statements here and meet you there shortly."

Sergeant Chang took out his pen and notebook. "Now, what happened here?" he asked his son as Brando was led away.

"Joe can tell you," Cody said. "He's the one who got him. Frank and I haven't even heard what happened yet."

Joe filled them in on his encounter in the backyard. Then Cody told him about the disaster at Bug Central.

Breathing a long "Wheeeeeew," Sergeant Chang leaned back in his chair. "You boys have been pretty busy, haven't you?" he said with a big grin.

Then he leaned forward again, and his manner and voice were serious. "Okay, guys, now it's time to turn the case over to the police. We'll put Brando back where he belongs and track down his accomplices, if any. You have done a great job, but there have been too many close calls."

Sergeant Chang stood up and put his notebook back in his pocket. "Joe, you might need to come to the station and go over your complaint again. Until then, I know it'll be hard, but you and Frank try to remember you're on vacation—not on assignment. If anything happened to you here in my city, your father would never forgive me. Cody, you leave Mike

Brando to me. I'm going to see how the questioning is going. I'll keep you all posted."

Sergeant Chang left and Frank, Joe, and Cody sank into comfortable chairs with fresh cans of soda.

"Okay, so we still go to Muir Woods tomorrow, right?" Cody asked.

"Absolutely," Joe said. "It's not possible for Brando to have done everything that's happened since we've been here—let alone all the things that have happened to you, Cody."

"Right," Frank said. "Either he has someone working with him, or we've got more than one culprit. The field trip tomorrow is still on."

"And don't forget," Joe reminded them. "We have to be back by late afternoon to help Jennifer Payton set up the haunted house for the dress rehearsal."

"Yikes!" Cody said. "I forgot about that."

"No problem," Frank said. "We'll get an early start. My tour book says Muir Woods opens at eight in the morning."

"Too early," Cody said, shaking his head. "We don't need to go that early."

A ringing phone interrupted him. Cody answered it, spoke for a few minutes, and then hung up.

"That was Dad," he said, walking back into the kitchen. He carried a small pile of mail. "Brando's in major trouble. Attacking you two plus breaking so many parole violations—he's not going to be out for quite a while."

"Did he give them any clues about accomplices?" Joe asked.

"He still says he didn't do any of the other stuff and doesn't know who did," Cody answered, "but they're going to keep questioning him. He'll break down eventually. They ran a check on the green car rental, but the name and the prints on the keys didn't bring anything up. Dad thinks the guy used a phony name and fake ID."

The Hardys and Cody agreed they deserved some serious sack time, so after going over the next day's plans one more time, they headed for their beds.

Thursday morning started with the usual fog, but the radio weather station predicted a sunnier afternoon.

Cody made a quick run over to Skin & Bones to make sure everything was okay after the fumigator's visit. Frank and Joe had breakfast and dressed in jeans, sweaters, and boots.

Cody arrived back in less than an hour. "Look who I found," he said. "She was at Skin and Bones picking up the mail. Since we can't work today anyway, I asked her if she wanted to go with us to the woods."

Deb walked in. She was carrying her briefcase, but was dressed in jeans, a white T-shirt, and a tan jacket. Her thick blond hair was caught up under a baseball cap.

"First you have to see the letter we got today," Deb said. She dug down into her briefcase. "You know, it's getting close to your anniversary date." She pulled out a long envelope. "Almost time to renew your lease for this building."

"So, what's the deal?" Cody asked. "They've raised the rent so much I can't afford to stay here any longer?"

"Actually, I don't know yet. We didn't receive the lease—just this letter."

Cody scanned the letter quickly. Frank watched as Cody's mouth dropped open. "What!" Cody said. "I don't believe it." He turned to Frank and Joe. "My building's been sold," he said. "And guess who the new owner is."

His dark eyes flashed from Joe to Frank. "It's Jennifer Payton."

12 The Skull in the Forest

"Jennifer Payton has bought my building," Cody said.

"And you didn't know anything about it?" Frank asked.

"This is a complete surprise," Cody answered. "She never said a word to me."

"She told me she's planning to expand her club," Frank said.

"Yeah, like maybe expand right into my building," Cody said. He slumped into his chair. "I'm just getting the business to a point where people know where I am, and then she buys the building and kicks me out."

"You don't suppose . . ." Deb started to say.

"Well, it is odd that she hasn't said anything to Cody

about it," Joe said. "And she's got some pretty big plans for that area."

"She told me that she's hoping to help convert this neighborhood from retail stores to an entertainment hub," Frank told Deb. "Clubs, restaurants, places like that."

"And she thinks Skin and Bones doesn't exactly fit that image, I suppose," Deb concluded.

"Could be," Frank said.

"What if maybe she thinks she can drive me out by messing with my business," Cody said. His words sounded clipped through his clenched jaw. "Maybe it's time to tell her just how wrong she is."

"Cool it," Frank said. "We're going to be there this afternoon. We can snoop around then—*and* in disguise."

"All right!" Cody said. "To the woods." He threw a couple of sweatshirts at the Hardys. "Here, take these," he said. "It can be really cool up there."

"Get your backpacks," Frank said to Joe and Cody. "We need to be prepared to bring back anything and keep our fingerprints off it. So we need flashlights, a couple of clean towels or rags, gloves, camera, army knife."

"How about tools," Joe added. "Cody, can we borrow one of your dad's screwdrivers and a small pair of pliers? You never know . . ."

"Do you have any brushes with you?" Deb asked Cody. "An archaeologist's brush—one of the ones you use to clean your specimens. You never know what you might find on the forest floor, and we may need to brush it off."

"Great idea, Deb," Frank said with a smile.

"No problem," Cody said. "I've plenty of them in my car. Deb, here's an extra backpack for you."

"Can we stop at a dry cleaner's?" Joe asked as they climbed into Cody's SUV. "This thing's a mess." He held up the sweatshirt he had been wearing when Dave fell against him. It was smeared with blood.

At the cleaner's he handed the stained sweatshirt to the clerk. The woman gave Joe an odd look when she saw it and acted as if she didn't even want to touch it. She carefully swept it into a bag, marked it for special treatment, and gave Joe a claim check.

Cody drove to the north end of the city and on to San Francisco's famous Golden Gate Bridge. They were headed north across the bay. Frank looked out the window. The dusky Pacific Ocean stretched out to the left. The sun topped off the waves with dazzling yellow light.

To the right, the water curved into San Francisco

Bay. Alcatraz Island sat in the middle, and from that distance, it almost looked like an oversize houseboat.

They reached the other side of the bridge and drove under the rainbow painted above the arch of the Marin Tunnel. Along the way Frank, Joe, and Cody told Deb about Dave's confrontation with Mike Brando, Frank's discovery in the mailing locker, and the boa that led to Joe's capture of Brando.

After a few miles Cody pulled off the main highway and on to the road leading to Muir Woods.

"Parts of the woods are really dense," Cody reminded them. "These are coastal redwoods, so they're huge. Some are two hundred fifty feet tall, and the trunks can be fourteen feet across."

"And they're old," Deb added. "The oldest tree in Muir Woods is one thousand years old. Most of the mature trees are between five hundred and eight hundred years old."

"Where will we be parking?" Frank asked.

"There's a parking area outside the entrance for visitors' cars and tour buses," Deb said.

"Let's not park in the lot," Frank suggested. "It might be better if Cody's car wasn't sitting empty in the parking area—just in case."

The two-lane road curled around deep canyons and up through Mount Tamalpais State Park. At times

Frank felt as if they were riding along the edge of the world.

Then they seemed to plunge into darkness as the road wound through a dark wilderness of trees and brush.

Finally Cody pulled off the road into a secluded grove of eucalyptus trees and parked the car. "We're a couple of miles from the Muir Woods entrance," he said. "I park here when I come up to mountain bike."

They all strapped on their backpacks. Cody and Frank pulled on sweatshirts. Joe and Deb tied theirs around their waists. Then they started up the road to Muir Woods.

It took them about half an hour to reach the park entrance. As they approached the visitor center, Frank felt a chill. Cody was right, he told himself. It is cooler in the redwoods.

They bought tickets and headed into the forest. "Take a look at this," Joe called to Frank. "It's amazing."

He stood next to an exhibit that was a slice of a tree trunk standing on its side like a wheel. The wood was divided into hundreds of rings. A chart showed how the rings helped define the age of the tree.

Frank was impatient to get moving, so he hustled the others on to the dirt path into the woods. The trees seemed to reach beyond their sight. When

110

Frank looked up, all he could see were hundreds of huge red-brown trunks. The branches with their green needles didn't start until way above them, and they seemed to form a far-off roof. He could just barely make out small patches of blue-white sky.

There was a group of young schoolchildren ahead on the main path. Otherwise, there were just a few visitors, scattered in twos and threes.

Occasionally they came across an enormous trunk that had fallen across the path. A small sign told them when the tree had fallen, how old it was, and that it would be left alone, as part of the natural evolution of the forest.

"This place is kind of spooky," Joe whispered. "I feel like I've gone back in time. Like I'm going to suddenly see a T. rex. Or a pterodactyl's going to make a surprise landing."

It was very quiet. The forest was so ancient, so mysterious, that everyone spoke in low voices.

Frank checked the map the courier had drawn for him. "It's up that way," he said, pointing. "That's where the delivery guy picked up the package with the anteater claw."

Frank led Joe, Deb, and Cody on to the upper path for a couple hundred yards. An older woman passed

111

them going in the opposite direction. No one else was on their path.

Finally Frank stopped. "Okay, we have to leave the path here. Let's do it so no one sees us."

They glanced around. There was no one in sight. Quickly they stepped off the path through a dense carpet of ferns and into a very dark, secluded area of the forest.

At last they came to the tree that the courier had drawn on the map. "This has to be it," Frank whispered. "This is where the courier picked up the package."

Using their flashlights and sticks to brush away the undergrowth, they scanned the area for clues—anything that might lead them to the person who had sent the anteater claw.

But they found nothing. Joe looked up. The forest was so dense in this area that he could see only one tiny patch of sky. A gray-blue veil of fog twisted down through the opening. He could hear occasional crackling noises and faint swishes and scurries. A chill across his shoulders sent his body into a shudder. He untied the sweatshirt and pulled it over his head.

As he looked around, the huge tree trunks made him feel as if he were gazing into a funhouse mirror that had reduced his size.

Joe concentrated his gaze on the ground off to the right. It was different from the forest floor where they stood.

He took a few steps in that direction. The ferns were bent and lying flat on the ground. Fallen tree bark was splintered and smashed. Occasional spots of dirt were stomped. It looked almost as if someone had forged a crude path.

Joe hurried along, following the trail of trampled plants and redwood chips. His breath caught in his throat when he saw blurry impressions in the dirt that might have been footprints.

He moved faster, casting his flashlight beam ahead. Behind him, he heard the others begin to follow.

There was no sound in front of him. Not even the scampering and slithering noises he had heard before. Just the stillness of the forest.

His eyes fixed intently on the flashlight beam, which bounced ahead of him with every footfall. Then something jarred the continuous dark picture of dirt and ferns and chips of redwood bark.

Something very pale glinted at the left edge of the flashlight beam. Joe stopped suddenly and realized he'd been holding his breath. As he took in a gulp of air, he turned the flashlight. He aimed it to capture the ghostly vision.

A thin stream of fog wove in and out of the tree trunks, and it almost seemed to blur Joe's vision as he stared at the pale object. He squinted to get a clearer picture.

As the fog drifted away, Joe's breath caught again. Resting on rust-colored shards of bark was a human skull.

13 A Werewolf Warning

As Joe stared at the human skull, a large brown spider slithered out of one of the eye sockets.

"Looks like something out of the shop, Cody," Deb added, standing next to Joe.

"Let's take a look," Cody said, moving ahead.

"Wait!" Frank ordered. "It could be a kind of trap." He swung his flashlight around, but they saw nothing but tree trunks and ferns. "It's probably not a setup," Frank added. "But let's be careful, just in case."

"You three stay here and keep your lights burning," Joe said. "I'll check it out."

Cautiously, he moved toward the skull. He took each step very carefully, tapping the ground with his toe first, then setting down his whole foot. When he got to the skull, he prodded it—very gently—with a stick.

The skull rolled on to its side, and another spider skittered out between two teeth. Finally Joe knelt beside the skull and rolled it a couple of times with the stick. The others joined him then, kneeling on the redwood bark chips.

"I don't see any marks or tattoos on the skull," Cody said. "Of course, you can remove marks pretty easily from bone. Most bones have a few knicks and dings in them anyway, so shaving off a mark is no big deal." He carefully wrapped the skull in a rag and put it in his backpack.

"Do we know where we are?" Joe asked, looking around. "We've come pretty far off the park trail."

Frank got out the Muir Woods map and laid it next to the map drawn by the courier. "We're about here, I think," he concluded, pointing to the Muir Woods map.

"You're right on, Frank," Cody said. "In fact, we're not far from a trail that leads to the beach. Dad used to take me fishing down there."

"I want to keep going this way," Joe said. "Okay, it's not a path exactly, but someone's been through here—maybe someone who dropped the skull."

The trail led deeper into the forest about sixty yards, and then the air changed. The heavy dank smell of wood and forest undergrowth gave way to the crisper air of ocean and fog.

Joe, Frank, Deb, and Cody followed the makeshift trail until they arrived at the edge of a bluff fringed with a wide stand of cypress trees. At last they could put away their flashlights. A steep path led down to a strip of beach.

"Hey, that's not my beach," Cody said, gazing down from the edge of the bluff. The ocean rolled in around several enormous rocks to a small strip of sand. The rocks served as a windbreak, protecting the small inlet.

"We've come this far," Joe said, "I'm not stopping now." He began the steep descent down the bluff. Frank, Deb, and Cody followed.

When they reached the bottom of the bluff, they came to a wire fence. "This probably means this is private property," Deb pointed out.

"Maybe," Joe said. "Maybe not."

"What's this?" Frank asked, stopping suddenly. He reached through the fence. Something had blown up against the other side and was stuck. It looked like a piece of fabric, about six inches square. But Frank was pretty sure it was something much more exotic.

"Cody, you have to see this," Deb said.

Gingerly Frank peeled the thin scrap off the wire

and pulled it through to his side of the fence. It was tan with a light pink pattern like patchwork. "Snakeskin?" he asked.

"It sure is," Cody said. "Probably an Argentine pink aboma," he added. "A pretty strange find out here."

"Why?" Joe asked.

"They're not native to California," Cody said.

"So how did it get here?" Frank wondered. "Come on, let's get closer." He was over the fence in seconds and walking toward a large rocky bluff.

The others followed quickly. They continued walking along the fence, but on the ocean side. As they neared the bluff, Frank stopped, gesturing for the others to be quiet. "Listen," he whispered. He could hear noises from around the bluff. There were no voices, just a few thuds and slamming noises.

His heart tripping in anticipation, Frank led the others around the bluff. When he reached the point where he could see the other side, he stopped again, holding the others back.

A large speedboat bobbed in the water, tied to a pier next to a small boatshack. As they watched, someone carried a wooden box from the shack onto the boat and disappeared belowdecks.

Using rocks and scrubgrass as shields, Frank, Joe,

Deb, and Cody crept toward the shack. But before they could reach it, the boat zoomed away.

Joe led the way to the shack. The door was padlocked. One window was locked, the other warped tightly shut. After a few minutes Frank and Joe pried it open, using sheer strength and Sergeant Chang's screwdriver.

A faint smell hit them immediately. It was the sweet sickening smell of meat that was old and going bad. It wasn't strong enough to make them gag, but it hung in the air, mingling with the fog that stole in through the window.

"There have been specimens stored in here," Cody said in a low voice.

"We get stuff sometimes from overseas that isn't cleaned well before it's sent," Deb told the Hardys. "This smell reminds me of that."

"Wood shavings—excelsior," Joe said, picking up a few shreds off the floor.

"Some countries still use this for packing. We get it sometimes with bones," Deb told him.

"Look, here's something," Deb cried out from the corner. She shone her flashlight on a piece of paper. It was shaped like a triangle, with two cut edges bordered in navy blue and one ragged edge.

Frank peeled the scrap of paper off the floor and

held it under his light beam. "It looks like a corner torn off some kind of label," he said.

"There's something on it," Deb pointed out. "A lowercase *g* and a number two."

"B-two-g," Joe said in a whisper. "The code at the mailing station," he said to Frank.

"Let's get back to town," Frank said. He was shot through with adrenaline. He felt as if he were straining to look at something from far away and if he could just get closer, he would see it clearly.

The four climbed out the window and retraced their steps down the beach and over the wire fence.

"We can catch Redwood Creek Trail over this way," Cody said. "It'll get us to the car quicker."

It took them half an hour, but they finally reached Cody's SUV, still parked safely in the eucalyptus grove.

Back in town, they picked up sandwiches for lunch, and then headed over to Skin & Bones.

There was a faint odor from the fumigation but not enough to bother anyone. They ate quickly, and it was two o'clock when they finished. Cody and Deb took the skull to the lab to clean it to see if they could find any identifying marks.

Joe got on the phone to check with Cody's network to see whether anyone knew anything about the boatshack, *b2g*, or a missing human skull.

Frank booted up the computer in Cody's office to check online public records that would tell him who owned the beach property they had found.

No one made a connection that helped the case.

About three o'clock Dave knocked on the shop door, and Joe let him in. Cody and Deb came down, and they all gathered in the kitchen of Cody's flat.

"Man, it is great to get Mike Brando back behind bars, isn't it?" Dave said. "That weasel."

"Yeah, but someone else has to be helping him," Cody reminded Dave. He was interrupted by a loud tapping on the door of Skin & Bones. Deb let in a frantic Jennifer Payton.

"Cody!" Jennifer called up the stairs. "Where are you guys? I need you desperately. You've got to come over to help me finish getting set up. The dress rehearsal's in less than two hours."

"Remember, Cody," Frank whispered to his friend, "we're going to check her out while we're over there. Don't let her know how you feel—or even that you know about her buying your building or her plans for the future of this area."

"What's going on?" Dave asked. "Don't tell me you suspect Jennifer Payton of something."

"Cody, where *are* you?" Jennifer called again.

"Later," Cody said to Dave. "It's showtime."

Cody led the Hardys and Dave down to the shop. "Jennifer, I'm sorry," he said. "We're on our way."

"Okay," she said, hurrying back to the door. "Don't forget your costumes."

"Costumes?" Dave repeated. "Is this for the charity fund-raiser? Do you have room for me?"

"We always have room for more volunteers," Jennifer said without turning around.

Frank, Joe, Cody, Dave, and Deb grabbed the costumes Jennifer had given them and went next door to Reflections. The transformation of the club was wonderfully spooky. Under the black draped ceiling with red twinkle lights, cubicles were set up and connected in a mazelike pattern, almost like train cars opening from one to the next. Each had a scary scene inside. Visitors would be ushered through the scene and past the costumed figures, who would interact with them.

The Hardys and the others joined the gang of volunteers to finish setting up the scenes—ghostly parlors and attics, sunken ships, alien spaceships, witch kitchens, crazy scientist labs, caveman lairs, vampire crypts, werewolf forests, pirate cabins, and monster basements. All had been reproduced. When the setup was finished, everyone got in costume.

"So, what do you think?" Joe asked, flashing his werewolf fangs and stroking his hair-covered face. "Pretty scary, hmm?" He was dressed in his own T-shirt and jeans, but mats of hair hung out from under the long sleeves.

"Awesome," Frank agreed. He wore a neon blue jumpsuit. A pale green skullcap matched his alien makeup.

"So, when are you going to get in costume, Deb?" Cody asked as she emerged from the dressing room. She was an apparition in ghostly blue-white with pale fluorescent makeup.

"Very funny," she said with a crooked smile.

"Be careful or I'll make you walk the plank." Cody whipped off his large plumed pirate hat and made a courtly bow.

"What about you?" Cody said to Dave. "Did Jennifer decide you are so scary as Dave Cloud that you don't need a costume or makeup?"

"You *are* funny," Dave responded. "I was too late to be a character—I'll take tickets or something like that. But for the dress rehearsal, Jennifer is going to have some of us pretend to be visitors. We'll walk through the gauntlet to make sure you guys are scary enough to be fun, but not enough to cause permanent damage."

Jennifer also had choreographed surprising confrontations between some of the characters, which would take place on the stage in the corner.

The dress rehearsal filled the room with a jumble of howls, moans, screams, and cackles. Jennifer finally took the microphone. "Okay, everyone, time to stop. I want you to have plenty of spooky spirit left for to-morrow. Report here at four o'clock. But right now, let's party!"

Jennifer had planned a party with lots of food, music, and fun for the volunteers. The deejay fired up his sound system, and the music was deaf-ening.

Frank, Cody, and Deb met up near Jennifer's of-fice. "Have you seen Joe?" Frank asked.

"Not yet," Cody answered.

"He's still rehearsing with the vampire," Deb said. Werewolf Joe was locked in a wrestling match on the stage. He was acting out the skit Jennifer had cooked up, pitting the two most famous biters in horror his-tory against each other.

"Okay," Frank said. "Jennifer's pretty distracted as it is. But you two keep an eye on her and keep her away from her office. I want to look around. When you see Joe, send him here."

Deb and Cody wove through the noisy crowd. Frank stood in the office door, but he couldn't take his eyes off the stage. "Come on, Joe," he muttered. "Get it over with. You can take him."

For a minute he was dazzled by what seemed like a thousand lights dancing around the room. He looked up to see a mirrored ball dangling and revolving from the ceiling. He thought of the piece of mirror that Joe had found on Cody's roof.

Then he remembered all the sports and fitness photos, awards, and certificates he had seen in Jennifer's office. He raced to the wall and scanned it eagerly. His eyes rested on one framed display, and he felt his pulse stop and then quicken. Hanging on the wall was a certificate attesting to Jennifer's championship karate skills.

"Excuse me," a young man said, coming into the office. Frank could hardly hear him over the noise. "Are you Jennifer's manager?"

"No, I just—"

"Tell her someone stole my costume," the young man said. "I was in the dressing room getting ready to change, and someone took it off the counter. It was the vampire costume she had made special for the fight with the werewolf, so she's not going to be happy about it. Had a full head mask and everything." He gave Frank a little wave and then rejoined the loud party.

Frank felt a wave of foreboding cascade through

him. "Joe!" he yelled as he left the office and focused on the stage in the corner. As he watched his brother struggling to take charge, the vampire got a stranglehold on Joe.

"Joe!" Frank yelled again, charging through the dense crowd. His voice was just one more in the crowd of party monsters.

14 Fear in the Fog

Frank barreled through the mass of costumed volunteers—some eating and drinking, some dancing. No one paid any attention to him as he yelled to Joe.

Still calling as he pushed through, Frank saw Joe dragged off the stage and into the wings. He spotted Cody and Deb and motioned them to follow him.

At last the three made it backstage. But neither Joe nor the vampire was there. Frank rushed to the back door of the club, a metal double door that led to a parking lot. One of the doors was being held open by a kickbar. There was no Joe, no car peeling away.

Frank went back in, saying, "Cody, call your dad. I

think Joe's been kidnapped. Deb, find Dave. We need all the help we can get."

Then Frank went to the deejay and told him to have Jennifer meet him backstage immediately. He also put out a call for Joe, just in case.

Frank paced the wings while the deejay's voice blasted through the sound system. "Jennifer, we have an emergency," he said. "Please report to the stage now. Joe Hardy, come to the stage."

Breathless, Jennifer was there in minutes. "What?" she said to Frank. "What's happening? Please—I can't take any more emergencies and disasters."

Quickly Frank told her about the stolen costume and the scene on the stage.

"Come on," she said. "So they fought and one of them won. It's over. They're probably out there scarfing up food now. Relax. Your brother will turn up."

"Listen to me," Frank said, his eyes narrowing as he glared at her. "This is not a joke. This is not a false alarm. Joe would have been here by now if he'd heard that announcement. He is either hurt and unable to respond or he's been taken away."

"What do you want me to do?" she asked. He could see the sparks of fear in her eyes.

"Were you on the roof of Skin and Bones Monday night?"

Jennifer's eyes widened and for a minute, he thought she was going to run. Then, still tense and looking as if she were going to sprint away any minute, she answered him.

"Yes, I was," she said. "But I wasn't trespassing. I own that building."

"We know that," Cody said, joining them. He turned to Frank. "Dad was out," he said, "but they'll find him. I also beeped him. He'll be in touch as soon as he can."

"I've been overwhelmed by this fund-raiser," Jennifer said to Cody. "Honestly, I wanted to tell you but decided to wait till this was over to sit down and talk with you."

"I know about your plans," Cody said. "And I bet they don't include my shop."

"Yes, they do," she said. She seemed to relax a little and not be so ready to jump away. "You're just the kind of quirky offbeat business I want to encourage here. In fact, I want you to move into the building on the other side of Reflections. It's bigger, and I'll let you have it at the same rent for a year if you'll stay."

"Why were you on the roof?" Frank asked.

"I didn't think anyone was in your building that evening. If Skin and Bones moves to the other side, I want to put a restaurant in your building, one with a rooftop café. I was just checking it out."

"But you attacked Joe," Frank said.

"Wait a minute," she said. "Is that what this is all about? You think because I kicked him then that I've done something to him now? You've got to believe me." Her tone changed as she pleaded. "I don't know what's happened to your brother."

Frank kept his eyes on her as she spoke.

"Monday night he surprised me and I panicked," Jennifer continued. "I didn't want to get into all this expansion stuff yet, so I just wanted to get away without being identified. I was defending myself. He was creeping toward me, and I didn't know who he was until I turned around. Then I pulled my kick so he wouldn't be hurt. Hey, I'm a champion. If I'd wanted to really hurt him, I could have. Is that how you figured out that it was me up there? The karate?" she asked.

"And a piece of mirror you left," Frank said.

"The mirrored ball." Jennifer nodded. "I've had trouble with pieces chipping off. I get them on my feet, and then I carry them around until I can reglue them. Look, if your brother's been hurt or kidnapped, I swear I don't know anything about it. But I'm ready to help any way I can."

Frank believed her. "I don't know of anything right now," he said. "Except report the stolen vampire costume and get the police here to interview everyone before they leave. Maybe someone knows the thief or saw him and can give a description. If you come up with anything, let us know or call Sergeant Thomas Chang, Cody's dad." He rushed out the back door with Cody and Deb close behind.

They raced through the parking lot, up the passageway between the buildings, around to the front, and into Skin & Bones.

Frank led them straight up to Cody's flat. He peeled off his jumpsuit and skullcap and washed off the alien makeup. Cody went into his bedroom to change. Deb stayed by the phone in the office, still dressed as a ghost.

"One of us has to stay here from now on," Frank said, joining her. "If Joe can call, he'll call here." He took out the triangular scrap of paper with *b2g* printed on it. He knew it held the answer, but he couldn't figure out how to break the code.

"Couldn't we call the bureau of public records and find out who owns that property with the boat shack on it?" Deb suggested.

"I thought of that," Frank said. "We've done it before in other cases. But in a metropolitan area of this

131

size, it would take days to get the job done. They're always backed up with requests. We can have Cody's dad get the information for us much quicker. I wish he'd call—or better yet, Joe."

Like magic, the phone rang. But it wasn't Joe or Sergeant Chang. Dressed in a red sweater and jeans, Cody came out of the bedroom to take the call. When he hung up, he turned to Frank and Deb. "That was the dry cleaners," he said with a puzzled expression. "Joe's sweatshirt is ruined, and they can't fix it. But get this—it wasn't blood. It was a red paint glaze!"

"Why would Dave have red paint all over his jacket?" Deb wondered.

"The real question is why did he tell us it was blood?" Frank asked. He felt as if his mind was zooming around a track, circling and circling the clues. Then one of them jumped out at him. "Did Dave have a set of keys to your car?" he asked Cody.

"Sure. We both used the SUV for pickups, so I got him a set of his own."

"Did he ever return them to you?"

Cody thought for a moment. "Now that you mention it, I don't think so. Why?"

"Does Dave have a boat?" Frank asked as he turned to Cody's computer.

"Yes, he does," Cody answered. "I've never seen it though. Why all the questions?"

"You said Dave started an online auction site for computer equipment, right?" Frank asked. "What's his company's name?"

"ComputerCloud-dot-com," Cody said.

Frank typed in the name. Nothing came up. Then he typed *b2g*. Nothing. "Okay," he muttered. "Let's start with this." He typed *2g*. An alphabetical list of *2g* names started running down the screen: ads2get-results.com, ask2getanswers.com, attorneys2go.com, avocados2go.com.

When he got to the last two, Frank stopped the search immediately and refined his search. He typed 2go.

Again, a long list of names started cascading down the screen. The names starting with *a* tumbled off the bottom of the screen, and then the *b*'s started. He felt a quickness in his breath that matched the rapid pumping in his temples. There it was: bonz2go.com.

Frank read aloud. The website explained that this site was owned by Dave Cloud, also owner of ComputerCloud. Bonz2go auctioned hard-to-find animal, fish, bird, and human bones and other body parts.

"It's Dave," Frank told the others. "He's been sabotaging you, Cody. Taking your merchandise, intercepting deliveries, and selling them on the Internet."

"Deb, keep beeping Sergeant Chang until he calls," Frank said, grabbing his jacket. "Tell him we've gone to Dave's."

Frank and Cody raced to Cody's car. Cody was in shock but didn't doubt Frank's deduction. "It's a perfect setup for him," Cody said. "He's got all my contacts, all my network available to him."

"That's why we couldn't find him at the party tonight. He'd stolen the vampire costume to kidnap Joe."

"But why?" Cody said. "I'm the one he's trying to ruin." He drove the car up onto the Golden Gate Bridge toward Sausalito, where Dave lived. It was dark, and a thick fog was rolling in through the arches of the bridge.

"To get us off the case," Frank guessed. "Also, Brando was the perfect dupe. Dave could throw suspicion on him. Now that Mike's back in prison, Dave has to keep the idea alive that Brando has an accomplice on the outside."

Cody pulled into Dave's long driveway up a hill. "Turn off your lights," Frank said.

They drove up to the house, but it was dark and Dave's car wasn't there. "Where's his boat?" Frank asked.

They drove back down the hill to the marina. Cody parked a block away, and they ran quickly to Dave's pier and his boat. It looked like the one they'd seen that morning near the boat shack.

One light was on belowdecks, but there was no sign of anyone. His ears straining for a sound, Frank led Cody aboard. They circled the deck, then crept down into the cabin.

In the dim light Frank saw a dreaded sight. "Joe," he whispered, running to the corner of the cabin. Joe was tied and gagged, his horror makeup still intact. But they could hear his celebration "Yesssss" from behind the gag and werewolf hair hanging off his face.

A sudden dip to one side told Frank that someone had boarded. He pushed Cody into the head, and Frank jumped into the bedroom closet.

"Okay, we're ready now for our little jaunt," Frank heard Dave Cloud say. "I take care of you and that's one less person trying to figure out my profitable little scheme. Plus, the others will be scared off the scent once and for all. Sort of like killing two wolves with one stone—or should I say, rock."

Frank heard footsteps going back up to the deck. In minutes the cruiser moved out.

Cautiously Frank left the closet and motioned Cody to come out of the head. They freed Joe. "We can take him," Cody said in a hushed voice. "There are three of us."

"I agree," Frank whispered. "But we have to be cautious. He might be armed."

"I didn't see a gun," Joe said, his voice low. "But that's no guarantee."

"Okay, let's go on up," Frank said.

"Let's wait until we get out farther," Joe warned. "There's a lot of traffic here. We don't want an accident with other craft."

They waited until they could feel Dave increase speed. From the porthole they saw that they were farther out into the bay and cruising parallel to the Golden Gate. As they started up the companionway, the boat swerved.

Then it lurched and swerved again. For an instant, Frank thought they were going to ditch. They hurried up the companionway.

It was nearly impossible to see in the thick cloudy air. From their left they could hear the loud intonation of a foghorn.

Ahead, Frank finally made out Dave's form. "He's

in trouble," Frank murmured. Dave was grunting and seemed to be frantically trying to get control of the wheel.

"He's trying to turn," Joe said. "We've got to help."

A large dark shadow seemed to be racing straight toward them. Joe pushed Dave to the deck and grabbed the wheel, but it was too late.

With a gut-grinding boom, the boat smashed into the huge black mass rising out of the fog.

...
...
...
...
...
...

15 Rock On!

Frank woke up first. He was sore and tired but okay. His right wrist was twisted under him, but it didn't seem to be broken. His clothes were wet, and he was shaking with cold.

"Joe! Cody!" he called. As his eyes adjusted to the foggy night, he realized he was lying in a cave. Waves crashed against the rock wall below. Sea water washed into the cave, dribbling foam around the edges.

He scrambled to his feet and stumbled around in the dark. At last he found the others. Cody was lying on the ledge close to the cave entrance. Joe was outside the cave on a rocky outcropping above the entrance.

"Joe! Come on, wake up." Frank walked to where Joe was lying and gently shook his shoulder.

"Ummmph," Joe said, twisting his body as he woke. "The last thing I remember I was turning the wheel of Dave's boat. We were barreling toward this big—"

He stopped talking and looked up the rocky wall above him. Through the fog he saw lights in the distance, forming the pattern of a long bridge. "Whoa, we crashed into Alcatraz!" He sat up quickly and rubbed his hairy face. "I thought when werewolves wake up, they're back to normal."

"Ooooohhh," Cody called from inside the cave. "My leg's numb. How long have we been here? What happened?" He sat up and looked around. "Hey, are we on the Rock? In one of the caves? A prisoner tried to escape once and didn't get any farther than one of the caves. He finally gave up and climbed back up to the prison."

"Yes, that's where we are." Frank leaned back and looked up. "I can see the water tower and the top of the cell-block wall and the building itself. I can see the road winding up from the dock."

"You're right, Frank," Joe said, following his brother's gaze. The Hardys had been on a tour of Alcatraz on a previous trip. "It looks so small from the city," Joe said. "But it's big when you're on it."

"Is everybody okay?" Frank asked. "No broken bones, no bloody cuts?"

"Not that I can tell," Joe said. "Any cuts have been sealed by all this salt water," he added with a lopsided smile.

"I wonder how Dave is—*where* he is," Cody said.

Frank and Joe shook their heads. "I thought I saw a piece of the boat drift by, but it's so dark, I couldn't really tell," Frank said.

"It's so cold," Cody said, shivering. Another wave splashed at them as it hit the island's rocky wall.

"It's time to strip down for business," Joe said. He peeled the werewolf hair off his face and arms. "Okay, let's go," he said.

"We've got to get up on top," Frank agreed, looking for a place to start climbing. He began his ascent, gripping the rocky wall and hoisting himself up. "Come on, guys, find something to hold on to and someplace to put your toes. It's just like any other rock climbing you've done."

"Except for having no equipment and a wet wall covered with slimy seaweed," Joe muttered.

It took them about twenty minutes, but they finally made it onto solid ground. The dock was about forty yards away, and the cell block about a quarter of a mile up the winding road.

Frank checked his watch. "The night tour should be landing in about an hour," he said. "We can get a ride back with them. Let's go check in with the rangers."

"I want to find Dave Cloud first," Joe said. "I have a few words for him about dragging me away from a party."

"Okay," Frank said. "Let's look around a little. Now, if you were Dave Cloud, where would you go?"

"Well, he can't go to the rangers," Joe said, "because if I made it through the accident and can identify him as my kidnapper, he's busted."

"He probably can't escape," Cody said. "In the twenty-nine years this was a federal prison, practically no one made a successful escape."

"If he can't escape on his own and he can't ask for help, there's only one other choice," Frank said.

"What?" Cody asked.

"He's got to hang out near the dock and try to stow away on the evening tour boat to hitch a ride back to the city."

Frank, Joe, and Cody crept along the dark rock at the base of Alcatraz toward the dock. "Let's split up," Joe suggested. "The first one to find him, force him onto the dock. Then the other two will close off his escape routes, and he'll be trapped there."

Joe was the first to spot Dave. He was huddling in

the bushes between the road and the dock. "Hey, pal, how about finishing the fight we started at Reflections," Joe said. Startled, Dave jumped up. Joe pressed forward, and within minutes Dave had backed up onto the dock. Joe and Cody joined Frank, blocking Dave from leaving. He was trapped.

"It's either us or the water," Joe said. "And you sure don't want to join the rest of those prisoners who tried to escape from the Rock."

"I can't believe it's been you all along," Cody said.

"Hey, one way to handle competition is to get rid of it altogether, right?" Dave said, with a half-smile. "I wasn't just going to beat you," he told Cody, "I decided to bury you and put you out of business permanently. Then the market would be pretty much mine to rule."

"So you did it all?" Cody asked. "You trashed my office Monday night, knocked me out?"

"I did it," Dave said with a shrug. "Actually, I was just looking for some paper files. I have no trouble hacking into your computer files, but some of the first customers and dealers we worked with never got put into the computer. So I was after those."

Dave shrugged again. "You surprised me, so I had to drop you. The zoo packages were a nice bonus. I sold the ostrich skeleton and three anteater claws in an hour on bonz2go. I saved one anteater claw for your present," he added, nodding toward the Hardys.

"I got pretty sick of you two butting in, trying to track me down. Thought you'd get the message, but you didn't. That's why I kidnapped you." His eyes narrowed to snakelike slits when he looked at Joe. "I figured if you disappeared for good, your brother here would get the message and back off."

"You don't know the Hardys very well," Cody said with a snort.

"You intercepted Cody's overseas orders and left him the computer threats?" Joe asked.

"Sure," Dave said. "Actually, that was the easiest part. It was a great scam until you two came along. I thought I'd been busted for sure yesterday at the windmill."

"You called to lure Cody to the Polo Field," Frank said. "Why?"

"I was pretty well disguised, if you'll recall," Dave said to Joe. "I was going to threaten him, maybe beat him up a little and dump him. When I saw Deb show up, I grabbed her instead."

Dave looked out across the bay. "I knew you'd been following me earlier."

"You'd followed us first," Frank reminded him, "from Sergeant Chang's."

"Yeah, well, I've been keeping pretty tight surveillance on you all," Dave replied. "Like I said, with all the extra help from out of town—you two—I've had to increase my guard a little, make sure I know where everyone is."

"So you grabbed Deb," Joe prompted.

"Right. When I saw Cody's car, I knew either you or Cody had tracked me to the Polo Field," Dave said to Joe. "I knew you had seen me in the green car, and Cody's was just sitting there, empty. I still had my old keys on my ring, so I took it. I figured Deb had blabbed about the meeting, and for all I knew, there were a lot of people out there looking for me."

"So you hadn't planned to go to the windmill?" Frank said.

"No." Dave chuckled. "At that point, I was playing it by ear, you know? I was mad at Deb, so I took her out to the windmill. I was going to tie her up and gag her, then lock her up in there and just let her sweat it out till someone found her. The whole point of the afternoon was to warn the three of you off. I figured that would do the trick."

"She wasn't so easy to handle," Cody reminded him proudly.

"She sure wasn't," Dave said. "When she broke free and went out to the deck, I really got mad. Then when you showed up," he said to Joe, "I thought I'd had it.

But fortunately, you were more interested in saving her life than nailing me."

"And you never had a fight last night with Brando, did you?" Frank asked.

"So you found out about the red paint, hmm?" Dave said, shaking his head. "Actually, I did scrape my arm. I was coming over to meet you guys for dinner, so I thought I'd capitalize on it and throw some more suspicion Brando's way. I had you believing it for a while, I could tell. Why didn't you just throw that sweatshirt away like a normal person, instead of having it analyzed?" he added, shaking his head.

As Dave talked, the sound of a Coast Guard siren wailed through the fog.

"You know, I can forgive you for almost everything but devastating Bug Central," Cody said. "Letting all the beetles loose was the lowest."

"Not all of them," Dave said with a grin. "I kept the colony in the second refrigerator for myself. After all I need the little munchers, too."

"Not anymore you don't," Frank said. "You're going to be out of business for a long time."

"Was it your human skull that we found in Muir Woods?" Joe asked as the Coast Guard boat came nearer.

The look on Dave's face was one of real shock. "Muir Woods? You mean you know about the boat shack? You found the skull in Muir Woods?"

"We did," Frank said. "Did it belong to you?"

"Yeah, but I didn't know for sure where I'd lost it."

Frank could see the Coast Guard boat shooting through the fog toward the dock.

"I got stuck once at the boat shack when my cruiser wouldn't start," Dave continued. "My only choice was to hike out to the highway to try to hitch to Sausalito. I put two skulls and some other bones in a bag and started through the forest. It was late at night, pitch-black, no flashlight. I got all turned around, lost, fell a few times. With one fall, all the bones emptied out of the bag. The skulls rolled around, and I never found one of them."

"You just left it there?" Frank said, astonished.

"Hey, I just wanted out of that black woods," Dave admitted. "I get claustrophobic in that place. Besides," he said jauntily, "there were plenty more where that came from. I just had to hack into Cody's computer files."

The Coast Guard siren stopped, and within minutes they heard Sergeant Chang's voice calling Cody's name.

"Yo, Dad!" Cody yelled.

"Boy, am I glad to see you guys," Sergeant Chang

said. "Dave, I understand you've got a lot of explaining to do."

"He's already told us a lot," Frank said, "and is pretty proud of it all, it seems."

Sergeant Chang handcuffed Dave and read him his rights. Then they all boarded the Coast Guard boat for the trip back to the city.

"As soon as I got your messages, I called your flat," Sergeant Chang said on the cruise back. "Deb told me you'd gone to Dave's and why. When we got to Sausalito, we saw your SUV near the marina, Cody. I found out that Dave had a boat and that it was gone. I knew no one would take a boat out in this fog unless it was an emergency, he was crazy, or he was doing something illegal. When I called the Coast Guard to have them search for Dave's boat, I insisted they take me along."

"How did you know we were here?" Cody asked.

"The Coast Guard got a call from some fishermen that a boat might have ditched on Alcatraz. We headed here immediately. I was pretty worried until I saw you on the dock."

Frank, Joe, and Cody told Sergeant Chang about their conversation with Dave.

"Well, Frank and Joe, there's no doubt about it. You are definitely chips off your father's block. He's going

147

to be very proud of you for putting Dave out of circulation. You were here on vacation, and you managed to save Cody's business in the process."

"Yeah," Cody said, giving the Hardys high-fives. "You might say your trip here has been a bone-anza for Skin and Bones!"

CAROLYN KEENE
NANCY DREW

GIRL DETECTIVE

Pageant Perfect Crime

Perfect Cover

Perfect Escape

Secret Identity

Identity Theft

Identity Revealed

INVESTIGATE THESE TWO THRILLING MYSTERY TRILOGIES!

Available wherever books are sold!

Aladdin • Simon & Schuster Children's Publishing • SimonSaysKids.com

FRANKLIN W. DIXON

THE HARDY BOYS

Undercover Brothers®

INVESTIGATE THESE TWO ADVENTUROUS MYSTERY TRILOGIES WITH AGENTS FRANK AND JOE HARDY!

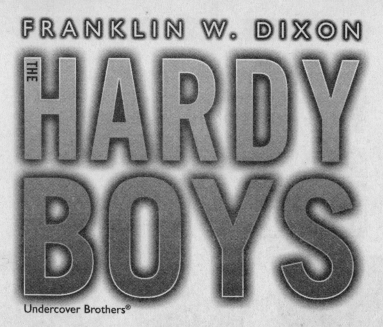

#25 Double Trouble

#26 Double Down

#28 Galaxy X

#29 X-plosion

#27 Double Deception

#30 The X-Factor

From Aladdin
Published by Simon & Schuster